Alpha Pair
by

Brenda Sparks

Alpha Council Chronicles

This is a work of fiction. Names, characters, places, and incidents are either the product of the author's imagination or are used fictitiously, and any resemblance to actual persons living or dead, business establishments, events, or locales, is entirely coincidental.

Alpha Pair

Cover Art by *Rae Monet Inc.*

The Wild Rose Press, Inc.
PO Box 708
Adams Basin, NY 14410-0708
Visit us at www.thewildrosepress.com

Publishing History
First Black Rose Edition, 2018
Print ISBN 978-1-5092-2071-7
Digital ISBN 978-1-5092-2072-4

Alpha Council Chronicles
Published in the United States of America

The Alpha swung a leg over the motorcycle and tugged on his helmet. "You coming anytime this century, woman?"

Tatiana pulled her helmet down over her dark hair, the blunt ends sticking out from under it like twigs in a nest.

"Hold your horses, Romanoff." She straddled her bike.

Demetri shifted the bike from its stand and rousted the thing with a kick of his booted heel. He gunned the throttle. "My horses want to go," he called over the roar of the sports bike.

Tatiana started the motorcycle she borrowed from Marcus with a push of a button. The black beast growled to life. "Well, what are we waiting for then? I bet I can get to the counseling center before you."

The howl of her engine made further conversation impossible when she revved the machine.

They tore off down the gravel drive, the bikes fishtailing. Bits of gravel spit out behind them. Demetri gunned his engine and took the lead. He flashed her a brilliant smile when he passed, making it almost worth being second place. But not quite.

As they rounded out of the gated fence onto the road, Tatiana cut under him to regain the lead.

He shook his head. *Life will never be dull with you, tigress warrior. You are a fierce competitor, but then so am I.*

Dedication

First and foremost, a special shout out goes to Chris King, without whom the Bachelor Brotherhood wouldn't be. Much gratitude to DW Adler and Barbara whose insights and feedback were invaluable to me while writing this story. To my family, thank you! I couldn't write without your love and support. Of course, my deepest appreciation and love goes out to my readers, who mean so much to me! And last but most certainly not least, I owe my sincere gratitude to my fabulous editor, Callie Lynn Wolfe, cover artist Rae Monet, and the wonderful staff at The Wild Rose Press for helping me share the Alphas with the world.

Prologue:
The recent past...

The half-moon shone down from above, through the bare trees, causing gray skeletal shadows on the snow-covered ground. Demetri Romanoff ghosted over the land, careful not to disturb the peaceful winter night as his breath frosted in the air.

His preternatural gaze glossed over the landscape as he moved, taking in the details of the night, nothing too small to escape his attention. He noted the lack of movement in the eerily still forest. No wind blew, no animal seen nor heard.

Even in Mason's Bluff, Wyoming, in the month of December, there was usually some movement, some sounds in the night. An animal scurrying home, tree branches bumping together in the wind, or perhaps a pinecone falling. However, tonight the silence was deafening.

He suddenly dropped to one knee, overcome with a sense of despair and grief. The feelings were not his own, but instead came to him through the mental channel he and his cousin, Nicholai, shared.

Nicholai had recently lost his heartmate, his one true love. She had fled after discovering Nicholai was a vampire.

The warrior had advised his cousin to go to England and get her. He didn't understand Nicholai's hesitation to do so. Nicholai needn't be in such pain. As his heartmate, his woman could not help but come to love him. There was no excuse for his cousin not to go, throw her over his shoulder if he had to, and bring her back to Russia. But for some reason, probably because the female was human, his cousin would not heed his advice on the matter.

Nicholai had mentioned something about wooing and needing time to work things out. In the meantime, his emotions came across their mindlink, and the warrior struggled to block them. It was a distraction he did not need.

The scent of the approaching storm tickled his nose. Clouds blanketed the moon, taking its light. The dampness settled on his shoulders as small flakes began to glide down.

He straightened once more to his full height. His six-foot-six, burly frame dwarfed all but the trees while his thick thighs took him through the woods. A leather cord drew his long, black hair from his storm-gray eyes. His neck and face, thickened by years of pumping iron, were taunt this night with foreboding.

The air tasted of malice and hatred. Demetri sent his senses out into the forest, spreading them wide in search of what might be the cause of his unrest. He detected a den of foxes nearby, and a bear hibernated some distance away. Neither of which gave him pause.

Then he sensed several blank spots, one coming from the mountain that loomed ahead and three at various spaces throughout the forest. He turned his preternatural vision in the direction of the spots, but found nothing of note, only the snow-covered underbrush and rocks. He listened carefully. Hearing nothing, he continued on.

There had been some trouble in these woods. People mauled. Others had gone missing. He'd patrolled the forest every evening in hopes of finding the cause and preventing more deaths. He and Stephan, the leader of the Alphas, had spent days searching for a pregnant female vampire that had gone missing under suspicious circumstances. Their search produced no results, and Stephan had decided to return home to his heartmate.

These were his woods. This was his home, and he would not allow any more of the people under his protection to be maimed or killed. Demetri breathed a heavy sigh as he came to a spot where the snow-covered ground lay disturbed. He knelt on one knee to examine the evidence.

He and his comrade, Stephan, had recently discovered signs of a struggle in the snow, animal tracks leading to and from the spot and human footprints. The two warriors had followed the tracks until they led into the side of the mountain. The same mountain where they had both sensed a large void.

Demetri pushed to his feet then squared his broad shoulders as another wave of grief rushed through his mind. The palpable force of Nicholai's pain demanded attention.

Demetri closed his mind to the powerful emotion as best he could. He needed to be alert, watchful, not distracted by his cousin.

Demetri headed toward the mountain, following the old set of tracks which were becoming less visible with each flake that fell from the sky. Soon the tracks would be covered entirely, but he remembered where they led.

As he neared the mountain, he heard a soft rustle of movement behind him. He stilled, then cast his awareness over the land. Sensing only a blank spot, he began to turn around just as a sting hit his back. Another sting bit into him. And another. By the time he had turned fully, a total of six stings pelted his back and side.

The large warrior took a step forward, determined to find the cause. Had he disturbed a beehive? Had an animal attacked?

His legs gave way, refusing to support the weight of his stony sinew and muscle. He tumbled forward. The Alpha tried to throw his arms out in front of his chest to catch his weight, but they refused to hold him. His face landed in the snowy detritus with a crunch of his straight nose.

The angle of his head allowed him to locate the two darts protruding from his side, their shafts and flights quivering from the jarring impact of hitting the ground. Something cold ran through his veins. As cold as the snow beneath his body, it burned through his blood.

Just before the darkness took him, he tried in vain to focus his blurry eyes as what appeared to be a pair of paws approached.

Chapter 1
Present Day...

Tatiana sat at the end of the bar. Her hair, blue-black like a raven's wing, matched the leather she wore. The ends, bluntly cut, brushed just above her shoulders. Her yellow, feline-like, eyes glanced around, glaring at the patrons in the place as if daring them to take her on.

She barely noticed the decor. It looked similar to the other places she had been during the past few months. These places were all the same: dark, smoky, with the stench of stale booze and sweat oozing from the walls.

Tatiana emptied the glass in one gulp before slamming it down on the bar while the whiskey burned down her throat. Like an old friend coming home, warmth spread through her body. She'd been cold for months, not just from the freezing temperatures outside, but also from the stark loneliness.

The Naugahyde creaked under her weight when she settled on the stool. Her spot at the end of the bar put her back to a wall and provided an unobstructed view of the door. Her training with the Vampire Enforcement Squad, commonly referred to as VES, had taught her well. She always made sure she placed herself in the best possible area to have the advantage should trouble arise. And trouble was exactly what she sought tonight.

Her eyes narrowed as a group of burly men entered. Dressed in jeans and leather jackets, their leather chaps suggested they rode motorcycles. As if to confirm her supposition, the odor of bike exhaust burned her nose when they passed.

They pushed their way through the crowd toward an occupied table in the back. The men stood silently around the table, still as statues, their glares the only communication needed. The current occupants scurried away like rodents, leaving the table for the group.

Tatiana shook her head. Always the same. A pack mentality. As long as they were together they thought themselves strong, but pick them apart and the biker group would crumple like a weakened house of cards.

She shrugged as her attention turned back to the bar. *Safety in numbers I suppose,* she thought as the barkeep placed another glass in front of her.

The woman beside her gestured toward her glass. "That's your fifth one of those, honey. You trying to drown your sorrows?"

Tatiana gave her an assessing look, noting the way her red dress appeared two sizes too small. It clung so tight she could have been wearing nothing at all. Each lump and bump were clearly visible. Her makeup had been applied liberally, the blue eye shadow a patriotic companion to her ruby red lips and white skin. The way she had slurred the word sorrows clearly indicated her inebriation.

"Hardly," Tatiana replied, effectively dismissing the woman by turning her attention back to the group in the back.

A waitress approached the table, and one of the men pinched her backside as she tried to take their orders. She shooed away the offending hand, only to have one of the men grab her and pull her onto his lap. His hands rough on her thighs, he started to make his way up under her skirt.

Someone should teach those guys a lesson, and I know just the person to do it.

Tatiana placed a fifty under her glass and slid away from the bar. She pushed up her leather bustier until the girls sat precariously close to slipping out then flung her leather duster carelessly over one shoulder.

This is going to be fun, she thought as she walked across the bar, putting a suggestive sway into her hips. She had been itching for a brawl, needed a little action.

She'd been frequenting bars in town after town, tracking the Alpha who had disappeared under mysterious circumstances. After months of investigating, she still believed he lived. Her instincts had told her that much, and she had learned long ago to trust those instincts.

She sauntered by the group, purposely brushing one of them on the shoulder when she passed. She sensed their collective gaze on her as she made her way toward the side exit door. The chairs slid in unison across the floor, and the sound brought a satisfied smile to her pretty face. Heavy boots clomped on the wooden floor behind her while she walked out into the night.

The frigid air bit her cheeks. It might be March, but it was still cold in Canada. The smell of crisp clean air mingled with the putrid stench of old garbage from the dumpster resting against the building. The malodorous combination made Tatiana's stomach roll. Perhaps she should not have downed quite so many drinks, but then again, she had not come to the bar expecting a fight.

However, that was exactly what she was about to have. And it was okay with her.

She trekked behind the building. Only a copse of trees, with their bare branches and shadowy outlines, would bear witness to what was about to happen. She glanced at the men over her shoulder. They wore similar expressions, a combination of lust in their eyes and violence in the hard lines of their faces. The leader stepped forward.

"My, my look what have we here, boys. Something to play with."

Tatiana turned slowly at the taunt. The menacing sound of their laughter slid down her spine, making it straighten in defiance. A large boulder sat next to where she stood. She placed her coat over the rock, taking time to smooth the leather out as she spoke. "You don't want to play with me, boys," she warned, pinning them with her steely gaze. "I suggest you get on your bikes and leave while you still can."

The men's arrogant laughter reached her ears just as the leader motioned toward her with a flick of his two fingers. Two of his gang raced forward, simultaneously grabbing Tatiana's arms. The bite of their fingers brought her senses to full attention. This was about to get interesting. She sent a silent prayer of thanks up to the heavens that these men were all action.

The leader approached her. "Time to play, bitch," the man bit out between clenched teeth as he reached for her leather bustier.

His hand never touched her skin. Tatiana's leg shot up. Her steel-toed boot caught the man under his chin. While his head snapped back, Tatiana jumped, allowing the two men holding her to take her weight as she kicked both legs out and propelled the leader flying backward into the building. His body hit the brick wall with a wicked cracking sound before he slumped onto the ground. Tatiana wasn't sure if he lay dead or unconscious, but it did not matter. Either way he was not a concern for the moment.

Her momentum took the men holding her to the ground, the three of them falling together as a unit. Air rushed from the lungs on either side of her as she turned her agile body to kneel between the two. She punched one in the face, breaking his nose. She savored the way it crunched flat under her knuckles, sending a splatter of blood down his face. As he moaned, her other hand contacted with his jaw. His head snapped to the side, his eyes closing slowly when the darkness took him.

Tatiana turned toward the man lying on her opposite side. She grabbed his head in her hands and squeezed. His hands shot up to cover hers, his fingers scraping against her skin in a desperate attempt to pull her away. She built pressure. His eyes bugged from his head. Just as they started to roll back in his sockets, Tatiana heard a pair of boots crunching on the frozen ground behind her. She turned in time to see a shiny metal object fly through the air. Releasing the head from her hands, she jumped up, landing on the balls of her feet. The strike came as she shifted her weight.

A searing pain coursed through her thigh. She tugged the blade from her leg. It burned as it slid past her muscle and sinew. Her brows narrowed in understanding, when she realized had she not jumped, it would have gone straight through her heart.

"Dammit, these were my favorite pants, you asshole." She swore a streak of curses as she inspected the hole caused by the blade.

The fourth biker backed away, a horrified look on his face. No doubt, he'd been in many fights in his time, but she'd bet he had never seen a woman react to being knifed as she had. His disbelieving eyes watched the wound on her leg heal, knitting itself back together from the inside out. The scent of fear rolled off him. He turned to run and hit the solid object in his path.

His eyes roamed skyward, coming to rest on a face. Blue eyes penetrated his gaze, and he went limp as a set of steel bands clamped around his biceps.

"What's going on out here?" asked Alex, while he held onto the man who had run into him.

"Nothing, I can't handle." Tatiana turned her attention once more to the man lying next to her feet. She reached for him, and he scrambled backward in an awkward half crab walk. Her fist closed around his leather jacket before she lifted him above her head. His hands went to hers, trying to get her to release her grip to no avail.

She reared back and let her closed fist fly. Like a ball of iron, it contacted with the biker's face, snapping his head back on his shoulders. A click-click behind her stilled her next movement.

"Put him down," the leader commanded as he pushed himself up against the wall, using the hand not holding a gun. "I said. Put. Him. Down."

Noting how surprisingly steady the gun trained on Tatiana appeared, she slowly lowered the man she held until his feet touched the ground. When she released him, he fell in a heap.

As the female warrior turned to face her aggressor, a shot rang out. The concussion echoed against the building. From the sound, Tatiana knew it must be a large caliber even before the bullet ripped through her arm.

In a blur, Alex grabbed the man who shot Tatiana. The gun was flung one way while the Alpha hurled the human body through the air in the opposite direction. Alex's breath frosted in the air as he leapt to where the man's body landed. The warrior picked the biker up by the lapels of his jacket and tossed him against a nearby tree as if he weighed no more than a small dog. The tree shook from the impact. The man fell into a crumpled to the ground with a thud.

Alex raced over to his counterpart.

They had been working together for months. During that time, she knew Alex had discovered she was meticulous, a true hunter who took her job seriously. So why then did he look at her like she had lost her mind?

"Mind telling me what all this was about?" His thick arm took in the surrounding area with a grand sweeping gesture. "You stalked them. Lured them out here for a fight. It isn't like you."

"We need to erase their memories," Tatiana replied, hoping to distract her partner. "I'll do this one first."

"We can't just erase their memories. They will wake up wondering where the bruises and broken bones came from. We need to plant a cover story."

Tatiana nodded. "Let's have them believe they attacked a group of preppy frat boys, and they got their asses kicked."

A smile spread across her partner's handsome face, and Tatiana couldn't restrain the answering grin which lifted the corners of her own mouth.

"As much as I'd like to deal their egos that kind of blow, I think it would be easier to make them believe an animal did this," Alex suggested.

Tatiana's smile turned downright evil. "I like that idea. We could add a few scratches on them, making the story seem more believable."

Tatiana's skin crawled, like large tarantulas walked over her flesh. Foreboding washed over her in a tidal wave of anxiety. She glanced around, knowing she would find nothing. These feelings had come for months though she had been careful not to let her partner in on them. She did not want the Alpha to know she sensed the feelings of the male they were hunting.

"Memories wiped," Alexander announced, pulling Tatiana from her reverie. "You want to do the honors of the memory implant, or shall I?"

Tatiana grabbed the duster from its resting place on the rock. After shrugging gingerly into the coat, cognizant of her injured arm, she glanced over her shoulder at the Alpha. "I'd be happy to do it." She pulled out a stiletto from her boot, bent down beside the man laying supine on the ground, and began scoring his skin to appear as if an animal had raked him with its claws.

"I think I'll make them believe a large mountain lion with yellow eyes and dark fur attacked them."

Chapter 2

Tatiana emerged from the small bath in her hotel room dressed in a pair of low riding jeans and a sweater that clung to her lithe body. She vigorously rubbed her wet hair with a towel trying to dry it. She hated staying in these cheap hotel rooms. They never had a hairdryer, and with the temperature outside dipping below freezing, the last thing she wanted was damp hair.

She supposed she should just be glad to have a place to sleep indoors, for there had been times on this mission when they had not been so fortunate.

Her thoughts traveled to Demetri Romanoff. She damned the day she had been injured during an operation, and the male had given her some of his blood to heal her. Taking the blood created a connection to him and his emotions.

It rarely worked that way. Usually when a vampire drank someone's blood, it was a simple act of nourishment and nothing more, but when they drank the blood of their heartmate, the blood of the one person who was the other half of their soul, they could then sense the person's emotion. Demetri's act of generosity had irrevocably connected them forever.

Tatiana marched back to the bath and draped the towel over the shower rod to dry then looked at her pale reflection in the mirror over the sink.

"Connected forever to that male. You better find

the chauvinist and quick, so you can get Stephan off your back and get Demetri out of your life."

She turned away and headed for the bed.

Thank the Fates Demetri didn't drink from me.

Doing so would have established a mindlink, a mental pathway that allowed two vampires to communicate. Without a way to communicate telepathically, Tatiana could only sense Demetri's emotions, which allowed her to know what Demetri was feeling, but not where he was being held. It was overwhelming and some nights, like tonight, she needed something to take her focus off her quarry.

Tonight, the worry was her own. The sensations from Demetri were less frequent, and she feared that meant he spent more time unconscious, or worse, dying. When his anxiety or pain hit her, she almost welcomed it now. Afraid there may come a time soon when she would stop sensing him altogether.

We must find him before it is too late.

A knock sounded on the door, pulling her from her thoughts. She reached for her Smith & Wesson, clicking off the safety as she moved toward the door. Laying her back to the wall next to the door jamb, she called out, "Yeah?"

A southern drawl answered back. "It's me. Open up."

A tired sigh escaped her lips before she cracked the door. Alex pushed through the entryway, a six-pack in one hand and a pizza box in the other.

"How's the arm?" the male asked as he crossed to the only table in the room.

Tatiana rolled her shoulder in demonstration. "It's healed thanks to the donation of blood supplied by those cretins we fought."

"Their blood might be regenerating, but I thought you'd like something to eat too." The Alpha gestured toward the pizza with a nod of his head.

"That smells fantastic." Tatiana moved her duffle bag off the rickety table and pulled out a chair for Alex while he placed the items down.

"Isn't it usually the man who holds the chair for the lady?" Alex quipped before he slid a second chair over to the table and held it for Tatiana.

"I'm no lady." Tatiana took a seat. A smell of mold and mildew from the tattered cushions wafted in the air when she sat.

"I'm afraid I'd have to disagree with that statement." Alex gave her an appreciative look. "The way that sweater and those jeans hug your curves, there is no doubt you're all woman."

Truth be told, he wasn't exactly hard on the eyes either.

"Easy tiger," she cautioned her partner. "I'll bring you up on sexual harassment charges."

"Tiger? Me? You're the one who looks like a cat with those yellow eyes of yours and that wild hair."

"Pbbbbbbbtttt!" She blew a loud, unladylike raspberry. "Just sit down, Hall, and stuff some pizza in that pretty boy face of yours."

Alex did as commanded, pulling a slice of pizza from the box and offering it to his partner. "You think my face is pretty, huh?"

"Don't flatter yourself."

"I believe it was you who was doing the flattering there, Bolovich."

They were total opposites and not just physically.

She was a natural-born vampire while Alex had once been human. He was a member of the Alpha Council, an elite Special Forces unit of the vampire world, and she was an agent for VES, the policing agency for vampires. But for all their differences, there was one way Tatiana Bolovich was exactly like Alexander Hall. They were both fierce fighters, and Tatiana respected her partner for his abilities.

Tatiana pulled a beer from the six-pack. With a flick of her finger, she opened the top and took a long pull. It wasn't as good as the firewater she slammed down earlier, but it helped to take the edge off. "You heard from Nicholai lately?"

The Alpha shook his head. "I was thinking we should contact him tonight. See if he has been able to reach Demetri using their mindlink."

Tatiana doubted Demetri's cousin would have any news for them. Nicholai had tried several times to contact Demetri through their mental connection, but the information he'd gleaned so far had been limited because Demetri quickly shut off the channel each time his cousin made contact. Nicholai feared it was because he was being tortured and did not want Nicholai to sense his pain.

That confirmed what she sensed. Demetri's constant feelings of confinement let her surmise he was being held against his will. His feelings of deep anxiety and pain led her to believe his was being tortured daily.

Alex took a bite of the pizza he had removed from the box. He pushed the lid closed as he swallowed. "He hasn't been very helpful yet. All he has given us is Demetri was abducted and being held in a place that is cold."

"I agree it isn't much to go on." Tatiana took a swig of her beer.

The Alpha clinked his bottle against hers. "Here's to finding out something useful for a change."

She stood. "No time like the present."

Tatiana grabbed a laptop from its protective bag and plugged it into the nearest outlet. She opened the computer as she placed it on top of the closed pizza box.

Alex gasped in horror. "Whoa!" He pulled the pizza out from underneath the laptop. "Show more respect for the equipment there, lady. I'll have you know this laptop is a top-of-the-line Alexander Hall Special."

The VES agent shook her head as the machine powered up. "Sorry." She put her hands up in mock surrender. "I lost my head for a second. I forgot this thing is your baby."

"Well, it is. And don't you forget it." Alex pet the keyboard and winked. "That's okay, baby. She didn't mean to hurt you."

Alex's fingers flew over the keys, working their magic. In seconds, Nicholai's face appeared on the screen. "Hey Nikko," Alex greeted his fellow Alpha.

"Greetings, Alexander and Tatiana. Do you have any news to report?" Hope shone in Nicholai's dark eyes.

Tatiana shifted in her chair. "Unfortunately, the only thing we learned was Demetri doesn't appear to be in this town."

"What about you, Nicholai? Have you been able to contact him?"

"Briefly," Nicholai informed the couple. "Demetri

is growing weak, very weak. I used our mindlink to push into his mind. He was unable to stop me."

Tatiana flinched. Being hundreds of years older, Demetri should have easily blocked Nicholai from his mind. His failure to do so, coupled with the lack of sensation she'd been feeling, did not bode well for his physical state.

"What did you take from his mind?" Tatiana asked.

"A name. Toulous."

Alex leaned forward in interest. "Is that a person or a place?"

"I am not sure. Just as I probed further, everything went black."

"I don't like the sound of that," murmured the VES agent.

"I cannot say I liked it either. It did not feel like Demetri was pushing me out. It was more like he went unconscious or…"

"Don't say it, man." Alex shook his head furiously. "Demetri is the biggest, baddest Vampire I know. He would take on an army and come out fighting. Hell, I've *seen* him take on a small army and win. I can't believe someone's going to be able to beat him down."

"A body can only take so much, even Demetri's body." Nicholai glanced between the two vampires. "We are all counting on you two to find him in time. Hopefully, the name Toulous will help you."

"I'll get right on it," the blond Alpha assured him. "Me and my magic fingers will search through databases until we come up with something."

"If anyone can find out what Toulous is, it would be you, my friend." A small round face appeared next to Nicholai as he spoke. Tatiana watched the Alpha drag the woman onto his lap, settling her sideways as he continued. "I will continue to try to reach Demetri. Please let me know when you discover what Toulous is."

"Of course," Alex assured his friend. "Hi, Juliette. You keepin' Nicholai in line?"

A smile graced the pretty face on the screen. "More like he's keeping me in line. Christina and I have been very busy making plans for our double wedding. She keeps going overboard in the ideas department, and Nicholai keeps reeling us back in. I swear if it were up to me, we'd elope and get it over with."

Nicholai gave his heartmate a squeeze. "Of course, we have all agreed that the wedding will wait until Demetri is found."

"We'll do our best to find him quickly." Alexander gave his partner a wayward glance. "Hopefully, this new lead will pan out. Let us go, so I can start working on it."

"Safe travels," Nicholai called as his hand reached around his heartmate to cut the connection.

The screen went blank. Even with his concern for his cousin paramount in his mind, Nicholai appeared happy. He had just found his heartmate at Christmas. They belonged to each other wholly, even though they had only been together for a few months. Tatiana almost envied them.

Almost.

She shook her head at the thought.

"They seem happy," Alex observed, his fingers tapping away on the keyboard.

"I never want to be like that with another person. I'm my own person, not half of a whole." Tatiana crossed her arms and stared sightlessly across the room. "I'd hate to be attached to someone else."

Alex shifted in his chair, glancing at her over the laptop, and continued to type. "But the Alphas I know who have found their mates all seem excited about the pairing."

"What's to be excited about since heartmates rarely survive being apart, especially if one passes before the other?"

She did not need someone else to care for deeply.

Especially Demetri Romanoff—a Neanderthal, who honored the old-world ways, in which the male dictated to the female. And didn't that just grate on her.

She had control issues and owned them. Tatiana refused to change who she was, even to be with her heartmate.

She was helping to locate Demetri because the leader of the Alphas had asked for her help. The VES and the Alphas had a tenuous relationship, and she only helped them out of respect for their leader.

It has nothing to do with wanting to find my heartmate, she assured herself.

She would have to be very careful around Demetri when they found him. He could never know she was his heartmate. A male vampire would stop at nothing to get his heartmate, and a male like Demetri would not think twice about throwing her over his shoulder and dragging her to his lair. If he knew they were mates, she would be locked up like some china doll, kept safe for Demetri to play with at his whim.

Just the thought had her back bristling and hairs standing on end. No one, especially Demetri Romanoff, would do that to her. Not again. She could take care of herself, and no one would cage her. Ever.

Alex misread her anger. "I'm going as fast as I can. It isn't easy to break into secured Wi-Fi. I've found three signals in the area, but they're all password protected."

"If we had a second computer, I could help."

"We've been over this. A second computer is just something else to tote about from place to place. We agreed to travel light, remember?"

"I remember." Tatiana glanced around the dingy hotel room. "I don't need a reminder of how everything is about efficiency and not convenience."

Alex smiled, and his fingers stilled. He turned her way. "Do I hear a hint of longing in your voice? Don't tell me the great Agent Bolovich is ready to leave all this luxury." He took in the room with a sweep of his hand.

Tatiana did not keep the laugh from spilling from her lips. "I admit I wouldn't mind seeing the inside of my home again."

Alex went back to his task. His fingers flew over the keys as he spoke. "Just where is home?"

"I have a place in the States."

"Me, too."

Another laugh burst from her lips. "I'd guessed that from your southern accent."

Alex chuckled. "Yeah. I guess you would. Where in the States?"

"I have a home in Florida."

"The Sunshine State?" Alex asked incredulously, as his light brows shot up. "I don't know many vampires who hang out in a place known for its sunshine."

"That's exactly why I chose there. I'm not likely to run into too many of our kind. I can stay anonymous, hidden. It makes my job a lot easier." Alex nodded in understanding as she continued. "And there is nothing prettier than a beach in the moonlight."

"Hoo-yah!"

The Alpha's yell made her jump.

"You found something," Tatiana said. It was more of a statement than a question.

"Yeah. Toulous is a town in Canada. Population three hundred and sixty-one. It's in the northern part of the country. It is remote, barren, the perfect place for an abduction."

Tatiana clamped a hand down on Alex's shoulder. "For the first time since we started this mission, I think we finally have a real lead."

"I agree. I'll gas up the car. It looks like we're headin' north."

Chapter 3

The bite of ice-cold water splashing across his bare chest and face brought him out of the darkness. Demetri sputtered as the sound of a woman screaming filled his ears. He recognized the voice. The female prisoner. The bastard must be experimenting again.

His mind, slow from weeks of starvation, gradually came online. With each second that passed, he registered a new sensation. The pain in his atrophied muscles was first, followed by the burning sensation in his stomach. Agony flooded each cell in his body as it died from a lack of sustenance.

His captors wanted him weak, wanted to push his body to the limit. They had burned him, then filleted the skin from his body. He had suffered through his bones being broken, sometimes just one or two, sometimes several at one time.

His tongue darted out to lick the drops of water from his parched mouth, the movement brought a fresh round of pain when his chapped lips cracked open. He had been reduced to this state by demons. He'd have spat at the thought if he could produce saliva. They were vicious, ruthless. Evil.

Shamed oozed over his skin. Never had he been a weak man, even as a human he had been known throughout his village as a man of strength. As a vampire, he made himself into a force of nature. His body had matched his personality—strong, large, fierce.

Now, he lay strapped to a cot, helpless for the first time in his life with a female screaming for help down the hall. It should have been easy to escape, with only leather straps to hold him in place. But too weak to lift his arms, he couldn't break the bindings.

He opened his eyes. Above him, stood two thickly muscled guards. It took effort to focus on the evil grins on their faces. Demetri fought to stay conscious. His eyes fluttered from the effort.

The guard closest to his head slapped his face.

"Wake up, sleepy head." He undid the restraints. "Lane wants to see you."

Demetri gave an involuntary wince that launched a wave of burning agony through his body. Lane, the most sadistic of all the demons, wanted to see him. *Lane*. Before the abduction, he had never known such cruelty could exist in one person.

Lane claimed his experiments were designed to enlighten him as to how vampires regenerated and fought off human disease, but having been the subject of the experiments for so long, Demetri knew better. The real reason behind the so-called experiments? Lane enjoyed inflicting pain which the poor female down the hall was no doubt finding out.

The two guards pulled Demetri to his feet. Each grabbed an arm when his legs refused to hold his slight weight. Repulsion and anger mixed as they dragged him from the cell. His condition sickened him. Too weak to fight, the demons would do whatever they wanted to him. His stomach knotted in anticipation.

The guards pushed a set of double doors open, and bright fluorescent light flooded his eyes. He tried to throw a hand over his face, but it refused to cooperate.

"Put him over there," instructed Lane without turning to see who had entered.

He tried to fight, tried to pull free of their grasps. They laughed at his puny efforts and hoisted him onto the metal gurney with more force than was necessary.

Shame and embarrassment heated his face. They had complete power over him. They decided where he went, when he ate, whether he lived or died. Never had he been so vulnerable—he hated it.

Lane crossed to his side holding a large needle in his gloved hand. He smiled down at the emaciated warrior. "Nice of you to join me, bloodsucker."

"Like I had a choice," Demetri bit out, his dry throat rasping the words.

"True. I need more of your blood."

"I doubt I have any left after the last time."

Lane's wicked laugh sent a shiver through Demetri's sore body. "Ironic, isn't it? You're the vampire, but I'm the one sucking out the blood. Funny how life works."

A sharp stick pricked the crook of his arm as Lane slid the large needle in and began taking his precious blood. "Yeah, real fucking funny."

Lane let out a foul curse. "I can't get any blood." He removed the needle and placed it in the opposite arm.

"That's because you have starved me so long."

Lane's gaze rose from the empty syringe to stare at Demetri's face. "I supposed I could give you a few sips. Just enough to take about twenty CC's from you."

Demetri's fangs lengthen. A few sips of blood would help, but he would need much more if he were to recover his strength.

Lane snapped his fingers and one of the guards brought him a bag of blood. Lane took the bag without a word to the guard and stuck the needle into it creating a tiny hole in the plastic.

Immediately, the scent of the crimson substance flooded Demetri's nose. His body spasmed in anticipation. He would have been salivating if he could.

Lane lowered the bag to Demetri's cracked lips, the weight of it split the delicate skin. A drop fell from the bag onto his tongue. It was cold. It was the wrong type.

It's the most amazing thing I've ever tasted in my life!

With the precious drops sliding down his throat, his cells screamed in relief, each fighting for their share of the life-giving sustenance.

For one exquisite moment, he knew bliss. The painful world in which he was being held prisoner melted away, and he floated in Heaven. A pain free, all-was-right-with-the-world, Heaven. Then in the next moment, reality crashed in.

Demetri opened his eyes. Horror struck as Demetri realized tears had formed in his eyes, threatening to spill over. He blinked them back, unsure if they came from the pain in his body, the knowledge the blood had been taken away, or the frustration of realizing once again the demon assumed control.

If he ever got out of here, Lane and his cohorts would be brought to justice. A justice that involved the same suffering inflicted on him.

Lane pushed the needle back into Demetri's arm and pulled back on the plunger. This time the demon was rewarded by a flow of blood that slowly filled the barrel.

A whimper came from across the room, and Demetri's head turned toward the soft sound. He eyes widened when his gaze rested on a female strapped to a chair. His fangs lengthened, nostrils flared when the aroma of the blood dripping from her wounds wafted toward him in the air. Her blood called to his body, but her helpless moans called to the hero in him.

He struggled against the restraints while Lane made his way over to the woman then filled her veins with the stolen blood.

Pure satisfaction grew on the scientist's face, and he watched the wounds heal on the female. "I've done it," he mumbled to himself, lost in his thoughts. "After months of experimenting, I have proven it's in their blood. Now I just have to figure out exactly what it is and how to reproduce it."

The bastard paced the room, his brows furrowing over his red eyes as he ruminated. "The bloodsucker must be kept alive a little longer." He stopped and glanced over his shoulder at Demetri. "I need more of the creature's blood. It will need to be fed regularly enough to produce the amount of blood I need, but not so often it can regain its strength."

A low growl emanated from Demetri's throat, stilling the demon's steps. Demetri swore a string of vile curses in his mind.

Lane resumed his pacing, his hands clasped behind his back. "Jara will be thrilled. Perhaps my discovery will win me her favor. She might allow me to share the discovery with her brother."

Demetri willed his hearing to block the constant droning of the mad scientist. The male could ramble on for hours. Most of the time, Demetri listened and learned about his enemy.

For example, this Jara, seemed to be the driving force behind the demon mission to discover the healing properties in the vampires. It was at her behest her brother, the Demon King, had agreed to fund Lane's experiments. She was responsible for acquiring the scientist this facility that had once belonged to her father as well as for blocking his ability to contact others through a mindlink. He'd overheard the guards saying she'd done a spell to block the communication.

If I ever get out of here, she'll be the second one to die.

Lane rubbed a thoughtful hand through the auburn beard that masked the gauntness of his cheekbones. "It will be tricky, making sure only just enough blood is given to the beast." The corners of his thin lips lifted into a malicious grin. "I'll have the lackeys supervise the feedings. That way if anything goes wrong, it will be their heads, not mine."

One of those lackeys cleared his throat. The demon appeared to come back to himself. The sadistic bastard straightened his lean frame, squaring his boney shoulders before turning to face the guards. "Take them back to his cell," instructed Lane before pulling the latex gloves from his hands and tossing them in the trash.

The guards hesitated, the larger of the two asking, "You want us to put them in the same cell?"

"That's what I said." Lane's irritation showed in his march across the room. "Put them in the same cell. I want him to be able to feed on the human."

"But, sir, won't it give him his strength back?" The

guards shifted back and forth on their feet.

"The girl is almost dead. Her injuries have all but bled her dry. She won't be able to supply the vampire with much blood. Let the beast suck her dry, it won't do him much good."

"But, sir—" the guard's words died in the throat at the look Lane shot at him.

"Just do it. I do not pay you to think."

Lane pushed through the doors, leaving the guards in stunned silence until one muttered, "I should probably get Jara to strengthen her spell to block communication, even though she recently did the spell."

Demetri closed his eyes, too tired to keep them open any longer. As the darkness took him, his last thoughts were of the girl. He would be damned if he would give that monster what he wanted, even if it killed him to deny himself the blood his body ached for.

****

Tatiana sat up with a start, grabbing the dash of the car with both hands so hard her fingers left a slight imprint in the plastic. Her heart raced in her chest, and air puffed from her lungs in heavy breaths.

"Easy now," Alex cooed in a soothing voice. "I'd like to return this rental in one piece. Mind taking your fingers off the dash?"

Tatiana blinked and glanced from side to side. She had been having a perfectly enjoyable dream until it morphed into something dark and ugly. The sensation of dread and frustration blurred her vision with tears.

There was no reason for her to feel thusly. They were on their way to Toulous. They had their first real lead toward finding Demetri. She knew they were getting closer because the emotions she sensed from him were growing stronger. Things were finally looking up, but the negative feelings she had awakened with lingered.

It must be Demetri's frustration and dread I'm sensing, she thought as the trees outside sped by. A fluttering sensation danced in her mind. Abruptly she snapped a mental wall into place and turned to glare at Alex.

"Sorry, I was just wondering what you were thinking about," he confessed.

"Demetri," Tatiana answered honestly. "And don't you try to read my mind, young one. It's rude."

Alex flinched. "I'm sorry. It's just you are so closed-lipped. I never know what you're thinkin' especially when you get those pained looks on your face."

Tatiana sighed. She should be able to tell Alex everything. After all, he was her partner on this case. It might help them if she let Alex share the information she'd picked up from Demetri, but she could not. If she let Alex into her mind to have access to her connection with Demetri, he might discover they were heartmates.

Determination straightened her spine, and she sneaked a quick glance in Alex's direction. If he knew the truth, it would just be a matter of time until Demetri found out. The last thing she needed was Demetri knowing they were mates.

"Don't worry about my looks, Hall. When I have something to share, you'll be the first to know. Otherwise, leave it alone. Understand?"

His hands tightened on the steering wheel until his knuckles went white at being chastised. "Understood, ma'am." The sarcasm dripped from his voice. "My apologies. I thought partners shared things with each other, but I guess I was wrong."

Tatiana's temper heated her face. "Look Alex. We might technically be partners. But this is only temporary. When we find Demetri I'm outta here, back to my life in VES, and we'll most likely never see each other again. So, if I don't feel like sharing, maybe it's because I know in a little while you will no longer be a part of my life."

The Alpha's eyes never left the road when he spoke. "I guess I'm just used to being on missions with the other Alphas. We are a family. We might fight from time to time, but we always have each other's backs. We share things about ourselves, because it helps make us better at reading each other. And the better we know each other the better we are at being a team.

"I thought you and I might get to know each other a little better since we are going to be stuck working together for a while. But, hey, if you want to be the strong silent type, then don't let me stop ya."

Tatiana's hand fisted in her lap. The Alpha was right, sharing did make people a better team, but she couldn't afford to get too close. She lived life by her rules. She needed no one—she preferred it that way. A lone wolf, a woman in complete control, she was not willing to risk giving even a little control away by getting close to or needing anyone. Especially, not some Alpha.

They rode in strained silence for hours, making their way along the highways and back roads that led to Toulous.

Alex pulled off the dirt road, and parked in front of

the hotel check-in. A dust cloud rolled from behind the car.

He shut down the engine and turned. The appearance of his serious face drew her attention. "I don't want to fight, Tatiana. I won't pry into your life. And in return I only ask if there is something I should know you'll tell me. I hate feeling like you are keeping secrets from me, but I'm willing to believe the secrets have nothing to do with finding Demetri.

"'Cause I have to tell you, if I thought for one minute you were keeping me from finding Demetri, I'd make you regret it. I might be younger than you, but I'm still an Alpha.

"Do we have an understanding?"

Tatiana didn't keep the smile from her face. She admired a male who would stick up for his friend, even at his own personal risk. In a physical altercation between them, she'd emerge the winner, but this young vampire obviously thought enough of Demetri to be willing to stick his neck out for him. Perhaps there was more to Demetri than she realized. She tucked the thought aside to examine later.

"I understand, Alex. I promise you, I am not hiding anything that would keep us from finding Demetri. I want to find him as much as you do." *So, I can get on with my life.*

The blond Alpha nodded in acknowledgment and folded his large frame from the rental car. While he acquired two rooms for the night, Tatiana paced in front of the vehicle. For a moment, a blanket of utter bliss coated her as if she had fallen into Nirvana itself. Then in an instant the feeling vanished, replaced by the need to play savior. She knew without a doubt these feelings were not her own.

While she and Alex made their way to their rooms, bags in hand, she tried to sort out Demetri's feelings. What could they mean? How could he experience complete euphoria one minute and utter helplessness the next?

She would have to locate him to find the answers to her questions. She bid Alex good morning and closed the door to her room.

"That is exactly what I need to do. Locate Demetri—and soon."

Chapter 4

Demetri watched wearily from his place on the floor as the viewing window opened in the titanium-lined, steel door to the cell. Red eyes peered through the small opening. It gave him a moment's pleasure to hear the string of curses which left the scientist's mouth as he looked around the room before slamming the window shut with a solid clunk that reverberated off the walls.

The loud noise startled the woman with him back to life, rousing her from her slumber. She pushed herself up from the cot upon which she lay, panting from the effort it took to lean her back against the unforgiving wall.

"What was that?" She slowly turned her head in his direction.

Demetri licked his parched lips in an attempt to moisten his mouth enough for it to function. When he eventually answered, his voice sounded low and raspy. "The one they call Lane. He came to see if I had killed you yet."

"Please," the woman's voice wavered as she shifted on the uncomfortable cot.

"Please what?"

"Kill me."

The request did not surprise Demetri for it was not the first time she had made such a demand of him.

Since being placed in his cell, the human female with him had asked for her death at his hands with startling regularity. Every conversation circled back to the same request.

Once the woman had learned he was a vampire, she pestered him incessantly about ending her miserable existence. Much to his surprise, her initial fear had lasted for the briefest of minutes. All too quickly, she'd accepted her fate, wanting, begging to die—the demand a testament to her mistreatment at the hands of the sick bastards who held them.

Bile rose in his stomach when images of the so-called experiments flashed in his mind of the quest to learn how Demetri's kind survived exposure to illness and injuries.

In the six centuries he had been alive, not once had he taken a human life by feeding, especially a woman's life. The very thought repulsed him. His capturers may have taken his dignity and pride, but he still had his morals. And those they could never take from him.

It was entirely up to him if he fed from the woman sitting in his cell, and not Lane nor anyone else would make him take her life. It was the one thing over which he had control, and he would not relinquish it.

Demetri shook his head. "I realize why you long for the ultimate escape death offers. Nevertheless, I will not be the one to give it to you."

"But I want to die. Please! It is the only way the pain will stop."

Demetri understood. Starvation burned through his body, coupled with the series of inflicted injuries, slow to heal due to the lack of nourishment. Respite lay feet away.

If I drained this woman, I might get enough blood to heal my body. He at least would get enough to take away the misery of starvation. The thought lengthened his fangs. His body knew what it needed and was prepared to get it.

Demetri pushed down hard on his desire and leaned back against the wall of his cell, allowing the hard surface to dig into the open wounds on his back. The pain drew his thoughts away from the woman across the room.

He put as much distance between them as the tiny cell would allow. Unfortunately, it was not far enough away to remove the temptation the bleeding woman posed. The scent of her blood closed around him like a thick fog, permeated his senses until he tasted it on his tongue. The thought of warm blood was almost enough to make him give into her death wish.

Almost.

Demetri pushed a compulsion into the deep timbre of his voice. "You need to suck it up a little longer. I'm sure someone will come for us."

The tiny woman let out a heavy sigh. "No one ever comes. Except the guards. And we both know what happens when they come."

Demetri flinched when thoughts of the sadistic experiments flashed through his mind yet again. The warrior in him wanted to fight, but his weakened body wouldn't obey.

He glanced down. His legs, once as thick as logs, were now the size of flagpoles. His arms, having been as large as a man's head, now sticks which hung limply from his shoulders. There was no mirror in the cell, so he could not see much more, but he felt the bones protruding on his body. He must look like a walking skeleton. Correction, a sitting skeleton, because in his weakened condition all he could do was sit. He had not walked under his own power in some time.

A growl escaped his dry throat, rumbling low in his hollow chest.

A member of the Alpha Council, Demetri was a proud, strong fighter like his brothers in arms. He possessed the powerful presence to back up his commands. Others trembled in his presence, ran from him in fear. He wore his power like a badge, proudly displaying it for all to see, his legendary strength known among his kind.

The things holding him here had reduced him to a shell of his former self in a matter of…weeks? Months? He lost his ability to sense the rise and setting of the sun when they starved him. Locked in the windowless cell, he had no concept of how long he had been held captive. And truth be told, he didn't really care. Thoughts of escape filled his mind during his few waking hours.

Another growl rumbled through the room as anger and rage consumed him. His hands fisted in his lap at his predicament. Across from him sat the very thing that might strengthen him. A willing partner, who would bare her neck to him, let him take from her what he so desperately needed. However, while his body would be sated, his conscience would forever hold him accountable for taking her life.

It was enough to drive a male insane.

Chapter 5

"We're here," announced Alex, pulling Tatiana from her thoughts as he expertly slid the car into a parking space.

"Just in time," murmured the female warrior before she exited from the vehicle. Tatiana watched from across the roof as Alex emerged from the opposite side. "This is exactly what I need tonight," she said, referring to the recon they were about to do.

"What do ya mean? Going into a shady bar and drinking with a handsome stud like myself."

Tatiana shrugged out of her duster and tossed the coat into the back seat on top of Alex's. No need for jackets when the bar was so close. Alex joined Tatiana, so the pair could enter the establishment together.

"Yeah, big boy. That's what I meant."

Alex threw an arm around her shoulders, drawing her to his side. "You know, darlin', if I didn't know better I'd think you've seen me naked with that 'big boy' comment."

Tatiana wrapped her arm about his waist to give the impression to the patrons inside they were a couple. "You wish."

"Why, yes, I do," his southern drawl purred the words as they entered.

Tatiana glanced around the bar decorated near identically to the last twenty-one they'd patronized.

Dimly lit, the various nondescript items tacked to the walls hardly showed. The music was too loud, the booze no doubt too weak. And the people, all human.

What she wouldn't give for a vampire bar, where the blood and booze flowed made to order. She and Alex had consumed a couple of bags they acquired from the local blood bank earlier, so her cells were not starving, but her mouth felt dry.

"Do me a favor, Hall, get us a couple of drinks while I find us some seats."

"Will do." The male gave her a wide grin.

Tatiana located an empty table for two and sat. Alex made his way from the bar with a long neck in each hand. She appreciated the way his warrior's body moved with predatory grace. The jeans and the turtleneck sweater he'd chosen to wear this evening hugged his body. He was a magnificent specimen of maleness. Broad shoulders, defined arms, not thickly muscled like Demetri, but corded. His flat abdomen led to a narrow waist, thinner than Demetri's. His legs were powerful, though not as big around as Demetri's.

Yes, Alexander Hall was a superlative example of the male body any woman could appreciate. Any woman, except Tatiana. Since realizing Demetri was her heartmate, every male was now compared to him, and if she were honest with herself, found to be lacking. She silently cursed the egotistical, chauvinistic Alpha for making it difficult to enjoy any other males.

As he sauntered over to their table, Tatiana admitted Alex was a hottie, with that short blond hair, those aquamarine eyes, and his flirtatious personality. A perfect mixture of mirth and danger rolled into one delicious hunky package, he would make the perfect mate for some lucky female.

Unfortunately, she would not be that female.

No, fate had destined her to be mated to a Neanderthal.

Tatiana shoved the thought from her head. She had no intention of being saddled with a mate like Demetri Romanoff.

Alex toed a chair around, set the bottles on their table and straddled it, resting his powerful forearms on the back. A suggestive smile graced his handsome face. "Want to dance?"

Tatiana took a long draw from her beer before putting it down on the table with a clink. "Not particularly."

"Ah, come on. Dance with me, baby." Alex leaned over closing the distance between them, whispering in her ear. "Don't blow our cover, Agent Bolovich. We're supposed to be a couple. Couples dance."

His warm breath tickled her lobe as her hair swayed gently. Alex eased back onto his seat and took a swig from his bottle. He appeared provocative, seductive.

His eyes seemed to undress her while he awaited her answer. Alex's full lips closed around the bottle when he took another pull. His Adam's apple bobbed with each swallow, bouncing near his pulse point.

His tongue eased out between his lips to lick the frothy foam from his mouth. His eyes never left hers as he spoke. "So, what do you say? Shall we dance?" Alex reached out a large hand toward his partner.

Tatiana hesitated, surprised by her reaction to the male sitting beside her. She glanced around the bar. Most of the women within looked their way. Not at *them*, she realized, but at Alex.

Tatiana shook her head, sending her raven hair skittering across her shoulders. "I don't want to dance. Why don't you go out on the dance floor and find a partner while I sit over here?"

His gaze darted across the dance floor on the opposite end of the building, Alex obviously understood what she intended. "Gotcha," he replied with a wink.

Tatiana had to smile at her partner's quick mind. Alex had instantly realized that by going to the dance floor while she remained at their table, the two of them would be able to visually cover the entire place.

He was as intelligent as he was handsome. A real catch…for some lucky female.

Alex made his way across the room. Once on the dance floor, his hips quickly took up the pace set by the music. She could not help but admire the gracefulness of his movements. Each rise of an arm, each gyration of his hips drove the women around him into meltdown. By the second verse of the song, a gaggle of women surrounded him, each displaying their goods for his approval. He commanded the enraptured attention of almost every female in the place, save one.

A woman stood at the bar. She diverted her gaze when Tatiana scanned the room, but not before the female warrior caught the expression of disdain she threw Alex's way.

Something's not right.

Tatiana sent her awareness throughout the room, slowly expanding it to reach into every corner. A man leaned against the jukebox. Two women chatted in the bathroom. Couples dined around her, and a man sat at the bar talking to the bartender. She heard the conversations, smelled the potent combination of lust and alcohol.

Taking in each sensation as it came, she examined them for any abnormality, any sign of Demetri. She sought his scent, his energy.

For the past few days, his emotions had been muted. She feared he was becoming weaker as they continued to torture him. The thought sickened her, made her determined to find him.

Tatiana focused again on the information from her senses, searching each one for some tiny sign she might have missed. There was something. No, not something…nothing. A peculiar blank spot, near the bar.

She turned to glance in the vicinity from which she sensed the void and found the woman who had shot the derisive look toward Alex. Tatiana noted the woman's features in detail.

Dressed like a local in jeans and a sweater, her frame was a medium build, not too small, not too large. She possessed womanly curves but wasn't over-weight. Average—yet not.

The vampire reached for her beer and continued the perusal. Her long hair was the color of snow. And her eyes…

Holy shit! She slowly lowered the beer back to the table without taking a sip.

Tatiana swallowed convulsively as she stared at the woman's golden-red eyes. Not a hazel or a shade of light brown, but a piercing gold with flecks of red. Barely noticeable to the humans in the dimly lit bar, they were clearly visible to Tatiana when the woman turned and met her stare.

A chill shimmied down the VES agent's spine. Something inherently evil shown in those eyes. A coldness that came from doing atrocious deeds without repercussions.

Tatiana pushed her energy into the woman's mind, searching for the memories that created those eyes. She found nothing, just a strange blankness as if the woman put up a barrier. Tatiana furrowed her dark brows in concentration and pushed harder, seeking information.

She blew out an exasperated breath as once again she got nothing from the woman's mind.

Tatiana instinctually realized the woman was not a vampire, but she had to be something. The female warrior wondered how the woman had cloaked her presence and blocked Tatiana from her mind. She had to find out what this woman was.

****

Goddess help me! Shira thought, meeting the penetrating gaze of the female vampire. *She's trying to read me. She'll know I'm not human.*

Shira, like all demons, recognized a vampire when she smelled them. The moment the two vamps had walked through the door of the bar, she'd made them. She'd been watching the couple all evening. They seemed innocent enough at first, like two beings out for a nice date, but the longer she watched she noticed something seemed off.

Their eyes constantly moved around like they were searching for something. They both sat with their backs to the wall. They did not touch or hold hands the way lovers often did. They appeared to be making a show of being together, but when other females blatantly flirted with the male, the female vampire did not respond.

Shira might not be an expert on vampires, but she understood enough to know they were a possessive lot who did not mind manipulating humans or killing demons. The thought no sooner passed through her head than the female vampire rose gracefully from her seat and stalked her way.

Panic widened her eyes. Her heart raced in her chest. Shira turned and pushed through the humans who stood between her and the exit. She burst through the door, causing it to ricochet off the front of the building with a loud bang and took off down the street as fast as her legs would take her.

Chapter 6

Tatiana's eyes widened as the woman with the platinum hair disappeared from sight in an instant.

Damn, she's fast. Too fast for a human.

Her supposition had been correct, this woman was no mere human.

Tatiana bolted through the crowd, careful to control her speed until she made it outside. She scanned up and down the street. Except for a car driving slowly down the middle, an eerie silence surrounded her.

She sent her awareness flaring out over the pavement, expanding, reaching beyond the buildings and into the neighborhoods beyond.

She stood stoically absorbing what she found; a shop owner closing for the night, a father tucking his child into bed, a teenage couple discussing the upcoming school dance. She pushed further, finding animals. There seemed to be a park of some kind in one of the neighborhoods. A park with birds...and a dog...and...

A blank spot!

Hope blossomed. Using her preternatural speed, Tatiana made a beeline for the void. On silent feet, she trekked through a subdivision of pretty two-story homes and discovered a local park. She slowed her pace, careful not to disturb so much as a blade of grass. The void remained just ahead in a copse of trees.

Movement, little more than a shadow, drew her attention. The female turned her way as Tatiana put on a burst of speed. She caught the woman around the middle, tackling her against the side of a tree.

The female's breath left her lungs. Without skipping a beat, she grabbed onto Tatiana's hair and yanked for all she was worth. Her hands came away with two black clumps. Tatiana screamed in shock. The female pushed out with both hands simultaneously, catching Tatiana in her ribs. The impact threw her off balance.

She pivoted and threw out a leg, giving Tatiana a roundhouse kick to her chest. The wind rushed past Tatiana's face as she flew through the air toward a tree. The tree's trunk cracked from the collision in unison with Tatiana's spine. Pain flooded her body, and she fell to the ground in a heap.

The female paused just long enough to give her a satisfied smile then headed deeper into the trees.

****

Having realized Tatiana left the bar, Alex used his senses to locate his partner. A burst of speed brought him to her. Alex's heart clenched in his chest. Tatiana lay ahead slumped against a tree. Alex ran to his partner and laid a steadying hand on her arm. "What's going on?" His eyes tracked a woman running away.

"Get her," Tatiana commanded with a winded breath. "I'll explain later."

Years of working missions with the Alpha Council had trained him well. Sometimes you just blindly followed orders and saved the questions for another time. Now seemed like one of those times.

The Alpha increased his strides. The platinum

blonde was quick, but his vampiric speed had him baring down in seconds. Easily overtaking the woman, he pinned her to the nearest tree by her neck, intending to hold her until his partner caught up.

"It's just not my night," the woman muttered between clenched teeth. "You're hurting me."

She wiggled beneath his fingers as if the tree bit into her back. Normally he would feel bad about hurting a woman, but this one had already proven how dangerous she could be when she took down his partner.

"Stay Still!" Alex squeezed slightly on her neck to emphasize the directive. "What is your name?"

"Sh-Shira."

"Now tell me why you attacked my partner."

Shira's eyes widened with dread as her throat constricted under his grip. Her eyes darted from side to side. If she sought a means of escape, she'd be sorely disappointed. There was no escape for her, he would make sure of it.

The sense of panic mingled with her enticing rosy scent to tickle his nose. He almost felt sorry for the pretty woman until she raised her knee with as much power as her muscles could give her and contacted his groin.

Fiery pain rushed through him in a crippling wave. Alex clutched his package and gagged. Nothing made a man drop like having his hootenannies pushed up into his chest. Before falling to his knees on the snow, Alex swore he felt his boys in the back of his throat. His stomach threatened to give the frozen ground a beer bath. As he fought for air, each breath sending a fresh round of agony below, his vision went wavy.

He blinked up at the woman standing over him and watched her form blur. Just as Alex was about to chalk it up to his wonky vision, her arms shortened, and the sound of bones crunching filled his ears.

What the hell?

Something white formed over her limbs as her body shrunk in on itself. Her face contorted, her mouth and nose elongated. Ears became pointy, moved to the top of her head. Her long hair was replaced by short white…

Fur!

Alex's gut heaved with the realization. His vision may not be working perfectly, but it worked enough to tell the female who he had been holding just moments before was transforming into something else. Before his eyes, the creature shrank into the woman's clothes.

Alex had spent much time in the wilderness. He knew a snow fox when he saw one. And one leapt from the woman's clothes, glanced at him over her shoulder, then fled between the trees.

Tatiana limped to Alex, her eyes following the animal scampering away as she approached.

"Shit, Hall! You okay?" Tatiana knelt beside him. It was all Alex could do to nod his head. She reached down, plucking the blonde's shirt from the ground. "What happened?"

Alex groaned. Unable to reply, he rocked in the snow.

"Where's the woman?" Tatiana dropped the shirt and stood to scan the area.

"That way," croaked the male vampire, removing one hand from his groin to point north.

"Guess I don't need any details to figure out what

happened here. She got you with the age-old Knee-Him-in-the-Family-Jewels play. Right?"

Alex nodded his head as a fresh wave of pain raced through his body. "I'll live. How are you?"

Tatiana brushed aside the inquiry. "I don't understand why her clothes are on the ground, but she isn't."

"She turned..." Alex grunted as he stood and placed his hands on both knees for support. "...into a fox."

Tatiana made a rude sound in disbelief. "Yeah, right. I've seen many things in my centuries, but I've never seen a person change into an animal. Are you seriously telling me the woman turned into a fox?"

"That was no woman," the Alpha informed his partner, wincing when he took a painful step forward. "That was some kind of shapeshifter. I'm telling you, she shifted right out of her clothes. She turned into a snow fox and ran off."

"I sensed a blank spot earlier."

"What's up with all these blank spots we've been sensing? Seems to be a common thread in the disappearances and strange occurrences."

Tatiana nodded. "It's happened one too many times to be a coincidence. It must be related. Here's what I know. I couldn't read the woman's mind," Tatiana shared, lifting a finger to count each point as she named them. "She had inhuman strength. And she isn't a vampire."

"Something is definitely out of the ordinary here, Tatiana. Perhaps we have discovered a new breed of beings. One strong enough to take on two vampires and escape."

Unease washed over him. Sure, he had read about creatures in folklore and myths, but he didn't believe they existed until he watched the woman change into the snow fox with his own eyes.

Replaying the event in his mind made him outwardly cringe. Hearing the shape shifter's bones break and shift, seeing the fur sprout from her pours disgusted him, but he pushed the mental image aside.

"If one of them could take on two vampires, then surely more than one of the beings could take down one vampire, even if that one vampire was three hundred pounds of muscle."

"You think the shifter might have something to do with Demetri's abduction?" Alex waited for her nod of agreement.

"You stay here, Alex. I'm going after her."

Tatiana did not wait for his response. His protest died on his lips as she bounded through the trees following the paw prints in the snow.

****

Demetri's eye snapped open at the sound of footsteps echoing down the hall. He recognized the heavy combat boots. Three of the larger guards he realized with a start, his curiosity piqued. *Why three*, he wondered. *Surely, they don't need three to subdue me. I'm too weak to put up much of a fight.*

The concrete floor bit into his back. His joints ached from dehydration. His cells withered as his muscles continued to atrophy. The cold seeped into his bones until even those throbbed. He needed blood, desperately, and it lay right beside him.

Demetri looked down his chest to find a wealth of blonde hair cascading over it. Hair he knew was attached to a pretty face and small naked body. A groan escaped his cracked lips.

At some point the human must have crawled over to him. He didn't need the temptation.

In stronger times, she would have been just his type. He had an infinity for beautiful blondes with petite bodies. One lying naked against him would once have seemed normal.

But normal had morphed into something dark and horrid. Normal now meant constant pain and degradation, weakness and impotency. Even blood had changed for him.

For Demetri, blood became all-consuming. With his body starved and tortured, his baser instincts dominated. More animal than man, the drive for blood devoured his rational thoughts until the rush of it through the veins of those around him screamed to him.

Blood which lay draped across his chest.

Blood for the taking.

The woman had begged him for death, had she not? If he took from her what he needed, it would take away some of the pain. She did not have much in her body, her stuttering heartbeat attested to that, but she probably had at least enough to strengthen him. Perhaps enough he might support his own weight long enough to discover a way to escape.

His hand fisted in her hair, the movement sent a fresh wave of pain through his body as each joint screamed in protest. His fangs pushed from his gums when his mouth opened, his parched lips cracked with the motion, sending a second wave of pain to his brain.

The added sensation awakened his primal instinct, but higher thinking broke through commanding him to stop. He knew if he penetrated the soft flesh of her throat, he would not be able to stop drinking until every last drop had been downed. His body's survival instinct would dominate, demanding he take all the life sustaining liquid available to him, and he refused to kill.

Déjà vu washed over him. This same internal struggle was no stranger to him, a constant war between his moral and physical needs which the temptation in his cell perpetuated. His thoughts jumbled, foreign yet familiar.

Demetri willed his hand open and let it drop to the hard floor as the booted feet stopped before the door to his cell. A loud metallic clank signaled the bolt had been thrown open. The metal door scraped along the floor, pushed wide so the three males could enter. The first through the door reached down and grabbed the human. Under Demetri's watchful gaze, he lifted the woman, pinning her against his large body with a hand held to her forehead. The blonde hung limply against the guard's body, her feet dangling a foot off the floor. *A blessing,* he thought, *she must be unconscious.*

His eyes widened as he noticed a flash in the male's free hand. The thick blade of the knife reflected the light from the hall. The glint flared in Demetri's eyes. He blinked, trying to clear the spots as the blade approached the woman's throat. A quick slash across the exposed flesh, and blood trickled down her body into the drain below her feet.

The coppery smell forced Demetri's fangs to explode through his gums. The second and third guards grabbed him. Each held him under an arm, so he stood limply in front of the woman. A growl escaped from his chest as one of them grabbed a fist full of his hair with hard fingers and forced him to witness the senseless sacrifice.

The guard to his left leaned in, his breath flowed across Demetri's ear when he spoke. "Look at her, bloodsucker. See the waste. You could have tasted that blood. You could have drunk from her, let her death be of some use.

"Instead you refused. Now look at what has happened. She is dead, and her blood wasted down the drain. You are an idiot for not taking what was offered. And Lane has some interesting plans for you as a result."

The guard carrying the woman's body left the cell first. He headed down the hall in the opposite direction from which the two guards took Demetri. The warrior hung between them. He might have been able to support a little of his weight, but he did not want to spare the strength.

Better conserve my strength for whatever lays ahead.

Demetri was not shocked to find the bearded red head standing beside the metal autopsy table when they entered the lab. His white lab coat flared around his legs when he turned to face them.

"We brought him as you requested, Lane," one guard said.

"Put him on the table and strap him down," the demon commanded with an arrogant wave of his hand.

As the cold of the metal burned his naked flesh, Demetri watched a female step around his torturer. His eyes tracked her hand run down the scientist's arm in an intimate gesture. Her sandy blonde hair hung in thick waves just past her shoulders. Sharp cheekbones stood out against her face, creating dark shadows on her cheeks which made them appear hollow. Her small mouth and almond-shaped eyes gave her face a distinctive leonine look. The female's scrutinizing gaze swept over the warrior's body with the objectivity of a clinical researcher, until it landed on his groin.

Her blonde brows arched in appreciation of the one part of his body that had not atrophied. Lane did not miss her regard. Quickly, he placed cloth the size of a hand towel across Demetri's hips.

"Guard, bring the bloodsucker a pair of shorts."

The brute exited with a huff.

The woman smiled. "Worried you might have some competition, Lane?" She tossed her hair with a flip of her hand.

The scientist snorted in disgust. "Hardly."

The smile fell from the blonde's face as her gaze once again raked the Alpha's body. "I see you've been hard at work. Why is he so damaged? Has his body stopped regenerating?"

The sting of the syringe in his arm drew his attention as Lane replied. "I believe the body isn't regenerating because it refuses to ingest blood. I put a human in its cell. I thought its natural instincts would take over and make it drink, but my hypothesis was incorrect."

"But if the bloodsucker isn't drinking enough blood for it to regenerate, then we will lose him like we did the pregnant female."

Demetri's stomach turned. The monsters who held him were the same ones who had taken the female he'd been searching for when he was captured. The bastards had killed her and the unborn baby. Anger flared white-hot in his veins.

Lane glanced down at the empty syringe. "Damned vampire," he spat out between clenched teeth. He leaned over, placing his face directly in front of Demetri's. If Demetri could have formed saliva, he would have spit in the bastard's face.

"You are dry, vampire. Your veins are collapsing. I can't draw any blood."

Demetri remained stoic, determined not to show how much the statement pleased him. He would gladly continue to suffer if it kept these monsters from getting what they wanted.

"What are you going to do now? I thought you needed his blood for Phase Two."

Lane moved across the lab and opened the door to the refrigerator. "I do, so I will force it to drink until I can get what I need."

Demetri clamped his teeth together, his lips drew into a fine line. Determination to do whatever was within his power to stop this male and his revolting experiments gave him strength. If this asshole wanted him to drink, he would refuse with every ounce of his fortitude.

"Hold his nose closed." Lane approached with a bag of blood.

The female moved behind Demetri's head. She pinched his nostrils shut, holding tight as Demetri thrashed his head from side to side.

"Come on," she coaxed. "Open up like a good little vampire. I know you are hungry. Mr. Lane has some yummy blood for you."

His lungs started to burn from the lack of oxygen.

His chest convulsed, desperate for air. If he didn't soon take a breath, he would go unconscious, then they would be able to do anything they wanted to him. The warrior decided it was worth a quick breath if it meant he could continue to fight their efforts.

As soon as his lips parted, Lane was there dumping the contents of the bag into his mouth. The Alpha tried to close his throat and refused to swallow. He thrashed his head to the side, spitting the blood as best he could, hoping to expel most of it. A small amount slid down his throat, but Demetri's pride expanded his chest as he realized he had been largely successful.

Lane cursed when the scarlet liquid stained his pristine white coat. "Wasteful," he admonished, giving Demetri a subjugating glare. "I'll make you drink."

"Bring me that tray, Jara." Lane gestured toward a metal surgical tray with wheels.

Demetri now knew two names, Lane and Jara. He tried to open the mind link to his cousin, wanting to share this new information, but found he couldn't make the connection. His hands fisted in frustration.

Jara rolled the tray around Demetri's body and brought it next to Lane. She ran her fire engine red nails across his back as she moved back at the head of the table. The scientist picked up a long rubber tube from the tray. An evil grin lifted one corner of his mouth.

His throat now lubricated by the blood, Demetri found his voice. "What are you going to do with that? Try to beat me into submission?"

Lane ruminated over the suggestion. "No. I don't believe you would bend to my will if I beat you. You have never submitted to me after your torture session before. No. I have another use for this tube." Looking up into the eyes of his companion, Lane continued. "Jara, hold his head."

Two hands clamped down on either side of Demetri's head, squeezing it tightly. His skull flexed under her grip. This was no mere human holding him. She had vampiric strength, but she was not a vampire. Of that Demetri was positive.

He had spent his months in captivity trying to discern what these creatures were. Until now, he had not seen a female. He'd wondered if the entire breed consisted only of males, but now he knew better.

"What are you?" Demetri looked up into Jara's red eyes.

A snarl raised one corner of her mouth. "I am a demon and your worst enemy, vampire."

A demon. The Alpha turned the word over in his mind as *déjà vu* washed over him yet again. Had he known he was being held by demons? His memories were blurry, distorted and muddled by his starvation, until they were a mass of contorted images and sounds.

The excruciating sensation of the tube being forced through his nostril pulled Demetri from his thoughts. He sucked in a deep breath when Lane shoved the rubber tube through his sinuses. Snaking its way down, the tube burned on its trip through his throat. Demetri gagged, coughing as the thick tube twisted into his stomach.

Demetri watched helplessly. Lane clipped off the top of a new bag of blood. The demon carefully poured the liquid into the end of the tube protruding from Demetri's nose. The cold fluid glided through the tubing to settle in his stomach. It was a heavy sensation.

Slowly his body began to respond as it absorbed

the life-giving nectar. His cells took in the regenerating nutrition. The pain in his joints intensified, then subsided into a blissful dull ache. As a second bag slid down, his muscles expanded slightly, the fibers filling with blood. Demetri's mind cleared while the agony ebbed. He attempted the mindlink again.

Nicholai, the warrior sent, *can you hear me cousin?* Getting no response, he tried again, this time trying to put more force behind the words. *Nicholai, are you awake? Can you hear me? I have news of my captors.*

Deafening silence was Demetri's only reply. The sharp sting of a needle brought his attention back to the demon standing over him. His head now freed from Jara's grasp, he looked down at his arm as his blood filled the tube attached to the syringe. Each time the tube filled, Lane snapped it off and replaced it with a new one. Again, and again an empty tube filled until his strength faded.

Demetri spat out a string of curses in his native Russian. How cruel to give him hope, make his body feel better only to take it all away an instant later. *Why don't they just kill me? What do they hope to do with my blood in this Phase Two they mentioned?*

Questions pinged around his head. Questions these demons wouldn't answer, but at least he learned something useful today. He now knew two of their names and what they called their breed.

Demons.

He turned the word over in his mind. He had read about demons in books, but these demons weren't anything like what he had read about. He wanted answers, more information about this breed. His intellectual curiosity gave him the strength to continue.

Lane ripped the hose from his body. "That's enough I believe. Wouldn't want you to regain your strength."

Demetri vowed to survive this. He would discover all he could about the demons and find a way to bring the knowledge to the Alphas. He pledged to endure everything the bastards did, until he discovered an escape, to get back to the Alphas.

To get home.

The guard reappeared with a pair of tiny shorts, and Demetri knew they'd never fit. When Lane and the demon guard slipped them on, anger coursed in his veins. They'd reduced him to a shell of his former self, literally and figuratively.

Demetri let the frustration build. It fed him. Fueled his strength.

The mighty roar that ripped from deep within his chest rattled the instruments in the room.

Chapter 7

Tatiana sprinted through the trees. Their skeletal branches swayed in the chilled air. Brisk wind whipped around her body, cold bit into her cheeks.

She and Alex had been tracking the snow fox in nothing but the clothes on their backs. They had left the bar in such a hurry to chase down the shapeshifter neither of them thought to grab their jackets from the car. The glacial air pierced the fabric of her clothes, her jeans and sweater providing no barrier to the crystallized molecules. It blanketed her body in an afghan of ice, making her skin ache, each step an experience in pain as her chapped skin rubbed against the cloth.

Tatiana glanced at her watch. *Half past midnight.*

The half-moon barely cast any light below. The pair ghosted through the frozen woods to follow the tiny tracks in the snow, careful not to disturb the impressions left by the female shifter in her fox form for fear of losing their bearing.

"Do you see her?" Alex asked in his deep southern drawl, wrapping his arms around his chest to tuck his hands beneath his armpits for warmth. "We've been at this for almost an hour now, and we have nothing to show for it but frozen body parts."

"Afraid of a little cold, Hall?" Tatiana taunted, a thin smile pulling at one corner of her mouth.

"There are certainly a few body parts I'd rather not get frostbite on." A wide grin pulled his blue lips taunt. "If we don't find something soon, I think we ought to head back."

More than once, in the past hour, he'd mentioned turning back, but Tatiana's instinct kept them moving forward. Her intuition told her the shifter would provide valuable information about Demetri's whereabouts, and she trusted that intuition explicitly.

"I disagree, Alex. We need to keep following the fox. I believe she can help us find Demetri."

"She certainly didn't seem in any mood to talk earlier when she kicked both our asses."

"Exactly my point. She was desperate to get away from us. Don't you wonder why?" Tatiana picked up the pace. "Why did she run from the bar when I tried to read her? Why did she fight me when I caught up to her?"

Alex lifted his broad shoulders in a shrug before Tatiana continued. "I'll tell you why, because she has something to hide."

"Maybe she was trying to hide the fact she is a shapeshifter." Alex quickened his long strides to keep pace.

"Perhaps, but I got the impression it was more than that." Tatiana stopped so abruptly Alex brushed against her side before he could stop his forward momentum. "Look."

Tatiana raised her arm to point ahead of them and used her preternatural vision to peer between the trees. Her gaze settled on a small figure creeping along the ground. Its white fur blended in with the surrounding snow, making it difficult to see. If not for the movement of the animal, the natural camouflage would have rendered it completely invisible.

"Our fox," Tatiana whispered.

The two warriors stood stone still, not moving so much as a finger, and watched the fox approach an abandoned warehouse. The building stretched over an expanse of the land. Rivers of rust rolled down the aluminum siding that covered the exterior, showing the building could not escape the ravages of time and the harsh climate of the region. The metal roof peaked into a triangle, reminding Tatiana of children's blocks.

The fox stopped next to the door of the structure. The small animal stood on its hind legs and braced its front paws against the door. Its fur began to recede, drawing into its skin, while its limbs lengthened. Flesh stretched over the growing muscle and sinew as its torso morphed from small and cylindrical to a thin hourglass. Snowy hair cascaded down her back until it reached her waist.

Tatiana put on a burst of blurring speed. She reached the shifter just as she completed the metamorphosis. The female warrior pinned her naked body against the side of the building by her neck and tightened her grip until only the smallest amount of air got to her lungs. The shapeshifter scratched at Tatiana's arm like a wild animal in a trap. Her red eyes widened with fear.

The last of the shifter's humanlike features formed on her face. Tatiana pushed her own face closer to the woman. "What is this place?" she asked in a throaty growl.

Alex grabbed the shifter's hands and pinned them to the wall by her sides. "I suggest you stop fighting and answer my friend's question."

"N-nothing. Just an old empty w-warehouse." The shifter's reddish-gold eyes darted back and forth between the two vampires.

Tatiana took a deep breath. "You're lying. I can smell it." She tightened her grip, cutting off the woman's air for several seconds before once again allowing her to breathe. "I'll only ask you one more time. What is this place?"

The woman glanced around nervously, as if looking for someone to help. With no help in sight, she finally answered, "It is a warehouse. I swear."

Alexander let go of one of the shifter's arms and used his sleeve to rub years of dirt and grime from the window next to them.

"This place is hardly abandoned." The Alpha looked back at his partner. "There are boxes stacked to the ceiling, and the building has electricity."

Tatiana turned her menacing glare back onto the woman. "Tell me what is in the warehouse?" Her austere tone brooked no argument.

Tears welled in the shapeshifter's eyes, threatening to spill down her cheeks. "I can't. They will kill me if I do."

"I will kill you if you don't." Tatiana leaned closer to the woman. "Now tell me what is in the building."

"I'd tell her if I were you," Alex suggested. "She doesn't make threats. She makes promises."

The shifter's gaze darted between the them again then around them, taking in the surrounding forest as if looking for something or someone. "Fine," the woman spit out in capitulation. "I'll tell you, if you promise to let me go."

"We'll release you unharmed, if you tell us the truth, Shira." Alexander dropped his hand from her arm in a show of good faith.

The woman looked down and closed her eyes as if to gather her courage, her mouth drawing into a tight line. She took a deep steadying breath before she opened her eyes and spoke, her voice so soft they would not have heard but for their preternatural hearing. "There is one of your kind being held in there."

Hope zinged up Tatiana's spine to lodge deep in her mind. One of their kind, inside, it must be Demetri.

"A male or a female?" she asked, trying to keep the hope from her voice.

"A male." The shapeshifter would not meet the vampires' eyes.

At her reply the two warriors looked at each other with a hopeful glance.

Have we finally found Demetri?

"Do you know his name?"

Shira shook her head.

"Tell us what he looks like," demanded Alex.

Golden fiery eyes flew to Alex's. "I only saw him twice. I don't really remember wh—"

"You better remember and quick!" Tatiana cut off the shifter's statement. A deprecating snarl pushed from between her lips.

"I-I…" The woman swallowed hard. "He had d-dark hair, I think, and he was tall. He was as long as the table."

"He was on a table?" prodded Alex.

"Yes, both times I saw him he lay strapped down to the table in the lab. I-I brought blood to put in the refrigerator, and he was strapped there."

"You mentioned you were bringing blood. Was the blood for the vampire?"

"I don't know." The woman's eyes roamed the area once more. "I only know I was ordered to get bags of blood from the local blood bank and bring them to the lab."

"Was that your only duty?"

"No, I was hired to do other things too."

Alexander scrubbed a hand across the back of his neck. "Do you know the layout of the building?"

"Only a few of the rooms. There were many rooms I was not allowed to enter."

"Why?" The Alpha crossed his arms over his chest.

"I never asked questions. I did what was asked of me and left each evening. Sometimes you just don't want to know the answers. You know?"

Tatiana knew all too well most people didn't want to know the answers, especially when they thought the answers might not be pleasant. That had been one of the reasons her captor had been able to keep her all those years. His servants had been paid well to keep their noses out of their master's business. She shook the memories away before they pressed in on her.

"What else can you tell us about the male?"

"He was very thin, all skin and bone really."

Tatiana's heart clenched in her chest. It might not be Demetri who was in the warehouse after all. Demetri would never be described as thin.

Her hope spiraled toward the ground like a wounded sparrow only to pull up and glide gracefully into a safe landing as she realized months of malnutrition could account for a spectrally thin appearance in a vampire. The male shifter described may be Demetri yet. In any case, they needed to get inside to rescue him.

"How do we get inside the building?"

Shira gave a moment's hesitation before answering. "There is a keypad. You have to push a code."

"What's the code?"

"I…" The woman's eyes darted around the woods. "I don't know."

Tatiana's grip tightened around the woman's neck before she slid the woman up the side of the building. Her feet dangled beneath her. The woman struggled to no avail against the grasp, her face turning red with the effort and lack of air.

Tatiana waited until her eyes started to roll back in her head, then she lowered the woman and slapped her face with her free hand. The shapeshifter startled back to the present. Her fearful gaze landed on Tatiana, and she gave the bitch a most menacing look. Her body shook with fear. The acidic smell of which burned Tatiana's nose.

"I warned you about lying to me. Do it again, and it will be the last thing you ever do on this earth."

"Tell us the code, Shira," Alex commanded, then rested a hand on Tatiana's shoulder.

The shifter's shoulders slumped in capitulation. "It's three, three, six, six, six. It spells demon on a phone keypad."

"Why the word dem…?" The Alpha's question was interrupted by a loud roar, heard echoing off walls of the warehouse.

Tatiana and Alexander turned simultaneously to stare at each other. "Demetri!" they exclaimed in unison as Tatiana flung Shira's naked form aside.

Chapter 8

A beep punctuated each number as Alex punched the code into the keypad. When Tatiana's hand clamped around the knob, it buckled slightly under the force. She pulled it wide. Drawing her gun from its resting place at the small of her back, she stalked into the building on silent feet.

Her partner ghosted up behind her, drawing his own weapon from its holster. He leaned over her shoulder to whisper in her ear. "You go straight. I'll come around from the side."

A nod of her head her only response, Tatiana forged ahead between the row of stacked crates and boxes, gun held tightly in both hands pointed toward the floor.

The VES agent cast her senses out through the warehouse. When they slowly expanded, she sensed several voids followed by a few humans and finally a familiar presence.

Demetri!

She drew in a deep breath. The scent of blood mixed with perspiration and the stringent scent of death stung her nose. Murmuring voices sounded in the distance—a male and a female. She followed the muffled sound. Her long strides ate up the concrete floor as she quickly reached the far wall of the building.

Her gaze swept over the wall and floor. There was

no sign of an entryway, just a solid surface that confounded her. With Alex coming up beside her, she ran her fingers over the wall, searching for the smallest crack or fissure, anything that might indicate an opening.

The Alpha immediately followed suit, sweeping his own hand along the wall in the opposite direction.

"Find anything?" he whispered, looking over one shoulder from across the room.

"Not yet, but there must be a way through."

Tatiana closed her eyes in concentration and listened to the voices. She focused on the muffled sounds, letting them draw her feet to their origin. She moved blindly away from the wall, one hand stretched out in front of her, the other holding the gun toward the floor.

She made her breathing shallow, barely audible under the noise of the voices. The voices grew louder as she walked. She could almost make out what they were saying when her outstretched hand pushed into a crate.

The crate was cold to the touch, abnormally so. She ran her hand up to the next crate in the stack, it too was cold.

That's odd.

Her hand traveled to the crates stacked on either side of the cold ones. Those crates were the same temperature as the air. Only the stack in the middle seemed to be a different temperature.

"Hall," Tatiana whispered, "come here and check this out."

Alex trotted over. Tatiana grabbed his hand, placing it on the cool box. He threw her a questioning look. With one brow raised, he whispered, "What the hell?"

"Exactly what I was thinking?"

The Alpha touched a few of the surrounding crates before his hand came to rest again over one of the cooler crates. "Why do you think these crates are so much colder than the rest?"

Tatiana shrugged. "Maybe it's a passage way of some kind."

Alex tucked his gun back into the waist band of his jeans. "Let's find out."

He ran his fingers along the surface of the crates, searching for an opening, a latch, anything indicating a secret passage. Tatiana's temper flared as a feeling of impotency grew. They were close to Demetri. His emotions pressed in on her. She began to pace the confined space between the wall and the stacks of boxes. Like a caged gorilla, she shifted in agitation back and forth, watching Alex run his hands over the crates.

Another roar. This one much louder than before, seeming to come from within the crates. Alex shot her a knowing look of concern. His hands flew faster, seeking, searching.

In frustration, Tatiana's hand shot out and punched the nearest crate. Much to her surprise, the front of the crate rose to reveal a red button. She blinked twice before the sight registered with her brain. Understanding brought a smirk to the corner of her mouth. Her fingers flew forward to depress the button.

The hushed whoosh sound was the only warning Alex had before the façade of the crates slid to one side to reveal a descending stairway. The dim florescent tubes that lined the top of the stairwell lit the stairs with an eerie light.

A blast of cool air poured from the opening. "Way to go, Tatiana. How'd you do it?"

She stepped behind him and peered down the stairs. Not one to lie, but wanting to seem like she had not discovered the button by accident, Tatiana gave in insignificant shrug of her shoulders. "Just found a button that seemed like it might be what we were looking for, so I pushed it."

Alex pulled his gun from its holster, gripping it tightly in both hands. "Let's go," he commanded, leading the way down the stairs. As Tatiana descended behind him she mimicked his stance with her own weapon, careful to point it away from the male in front of her. The pair reached the bottom in record time to find a T-intersection. Long hallways flowed out in three directions.

Alex motioned with one hand, pointing at himself then down one of the halls before pointing at Tatiana then down one of the other hallways. With a nod, Tatiana took off, the Alpha heading in the opposite direction.

****

A warrior's calm settled over Alex as he went into combat mode. He held his weapon at the ready in front of him. He came to a thick metal door with a window and glanced through the opening. Three bodies lay piled on the floor. As he gazed around the room, he noticed a large cylinder with a door on it. Seeing no threats in the room he entered.

The scent of burned flesh accosted his nose, so pungent it overpowered the decay from the bodies. He knelt on one knee by the people. They were human, two females, and one male.

Not Demetri!

Relief pushed from his lips in a sigh, relief quickly followed by a gulp of guilt for the mollification that none of the dead were his comrade, for surely these people had families and friends who would never see them again.

In a fluid movement, he rose and stepped around the bodies to examine the cylinder. He unlocked the latch and opened the thickly reinforced square door. The hinges groaned under the pressure of the heavy door as it opened to reveal a pile of ash.

Alexander stepped closer. Bits of bones lay mixed in the ash. His gut twisted at the realization that he stared into a crematorium oven. The amount of ash made it apparent several bodies had already been burned in the large oven, and no doubt the ones on the floor would be next.

A noise drew his attention away from the gruesome discovery. His head snapped in the direction from which it came and cocked to one side as he listened for the noise again. As if on cue, it obliged—a faint clunk like tin striking against concrete.

Alex ran at blurring speed, exiting the cremation room and heading down the hall toward the sound. He passed two more metal doors with windows before coming to a door with a mail slot size opening.

He bent down and peered through the opening. Inside a young woman lay on a cot. Her hair appeared matted, her skin dirty. Her clothes were tattered, and her pallor ghostly pale. Alex's preternatural hearing easily discerned her heart stutter its beat.

A man stood beside her, shoving a needle into her

arm. Ruthlessly, he pushed it into the vein. She winced. He snapped the rubber tourniquet off her arm and blood trickled slowly out into a bag lying on the concrete floor.

Alex sent his senses flowing into the room. One human. One void. Nothing. Zero.

Alex would have felt a vampiric presence at this close range, even if the man was blocking his senses. The male standing over the woman was definitely something else, something Alex had never encountered, something that seemed bent on hurting the helpless human.

"You're running slow today," the male observed. "Perhaps if I scare you, your heart will pump the blood faster."

Fear came from the woman at the threat in astringent waves. Her heartbeat quickened its pace, stuttered with increasing frequency. This bastard was going to kill her if he didn't do something.

Alex pushed through the door, firing his weapon. The concussion in the confined space reverberated off the walls in deafening decibels. The muzzle flashes illuminated the small room like a nuclear explosion, orange and reds painting their bodies in vivid color.

The male collapsed in a heap, instantly. Twin trails of blood oozed from the two holes in his forehead. The woman gaped up at Alex, shock and awe on her face.

"It's going to be all right." He gently removed the needle from her arm. The confused expression on her face indicated she had not heard what he said. As he pushed down the ringing in his ears, he realized her own ringing would have made it impossible for her to hear him. He shook his head at the mistake.

He needed to get them out of here. The shots would have been heard throughout the complex. Others were sure to be here soon to investigate.

Alex waved a hand in front of her eyes, gaining her attention. He stood two fingers in the palm of one hand, indicating the woman should stand up. She nodded and pushed up onto her elbows. Her eyes rolled back in her head before she collapsed onto the bed.

Alex reached down and grasped her shoulders in his large hands. Giving her a gentle shake, he roused her. She blinked up at him from under her long lashes and tried to rise again.

This time, Alex kept a firm hold on her. Once on her feet, she swayed slightly. One hand on her arm, the other on his gun, the pair made their way to the door.

Alex took one step into the hall and headed in the direction from which he came, but the woman dug in her heels.

She was surprisingly strong for one who looked so ill.

Alex glanced over his broad shoulder at her. She pointed across the hall at another door with a mail slot size opening.

Alex leaned the woman up against the wall and went over to the door. Looking through the slot he saw two more humans, one a man and the other a woman.

Shit! Just how many people were being held in this place? Alex wondered, knowing neither he nor Tatiana would be leaving anyone behind, even though the more people they had to rescue the more difficult the rescue would be.

Their condition appeared slightly better than the woman leaning up against the wall, but he wasn't sure they would be able to move under their own power. *Only one way to find out how bad off they are.*

****

Having left one of his techs to finish draining the vampire, Lane sat behind the desk in his office. Jara leaned on the edge of the desk.

"I can't believe you have begun Phase Two." Jara's naughty grin spread across her face. "You deserve a bonus."

Lane's auburn brows rose in curiosity. "What did you have in mind?"

"What would you like?"

Desire coursed through his veins the first time he'd seen Jara. Working closely while she supervised his experiments, having her near as he discussed his findings, it had been as much a punishment as a pleasure.

"A kiss," he answered cautiously and braced for her response.

Jara threw her head back and laughed. "Well, you certainly work cheap. Sure. Why not?"

She slid onto his lap and lowered her head. Her wavy blonde locks surrounded his head like a veil, keeping out the world around them. Her tongue thrust between his lips in a violent motion he could come to crave. The kiss, rough and demanding, made him relish every minute of it. His hands snaked around her back, pulling her close so her breasts pushed against his chest.

The sound of gun shots reverberating throughout the complex tore their lips apart. "What the f—" The sound of his office door being taken from its hinges cut off Lane's expletive. The wooden panel splintered apart when it bounced off the wall.

"Where is he?" a tall, lithe figure demanded as she breezed into the room. Lane jumped to his feet. Jara fell onto the concrete floor between him and the desk. The demon's eyes narrowed on the gun leveled at his face and the long fingers tightening around the grip.

"Who are you—" Before Lane could complete the question, the female warrior bound across the room in one fluid, instant motion to land in a couched position on his desk, sending papers scattering to the floor on top of Jara. "—talking about?"

Lane swallowed hard when he locked eyes with her deadly yellow eyes.

"Where is Demetri?" the woman asked, her voice hard as stone.

The scientist carefully slid his hand along the underside of his desk, searching for the button that would sound the alarm. *Where's that damned button?* It was there somewhere. His hand inched forward. *Just a little further.*

"I wouldn't do that if I were you." The woman's tone brooked no argument as she cocked her weapon.

Chapter 9

Sweat broke out on the male's face. Staring down the barrel of a gun would do that.

Tatiana gestured toward the desk with her gun. "Tell the woman to stand up and get your hands where I can see them."

Tatiana leapt from the desk and landed next to the male in the white lab coat. A female with red eyes rose slowly from beneath the desk, gripping the edge of the desk as if to steady herself.

Her long fingers lingered under the desk. Tatiana eyes narrowed as the woman's digits closed over a button and depressed it. She held both hands up in surrender when the siren blared, screaming its warning intruders had entered the compound.

"What did you do, Jara?" the man behind her asked with an expression of horror on his face.

"What you couldn't, Lane."

"She'll kill you." The male nodded in Tatiana's direction.

Footsteps pounded down the hall in unison to people yelling instructions over the loud noise. Tatiana turned in time to witness three large males pour through the door jamb, weapons drawn.

A sudden report of gunfire rang out. With four sharp staccatos, the guards discharged their weapons. Tatiana dove, hitting the floor in a roll. She landed crouched on the balls of her feet, her weapon pointed in the direction of the guards.

A quick glance at the couple behind the desk told her the guards had fired not to kill but to stop. She stared up at the tranquilizer darts which protruded from the woman's body and watched her eyes roll back in her head before she slumped into the man's arms.

Tatiana's senses flowed throughout the room to discern whether any of the guards were human. Sensing only five empty spots where the people now stood, she realized they were all preternatural.

That makes them fair game.

She squeezed the trigger, sending a bullet into the leg of one of the guards. He dropped to one knee with a howl of pain. His gun flew from his hand as he gripped his thigh to stay the bleeding.

"Get us out of here," Lane bellowed and lifted Jara over his shoulder in a fireman's carry.

A guard rounded on Tatiana and laid down a stream of bullets as cover for Lane to make his way to the door. Tatiana had no choice but to crouch low behind a metal file cabinet for refuge.

I guess they changed their mind about not killing me. Well, they'll find out it'll take more than a few bullets to take me down.

Tatiana rose. With blurring speed, she crossed the room in a blink of time, grabbed the barrel of the gun the guard used to shoot at her and turned the thing back on its owner. Her finger slipped over the guard's thick trigger finger. She squeezed, sending a round through his heart, instantly stopping its beat. The large male slumped to the floor in a heap, his sightless eyes staring up at Tatiana.

The sound of a soft click brought her head around. Having dragged himself to where his gun had slid, the wounded guard now pointed the weapon directly at Tatiana's chest with the hammer cocked back. His hand shook slightly. His eyes glassy with pain, he worked himself into a sitting position.

Tatiana leapt across the room in a single, fluid bound. With a swipe of her hand, she disarmed the guard, using his own gun to knock him unconscious before she turned. Lane and the last guard pushed out the door with Jara in tow.

The female warrior stalked to the door and carefully peeked down the corridor to assess the situation. A hail of bullets rained down when her head emerged. She ducked back into the office. Holding her gun close to her body with both hands, she took two deep, steadying breaths, then rolled out into the hall. Tatiana came to a stop in a crouch. Her gun aimed at the male who had fired on her as he ran down the hall, pushing Lane in front of him.

Just as the guard and Lane turned the corner, the sound of heavily booted footsteps behind spun her around. Her eyes tracked up the long length of the muscular body in front of her. This male was huge, as large as Demetri and just as wide. Every muscle twitched and flexed, ready for action. In his large hand, he held a rather sizeable, though rusty, machete.

Tatiana rose to her full height and squared her shoulders. "I hate to tell you this, but you brought a knife to a gun fight." She raised her weapon in one hand and aimed it at his forehead. "If you turn around right now, I'll let you live."

Without a sound, the male lunged forward, raising

the machete over his head. Tatiana fired, the report of the gun echoing off the cinderblock walls. The bullet hit its mark. A spray of blood splattered from the back of the male's head, coating the wall and floor behind him in a splash of crimson.

"Warned you." The VES agent stepped over the body.

She prowled down the hall, her body pressed tightly against the wall. The coolness of the cinderblock seeped through her clothes.

People rushed by her in a flurry. A few glanced her way, most appeared too concerned with getting out of the compound under the screaming noise of the alarm to pay her any attention. She allowed them to pass unharmed. She had no wish to injure anyone unless it was in self-defense.

Tatiana came to an open door and paused to glance inside. The smell of blood, both human and vampire filled her nose. A man lay motionless on the table, clothed only in a shredded pair of shorts. His skeletal frame as sharp as the edges of the table upon which he lay strapped. His chest rose slightly under her perusal.

He's alive.

Tatiana moved toward the man, shocked by the emaciated form. He was so thin he should not be alive, yet he breathed. Each breath seemed labored, evidenced by the pained expression on his face.

His dark brows furrowed, lines creased his forehead and the corners of his eyes. His gaunt cheeks and eyes stood out against the ghostly parlor of his skin. Large, gray eyes looked up at her with recognition.

Her breath left her lungs in a rush. A heavy, leaden weight threatened to crush her spirit. She recognized those eyes, those beautiful steel-gray eyes.

"Demetri," she whispered on an intake of breath as she tucked the gun in the waistband of her jeans.

He closed his lids once in affirmation before his dark lashes raised, and he pinned her with a hard stare.

"What have they done to you?" Tatiana's fingers flew over the restraints, snapping the leather straps and metal cuffs like they were rubber bands.

She helped Demetri into a sitting position, eliciting a groan from his parched, cracked lips. "You need blood."

Tatiana brought her wrist to her mouth. As her lips parted, a thought stuck her mind with such force, it almost knocked her back. If she gave Demetri her blood, he would know they were heartmates. It would only take one drop.

He'd never let her go. And going was exactly what she planned to do once he was safe.

No. She couldn't feed him from her vein. Perhaps she could locate some bagged blood. She glanced around the room. Her eyes alighted on a small refrigerator sitting inconspicuously against one wall.

Tatiana reached the fridge and opened the door. Her hope sank to her toes.

It stood empty.

She noted the equipment and dissection tools about the room. Had they used those on Demetri? She imagined the torture he must have endured all the months he had been held here. Bile rose in her throat.

Demetri's heart stuttered a beat before he fell back down onto the table. He lay dying!

She had no choice, Demetri needed blood. *Now!* Her baser instinct would not allow her mate to die.

On anxious feet, she returned to Demetri's side and brought her wrist to her mouth once again. She let her fangs extend from her gums, feeling every millimeter of the slide. She scored her delicate flesh.

Alex bound into the room, carrying a person over one shoulder, with three others on his heels. A quick flare of senses told her everyone was human. The Alpha skidded to a halt at the head of the table and looked down on the thin figure.

"Holy shit, that's Demetri."

Tatiana licked the wounds closed on her wrist. "I figured that out already."

"Yeah, but look at him. I mean…shit. He looks—"

Tatiana nodded her head, sending her blunt-cut ends swishing around her face. "He's in bad shape, Alex. He needs blood. Can one of the humans feed him?"

The blond Alpha kept his unwavering gaze on Demetri as he answered. "The man probably could. He seems in a little better shape than the women."

Tatiana pushed into the mind of the male and commanded him to come over. His eyes fogged as he obeyed the silent command. He obediently raised his wrist to her lips. She scored his flesh with her fangs then placed his open wounds over Demetri's lips.

****

Though his eyes were closed, the smell of blood roused his senses. It called to him like a drug does its addict. Demetri's nostrils flared wide to take in the delicious scent. His mouth parted of its own volition to down the dark, rich ambrosia that danced on his lips.

He swallowed once, twice. His stomach cramped, not used to taking so much at one time, but it didn't slow his drawls. Instinct took over. Demetri's will to live stronger than his desire not to hurt the human. He swallowed, gulping as he drank his fill. Again, and again he swallowed the warm liquid.

His cells filled with the life sustaining fluid. It fed his muscles, his tissue, his sinew…his very soul. Euphoria was tantamount to the strength that coursed through his body. One and the same, pure ecstasy.

When the source of his pleasure ripped away from his mouth, his eyes snapped open and a mighty growl pushed through his lips. The women covered their ears and whimpered at the animalistic sound.

"That's enough for now, Demetri."

The sound of Tatiana's soft voice drew the warrior's gaze. He turned his head toward the sweet sound. She looked good, a sight for sore eyes. *Both she and Alex*, he thought as he shifted to peer up at his fellow Alpha.

With a sigh, Demetri pushed himself up onto one elbow, testing his strength. Still weak, he needed much more blood after so many months of starvation, but he could at least move.

"Take it slow, big guy." Alex's hand shot out to steady him as he moved into a seated position, his feet dangling off the side of the table.

He braced himself with his hands on either side of his thighs, holding his arms taunt.

Tatiana moved directly in front of him. "Do you think you can walk?"

"I'll try," Demetri rasped, licking his dry lips.

He pushed away from the table. With his muscles atrophied, his knees threatened to collapse from his slight weight. Tatiana was there in an instant. She took one of his arms and wrapped it around her shoulders, helping to take most of his weight off his weak legs.

"We need to get out of here," Alex stated the obvious.

"How do you propose we do that?" Tatiana helped Demetri toward the door. "It's too far to go back to the town on foot, especially with four injured humans and one weak vampire."

Demetri tried to straighten, taking great offence at Tatiana's comment. The effort was for naught as his muscles did not comply, confirming the female's assertion. He was weak, even with the blood from the human, and it angered him. His fury at the impotence rose with each step he attempted to take. Being dragged down the hall embarrassed him but being dragged by a female…well that was just about unbearable.

Alexander glanced behind them, making sure the humans were in tow before he reached into his front pocket and pulled out a phone. His expression hardened when he looked at the screen. He slipped it back into a pocket saying grimly, "No signal."

"Great, we can't call for help. We can't walk back to town. This just keeps getting better and better." Tatiana blew a fallen wisp away from her forehead.

"Perhaps you should have planned the rescue a bit better," croaked Demetri.

"Listen, buddy," Tatiana bit out between clenched teeth. "Alex and I are doing the best we can. We're making this up on the fly. We weren't planning on rescuing you tonight."

"I can tell. Alex what were you thinking, bringing only Tatiana to back you up?"

The Alpha exchanged an exasperated look with the

VES agent. "I don't think now is the time to critique our *modus operandi*, big guy. Let's just figure out how we are going to get away from here then later you can assess our escape once we have you and the humans someplace safe and sound. Okay?"

A grunting sound from Demetri's throat served as his acquiescence while they maneuvered down the hall. Not a soul roamed the abandoned hallway as they walked. Only the sound of their feet and the scream of the alarm evidenced any signs of life.

When they finally emerged from the front of the building, it was Alexander who spoke first. "We must find some transportation."

"Alex, you come with me," ordered Tatiana. "We'll go around back to see if there is a garage or something back there. Demetri, you wait here with the humans. We'll come back for you."

Before the protest left his lips, the two vampires disappeared into the darkness. Demetri crossed his arms over his chest, the effort winding him before he leaned back against the building for support. The humans sat huddled together for warmth, seemingly oblivious to the frozen ground, thanks no doubt to shock.

The sound of an engine carried to them on the wind moments before a set of blinding headlights blazed through the darkness. A sport utility vehicle came to a stop in front of the humans. Alex jumped out and set to work helping the humans into the vehicle.

Once the last person got into the SUV, Alex closed the passenger door and turned toward Demetri. "Tatiana is on her way. You'll ride with her."

A sheepish smile threatened to spill across his lips, the dimple in his left cheek barely showed. But as

Demetri started to ask what type of vehicle he would be riding in, Alex jumped across the hood and slid in behind the steering wheel, before bringing the engine to life. The SUV drove away as the high-pitched sound of an engine registered in Demetri's ear.

He turned, and a single headlight blinded him momentarily. He didn't need his sight to recognize the sound of a motorcycle engine. Not the best vehicle to escape in, but he had ridden motorcycles since their inception, and if that was all Tatiana could find, then at least he would be able to drive them to safety.

Debris spit from the rear tire as Tatiana slid to a halt by Demetri's feet. "Jump on," she commanded over the growl of the engine, while she gestured with her thumb over her shoulder. "You're riding bitch."

Chapter 10

Demetri pushed away from the building. The effort forced a grunt from deep within his chest. "I think not, woman." One long stride took him beside the motorcycle to peer down menacingly onto Tatiana's upturned face. "I will drive. Slide back."

Tatiana wasn't impressed. The male could barely stand, let alone threaten her. "I'm trying to save your ass, and you're concerned about who is driving? Give me a break. Just get on and hold tight. Now!"

"I'll drive," he repeated and grabbed the handlebar.

His fingers closed around the throttle. Her acute vision noticed a slight sway of his body. The drawn lines on his face appeared like deep valleys. Even in the darkness, she noted the shadows that eclipsed his skin under each rib where his flesh stretched tight across the bones.

She knew a moment of pity for the warrior. He'd been put through much, his unnaturally thin, skeletal physique a testament of his torture and starvation.

His hair lay matted around his face, framing those sunken gray eyes. Eyes now trained on her, filled with the same commanding presence and determination they had always shown.

Used to being in charge and giving orders, Tatiana swallowed hard, suppressing her own instinctual commanding demeanor. Demetri was in no condition to drive them out through the forest. However, she also realized forcing him on the back of the bike could be a battle easily lost. She needed him to be reasonable, and Demetri was the type of male who would become an immovable wall should someone try to force him.

It is probably that very characteristic which kept him alive all these months.

"Demetri." The softness of her voice snapped his steel eyes to hers. "Surely, you realize that you need more than just the one feeding you had tonight to be in top condition. We will be going through woods unfamiliar to you. You do not know where the hotel is. It makes sense for me to drive. Get on the back. Please."

The VES agent silently observed the warrior process the request. His eyes lowered in defeat. His head tipped to one side as if he heard something strange. He quickly threw one leg over the back of the bike. The motorcycle sank on its struts under his weight. Tatiana throttled the engine.

A pair of arms encircled her. She barely repressed the shudder when his chest pressed against her back.

"Hang on, Romanoff," she called over the roar of the engine.

A figure, shadowed by the building, rounded the corner. Deciding not to stick around and investigate, Tatiana throttled the bike hard. The rear wheel spit debris behind them, and they flew off into the woods. In tandem, they leaned forward over the bike. Demetri's body curled over hers, trapping her between the warmth of his chest and the coolness of the fuel tank. The stark contrast made her acutely aware of the male behind her.

Her heart pumped harder. Blood coursed through

her veins. Every nerve ending tingled. The exhilarating rush spurred her faster.

Surely, the excitement from the speeding bike and not Demetri caused the sensation. She refused to entertain the thought that it might be sitting with her heartmate's arms around her.

Tatiana weaved the bike between the trees, dodging the low-lying branches as much as possible. She cringed inwardly each time one smacked against Demetri, knowing the last thing he needed was more pain.

To his credit, she thought, *he has not flinched once, even though the stings must be sharp.*

A sigh of relief blew along her neck when they emerged from the forest. The lights of the town glowed dimly in front of them. They bounced over the open terrain. Each bump rubbed their bodies together.

The caress of his thighs against her jeans, his chest against her back, coupled with his lap cradling her bottom was a stimulating combination.

Whoa! Not going there. The last thing I need is to respond physically to this male. Better get to the hotel and get some distance quick.

Tatiana cranked the throttle and put on a burst of speed.

****

Demetri breathed deeply.

The ocean! The female smells like the sea.

When not dodging the low-lying branches, the woman seemed determine to hit, he had been trying to figure out the fragrance coming from her body. It had been tantalizing. A reminder of a lost memory from long ago. The recollection eluding him until at last he placed the scent. Like a summer's day, her bouquet surrounded him, filled his lungs while he lay over her.

Her warmth seeped into his body, and he welcomed it. Dressed only in a pair of shredded shorts, he fought to block the cold from his mind while they rode through the night. The arctic air blanketed him, biting at the flesh like a thousand bee stings. Little pin pricks danced along his skin while they made their way over the snow. A shiver shook his body though he was not sure whether it was from the cold or from the female beneath him.

Demetri assumed it must be the cold, for he could not find anything remotely interesting about the female sitting in front of him. Oh yes, her smell was perhaps enticing, but that was all. She was not his type. He preferred blondes with lush curves and a penchant for pleasing him.

Everything Tatiana was not.

Used to being in charge, whether on the battlefield or in the bedroom, he liked things his way. The female driving toward the town was the antithesis of obedient. She was a fighter, used to giving orders, not taking them. She seemed cold, unemotional. Everything he did not find attractive in a woman.

Yes, the shiver is definitely due to the cold, he thought as they bumped along with the air flowing around their bodies.

Thank goodness Alex had gone ahead with the humans. He didn't want his fellow Alpha to see him like this. Holding onto a female, allowing her to take them to safety. Just one more humiliation to add to the long list from his capture. He'd believed his degradation would end once freed from his captors, but fate apparently had other designs.

To be in a position where he needed rescuing had been bad enough. The fact a female had not only been one of his rescuers but had also witnessed him strapped helplessly to a table with the instruments of his torture around him on display, grated on his last shred of self-worth, threatening to cut the last of his self-respect into a million pieces. He was a proud man; at least he had been before his capture.

He endured constant physical and psychological abuse at the hands of the kidnappers. The effects of which would never be completely erased from his body or mind. In his weaker moments, he longed for death to release him from the torment. Welcomed the Reaper of souls with outstretched arms and a prayer to the Fates, but the Reaper had not come. Instead, he'd been rescued from the Hell created by the demons not by a team of his fellow Alphas, but instead by a female.

A female with whom he had an unpleasant history. A female who had last left him kneeling in pain on the ground when she had kneed him in his groin after they kissed, a kiss which had been as powerful to her as it was to him.

He'd been sure of it.

But for some unfathomable reason, she brought him to his knees then dematerialized without so much as an explanation or a goodbye. And now that same female had complete control of him. Helplessness tightened his arms and anger curled in his stomach.

****

Demetri had been eerily still as they rode along. It was like the warrior to be pensive and quiet. In fact, Tatiana preferred him that way because when he spoke

91

he tended to piss her off by saying something sexist.

As if hearing her inner thoughts, his arms tightened around her middle, making it difficult to breathe. The strength of his thin arms surprised her. She chalked it up to his recent feeding.

Good, he'll need his strength. I'll have to make sure he feeds again before tonight is over, so he'll have enough strength to travel tomorrow night.

Movement ahead caught her eye. In the predawn light, a petite figure jogged down the opposite side of the street toward them. Tatiana slowed the bike to a stop and killed the engine.

"It's almost dawn. What are you doing?" asked Demetri as they sat up.

A groan of pain sounded behind her.

"You need to feed." Tatiana nodded toward the woman. "Beggars can't be choosers."

Demetri nodded. He lifted a leg off the bike and straightened to his full height testing his muscles. Tatiana noted the slowness of his movements. "You want me to compel her?" she offered over her shoulder as she dismounted the motorcycle.

"Not necessary. I can take care of myself." The tone in his deep voice allowed no argument.

Tatiana shrugged. "Suit yourself. If you need any help, I'll be over here."

"You have helped enough for one night."

The sound of the insult in Demetri's voice caused the VES agent to lift her brows and cross her arms in response.

Demetri approached the woman. Unsure if he would require her help, Tatiana's body tensed, ready to leap across the road if assistance seemed needed. She might not like the guy, but she'd been charged with getting him back home safe and sound, and she intended to complete the mission. To accomplish it, he needed to be strong enough to travel.

The woman's face went blank before she cocked her head to one side and bared the slim column of her neck to Demetri. He lowered his mouth, hovering over the spot where her pulse beat below the skin. His tongue darted out, tasting the spot. The sight made Tatiana's gut twist. Her heart clenched in her chest when he lowered his lips to the woman's flesh. An emotion akin to jealousy flashed through her mind, but as quickly as it came, confusion pushed it aside when Demetri straightened.

Tatiana noted the absence of puncture wounds on the woman's neck. Demetri murmured something while he looked deeply into the runner's eyes then sent her on her way.

The Alpha crossed the road in three strides.

Tatiana's hands fisted at her sides. "What the hell? Why didn't you feed?"

"She was not a good candidate to feed from," he replied as his stomach growled its objection.

"She was the only person around. That made her perfect to feed from. I told you I could help if you needed me." *Stubborn man.*

Demetri's hands balled into fists. "I did not need your assistance. I am perfectly capable of putting a compulsion on a human mind."

"Then why didn't you feed after you compelled her?"

"Because she was with child." The news shocked Tatiana into silence, allowing Demetri to continue unabated. "When I bent to take her neck, I heard a second heartbeat. I missed it at first because it beat so quickly it sounded like a hummingbird's wings, but as I was about to drink, I realized what it was."

"Are you sure? I mean her stomach was flat. She definitely didn't look pregnant."

"I took the information from her mind after I became suspicious. She is seven weeks into the pregnancy." Demetri swung a leg over the back of the bike. "It is almost dawn. We must get going, Tatiana." The sound of her name on his lips launched a shiver down her spine.

"You need to feed. Alex may have some bagged blood back at the hotel. It won't make you as strong as taking from the vein, but it will help ease your hunger pangs."

Tatiana climbed back onto the bike, brought it to life, then headed for the hotel.

Demetri's hunger remained a tangible force beating at her back. She remembered that pain, the pain of cells crying out for nourishment, joints refusing to work, muscle seizing in their need for sustenance.

The control it took for him to walk away from the willing meal in front of him impressed her. To turn down the one thing that could ease his suffering to keep the unborn child safe—remarkable.

As she pulled into the parking lot of the hotel, Tatiana reluctantly admitted maybe, just maybe, there was more to Demetri Romanoff than the male chauvinist she had come to expect.

Chapter 11

Parked between two nondescript buildings in the town, Jara sat in the small car tapping her nails impatiently on the dash. The blonde hair that normally hung in waves just past her shoulders floated away from her head, held suspended like a golden halo. The long locks crackled with sparks of demonic ire. Her cheekbones stood out against her face, creating dark shadows on her cheeks. Jara's almond shaped eyes narrowed menacingly in Lane's direction.

Lane cowered behind the steering wheel. He dropped his hands to his lap and lowered his gaze to avoid the red eyes of the woman sitting next to him. The vehicle seemed suddenly small. He tamped down the instinct to leap from the car. He knew better.

The demon beside him was royalty, the sister of the Demon King. She was used to sycophants, expected all to kowtow to her every whim. If he ran, she would follow. Not to retrieve, but to kill him for his perfidy.

His heart raced, and he worked to calm it as he mustered some courage, then turned toward Jara. He bowed his head. Hoping she would not take her anger out on him, he kept is eyes lowered to his own chest.

"How could you let this happen?" Jara demanded from between clenched teeth.

The muscle in Lane's jaw twitched, the only outward sign of distress he showed as he considered the answer carefully. He wasn't responsible for what had happened at the warehouse. He had not led the vampires to their complex. They could not have followed him there because he never left.

"Don't blame me. Like most demons, I have agoraphobia. I never left the safety of the compound since every exposure to humans is a deadly risk."

"A risk Varrick has forgotten ever since he found that human queen of his."

"I've noticed a few of the younger demons are equally reckless. Perhaps one in our employ went to town, and the vampires followed him back to the compound."

The sound of the impatient clicking of Jara's long nails on the dash broke his train of thought.

"An interesting supposition. I still hold you responsible."

A horrified expression widened his eyes. "I took every precaution. We had the door key-coded, the passage to the lab concealed, and armed guards stationed about the complex. I even had an emergency alarm installed. I don't know what more I could have done."

"You obviously didn't think of everything, did you? We were lucky to escape with our lives."

Lane's head snapped up, and he pinned the demonic princess with his crimson eyes. "I never would have let those bloodsuckers lay a finger on you. As long as I breathed, they would not have hurt you."

"A nice sentiment, but that's not what happened. You grabbed me and ran like a coward. You allowed the vampires to remain in the complex. As we speak, they are probably taking the specimen while our people flee.

"We've not only lost our people but the creature that could have helped us to fulfill my brother's directive. And it's all. Your. Fault."

Her power coiled around him like a Burmese python, encasing him. The constricting began at his feet, binding them together before continuing up his body to stop around his throat. He struggled to breathe. Each breath pushed against the invisible barrier.

"Please, Jara," he begged.

"Someone must pay for what happened tonight!"

The pressure tightened. When his ribs snapped, a yowl ripped from his throat.

"Don't...kill...me," the demon pleaded, taking small breaths during the pauses between his words. "I...I can still...save our people."

The pressure around his throat and chest eased slightly. "I know the secret...to the vampire immunity is...in their blood. I've proven that...it can heal most human injuries. I-I was ready to begin the demon trials...when we were attacked." Lane took a deep breath, sending a stabbing pain from his ribs throughout his body. Agony contorted his face. "If my store of vampire blood...is still at the warehouse...all is not lost."

Jara leaned back into the seat as if considering the male next to her. "Fortunately for you, Lane, Varrick would not be happy if I killed our people's best hope for discovering the secret to immunity."

The pressure around his body eased slightly as she continued. "I will allow you to live. We need more time for your experiments. More time and some demons. Of course, the workers from the warehouse scattered to the winds when the alarm had sounded. Unfaithful wretches.

"How do you propose we find our kind? With the warehouse compromised, they will not return there. Was there a safe house in the area?"

The scientist shook his head slowly, careful not to disturb his broken rib. "No…I have a few of the guards' numbers programmed…into my cell…but it is back in the lab."

Jara gave a very unladylike snort. "Of course, it is."

"Look at the sky," Lane continued, unabated by the sarcastic retort. "The sun…will be up soon."

"So." Jara crossed her arms over her bosom.

"The vampires will have to be inside by the time…the sun rises." Lane wrapped a bracing arm around his middle. "We can go back to the warehouse…get what we need to continue my experiments."

"If we are lucky enough to find the vampire's blood still there, how do you intend to get the demons for your experiments? Surely you don't plan on using the guards. We'll need them to protect us should the vampires strike again."

As Lane rubbed a thoughtful hand over his bearded chin, Jara's arm jutted out with one finger pointing out the windshield. "Look! Isn't that one of our vehicles?"

Lane tracked the SUV as it passed. "Yes, that is Manon's. I recognize the dent near the gas tank."

"Well, don't just sit there, idiot. Follow them." Lane started the engine and pulled onto the street as Jara continued excitedly. "I think I saw multiple bodies in the vehicle. Hopefully some of them will know where the other demons are. Maybe we can salvage something from this disaster after all."

Lane raced to catch up to the sport utility, following it as it turned into a hospital parking lot.

"Where are they going? All demons know we can't go to a human hospital for help. Are they crazy?" Jara's eye widened as she spoke. "Lane, get out and stop them! NOW!"

She gave him a shove as if to push him from the moving vehicle. The motion made him jerk the steering wheel. Their car jumped over a curb and headed for a concrete light post. Lane stomped on the brake and skidded to a halt just inches from the post. The scientist ran a sweaty hand through his auburn hair, disheveling the short strands.

"Get out!" ordered the princess as she reached for her own door handle. "We must stop them!"

Lane reached over and stilled her movement by laying his hand on her wrist. "Wait! Look."

Lane nodded in the SUV's direction.

Jara froze.

The blond vampire, who had attacked them, exited from the vehicle. He moved swiftly taking one human after another from the car to place them on a bench located just outside the automatic doors to the hospital. Once all the humans were seated, he entered the hospital.

Minutes later, three orderlies and a nurse pushing wheelchairs followed him outside.

"See, humans not demons." Lane put their vehicle into reverse and backed the car away from the light post. He maneuvered from the curb and came to a stop a discreet distance from where the vampire had parked.

"I have an idea." A fiendish grin overtook Jara'sface. "The vampire will not remain at the hospital, and the sun will be up soon. He'll have to go someplace safe, someplace he knows. Let's follow him. Maybe he'll lead us to the other bloodsuckers."

Relief flooded Lane's body. "Goddess be praised. Our luck may have just turned around."

He flashed Jara a wide smile that reached his ears.

****

With Demetri's arm draped around her shoulders, Tatiana wrapped her arm around his waist and helped him to lie down on her bed.

When they had arrived at the hotel, she expected Alex to have beaten them there. She had knocked on the door to his room to discover they had arrived before him. He was nowhere to be found, nor was the SUV he'd been driving. Consequently, she'd had no choice but to take Demetri to her room.

She glanced at him sprawled out on the bed and wished she had requested two full sized beds instead of a queen. Even emaciated, he still took up a good portion of the bed. It would be difficult to sleep and not accidentally touch him.

The thought sent heat racing through her veins. Every time their bodies came in contact, hers responded as any heartmate's would, with a rush of desire. It was chemistry, pure and simple, but she could no more stop her body's reaction than she could stop flow of the mighty Mississippi River. Heartmates never tired of each other. Even if they were blessed to have hundreds of years together, they always desired each other. Heartmates were faithful until the end. Once they found each other they could never touch or care for anyone else.

Tatiana chose to believe it was a chemical bonding between the pair that caused all the physical ties and emotional baggage. She also believed, if she kept her distance from Demetri, the chemicals racing through her blood would not bond them.

The minute Alex arrived back at the hotel, she intended to have him help Demetri into his room for the day, then tonight they would get Demetri back to his home in Wyoming, and she would be free.

Free to go back to Florida.

Free to resume her duties with VES.

Free to live her life unattached to an overbearing heartmate.

"You need anything, Romanoff?" She tossed over her shoulder as she meandered to the window.

"Sleep," mumbled the deep voice behind her.

Her heart sank as she reached for the drapes. She felt the sun through the crack in the material. Morning had arrived. Even if Alex made it back to the hotel in the next few minutes, Demetri was too weak from starvation to be exposed to the sun's direct rays.

A sigh escaped her lips as she pulled the heavy drapes closed, overlapping the material so no light would stream through.

Dammit!

Tatiana pulled her cell from her jeans and punched in Alex's number. It rang once before he picked up.

"Hall here."

"Mind if I pop into your hotel room?"

"Of course, not, Tatiana. But what do you need?"

"Blood. For Demetri."

"Can't help. I'm all out. We finished the last of it."

"Can you get more? Where are you?"

"No can do. I'm on my way there now with the sun baring down on my back."

Shit, he's no help. Demetri would just have to suffer a little longer. At least his day sleep would take some of the pain away.

"Safe travels, Alex. Get here soon."

"Will do. Watch over my boy for me."

Tatiana grunted her agreement, clicked the phone off and stood at the foot of the bed looking down on the male sleeping in it. Still wearing his tattered shorts, he had crawled under the covers and now had them tucked up under his chin. He lay curled onto one side. His face appeared innocent, almost angelic. A sleepy grin pulled at one corner of his mouth as if in response to a pleasant dream. Sleep eased the lines of his face, made him seem almost peaceful.

Handsome.

Whoa! Where had that thought come from?

Tatiana ran a tired hand through her dark hair. She must need some rest herself, but she smelled of bike exhaust and blood, so a shower was in order.

After taking a quick shower to wash the thoughts of Demetri from her mind as the soap washed the signs of battle from her body, she completed her daily ritual of brushing her teeth and…

A thought gave her pause. Normally she would have put on a nightgown to sleep, but having to share a bed with Demetri crushed that plan. She would sleep fully clothed tonight.

She wrapped a towel around her body and crept on silent feet to her suitcase. Careful not to make much noise, she unzipped the bag then took out a pair of jeans, underwear, and a sweater.

Making her way back to the bath to slip into her clothes a loud zZZzzzZZ- hngGGggh-Ppbhww-zZZzzzZZ startled her. Years of training suppressed the jump her body wanted to make at the noise.

Great, just great. On top of everything else, he snores.

She donned the clothing and snuck into the bed, careful not to disturb the sleeping giant who lay on his side with his back toward her. A weary sigh blew though her lips as she rolled onto her side away from Demetri. They might have to share a bed, but they did not have to touch.

Her eyes, leaden from exhaustion, closed when she yawned. Her thoughts stilled, and the blackness settled in, taking her to her dreams.

****

"You're losing him. You're losing him," squawked Jara, her nails digging into Lane's arm with enough force to draw blood from his flesh.

"I see him. He just turned off. Relax. I won't lose him." Lane maneuvered the car into the hotel parking lot in time to see the SUV disappear behind the building. He made his way slowly over the asphalt, wanting to avoid drawing any unwanted attention.

When they rounded the corner of the structure, their eyes went to the tall male walking briskly toward one of the hotel room doors. Steam rose from his exposed skin, providing absolute proof of what he was. After a swipe of a keycard, he opened the door and disappeared into the darkness within.

Lane brought the vehicle to a stop several doors down from the one which held the vampire and put the car into park. "Guess we know where he is staying."

A genuine smile graced Jara's haunted face. "We also know where he will be until sunset." She glanced down at the clock in the dash. "That gives us about twelve hours. We need to go back to the warehouse, get your cell, and gather all the guards we can find."

Lane put the car into reverse. "I take it you have a plan."

Jara turned the full effect of her iniquitous stare on Lane, her eyes wide with bloodlust. "Oh yeah, I have a plan."

Chapter 12

The sound of wood splintering pierced his consciousness. Metal hinges screamed their pain as they ripped in two. Alex struggled to gain consciousness, his body still lethargic since the sun had yet to set. His eyes peeled open slowly; his senses fuzzy. His mind resisted the commotion in the room.

"What the—" A thick hand squeezed his throat, stopping not only his next word, but the air as well.

The Alpha's hand flew to his neck to discover fingers of the one pinning him to the bed. He gripped the digits, peeled them from his skin, and rolled away. Alex rose from the bed and settled into a fighting stance with fists raised, his weight balanced on the balls of his feet.

A large male approached him with surprising agility and speed. His fist connected with the warrior's face, sending it flying to the side. Pain radiated through Alex's cheek and down his neck, bringing with it awareness that this was no human. He sent his senses out into the room and discovered the beings were not vampires either.

"Shifters," Alex spit out between teeth clenched in pain.

"Demons."

The Alpha's gaze turned toward the source of the female voice, watching as a woman with leonine features breezed through the tattered doorway. Her long blonde hair hung about her shoulders in waves. Her red eyes burned with hatred when she pinned Alex with her evil stare.

The Alpha launched an attack. Catching the male in front of him around the waist, he took the demon to the floor. He landed on his back with a grunt as the air was knocked from his lungs.

Alex drew his fist back, preparing to connect with the man's face with as much strength as he could muster with the sun still in the sky.

"Get him!" The female shrieked, her voice filling the small hotel room. "Shackle him, quickly!"

When two more demons ran toward him with restrains dangling from their hands, Alex leapt from the male. He backed away, keeping an arm's length between him and the demons until the unforgiving wall hit his back.

One of the demons smiled a sinister grin seconds before his hand clamped around Alex's wrist. The blond warrior struggled as the second demon wrapped a thick hand around his opposite forearm. In his weakened condition, he was no match for the pair. They easily held his arms in place.

Alex kicked at them while they attempted to place the cuffs on his wrists, but two more demons leapt across the bed at his legs. Their effort brought Alex's limbs out from underneath him, taking the Alpha to the floor. The four demons followed him down, their shackles clanking with the movement.

His limbs ached from the effort to break free from the enemy's holds. The sun-induced lethargy took the fight from his body. However, the Alpha would not go down quietly. A roar ripped from his chest as he poured all his power into his appendages. One leg broke loose of its hold.

He kicked it wildly, contacting with the shoulder of one of the demons kneeling by his legs. The demon swayed. The movement spurred the male into action. The large man tackled Alex's leg in a bear hug and immobilized it with the weight of his body.

The Alpha felt the last of his power drain. He lay pinned like an insect in a collection box, his arms and legs splayed out like the wings of a dragonfly.

He was in trouble.

The Alpha's eye darted between the four cuffs. He quickly realized they were made of titanium. *Clever demons.* How the hell did they know titanium could hold a vampire? If they got those cuffs on him, he would not be able to dematerialize.

Dematerialize!

The thought immediately triggered the action. Alex's form coalesced into an obsidian pinpoint before disappearing completely, leaving only a puff of black smoke wafting between the fingers of the demons as they scrambled in vain to grasp at the flesh no longer there.

****

Demetri made his way down the street of his hometown, his cell phone to his ear. He and the leader of the Alphas, Stephan von Haas, had decided to do a little recon to see if they could find any clues as to why there had been a series of possible animal attacks in the area. Finding nothing of note, Demetri decided to call his cousin.

"Hello Demetri," Nicholai greeted him in their

native Russian. "How are you this evening?"

"I'm fine and you?"

"I am doing well enough."

Demetri heard Nicholai closing a door before he spoke. "You sound bored."

He nodded, though he knew Nicholai could not see. "I am bored. You know how recognizance can be."

"Since you haven't found anything yet, have you considered contacting VES? What do they have to say?" Nicholai inquired.

Demetri hesitated. "No, I haven't contacted the Vampire Enforcement Squad yet."

"Would you like me to call Agent Bolovich and try to find out if they have any information about the attacks?"

"No!" Demetri said a little too quickly, hoping his cousin would not notice.

Demetri flashed back to when he and Tatiana worked together to rescue Marcus' heartmate, Christina. After a passionate kiss, she disappeared from his life, leaving him hurt and confused. Of course, he'd eventually shaken both feelings and taken solace in the knowledge that he would never see her again.

Demetri took a deep breath. "Until we know for sure if it is just an animal attack, Stephan and I do not think it was a good idea to involve…"

Demetri stopped mid-sentence, his words taken by a beautiful blonde approaching him. Déjà vu took him. He realized he dreamed of a time in the recent past. But one more glance into the woman's gorgeous face and he quickly decided he'd go where the dream took him.

He memorized the sway of her hips as she walked, the graceful way her delicate arms swung at her sides.

She was petite, with long hair that begged for his fingers to run through the straight silky strands.

The phone at his ear long forgotten, Demetri muttered under his breath. "I could really take a bite out of that. She's gorgeous. I wouldn't mind having her in my bed. I bet she'd be a tiger."

Nicholai chuckled. "Demetri, you do realize you said that out loud."

"Yes, but I said it quietly enough no human could hear." Demetri laughed. "I couldn't help myself cousin, sometimes when they look that good, you just have to say something."

"Sounds like you found something interesting. Tell me about her. What does she look like?"

"She's beautiful. Long blonde hair, tiny little body, curves in all the right places. She looks scrumptious."

"Sounds like your type, Demetri."

"She certainly is," he agreed. "I think I better go now."

Demetri hit the end button on his phone, stuffing it into his jacket pocket before doing an about-face to follow the tiny blonde. Duty could wait.

He strolled on silent feet behind the woman, watching as she wrapped her arms about her royal-blue parka. The fur lined hood, pulled tight around her face, left only her eyes, red little nose, and a wisp of blonde bang sticking out from underneath.

Her hips swayed like sensual waves on the sea. His body hardened.

Nicholai had not been wrong. She was exactly his type. He had always preferred soft, supple, helpless females in his bed. The thought of her writhing under him, screaming his name in passion, empowered him.

How he would love to hold her tiny wrists above her head as he took her. He wiped one hand through his hair and quietly stalked behind her waiting for just the right moment.

She would be just another of his conquest. He would take his pleasure and leave just like every other time. Demetri had no use for a relationship, no desire to have a female around on a permanent basis. He preferred to have his fun and go.

Of course, he gave as good as he got, sometimes he gave more. A considerate, passionate lover, he always saw to his partner's pleasure. No one left his bed unsated, ever.

He approached the woman and wrapped his long fingers around her delicate arm, careful not to mar her flesh with his bruising grip. Her steps halted. She remained still, eyes cast down at the phone she held in her hand. Her small frame could not be more than five foot tall. He towered over her, his large body casting a shadow around her from the streetlight overhead.

He reached out to grasp a strand of her hair, unable to refrain from touching the sunny strands. Her lids pulled back slowly as she raised her face to gaze at him, revealing her eyes. Eyes that took his breath away. Her golden eyes matched her hair, hair every bit as soft and silky as it looked.

Without a word, she removed her parka, oblivious to the chill in the air, to reveal a snug sweater beneath. His gut twisted at the site of the green material hugging her amble breasts, molding to her slim ribs and waist. A goddess, she possessed a perfect hourglass figure.

Demetri pushed her against the storefront and took her lips in a searing kiss that drove the heat of desire through his veins. Her lips parted allowing his tongue entrance. She tasted like sweet honey.

He broke the kiss, turned her away from him. He placed her hands against the wall of the store, knowing she would need an anchor, something to keep her bound to this earth when he sent her soaring.

He lowered his mouth to her neck. His tongue flicked out between his lips to taste her flesh. She tasted like the forest—wild, untamed. He suckled at her neck, careful not to break her flesh with his fangs.

His hand wandered up her arm and over her shoulder, trailed down her back to find her hip. He splayed his fingers wide, covering her stomach with his large hand. He inched his palm up until he found the tantalizing mound of flesh begging for his touch.

His long fingers wrapped around her breast and squeezed, soliciting a moan. The sound zinged straight to his groin. A responsive little thing, she'd reacted just as he knew she would.

Her breast seemed smaller than it looked, not the oversized handful he expected, but it was soft and melted in his palm as he kneaded the creamy flesh. Her nipple pebbled under his ministrations, and Demetri could not help the smug smile of male satisfaction that crept onto his lips.

****

Burning throughout Tatiana's body brought her into a semiconscious state. A vague awareness of a hand messaging her breast stirred in her mind. Desire for the gentle touch flowed through her like a warm bath; soothing and comforting, lulling her into a contented state of listlessness.

She remained motionless, allowed the fingertips to

stroke, feather-light, over the swell of her breast. The pad of a thumb brushed along her nipple, sending hunger streaking from the breast to her belly then lower, so that her core grew hotter, and her thighs spasmed.

The hand slipped down, following the track of her hunger, to glide over her stomach before settling on her thigh. Fingers caressed and stroked over her pants, moving higher to brush over the junction of her thighs. Tatiana pushed against the hand like a cat preening for affection, wishing the cumbersome material that blocked the feel of skin on skin gone.

Her body welcomed each stroke, each brush of the fingers as they roamed, creating a craving only they could satisfy. She needed the touch, wanted more. Wanted it to never end.

She lay in her dreamlike state, enjoying the sinuous sensation. Her mind refused to think, only enjoy. She barely registered the significant and very admirable male part pressed against her bottom, her mind instead focusing on the pleasure circulating throughout her body.

Her eyes snapped open when a deep male voice tore her from the euphoria. "Tatiana, wake up."

Tatiana's confused gaze met Alex's for a second before his eyes lowered to the hand under the sheet as it slid over her thigh on a path that led to her breast.

Alex cleared his throat and adverted his eyes. "Don't mean to barge in on you, but we've got a problem."

Tatiana blinked, trying hard to process what the Alpha said. She forced the haze from her brain and pushed up on one arm. A large hand slid down her body as she moved into a seated position. Realization flooded her brain like a tsunami crashing onto a coast. The dream fingers belonged to the male sharing her bed. The very male with whom she wanted nothing to do with.

Repulsion at the thought of the way her body responded to his touch took the last of the lethargy from her body. She bound from the bed as if it was on fire and turned in fury to glare at the male lying in the bed.

At some point during the day, Demetri had rolled over to her side of the bed, taking advantage of her day sleep to molest her. "How dare…" Her admonishment died in her throat as the slight sound of a snore made her realized the Alpha lay sound asleep.

Alex laid a hand on Tatiana's shoulder. "We have a problem," he repeated, taking her attention away from Demetri. "I was attacked."

"Are you okay?" Concern furrowed her brows when she noted a bruise darkened the Alpha's jaw.

Alex nodded his head. "I'm fine."

"Your face."

"Yeah, they got the drop on me. Came in while I was in day sleep."

"Who attacked you? The shifter?"

Alex shook his head, the motion obviously making his bruised face throb in response for his hand rubbed over the bruise. "They aren't shifters. They called themselves demons."

Demons. Tatiana rolled the word over in her mind before turning her attention to their present situation. "Where are they now?"

Alex crossed to the window, carefully peeling back one corner of the thick drapes to look out onto the walkway. "Coming this way." Alex dropped the drape back into place, plunging the room into partial darkness.

Tatiana crossed to her bag and withdrew a gun. She thumbed off the safety as she turned back toward the Alpha who scrubbed a hand down his handsome face. "There are a lot of them, Tatiana."

The agent dropped the clip from the gun and noted the amount of ammunition before slamming it back into place. "Shit, it isn't even a full magazine. I haven't had time to replace the ammo we used up last night."

"My weapon is back in my room. I didn't have time to grab it."

"What are we going to do?"

"The only thing we can do. Dematerialize out of here. Fast."

It was Tatiana's turn to nod, knowing sometimes it was smart to retreat if it meant you got to fight another day. "Where should we meet?"

"How about the inn we stayed in back at that little town outside of Sherbrooke? You know the one two towns ago. The owner reminded you of a mouse."

"I don't know where that is," said a rough voice. Demetri pushed up to sit. The sheet fell away from his chest and pooled in his lap. Tatiana did not miss the way he bunched the material to hide the evidence of his arousal beneath the cloth. "I can't go far in my condition."

"How about your place in Wyoming then?" Alex suggested. "It's not too far from here, and we all know where it is."

Demetri nodded weakly, the pissed look on his face indicating he did not appreciate his feebleness. "Perfect.

I can't wait to get home."

Alexander smiled, showing the dimple in his left cheek. "I bet you can't, big guy. I'll see ya there."

Alex popped out of the room, only a puff of black smoke to indicate he had ever been there.

Tatiana put her gun back into the bag and pulled the zipper closed.

"Okay. Your turn." She turned and faced Demetri. His form blurred. Her eyes widened as his body solidified on the bed, his chest expanding with each deep breath he took.

"What's wrong?"

"Can't…fade…too…weak." Demetri took a breath between each word, his body obviously exhausted from the effort. "Need…blood."

"We don't have any blood," Tatiana informed him, "or I would have given you some last night."

The sound of heavy footsteps drew their attention.

"Down here. I think I smell the stench of the bloodsucker."

The deep voice traveled easily through the thin walls.

Tatiana grabbed her bag and sat next to Demetri on the bed. They could not fight their way out, Demetri was too weak and according to Alex, there were too many of them for her to take on alone.

Demetri eyed her wearily. He looked at her like a wolf does its prey. She realized what he would say before he opened his mouth.

"Your blood is strong…Tatiana. If I…take from you, I…might gain enough strength to…dematerialize." As if trying to gather his courage, his next intake of breath was slow, and determination took his face. "May

I…drink from you?"

A shiver straightened her spine. She knew it would give him the strength he needed to dematerialize the distance to his home. She was not an ancient like him, but she was several centuries old. Her blood was powerful and would be able to nourish the Russian warrior.

It would also give away her secret; tell him they were heartmates. But he must survive. Her honor, her duty required it. He must get home safely, and this one last act would ensure it.

Knowing it was their best hope, their only hope, she begrudgingly offered him her wrist.

Chapter 13

The weary Alpha took her proffered wrist. When Demetri's fingers closed around her flesh, a shiver raced through her. His fangs lengthen. The smell of the ocean flooded his nostrils.

His teeth pierced the creamy flesh, sliding in slowly to find the ambrosia that ran beneath. Demetri's eyes closed in ecstasy as the first drop fell on his tongue.

Pure bliss. The sweet taste, unlike any he'd consumed before, warmed him to the core, made his body come alive. Each cell sang. His muscles danced. Demetri's body reacted like a schoolboy while he took in the scarlet essence. She filled him, sustained him in a way no other could.

The earth tilted. The room swayed. His body reacted with every cell screaming, *MINE*! His muscles and sinew tightened, cried for more. More of the delicious nectar. He gulped another mouthful, allowing the life-giving nutrients to flow over his tongue, the next swallow so large it felt like a block in his throat. More of her. He drew harder, the need consuming him.

More of my heartmate.

The realization stunned him. His lips stilled on her wrists, his purpose forgotten.

His heartmate! The other half of his soul. A half he had not missed until this moment.

117

Someone to spend eternity with. Someone to love him, to be loved by him. The future seemed bright, hopeful, and he began to imagine what it would be like with his mate.

His eyes locked with Tatiana's. Like an invisible thread weaving between their minds and hearts, something slid into place. A force greater than themselves linked them. A force nothing could undo. Bonded in a way only possible between heartmates.

"We have to go." Tatiana broke the spell, bringing Demetri back to the present. "I hear the demons. They are just outside the door."

Demetri nodded his head once, afraid to use any more energy by speaking. He wanted to tell her they were mates, wanted to take her into his arms and kiss her senseless, but that would have to wait. And he could wait, knowing she would be materializing into his home.

Home.

The word had taken on a new context now that he would have someone to share it with. He could not wait to share the discovery with the VES agent. *His* VES agent. The thought made him smile.

****

Tatiana watched Demetri's smile fade as his body coalesced in on itself to an ebony pinpoint inside a bit of smoke.

A string of curses left the female agent's mouth. That smile could only mean one thing—Demetri knew.

She hesitated then pulled her bag into her hand. The stupid grin on his face told her more than any words could. Her fears had come to fruition, he knew they were heartmates and no doubt expected her to be a willing mate. He would expect her to stay at home, barefoot and pregnant.

Naked and pregnant is more like it.

The chemistry between them was explosive, consuming, even in his weakened condition. Fates help her when he recovered physically from his ordeal. No doubt a physical relationship would be mind-blowing, but Demetri would demand total submission. He would need to be in charge, expect her to quietly follow his lead.

Not gonna happen, she thought when the first demon burst through the flimsy door to her room.

She gave the man a middle-finger salute before dematerializing.

Chapter 14

Tatiana materialized into the great room. She scanned the area, looking for any possible threats, noting every entry point as training had taught her to do.

Always know your surroundings. Always have an exit. Know from where your enemies might attack. It was as much an automated response to her as the beating of her heart.

The walls in this house, like Demetri, were hard, abrasive. The home fit him, large, manly. No frills or fancy decorating. Simple, rustic furnishings sat on the oak floor. The ceiling, made of thick arched timbers, was roughly cut.

Her eyes came to rest on Demetri. He sat heavily in a chair as if the elk antler furniture called to his tired body. Concern furrowed her dark brows. His breathing seemed laborious. His chest pushed up and down. She noted the way the pulse beat hard, straining under the skin of his neck.

He appeared drawn. The bones of his cheeks stood out in sharp contrast to his strong jaw. A fine sheen of perspiration coated his body as if he had been exercising.

Surprise cocked her head to the side as she considered him. She would have expected her blood to give him more than enough strength to dematerialize this relatively short distance. She took a moment to assess each bruise and scar.

One particularly angry looking scar ran down the middle of his chest from the base of his breastbone to disappear under the waistband of the shorts he wore. A reddish line ran in a jagged diagonal line from his shoulder to his breastbone. Another scar mirrored the one on the opposite side to create a vee that connected to the scar running down the center of his body.

This pattern looked familiar to her. She had seen it before.

It was the "Y" incision done during an autopsy.

Bile rose in her throat. Demetri had endured a vivisection!

Horror twisted her stomach. She could not imagine the pain of such a procedure and hoped Demetri would have been knocked out for the dissection. The thought was despicable.

She put her bag down and started toward him, needing to touch the evidence of his torture. To feel would be to believe. To understand.

Alex popping into the room stayed her feet. He lifted the cooler in his hand. "Blood anyone?"

Demetri turned, resting his arm on the back of the couch, palm up. "Fates, yes! Give me a bag."

Alex placed a bag into Demetri's open hand. Faster than her eyes could register, Demetri popped the bag on his fangs. He moaned around the plastic while the cold liquid seeped into his mouth.

Tatiana crossed to the kitchen. She opened three cabinets before finding the one containing glasses. After bringing one down in each hand, she turned her attention to Alex. "You want a glass for your blood?"

The blond warrior shook his head then tossed a bag at Tatiana. "Nah, I had a bag before coming over here."

She caught the bag easily and poured it into one of the glasses. "Where did you get the blood, anyway?"

"From my place in Virginia. I stopped by there before coming here."

Tatiana nodded. She took a sip of the crimson liquid. AB negative. Her favorite.

Her body needed the fuel, depleted from a lack of regular feeding coupled with the energy expended during the rescue. She barely stifled the moan threatening to spill from her throat.

Nothing better than a little AB negative. Demetri liked the same type, something they had in common.

She poured the remainder of the bag into the second glass. "Got any more?" she asked, looking expectantly at Alex.

"Of course." The Alpha tossed her another two bags.

After filling both glasses, she brought one to Demetri. He pulled the now empty bag from his mouth. Tatiana could not help but note the possessive glare in Demetri's eyes when she crossed the room and hoped it was because of the blood. She should have made him get up and retrieve the blood himself, but he seemed so tired. Bringing it to him was the least she could do.

She had agreed to see him home safe and sound. Once he drank, he would get his strength back, and she could leave, knowing she'd fulfilled her duty.

Yep, now that he was safe in his home, he just needed to regain some strength for her not to feel guilty leaving him alone. It wasn't the fact they were heartmates that caused her concern. That couldn't be it.

It had to be her strong sense of duty that made her want to be sure he would be safe.

Of course, he wouldn't necessarily be alone. Alex could stay. She wasn't needed at all, really. She would just stay long enough to replenish her own strength. One more glass should do it, then she would go home.

Back to her normal life.

A life which did not include a heartmate.

Tatiana smiled as she handed a glass to Demetri.

"Thank you," he croaked, his voice still raspy. He downed the blood in one long gulp and looked expectantly at Tatiana when she sat on the couch opposite him.

"More." When Tatiana lifted one brow, he amended his demand. "Please."

"Here you go, big guy." Alex ripped off the top of another bag of blood and poured it in a glass.

Alex took the crumpled bag from Demetri's hand and tossed it in the trash. "All right guys, looks like everything is under control. I'm outta here."

Tatiana shot to her feet. "What?"

"I gotta go. Stephan called me while I was in Virginia. He wants a debriefing, and I told him I'd do it as soon as I got you guys the blood."

Tatiana put her glass on the coffee table. "You have to do it tonight? Can't Stephan wait until tomorrow for his briefing?"

The blond Alpha shook his head. "Apparently not. He said he didn't care what time it was, I needed to come to his place in Vegas as soon as I got you guys the blood."

"But what about Demetri? I thought you would stay with him tonight."

"I don't need a babysitter," Demetri growled around the glass in his mouth, earning him a dubious look from Tatiana.

Panic quickened her pulse. Demetri knew they were mates. No way would she remain in his home. The longer they were together the more possessive he'd become. She needed to get out while the getting was good. She could *not* be the one to watch over him tonight.

"I'll go and brief Stephan," Tatiana offered, struggling to keep the desperation from her face.

"No can do. He requested me and what the Alpha leader wants, the Alpha leader gets." Alex shrugged into his jacket. "Bye ya'll."

Before Tatiana's disbelieving eyes, Alex's form coalesced to nothing, stopping the forth-coming protest in her throat.

Think, think, THINK! Desperately needing something to occupy her, Tatiana crossed the room to fetch another two bags of blood from the cooler as she struggled with what to do about Demetri.

She couldn't leave him in this weakened condition. What if he was attacked? He'd been kidnapped not far from here. He may not be safe here.

But she couldn't stay. She just couldn't. The longer they were together, the more dependent they would become on one another.

He just needed to be a little stronger. Needed to be able to defend himself, then she could go. Maybe another bag of blood would do it.

She sent a weary glance his way, noting the condition of his body.

Then again maybe not.

****

Demetri accepted the opened bag of blood from Tatiana. Pouring it into his glass, he mused about how much he enjoyed her taking care of him. He was a proud male, a strong male, but having his mate dote on him was something he might be able to get used to.

When she sat down across from him, he took a sip.

He wanted, no needed, to know more about his heartmate. Wanted to know her past, her present. He wondered what her favorite color was, her favorite flower. Did she even have a favorite flower? *Probably not,* he decided. Her favorite weapon, then.

He decided to start with an easy question. "So, tell me where you live?"

Though, soon we will sell the place, so you can live here with me.

"I have a place in Florida."

Demetri nearly spit the blood from his mouth in surprise. "Florida! Why in the world would anyone live in Florida?"

"I like the beach," Tatiana replied succinctly with a casual shrug of her shoulders.

"But *Florida*, It's so hot. And the humidity. Don't you miss the change of seasons, cold weather…snow?"

Tatiana hands fisted in her lap in pique. "Why am I not surprised you don't like a place known throughout the world for its warmth and hospitality?"

Hostility prickled against his skin as it radiated from the female across from him. He noted the fire in her yellow eyes. Her temperature rose—she was going to blow.

He had no idea what may be wrong but decided a change in subject could not hurt. "So, tell me how you and Alex were able to find me."

Tatiana shifted in the seat and crossed her legs. She took a deep breath, then blew it out slowly before answering. "It took us a while to locate you. We were hopping from town to town for almost three months before we found you."

Demetri nodded. So, he had only been gone for a few months. It seemed like years.

"We would scour the towns looking for clues as to where they had taken you. We weren't even sure at first who had you, but then we got lucky."

"How's that?"

"We ran into a shifter, I mean demon, in a bar. I followed her. Found out she knew about a vampire being held in a warehouse."

Demetri's smile reached his eyes. "I can only imagine how you were able to persuade her to share the information."

Tatiana laughed. The rich sound warmed Demetri's heart as he continued. "Did she tell you the name of the city I was in?"

He drained the last of the blood from his glass while she spoke.

"She didn't have to. By the time we found her, we were already in the same town as the warehouse where you were being kept."

Surprise raised his brows. His little mate was smart and resourceful to have found him with such little help. "How were you able to locate the town where I was being held?"

"A tip from Nicholai and your blood." The moment the answer left her mouth regret took her pretty face.

The Alpha's eyes widened in surprise while his

mind replayed their brief encounters together. Their first meeting had them sparring and ended with her spilling a drop of his blood, but she had not tasted it. During their first mission, more than a year ago, he had accidentally injured her and given her some of his blood to help heal her.

She had taken his blood!

More than a *year* ago, she ingested his blood. She would have known that instant they were heartmates. Anger heated his face. They shared a kiss after that night. A passionate kiss that had ended with her disappearing from his life.

For over a year!

Despite knowing they were mates, she stayed away from him. She had purposely denied him his heartmate.

She was a natural-born vampire and knew how special, how sacred, the pairing of heartmates was. Yet she had not come to him when she'd discovered they were a fated pair.

Disbelief mixed with the anger to sour his stomach. Demetri did not keep the hurt from showing on his face.

Chapter 15

Demetri quickly steeled his features as the hurt transformed into anger. He would not give his mate the satisfaction of seeing how much her deception affected him.

How dare she keep the knowledge they were heartmates from him! Many vampires went their entire existence never finding their one true mate. How could she not have run to him once she realized?

It was proof of just how selfish and narcissistic she must be. She had probably grown up being treated like a princess, always getting her way. Her vampiric parents doting over her, spoiling her by giving into her every whim. No doubt she ran her childhood home.

That would certainly explain why she joined VES and was allowed to fight. It would also explain why she constantly struggled to control every situation.

His anger rose bunching his tired muscles. He rolled his neck to relax the tension, tried to take the stiffness from his sinew. His hand came up to rub the knot, the movement tracked by the female sitting across from him.

She was obviously used to being in control. Well, that was going to have to change. His mate would be a dutiful heartmate, seeing to his needs as he saw to hers.

Their eyes locked, and he stared at her in silence, assessing the situation. He reluctantly had to give her credit. She did not lower her eyes, instead met his gaze as if daring him to call her out on her deception.

Too tired to deal with it now, Demetri gave up trying to ease the knotted muscles and pulled his hand from his neck. He looked down, noticing the dirt and grime.

The Alpha flipped his hand over, then held up his other arm. Both were equally filthy. For the first time since his escape, he took a long assessing glance at his body.

Dirt and sweat from months of imprisonment had mixed with dried blood from his torture sessions to create a thick film which covered his entire body. The sight repulsed him. A reminder of all he had suffered at the hands of his enemies; the degradation, the humiliation, the misery.

He needed to wash away the physical reminder of his time with the demons. Cleanse not only his body, but the thoughts from his mind.

Demetri felt bone tired. The blood had helped, but he needed more rest and a shower.

No, not a shower, a bath instead. A long, hot bath to melt away the residue of his torture and the anger toward his mate.

"I'm going to take a bath," Demetri announced.

Her eyes widened in surprise. "I'd have thought you would be more of a shower man."

"Normally I am, but my muscles could use a good soak."

Tatiana stood and delivered their empty glasses to the kitchen sink. "I'll leave you to it then. But before you go, could you show me to the guest room? I have some calls to make while you are in the bath."

"To whom?" Demetri eyed the female with a wary look.

"VES, for one. I need to let them know they can put me back in the rotation by the end of the week."

No heartmate of mine will be going out risking her life to police our kind. I need to find a way to stop her from going back to that dangerous occupation.

"The guest room is downstairs. I'll show you."

He watched the sway of her hips as Tatiana sauntered across the room to retrieve her bag. All lithe muscle, she possessed a catlike grace. His eyes tracked up her strong legs, the jeans she wore hugged the muscles which flexed when she walked. Her thin hips and matching waist led up to small round breasts. His gaze continued upward to rest on pale eyes. Eyes that shimmered under the darkness of her bluntly cut black hair.

His male libido automatically registered the subtle curves of her body, the shift of her muscles as she moved toward him holding her bag in her hands. Normally, he preferred a curvaceous blonde, but this lissome raven-haired beauty was sexy, nonetheless. Watching her move sent a wave of desire flooding his body.

The Fates had truly blessed him. His woman was strong, beautiful, if not a bit deceptive.

She would be a challenge, but he never shied from a good challenge.

Tatiana followed the Alpha through the house and down a set of stairs. As they arrived at the bottom, lights automatically lit their way down a long hall.

Nicholai, Demetri used the private mindlink he had established centuries ago with his cousin. *Can you hear me cousin?*

Demetri, it is so good to hear your voice. Alex said you were safe. Are you well, cousin?

I am as well as can be expected, Demetri answered truthfully. *I need a favor from you if you please.*

Of course, Demetri. Anything. You know you have only to ask.

I need you to call VES and have them give Tatiana Bolovich an extended leave of absence.

Alex mentioned she was staying with you tonight. Any particular reason why I should request her continued leave?

Because she is my heartmate.

The surprise Nicholai experienced hearing the declaration passed through their link. *She is your heartmate? Are you sure?*

Do you think I wouldn't know my own heartmate when I tasted her?

Too tired to keep his outrage from crossing their mindlink, Demetri let it flow like a mental slap.

No, of course not. Nicholai responded to the rhetorical question. *But if she is your mate, do you really want to force a leave of absence on her? Tatiana does not strike me as the kind of woman who would want a male to step up and take control of her life.*

Exactly why I am asking you to do this. Demetri delivered the mental equivalent of an eye roll. *I want plausible deniability.*

No. What you want is for me to do your dirty work for you.

That too.

I don't think—

It is the only way. I must keep her with me a little

longer, at least until she has come to accept we are mates.

A little *longer?* Nicholai's skepticism came across loud and clear.

Just do me a favor and work everything out with VES.

I will try.

Thank you, Nicholai.

I hope you know what you are doing. I don't think this is a good idea. I am here if you need any advice.

Just get VES to agree to an extended leave of absence. I'll do the rest.

Demetri closed the line of communication, snapping a mental barrier down into place.

****

The expression on Demetri's face when he realized she'd kept herself from him had torn at her heart, nearly ripping it in two. Heartmates were supposed to want to be together. They should experience a magical feeling of completeness, but she had not wanted Demetri and now her heartmate knew she'd kept herself from completing him.

There would be hell to pay.

Demetri's gaze burned on her back as they made their way down the hall. He assessed her like a deadly tiger stalking his prey, looking for weakness. He wouldn't find any.

She had been weak once, and it had cost her dearly. She had vowed long ago never to allow herself to be placed into a situation where all control was taken away, and she intended to keep the vow, regardless of whatever plans the male behind her might be conjuring in that big head of his.

As they walked through a simple entryway, Tatiana noted the hesitation in Demetri's steps. He turned and punched in a code onto the keypad located next to the entryway with speed too fast for even Tatiana's preternatural sight to register. With a breathy whish, a metal door slid down from the top of the entry way.

Tatiana turned and faced Demetri, searching his face for an explanation. "Did you just seal us in?"

He gave an insouciant shrug. "And if I did?" Demetri asked, his sonorous voice daring her dissention.

"Open the door," she commanded. Her eyes narrowed.

His dark brows furrowed over eyes narrowed in pique. "I don't think so."

Tatiana's past pushed in on her. Panic rose within. Claustrophobia, a side effect of years of captivity, closed around her. She fought her body for control when her heart raced, and her breathing came in quick shallow breaths.

Her hand shot to the keypad. Fingers flew over the keys desperately trying to repeat the numbers Demetri entered. A long beep indicating she had not hit the buttons in the correct sequence sounded with each attempt.

"Give me the code," she demanded then rounded on the Alpha. "I need to be able to get out of here."

A smile threatened to take the Alpha's face. "I appreciate your obvious concern for your safety. *Our* safety."

Did he think she worried about him? Them? He couldn't be more wrong.

"It's all right, Tatiana. The door is lined with

titanium as is the entire bunker of rooms down here. No one can get in."

Or out. Tatiana fought to slow her breathing.

"We are perfectly safe in here. Come, let me show you around."

I'm going to kill him...No, better not. At least not until I get the code.

The VES agent, ruminating over the situation, dutifully followed Demetri as he led her on a tour of the bunker.

How dare he lock me in here with him! I must get out of here. Her eyes skittered around the room, noting every detail. *I'll play along just until I can get the code from him, then I'll dematerialize out of here and get this pushy male out of my life for good.*

The muscle in her jaw ticced. *I can't believe I was ever concerned about his safety tonight. Obviously, he can take care of himself...not that I care.*

Demetri led Tatiana through the maze of rooms. He showed her the large gym and the small utilitarian kitchen which connected the gym to his bedroom. With each room, she found it a little easier to breathe.

His bedroom appeared impressive. As big as the gym, it boasted a large four poster platform bed. The onyx frame stood in stark contrast against the beige walls and cream-colored carpet. A dresser, painted black to match the bed, stood against one wall. Directly at the end of the bed stood a large black hope chest.

The room, simple, yet masculine, was orderly and efficient, like Demetri. A man's room with large, dark furniture that was carved intricately. Tatiana ran her hand over the top of the hope chest. "What's in here?" she asked.

"A flat screen TV."

Demetri removed his shorts. They fell to the floor. Leaving them where they landed, he stepped out of them.

Tatiana shook her head. A slight smile raised one corner of her mouth.

The male obviously has no issues with nudity, she thought, peeking at his *derrière* for the briefest of seconds before she adverted her eyes to the discarded shorts on the floor.

Typical male, just leaves his dirty clothes lying around.

She bent to retrieve the shorts and looked around for a hamper. Finding none, she asked, "What do you want me to do with your shorts?"

"Burn them." The deep timbre of his voice drove a shiver down her spine.

The four bags of blood had obviously helped Demetri to heal. He sounded strong, more like a warrior as he issued the command. It echoed slightly in the bathroom.

Tatiana dropped the shorts and allowed them to remain where they fell. She was not his to command. If he wanted the shorts burned, he could do it himself. It might even be good for him, like burning the last of the evidence of his capture.

She would not take that away from him.

Tatiana heard the water turn on. Twice? Curiosity spurring her into action, she peered around the door to the room.

Her eyes traveled the bath. A brown granite vanity matched the sink. A large garden tub sat wedged between the vanity and a wall. A closed door hid what she assumed would be a toilet and by the sound that came to her ears, a shower as well.

The VES agent listened to the sounds from the tiny room. The sloshing water and a soapy lather sound indicated Demetri must be washing himself.

"You know water is filling the tub."

"I know. I'm too filthy to jump in the bath. Thought I should rinse off before I bathe."

Demetri remained in the shower much longer than she expected, much longer than would have been necessary to remove the grime from his body.

Was he trying to not only wash away the evidence of his torture but also the memories?

It wouldn't work. Tatiana had scrubbed her body raw many times trying to wash the memories away, but it never helped. Nothing could change what had happened to him. He needed to learn how to accept it and move on. Not that she was exactly there herself yet, but she at least no longer tried to scrub herself raw.

When the shower cut off, Tatiana backed out of the room just in time to avoid Demetri stepping through the door to get into the tub. From the bedroom, she heard the telltale splash of water slosh in the tub as his body slid in. The running water turned off seconds later, sending the room into an uncomfortable silence which brought her claustrophobia back to her mind.

The room shrank. Walls closed in around her, threatening to squeeze the air from her lungs. She needed to get a grip, needed a distraction. The sound of sloshing water gave it to her.

"You okay in there, Demetri?" Tatiana asked, hoping a conversation might help calm her frazzled nerves.

"I'm fine. Just getting comfortable."

Tatiana sat on the platform bed and sank into the thick blanket covering it. "Wish I could say the same." Tatiana rolled her shoulders trying to work the kinks from them. Fear had knotted them, and they refused to unclench.

"You could always come join me. There's room for two in here." Demetri's voice held a hint of amusement.

"I'm fine out here thanks."

"Your loss. The water's wonderful." His R's rolled from his throat in a sinuous purr, a tribute to an accent she rarely heard from him. She found it sexy.

"You know when you get tired, your accent comes out?"

"I didn't realize that."

"It does. Where are you from anyway?"

"Curious about me, heartmate?"

She heard a smile in the tone of his voice. "Just making polite conversation."

"I'm from Russia."

"I like Russia. We lived there for a while when I was a child. Beautiful country."

"Tell me about when you were a child, Tatiana. I bet you were a brat."

"I was not a brat."

She heard Demetri settle deeper into the water and released a long sigh as if he was letting lassitude sink into his bones. "I know you were. Of this I have no doubt."

Tatiana crossed her arms over her chest. "How would you know?"

"Because you are still a brat," he teased.

"Am not."

A deep, answering chuckle emanated from the bath, and Tatiana could not help the giggle from her own lips as the childishness of her words struck her.

"I love the sound of your laughter." His voice sounded softer, more at ease. "Tell me about your childhood. What funny stories do you have about your time in Russia?"

No doubt he sought a distraction, something to concentrate on other than his ordeal. She regaled him with stories from her youth, trying to entertain him. She worked hard to remember the funniest things from her life to share with the man in the next room.

"…so then he took off with my Easter bonnet tied to his tail. Mom and I laughed until we cried." Tatiana concluded her story, waiting to hear a deep chuckle. When none came, she pushed off the bed and made her way into the bath to check on the Alpha.

Her gazed trailed over his body, distorted as it was by the water. The bruises had faded to a yellowish-brown. His scars appeared more pink than red.

Demetri's body had filled out slightly from the blood he ingested earlier. He appeared leanly muscled. Not exactly the body of an athlete, but lean muscle and sinew under pale skin. His neck, once thick from years of lifting weights, now a thin column on which his head lolled to one side. The dark circles under his eyes and the pale pallor of his skin were like physical blows to her. Each hit bringing a powerful guilt for not having rescued him sooner.

He rolled sleepily to his side, showing his back to her.

"He was excoriated!" she exclaimed in a horrified whisper while she gazed upon the healing strips of skin.

The grime had concealed the extent of his injuries well, but with it now gone, the full force of the torture he endured was plainly visible. His back looked like a child's first attempt at making a quilt. The skin was a jagged patchwork of pink healing flesh with scars creating a crisscross pattern. They laced across the entire length of his back and around both sides.

The sight brought bile to her throat as her stomach heaved its contents. With unshed tears blurring her vision, she ran for the toilet, quietly shutting the door behind her to keep from waking Demetri.

Chapter 16

Fire raced through Tatiana's veins to pool low in her belly. Her sensitive nipples puckered into hard, aching pebbles, the soft cotton sheets slid along them causing a pleasurable pain. A burning trail ran down the skin of her thigh. The sensation caused her legs to rub together, resulting in an entirely different sensation at the juncture of her thighs.

Her feminine core throbbed in time with her heart. Her body, achy and needy, craved the touch of another in a way entirely beyond her control.

A rush of moist heat gushed from her core when large fingers began to manipulate her left nipple, pinching it ever so slightly. The faint pain brought her body higher.

Unable to stop it, a moan escaped from her throat as fangs scraped the delicate flesh where her shoulder met her neck. Pleasure zinged through her body straight to another rush of heat below that made her arch into the body behind her.

Her mind was a sleepy haze of desire, every cell responding to the male holding her. She pushed her bottom back to discover evidence of the equally aroused partner. His hard, thick shaft pressed against her back and buttocks, the sensation shocking her into action.

Her mind struggled for a moment, trying to

remember who would be bringing her such pleasure. Tatiana's body coiled tighter as the fingers moved from her breast and traveled lower, seeking her feminine heat. The action reminding her of a dream, the dream she had recently, in which Demetri Romanoff had been caressing her.

Demetri!

She pushed into a seated position, held the sheet to her chest, and stared down with wide eyes at the male laying on the bed.

"What the hell?" She glanced around the room. "How did I get here?"

Demetri pushed up on one elbow and ran a finger down her sheet-covered leg. "You came down with me last night. Remember?"

"Of course, I remember. I meant, how did I get into your bed? The last thing I remember was..." her train of thought stopped her voice in her throat.

Her mind raced through the memories of the previous day. She recalled seeing Demetri's back and realizing the degree of torture he'd suffered. Tatiana remembered getting sick from the sight. She came out of the water closet and discovered a naked Demetri standing between her and the door to the bedroom. He had led her by the elbow to the bed and instructed her to get some rest. When she requested a separate room, her world had gone dark.

That highhanded son of a bitch! He put me to sleep. She pulled the sheet away from her body. *And he undressed me.*

Her blood boiled once again though for a much different reason. Anger heated her cheeks.

"You forced me to sleep!" Contempt filled

Tatiana's accusation.

"You were so tired, I could feel it pushing at me. You needed to rest. I could do no other but to see to your need. You know how it is between heartmates, Tatiana."

Her name on his lips stirred a fluttering in her heart. Like flattening a dragonfly, she ruthlessly squashed down the feeling. "You had no right."

"I had every right to see to your needs." Demetri's calm expression goaded her ire.

"How dare you force me to do anything!" Her voice rose to a fevered pitch. She leapt from the bed, still clutching the sheet to her body.

The action left Demetri completely exposed. Her eyes wondered the length of his body and a shiver of awareness snaked down her spine. She turned her back to the sight.

She possessed no feelings for this man. Well, that was not exactly true. She felt something at the moment. Hate!

His heartmate paced like a caged jaguar, her cat-like eyes blazing with a fiery passion. As she prowled, her feline grace emphasized just how similar to a jaguar she was. Beautiful, dark, with a deadly power that underlay all her movements.

Tatiana moved like a warrior, her strides purposeful and confident. She thought herself capable of winning every fight, but she would find him a much stronger competitor than she was used to.

Demetri realized upon waking, she would be upset he had forced her to sleep. It was one of the reasons he had worked her body up into a passionate frenzy before completely releasing her mind. He'd hoped the physical call of her mate would have been strong enough to override any umbrage she would take of his treatment.

She hadn't left him much choice. When he'd awoken in the bath to find his mate getting sick, the protective male within surfaced. When she had requested a separate bedroom to sleep in, he could not allow that. The only other bedrooms were upstairs, and he'd never allow his mate to sleep in an unprotected part of his home.

Knowing an argument was the inevitable outcome and the rising sun would zap his strength, he'd had no option but to push into her mind and send her to sleep. It had taken the last of his energy to get her ready for bed, but he had gladly spent the strength, so she would have a more comfortable sleep.

"Tatiana." Her yellow eyes pinned him with their penetrating stare. Demetri patted the bed. "Come. Sit."

"I don't think so." Tatiana stilled her feet and turned to face him straight on. "And stop giving me orders, Romanoff."

His mate sounded so proud, used to being in charge. Perhaps he needed to change his tactics. A strategic retreat might work. "If I stop giving you orders, will you calm down and talk to me?"

"Maybe."

Well, that is better than a no, Demetri decided. "If I promise to behave, will you at least sit down so we can talk?"

Tatiana gave him an assessing glare as if she was leery of him being so reasonable. She did not appear to trust the change in his demeanor. He heard her pulse rate kick up. Her eyes darted to the closed door and then the keypad. She looked like a deer desperately searching for an escape.

"Open the door, and we can talk," the VES agent demanded.

Demetri rose from the bed, glided to the door, and opened it wide. The process brought him beside his mate.

Demetri gazed down onto Tatiana's beautiful face, noting her concern. Something worried her.

He gingerly pushed into her mind, careful not to alert her to his presence, to discover the phobia. Her fear tasted rancid. He needed to cleanse it from her.

He sent her warmth and comfort, seeking to reassure her. It cocooned around her, smothering the fear like a blanket smothers a fire. Her tension eased. Her muscles relaxed, her breathing slowed. A peaceful calm came over her, the need to flee no longer in the forefront of her mind.

He withdrew from her mind, surprised to discover she wanted to leave him. As his mate, she should want to be with him. His physical presence called to her, he'd felt it ever since she arrived at the warehouse, but for some reason she fought the pull.

To find the reason why would require him to push harder into her mind. So deep, she would know he was there. Surely, she would see that as an invasion. Demetri subdued the instinct to take the information by force.

"Tell me why you wish to leave, Tatiana."

Judging by the look on her face, the question disarmed the VES agent. Did she really find it so surprising he would want to know? Maybe the soft tone he used to ask the question surprised her.

"I can't stay with you, Demetri."

"Why not?"

"Because I have a life back in Florida. A life I like, by the way."

"But we could have a life here, together. Don't you want that?"

"I want to get back to my friends, my job."

Demetri took her hand in his, reveling at the sensation of her delicate fingers encased by his large hand. He led her to the bed and sat beside her. "What can I do to get you to agree to stay with me?"

"Nothing." Tatiana looked down at their hands and slid hers from under his before her gaze returned to his face. "I can't stay. I need to get back to VES. I can't take any more time off. "

"But VES allowed you the time to find me. Obviously, they are willing to let you have some time off."

"When Stephan requested my help, they only agreed because they wanted to foster their relationship with the Alphas. I've found you, so it's time to get back to my job at VES."

"If you remained with me, you would still be fostering a relationship between VES and an Alpha."

A smile tugged at one corner of her mouth as if she found his remark clever. Before she replied, her phone sounded from across the room. She rose to retrieve it. As she pulled it from her bag, she noted the number. Keeping her back to Demetri, she answered, "This is Agent Bolovich."

Demetri registered the change in her voice. She instantly snapped into VES agent mode. She'd used the same tone of voice to speak to him the first time they met. His mind began to play scenes of their first sparring match.

"But, sir—" The desperation in her tone brought Demetri from his reverie. "I'm not needed here. I—"

Her shoulders tensed. She hugged the sheet tighter around her. "I don't think—"

She turned and looked at Demetri. Her face went pale, making the dark lashes and ruby lips stand out in stark contrast. "But I…Did Demetri put you up to this?"

She gave a heavy sigh. "Yes, sir. I understand."

Tatiana hurled the phone toward the wall behind him. Demetri's hand shot out, catching the device before it shattered. It stung his hand when it hit, the sensation bringing a question to his lips.

"What was all that about?"

"As if you didn't know!" Tatiana accused him, storming across the room.

The anger radiating off her made Demetri rise from the bed, wanting his height advantage for the coming confrontation.

"How did you do it?" Anger flashed in her yellow eyes. "How did you get VES to extend my leave? Did you call VES while I was under your sleep command?"

Demetri put his hands up in surrender and flashed a knowing smile. "That would have been a good idea, but alas I didn't think of it. I can honestly say I didn't call them."

"Bullshit!" Tatiana's voice rose.

"I didn't call them, I swear, but I can't say I'm sorry you won't be going back to work anytime soon."

Tatiana narrowed her eyes in disbelief. "What?"

Demetri shrugged. "I didn't want you fighting before, Tatiana. I certainly don't want you fighting now that I know you are my heartmate."

"I think you are forgetting who rescued your ass out of the warehouse." Tatiana poked a finger into the Alpha's boney chest. "I walked out unscathed, not you."

Demetri looked down at the scar her finger lay upon, the reminder of just what condition he'd left the warehouse in.

An eerie silence took the room. The muscle of his jaw twitched, the only movement visible as the warrior began to seethe.

When Demetri spoke, it was through clenched teeth. "I don't need any reminders about the shape I was in when I walked out of that warehouse. I remember quite well every minute of the torture I suffered at the hands of my enemies. I remember ever helpless second, every cut, every time I was bled dry."

Her regret hit him like a rushing deluge, combined with a wave of guilt. The pity on her face told him she realized her words hurt.

Males were physical when attacked. Their solution involved action. Punishment. Justice. An eye for an eye was the Alpha way. Tatiana couldn't begin to imagine the helplessness Demetri suffered at the hands of his captors. She had no idea the despair and desperation that came from feeling like your life was not your own, like the whim of another could end you.

Remorse softened her eyes when their gaze met.

Demetri's lips drew into a tight line. She viewed him as timid. His mate found him weak, a male to be pitied. "I'm not a victim, Tatiana!"

Her finger traced the scar on his chest. Her eyes followed the digit as it rose diagonally toward his shoulder. Upon reaching the end of the scar, her hand grasped his shoulder in a firm grip. Her eyes met his. "No, Demetri, you're not a victim. You're a survivor."

His gaze searched hers, finding a depth of sincerity one could only come by through an understanding of what it was like to suffer greatly at the hands of another. The knowledge turned his stomach. The phone dropped to the floor with a soft thud, the device unnoticed as his hands snaked out to cup her face. "Who hurt you, Tatiana?"

Her eyes darted from his. To no avail, she attempted to pull her head from his grasp. He kept her in place, this moment too important to allow her to run from it; from him.

"Let me go, Demetri."

"Answer me, and I will." His voice softened with concern.

Her hands gripped his wrist. "Please," she said, tears wetting her eyes. "Let me go."

The Alpha gazed into her eyes, bewitched by the sudden flood of emotion there. The unshed tears tugged at his heart. It was not like his warrior woman, this tigress, to be forlorn. Seeing her vulnerable made him want to kiss away the tears before they fell. His heart shattered into a thousand pieces.

Demetri's lips lowered to hers in a gentle kiss. Tatiana's eyes closed at the contact, her body melting into his. No force, no thrusting of his tongue between her lips to invade her mouth, just a slight press of his lips to hers. His lips moved faintly, the motion soothing, consoling.

She gave into the comfort he offered. Having her in his care, seemed right. The firm press of his body against hers, an anchor upon which she could tether herself during this storm.

What was done was done. There was nothing he could do to change what had happened to her. To him.

He had a heartmate who needed him to be the strong warrior he once was. For her, he would regain his strength. He needed to watch over and protect her, and he would see to it that he fulfilled his duty. He'd be a good provider, a tower of strength for her to lean on for support. He silently vowed to be a good mate.

Tatiana's hands left his wrists. Her arms circled his waist, holding him to her. Tears escaped down her cheeks. They tore his heart in two. His thumbs brushed her cheeks, trying to stay the weeping.

Tatiana deepened the kiss, testing the seam of his lips with her tongue. His lips parted allowing her entry. She tasted sweet, a delicious feminine flavor he found instantly addictive.

Demetri held back, letting her lead, instinct telling him she needed to feel some control.

Control.

That little word held such meaning to him, to them. If, as he suspected, she had once suffered at the hands of another, power would have been taken from her. No wonder she had control issues, but then so did he.

He was an Alpha in every sense of the word. Domination his middle name.

Before being taken by the demons, he had what some would consider control issues.

Now?

Well, now control had taken on a whole new meaning in his life. If she experienced even half the need he did for control, they were in for a bumpy ride.

But I want that ride. He was willing to strap on his

seatbelt and hold on for dear life if it meant having this woman in his life. *I might even be willing to give up some control to her...for her,* he corrected as their tongues danced between their lips in a waltz as old as time.

Chapter 17

The sound of a phone ringing broke their kiss as Demetri turned to glare at the offending apparatus sitting next to the bed. He rested his forehead against hers, drying the fallen tears from her cheeks with the pads of his thumbs.

"You'd better get that." Tatiana's tongue darted out to trace her kiss-swollen lips.

Demetri's gazed followed the movement before he tore it away to look once more at the phone screaming to be answered. "This had better be important," he growled, releasing her face to snatch it up.

"What," he demanded.

"And a fine hello to you too, cousin."

"Nicholai." The Alpha blew out a heavy breath.

"One and the same. I hope this is a good time."

"Not really." Demetri raked his heated gaze over Tatiana's body.

"Is Tatiana there? Juliette wishes to speak to her."

"She is here. What does your mate wish to speak with her about?"

Tatiana rewrapped the sheet around her body and shifted nervously from foot to foot.

"Jules has this idea that we should invite her to be a part of the wedding since she brought you home to us safe and sound. She intends to invite Tatiana to be a bridesmaid at our wedding."

Demetri's laugh rolled from his chest. "I doubt she will say yes. I can't imagine anything she would like to do less."

"I agree, but my heartmate wishes to extend the invitation, and I can do no less than see she is given the opportunity to do so."

He blew out a heavy sigh. "Put Juliette on."

****

Tatiana tucked in a corner of the sheet to hold it around her body and ignored her mate, lost in thoughts of the kiss they shared. The chemistry between heartmates was stronger than she thought, for it must have been the reason for the lapse in judgment. To think otherwise would mean she had to admit she cared for her heartmate, and she wasn't willing to admit that, not even to herself.

She must get away, put some distance between her and that male. Distance would calm their chemistry before it turned into genuine feelings.

"Here. Juliette wants to speak to you." Demetri held the phone in her direction.

Tatiana stepped forward and grabbed it from his hand. Their fingers brushed, sending an electric current zinging through her body.

"Hello." She really needed some space from this potent male.

"Tatiana? It's Julie, Nicholai's heartmate."

"Hello, Julie," she greeted wearily, wondering what this woman could possibly want with her.

"Yes, well, first I want to thank you for bringing Demetri home to us."

Tatiana shifted her feet. "I did my duty. No thanks are needed."

"But thank you just the same. It means the world to us that you were able to find Nicholai's cousin. Did you know we were postponing our wedding until Demetri was found?"

"I believe I remember something to that effect," Tatiana admitted reluctantly as she looked up into the face of Demetri who wore a wide grin.

"Good, so you know Marcus and Christina and Nicholai and I are having a double wedding."

The hopeful tone of Julie's voice piqued Tatiana's curiosity. "I'd forgotten that, but okay."

"So, we all were thinking it would be great if you would be a part of the wedding, since you helped save Demetri and all."

Tatiana's face blanch. Her ghostly pallor was blanched almost enough to pull the smile from Demetri's face. Almost.

Tatiana swallowed her initial reply, knowing it would be impolite to inform this virtual stranger just what she thought about the idea of being in a puffy bridesmaid's dress. The thought of having her hair styled, nails done, and wearing some fugly froufrou dress brought a scowl to her face.

"Before you answer," continued the sweet voice across the line, "let me tell you this. We would need you to come to Savannah ASAP. We're having the wedding at Marcus' estate. Nicholai said you have been there before."

During a slight pause, Tatiana managed to get out a quiet uh-huh before Julie continued.

"Anyway, we decided to have the wedding in about two weeks. We'll need you here to get the fitting done, help us with the arrangements, get your hair done. You know, all that weddingy stuff."

Tatiana's mind raced for an appropriate way to say *no frickin' way.* She did not wish to insult the heartmate of Nicholai Peterhoff, but she had no desire to go to Georgia immediately to do a bunch of *"weddingy"* stuff, as Julie had so aptly put it. As Demetri had said, she could not imagine anything she would like to do less. Imagine the look on Demetri's face if she said yes.

A smile lifted the corners of her mouth as she pictured Demetri doing all the wedding activities Julie had mentioned. Tatiana could not help but laugh when she imagined Demetri going to the fitting with her. A dress shop would be the last place on this earth he would want to be.

The last place he would want to be, she thought to herself. An idea struck her. *If I agree to be in this stupid wedding, I'll have an excuse to leave. Even Demetri wouldn't keep me from being in his cousin's wedding.*

Julie said she needed me in Savannah now. I could use the wedding as an excuse to dematerialize out of here tonight. Doing all the wedding stuff would allow me to be away from Demetri. There is no way he would follow me to do all that girly stuff. It's a great excuse to put some much-needed space between us.

"I'll do it," Tatiana announced. The surprise on Demetri's face brought a smug smile to her lips. "I'll come to Savannah tonight."

"That's great, Tatiana!" Julie's exuberance came through the line. "I'll let Christina know. Nicholai and I are staying at Marcus' plantation. We'll see you when you get here…Oh, huh…Listen, put Demetri back on Nicholai wants to talk to him."

Tatiana didn't quite hide the priggish look on her

face. She had found a way to get away from Demetri. It might not be entirely pleasant for her, but the means would justify the end in this particular case.

****

Demetri took the phone from his heartmate and placed the receiver to his ear. "Hello?"

"It's me again. So, I guess you heard, Tatiana said yes."

"I heard." Demetri noted the smug look on her face and gave his mate a dubious glance.

"Of course, I expect you to stand up for me at the altar. You have been like a father to me. I owe you my life, in more ways than I can count on two hands. You won't let me down, will you?"

I'll be following Tatiana to Savannah anyway, and Nicholai is dear to me. "Why not," Demetri answered. "I wouldn't miss it for the world."

Tatiana's eyes narrowed as she mouthed, "Miss what?"

Demetri held up one finger in her direction when Nicholai spoke. "Great! So, we should expect you later than?"

Demetri nodded his head, more for Tatiana's benefit then in answer to his cousin's question. "We'll meet you at Marcus' home later this evening."

"Safe travels, cousin, to both you and your heartmate."

The line went dead, and Demetri hung up the phone.

"'*We'll* meet you at Marcus' home'," Tatiana repeated as she bent to retrieve her phone from the floor. "Didn't you mean to say *she'll* meet you at Marcus' home?"

155

Demetri crossed the room, his long stride eating up the floor in his haste. "No, I meant we." He pulled some clothing from the drawers of his dresser and began to dress.

Tatiana marched toward him, the bed sheet flowing behind her. "Why are you going to Savannah? Nicholai's heartmate said the wedding isn't for a few weeks."

Demetri pulled a turtleneck over his head. The fabric hung loosely about his form stressing just how much smaller he had become. "True, but like you, I need to be there for a fitting and such."

"Fitting? You mean you are going to be in the wedding too?"

"Yes," he answered, pulling his pants up and snapping them. When he let go of the waistband, they fell around his ankles.

"Damn," he hissed.

His anger rose. His body shrunk to the point none of his clothes fit him properly. He would need a lot of blood and working out to get his old physique back. Those damned demons! He'd see each and every one of them pay for what they did to him.

I will strangle them with their own intestines, he vowed silently as he forcefully pushed his thin legs into a pair of sweatpants. They too were large, but at least they stayed up thanks to the draw string in the waistband.

Savannah here we come.

Chapter 18

Tatiana's sank down on the bed. She was not *getting* away from Demetri; she was *going* away with Demetri. How did this happen? The only reason she had agreed to be in the wedding was to have an excuse to have time away from Demetri, now they were off to Savannah together. Moreover, she had agreed to do all the girly stuff she hated.

The girly stuff!

That was the key. Her plan might still work. Demetri would never want to do anything girly. He might come to Savannah with her, but she would make sure she was constantly off doing wedding stuff with Julie and Marcus' heartmate.

There was always a bunch of stuff to do to get ready for a wedding, right? Last minute errands, vendors to confirm. She'd make sure every minute detail included her, volunteer to do anything that would put space between her and that male.

She dropped the sheet and headed for her bag to find something to wear thinking, *Savannah here we come.*

****

Lane ran the palm of his hand over his rough auburn beard. "We need to find another vampire, Jara."

"You know very well that Varrick will not approve of another abduction. I barely obtained his approval for the male."

Lane shook his head. "The king just does not understand. There is always collateral damage in the name of scientific discovery. Why can he not support the loss of a few vampiric lives for the salvation of our race?"

"I'm afraid my brother is a bit soft," said the demon princess with a sigh, as she gathered supplies. "We'll just have to locate the male and retrieve him."

Lane crossed his arms over his chest. "It would be easier to simply go behind the king's back to acquire another one."

Jara's red eyes pinned the scientist with a quelling look. "Be careful, Lane." Her voice pitched low in warning. "You speak of heresy to one who has the king's ear. I may not agree with my brother in all matters, but he is our king, and as such we are his to command."

Lane's eyes cast down in contrition to stare in silence at the tattered rug covering the floor.

The female demon noted his kowtowing as she unfolded the world map they had recently purchased. "Do not mistake my fondness for you as permission to see yourself as an equal." Her voice sounded dry, almost pedantic.

She smoothed out the map, running her hands in opposite directions across its face to push it flat against the table in their hotel room.

Looking properly penitent, Lane did not take his eyes from the floor when he spoke softly. "Forgive me. I meant no disrespect toward your brother."

The princess straightened and pushed her shoulders back as she turned on Lane. "You can make amends by helping me scry for the one you lost."

Jara pushed the wavy hair back from her face as she went across the room to pick up a bowl from the Formica chest of drawers. "Fill this bowl with water," she commanded, handing the bowl to Lane before she palmed a velvet bag.

She turned the soft black bag upside down and dropped a stone into her open hand. It felt heavy, solid. Her skin tingled at its touch, magic flowing through her veins.

Jara looked down at the map. Her patrician features hardened in concentration. The topographical image blurred as she focused her inner mind on the male vampire. Her hair hovered out from about her head, and a blue aura bathed her body in light, causing her caftan to take on an ethereal glow.

The scrying stone in her hand felt ice cold despite having been kept in a bag at room temperature. She held the stone over the map and closed her eyes in meditation. Slowly, she moved the stone over the landscape depicted below. Centimeter by centimeter she moved along, starting from where they were in Canada.

As her hand traveled south, the stone began to warm. With great restraint, Jara continued to move her hand at a snail's pace. With each inch the stone's warmth increased until it nearly seared her flesh. Pain radiated through her, but she pressed on.

She opened her eyes. The stone in her hand became translucent. Its crystalline beauty a sight to behold when the scintillation of the stone burned brightly in the dim room.

Her hand shook with the effort to contain the stone.

The stench of smoldering flesh burned her nose. Lane swallowed hard and gazed down upon the stone in Jara's hand.

The pain in her hand became unbearable. Her eyes flew down to the map to note the location over which the hand hovered. "Wyoming," she gritted out, her voice hoarse from the effort to hold the stone through the pain. She allowed the stone to fall from her hand. It took some flesh with it when it dropped to the map below. A hiss escaped her ruby lips.

"The bowl," she commanded.

Lane handed her the bowl of water absently, his gaze riveted to the stone when it returned to its solid gray color. His eyes flared as the map was scorched around the edges of the stone. His gaze flew to her hand. "Let me see your hand."

Jara shook her head, sending her floating hair twirling. "First, I must find where in Wyoming he is."

She cupped the bowl between the palms of her hands and bent over the container, concentrating on the water within. She took several deep cleansing breaths, forcing the pain away so she could concentrate properly.

The water spun counterclockwise, swirling until a blurry image began to form. Like a specimen in a microscope, the image in the water cleared, showing Jara where the one she sought could be found.

At first, a mountain range appeared. It seemed familiar, the tree line, the rock face were known to her. She recognized it as the home of her brother, her home. This was Mason's Bluff.

Like a panoramic shot on a movie screen, the image narrowed until the surrounding trees were lost from view and only a house remained. It was large, constructed to resemble a log cabin. *Make that a log mansion*, Jara corrected herself.

She recognized the house. She'd passed by it many times while running through the forest in her mountain lion form.

What luck!

She pulled her mind away from the image. Her body swayed. Lane reached out a steadying hand and grabbed her arm in support. Her hands released the bowl to grab the edge of the table and allowed it to support her weight. Her arms shook from the effort.

"I know where he is," she announced in a small voice.

An hour later, Jara and Lane stood in the middle of a large rustic living room. After materializing inside the cabin, a quick search of the home had produced little results.

"Not to impugn your scrying abilities, but are you sure you have the right location?"

Jara crossed the kitchen and discovered empty bags of blood in the trash bin and some red stained glasses in the sink.

Jara retrieved a bag from the trash and held it from her body between her index finger and thumb. Her scrunched face clearly showed her disgust. "Oh, I have the right location. He was here."

Lane watched her toss the bag back into the bin. "Now we will have a well fed, strong vampire on our hands when we find him. I'm not sure going after the bloodsucker is wise."

Jara's hands fisted in ire. "Of course, we cannot retrieve the vampire ourselves. We need to get some of the guards to help."

"If we go to the mountain fortress, Varrick will want to know why we are there, and we will have to inform him about the vampire's escape." Lane ran a hand across his thickly bearded chin in thought before continuing. "We should stay in a hotel in town. The guards are familiar with the area. They could materialize to meet us there."

Jara threw up her arms in derision. "Gee, why didn't I think of that? I was planning on making a sojourn to the court of the Demon King. Of course, we can't go to the mountain. The last person I want to run into is my brother.

"Meet me at the Lone Horse Motel. We'll get a room, and you can arrange for the guards to meet us while I scry again to find out where the bloodsucker has gone."

Chapter 19

Nicholai opened the double doors of Marcus' plantation wide in welcome. Centuries of practice steeling his features did not keep the shock from registering on Nicholai's face as his gaze raked his cousin. His mouth gaped open, his eyes widened.

Once thickly muscled, Demetri now stood before him slim and emaciated, clothes hanging loosely about his body. The spectrally thin figure in front of him was but a shell of the male he once knew.

The Alpha reached forward grasping the fellow warrior's forearms. Nicholai's large hand easily wrapped around Demetri's arms. For the first time in Nicholai's centuries of life, his fingers touched his thumbs emphasizing just how underweight his cousin was. He noted the way Demetri's body shook slightly as he held on, how his chest heaved in and out like he had just run across the town.

"It is so good to see you, cousin. Come in, come in." Nicholai stepped aside and gestured into the foyer with a grand sweep of his arm.

"Tatiana, welcome." Nicholai reached for her as she passed by and planted a kiss on each cheek in greeting.

A growl emanated from Demetri's throat. Nicholai's eyes flew to his cousin's face in time to watch fangs lengthen from his gums. They slid down to their full length, poking his lower lip.

Cousin, all is well. I was only greeting your mate.

I know you are an honorable male. You would never betray me, especially with my mate.

Through their mindlink, Nicholai sensed his cousin warring with his inner beast. Demetri knew he could trust Nicholai, but that did not stop the possessiveness when another male touched his mate.

It took all his self-control for Nicholai not to show a reaction when he discovered Demetri had not claimed Tatiana. No wonder he acted so possessive. Add to that the exhaustion he experienced from dematerializing across the U. S. and you had a dangerous mix—a caged tiger who did not need to be poked with a proverbial stick.

Demetri followed Tatiana into Marcus' home, and Nicholai closed the door. Demetri watched his mate while her gaze scanned the grand foyer, noting the dark hardwood floors, glossing over the crown molding and the Mort Kunstler paintings depicting the civil war which hung on both walls. Tension between the pair prickled over Nicholai's skin. He pushed past them, and the pair followed him through a set of French doors into the sitting room.

Tatiana headed for the striped Louis the Fourteenth couch, glancing covertly at the male behind her. It was as if she felt her heartmate's gaze roaming over her body while she sauntered across the room.

When the couple sat next to one another, the pheromones flowing between them tickled Nicholai's nose. Their bodies seemed to feed off one another. Their hearts pounded in unison.

Nicholai sank gracefully into a chair that perfectly

matched the couch. From the position, he noted the way their bodies sat stiffly, not touching, the tension between them palatable.

Nicholai's heart sank for his cousin. He had suffered greatly at the hands of the shifters and been rescued only to find a heartmate who did not want to be mated.

The relationship between heartmates should be celebrated and embraced. A treasure, a sacred connection between two people. He had almost lost his mate once, and the despair of that loss allowed him to sympathize with his cousin.

From the body language of the pair on the couch, the younger warrior realized this mating would not be an easy one. The awkward silence spoke volumes, and relief flooded Nicholai when a bubbly red head materialized in front of the fireplace.

"Hi, guys," Christina's southern drawl filled the room. "We are so glad you're safe, Demetri!"

Nicholai admired the way her cheery demeanor was not affected in the slightest by the sight of his cousin.

Ever the gracious host, Christina welcomed all with open arms. It was one of the reasons the clientele at her counseling center had grown to where she had needed to open a second center to accommodate the people wanting sessions.

Marcus entered the room through the open doors, then crossed it in long strides to take his mate in his arms and give her a kiss. "When you said you wanted to race in here, I didn't think you would cheat," he teased, one corner of his mouth turning up in a half smile.

"All's fair in love and racing." Christina ran her

left hand along his cheek. The love in her eyes outshone the large diamond on her ring finger. She laughed as Marcus scooped her up into his arms and spun them around until he plopped down into the empty chair across from Nicholai with Christina in his lap.

The pride on Marcus' face shone in his eyes. "Have any of you ever known a converted vampire learn how to dematerialize in only a few months?" The heads in the room shook as Marcus continued. "I swear this woman was made to be a vampire. She is constantly learning new vamp skills and using them to their fullest advantage. Just a few minutes ago, she moved around the kitchen making dinner for six so fast she was a blur."

Christina shrugged. "Hey, I've always said if you got it flaunt it."

"And you've got it in spades, *cara*." Marcus nuzzled her neck.

"Where is Payton?" Demetri asked, referring to the elderly valet who usually answered Marcus' door.

"I gave the man the night off. He's been working overtime helping Christina and Juliette prep for the wedding."

Christina nodded her head enthusiastically. "I don't know what Julie and I would do without him."

"Did I hear my name?"

Nicholai's smile reached his ears as the curvaceous brunette who had spoken entered the room. He stood, holding out his hand.

"Demetri." Due to his Russian accent, Nicholai purred the R in his cousin's name as his heartmate took his outstretched hand. "I'd like you to meet my heartmate, Juliette."

Demetri rose from the couch. "It is a pleasure to meet my cousin's better half," he said, two strides taking him to Nicholai's mate.

He bowed over Julie's hand and placed a light kiss on the back before straightening to his full height. "Anything you ever need, you have only to ask. You are now blood of mine, and there is nothing I would not do for my blood."

He turned and shot a pointed look at his mate as he returned to the couch.

Nicholai settled back in the seat as his heartmate alighted on the arm of the chair. He rested a hand on her thigh when he spoke. "Tatiana, we will never be able to thank you enough for all you have done for Demetri."

"Oh, yeah," chimed in Christina. "We wouldn't be having the wedding if it wasn't for you. I'm so glad you agreed to come to Savannah and be in the wedding. Will you be staying here with us?"

"Yes," said Tatiana at the same time Demetri said, "No."

One brow shot up on Marcus' face when Demetri continued. "We'll be staying at my townhouse on Troup Square."

"Speak for yourself." Tatiana looked at the male sitting beside her before turning her attention to the mistress of the house. "I'd prefer to stay with you, if you don't mind."

Christina's face lit with pleasure, her smile wide enough to show her petite fangs. "Great! I love having company. Come on, I'll show you which room you'll be staying in. You want to join us, Jules?"

"Definitely," his mate replied.

Anger swirled in the air around Demetri.

****

The males watched their mates leave the room, listening to the three pairs of footsteps ascend the stairs before anyone spoke.

"Fates, how I want that woman," Demetri murmured. His body, though tired from the effort of the trip here, responded to its mate, every cell screaming its desire for the female with the raven hair.

"Cousin, I know you don't want any advice on your love life, but I'm going to give it to you anyway. You can't control Tatiana. You need to be romantic, try to woo her."

Marcus cleared his throat. "She is hardly the flowers and candy type, Nicholai."

"No, but every woman likes her male to be attentive to her needs and seek to please her."

"So, you are saying, I can't just throw the woman over my shoulder and carry her off to my lair?"

That earned Demetri a hearty laugh from the two Alphas with him. Not long ago he had given similar advice to them both as they were working to win their mates. They had not followed his advice, and yet both won their heartmates. Perhaps he should consider their advice. It wasn't as if he was winning any awards for getting-the-girl.

Hell, she wouldn't even stay with me at the townhouse in the city.

Nicholai braced his forearms on his knees. "In matters of the heart, it is best to tread lightly. Go easy; let her get to know you. For in the words of Sir W. Temple, 'The greatest pleasure of life is love.'"

"I'm afraid she already knows me too well. She is

fighting our mating."

"Then show her you can change, cousin. Be the kind of male she wants. Allow her to take control once in a while."

"I don't know if I can." *Especially after what I have been through the past few months.*

Marcus crossed his leg, resting an ankle on the opposite knee. "Trust me. Giving up a little control can be a good thing, especially in the bedroom."

Marcus' eyes glazed over as if he was reliving a moment between him and his mate. Given how Demetri's body responded to Tatiana, they most likely would not have any troubles regardless of who was in control in the bedroom.

The air in the room scented with the scent of aroused males. Their combined aroma filled their nostrils in a way in which made them shift uncomfortably in their seats.

"Perhaps we should discuss something else," Nicholai suggested. "Tell us about your time with the shifters."

Demetri wasn't sure he found this subject any more comfortable, but he capitulated. "First, they are demons, at least that is what they called themselves, and they are the most inhumane creatures I have ever set eyes upon."

"Where did they hold you?" Marcus asked.

"Alex said they found you in Canada," Nicholai answered.

Demetri shifted on his seat as he recalled his prison. "I was kept in a cell, starved, tortured, and bled."

Both males blanched, their pale skin going ever

paler as he recounted the less gruesome details of his imprisonment. When he finished, they sat utterly silent until his cousin broke the hush.

"Demetri, we had no idea the extent of your suffering. Why did the demons do that to you?"

"The scientist mentioned little about his experiments, but the guards were freer with their tongues, especially when they thought I was unconscious." Demetri put one arm across the back of the couch in a forced gesture of causality. "Apparently, the demons are looking for the secret to our long lives. They are susceptible to human ailments and are hoping to find a way to become immune."

"Through vampire blood?" Marcus asked, scrubbing a hand through his thick chestnut hair. "That's unbelievable."

"Believe it." *I have the scars to prove it.* Demetri pulled at the collar of his black turtleneck.

"Shit," Marcus muttered, staring vacantly across the room.

"Precisely," Demetri whispered, memories crushing down on him.

The males sat in uncomfortable silence for several minutes, until at last Marcus rose to his feet saying, "Let's eat."

Demetri followed his fellow warriors to the kitchen, grateful for the distraction.

After their meal, the women began discussing the wedding. Luckily, Marcus mentioned he had recently completed an addition to the property. Demetri seized the opportunity.

"Let's go see it," Demetri suggested, not keeping the desperation from his voice.

"Great idea." Nicholai looked at Juliette. "Can you get by without us for a little while?"

She gave him a resplendent smile. "Absolutely, my dear. We will be here when you get back."

Demetri stood, and the Alphas followed suit. With Marcus in the lead, Demetri and Nicholai followed him outside to a warehouse-type building located in what used to be cotton fields. The building appeared plain, encased on all sides by metal siding. It stretched three stories high and seemed at least the length of five football fields.

"What the hell is this place?" Demetri took in the structure.

"It is a combat simulation room," Marcus explained with a wide grin as they went inside.

In the anteroom, he brought a set of computers to life. Demetri and Nicholai stood in stunned silence as Marcus explained the special traps throughout the building. "The purpose is to surprise the fighter inside, throwing various weapons at him, trying to help the warrior hone his battle skills."

Marcus brought the lights up in the next room, and the place lit up like a Vegas hotel, displaying a large interior room with a series of tall columns strewn throughout. "The computer system controls the traps inside, so each time the program runs the fighter gets a different set of traps. I can even set the level of the program by turning a dial on the console. With levels one through ten and never knowing which traps will be sprung, you have an infinite amount of fighting scenarios available to keep you surprised and on your guard no matter how many sessions you do."

"That is something straight from an action movie,"

Nicholai commented.

"Want to try it out?" offered Marcus.

Nicholai crossed his arms over his chest. "Not now."

"How about you, Demetri?"

The Alpha shook his head. "Not right now."

"Fine." Marcus shut down the lights in the combat room. "Anyone want to watch a DVD?"

"I thought you would never ask," said Nicholai. "I'm always up for a good movie. Maybe Tomb Raiders of the Lost Continent."

Not in the mood for a movie, Demetri opted instead for a workout in Marcus' gym once they were back in the plantation. Determination to get his strength back motivated him. Even for a vampire, muscle took time to build and there had been no time like the present to start.

Maybe Tatiana will be there, he thought as he pushed through the doors to the gym.

Alas the room stood empty. Disappointment gave him power as he grabbed a set of weights.

He pushed his body hard, needing to feel the burn. His aching muscles protested each rep. Only his desire to regain his former strength gave him purpose to put himself through the self-imposed torture routine.

After his workout, he walked down the hall and came upon Marcus and Christina retiring to their suite. Knowing there was no way in hell his mate would be sleeping in a different home than he and hoping to avoid throwing her over his shoulder to take her to his townhouse, he approached Marcus.

"Do you have an extra room for me?"

"Of course, we do." Christina nodded. "You can

have this room. And wouldn't you know, it just happens to be next to the one Tatiana is staying in."

A grateful smile came to his face.

As soon as he stood behind the closed door, he headed for the shower, needing to feel clean.

Demetri stood under the water, letting it rinse off much of the grime from his body. He soaped his hands and scrubbed them over his thin physique to cleanse his pale skin. The pads of his fingers rubbed over the evidence of his torture.

He scrubbed harder, trying to scourer the scars away. Memories crashed down on him. Memories that could no more be washed away than could his scars.

His capturer's face loomed before his closed eyes. He forced his eyes open under the onslaught of the running water, needing to rid himself of the images. The pounding did nothing other than give him more pain. He could not change what had happened to him, and he had a heartmate who needed him to be the strong warrior he once was.

For her, he would regain his strength. She was his to watch over and protect. He would see his duty to her fulfilled, be a good provider, a tower of strength for her to lean on for support. He would be a good mate to her.

After turning off the water, he roughly dried with a towel then got re-dressed, all the while thinking about his mate. Words seemed difficult for her when it came to him. He hoped that might change one day. He wanted to hear his mate say words of comfort, ask him to give her the kind of pleasure only he could. He longed to hear her say all the things other males were blessed to hear from their mates.

But those things were not in his near future. He had

to find a way to draw them from Tatiana.

As he dressed, his mind continued to focus on the female in the next room. After settling into his room, Demetri noticed a set of French doors on the wall next to his bed. Curiosity made him push through them to discover a terrace which just happened to join his room with Tatiana's.

A mischievous smile raised the corners of his mouth. Unable to help himself, he went on the terrace and spied his mate through the door leading to the room. It was pure torture, watching her snuggled under the covers of the bed, wishing he lay beside her.

He waited until she was asleep, then let himself into the room.

On silent feet, he made his way over beside the bed. His heart softened when he gazed down onto her beautiful face. Her dark lashes stood out in contrast to the pale skin. Her raven hair had fallen away from her face to caress the golden pillow beneath.

Another male might have found it romantic, the way she looked, but Demetri found her fierce. Her hand fisted over her stomach and furrowed brows made her warrior spirit evident even in sleep. Like a sleeping tigress, Tatiana appeared ready to pounce at the slightest provocation.

In that moment, Demetri realized he was in for a fight.

His tigress warrior would not simply lie down and accept their mating. He would have to fight for her, win her approval before she would accept him. He'd need to prove to her he was a man of worth, could see to her needs, and provide for her in a way that did not make her feel inferior. And he would have to be subtle about doing so, because if she suspected, her pride would push him away.

A tower of feminine strength, she wanted her independence when all he wanted was her dependence on him. It would not be easy fighting the instincts stirring within him, but to win her he'd do anything.

He pushed into her mind and took control of her dream, a trick he knew Nicholai used on his own mate. She did a series of martial arts *Katas* beside a lake. Her dream body moved back and forth through the exercises of kicks, punches, and blocks, looking like a master sensei.

Anticipation warmed his stomach as he inserted himself into the dream.

Chapter 20

Tatiana struggled to wake, swimming in the waters between consciousness and sleep. Hot breath on her cheek and a thump-thump-thumping sound roused her, but the vibration in her body, timed to the thumping noise, gave her enough stimulation to open her eyes.

A set of milk chocolate eyes stared back at her as a thick tongue flicked out to make a wet trail from her chin to her forehead.

"Ugh! Yuck!" Tatiana wiped the stinky saliva from her face.

"Talk about morning breath," she mumbled and reached out to run her hand through the coarse brown fur.

"How did you get in here, Connor?" The question earned her a happy thrashing of the dog's tail, causing the bed to vibrate when the long appendage gave the mattress a good beating.

The female warrior flopped onto her back and threw an arm over her face. "It's early, dog, the sun hasn't even set yet."

Connor barked then leapt on the bed. He stretched out beside her, resting his head on the spare pillow. She turned to face the animal. A grin played over her lips. "Look at you. You are as long as the bed."

Tatiana ran a hand down the dog's side in long rhythmic strokes, earning her another ride on the vibrating mattress when his tail beat its approval.

She picked up one of his front paws and pretended to examine it. "Yep, just as I thought. No opposable thumbs. So how did you get in here? I could have sworn I closed my door last night."

As she lay petting the Irish wolfhound, she ruminated on the previous evening. After Christina had given her a quick tour of the plantation, they had eaten the meal Marcus' mate had made, then she had gone down into the gym for a hard workout.

She stretched, her sore muscles attesting to just how hard she had pushed herself.

After her workout and a shower, she had joined everyone in the media room to watch a DVD, a romantic comedy. Not her kind of movie, but whatever. She had stayed because Demetri had been curiously absent. Enjoying the separation, she'd hoped he had gone to his townhouse for the evening. After the movie, everyone retired for the day, each of them separating to their respective rooms. She remembered closing the door to her room before retiring.

Glancing across the room, she found the door opened wide. Her gaze returned to the form beside her. "You know, I'm getting tired of the men around here assuming they were welcome to just barge into my life."

Connor raised his head, and his ear pitched forward as if he concentrated on what she had to say.

"I just wish Demetri was as easy to get along with as you."

She scratched him behind his ears, making his leg pound in a thumping motion.

"Tickle spot?" She chuckled. "I bet you aren't

supposed to be on the bed. This thing probably cost Marcus a fortune."

The bed she lay on had four ornately carved posts that stretched up to support a wooden canopy. Sheer blue material covered the canopy and hung on the posts, gathered as it cascaded down. The sheets matched the pillowy comforter in their golden hue. The matching throw pillows sat where she placed them the previous day, on the delicate wooden bench at the foot of the bed.

The beige ceiling, framed by plaster cornices that had been carved with a leaf pattern, accented the powder blue walls and the light brown antique sofa in front of a window. A window whose specially designed shutters were still closed. Though no sunlight entered through the window, light from the hall bathed the room in a bright glow, allowing Tatiana to easily see the ornately carved but delicate details in the room.

"And so, the froufrou stuff begins," she murmured on a sigh while she took in the room. "Guess I better get ready to face the night ahead, only the Fates know what girly torture Juliette and Christina have in mind, but first I need a shower and a workout, not necessarily in that order."

She smiled, gave Connor one last pet on the head, then rose from the bed. Her stiff muscles protested every movement.

Thirty minutes later, commotion up above signaled the others had risen to start their night. *Sleepy heads.*

Tatiana'd already completed her series of reps using the professional weight machines in Marcus' gym and was running on a treadmill. Her feet pounded a furious rhythm in time to the music piped in over the stereo system. She pushed hard, wanting the feel of the sweat dripping from her body. The physical exertion reminded her of the warrior she was, and it felt good. Surrounded by romantic movies, frilly furniture, and the two women who were consumed with wedding planning, she worried she might lose her edge.

The bed upstairs was so soft and girly, she had dreamt last night of her heartmate. They sat beside a lake having a picnic and just like in the movie she had watched earlier, they had gone skinny-dipping. Butterflies fluttered in her stomach as she recalled the dream.

Demetri looked sinfully delicious when he rose from the water, beads dripping from his dark hair to slide down his defined chest and abs. He stalked toward her, his body sluicing through the water with an erotic swagger that promised long Tantric sex.

The memory made Tatiana's pulse kick up, as did her speed. She ran, desperately trying to outpace the sensual images in her mind. She needed to stop thinking about her mate. It should be easier to do now since he stayed in a different location than her.

She gritted her teeth. *How can I let that male get to me?*

It had to be all the girly stuff that surrounded her constantly since arriving at the plantation. As soon as the wedding ended, she would return to Florida, back to her job with the Vampire Enforcement Squad, leaving this girly stuff and Demetri behind for good.

Chapter 21

Despite the gym's smell of spices and musk, Tatiana did not miss the sudden aroma of her mate when he entered. His presence caused her steps to falter. She grabbed the handrails of the treadmill and jumped both feet to the deck before she turned to look at Demetri.

He must have fed again. His body now took on the appearance of a marathon runner. Thin, but muscular.

He approached the weight bench and removed some of the weights from both sides of the barbell. The barbell had contained four hundred pounds, she knew because she'd been the one last lifting it. Quickly calculating the weight in her head, she realized Demetri had lowered the bar to only one hundred and fifty pounds. He benched little more than most human males could do.

The realization ratcheted her heart. Demetri had been a fierce warrior, his strength unmatched. But that was before the demons had taken him. Pity softened her eyes.

He gritted his teeth, took the bar from its resting place, and pushed it above his head. She admired the determination on his face as the muscles in his neck flexed and strained with effort.

With determination like that, Demetri would be back to his old form in no time. Pride replaced pity.

Her mate was strong, mentally if not yet physically. No doubt he could achieve anything he wanted, and by the way he forced his muscles to go through the reps, he wanted his physical strength back in a big hurry.

She just hoped he did not want her as badly or getting back to her old life might be harder than she thought. She mounted the treadmill again and increased the speed by one.

As her mate moved through the exercise on each machine, Tatiana continued to run until her legs went liquid. Satisfied, she cut power to the treadmill and headed for the sauna.

"Where are you going?" Demetri's deep voice echoed in the cavernous room.

"I thought my muscles could use a good steaming. I worked them pretty hard tonight."

Demetri let the LAT pulldown bar go, sending the weights clanking to the stack, and stood. His gray eyes captured Tatiana's. Holding her in his gaze, he crossed the room with his long strides quickly eating up the floor between them.

"I know something better than the sauna for your muscles. Follow me." Demetri offered his hand.

"What's that?" She glanced at his hand but did not move.

"Don't trust me, Tatiana?" His cheeky grin melted her heart—a little. "I promise it will be worth your trust."

Reluctantly, Tatiana placed her hand in his. He did not keep the small smile of male satisfaction from his lips while he led her through a set of double doors and into a training room which looked like it could belong in a professional football locker room.

Tatiana took in the room with awe-widened eyes. A hot tub, large enough to hold everyone in the house, sat against one wall. A set of cabinets with glass doors held everything an athlete might need from bandages for sprains to tape for wrapping knuckles before putting on a boxing glove. Several padded tables stood in neat rows in the center of the room.

Demetri dropped her hand. "Get on," he commanded, nodding toward the tables.

He crossed the room to retrieve a bottle from the cabinet.

Tatiana eyed him wearily. "What you got there?"

A sexy smile played over his face. "Trust me."

He almost sounds anxious, wonder why.

Tatiana moved to the table. The breath left his lungs when Tatiana laid down.

He made his way over to her prone form.

The contents of the bottle squirted into the palm of his hand. Her heart raced. He intended to give her a massage. Using oil. *Correction, hot oil,* she realized when a set of large hands descended onto her shoulders.

She had only a moment to wonder how he managed to heat the oil before the sinuous feel of his fingers robbed her of thought. Thick fingers worked the knots in the muscles of her neck, kneading each fiber until all were loose.

His hands roamed down each side of her back, stretching the muscles downward before they made the return trip north following the indention of her spine. Up and down. Back up and down again, his hands moved, kneading the tired muscles until a moan escaped her parted lips.

Demetri took a leg between his hands and pulled it slightly until the joints and muscles sighed in relief. Next, his fingers wrapped their magic touch around her calf. He worked down toward her foot, taking each toe between his strong fingers one by one.

She'd give him one thing—he was thorough.

Yep, definitely gets points for thoroughness, she thought when he reached for her other foot to continue his sinuous ministrations.

His hands left her foot heading north once more, only this time it was the other leg getting its reward. He worked the calf until it nearly mooed in pleasure. Her thigh quivered as his hands roamed over her flesh, taking their time to sooth every inch of her sore muscle.

He worked his way up the thigh, the tips of his fingers going under the cuff of her shorts until she believed he might touch her most feminine spot. Her core clenched. Her body reacted to his touch of its own volition. She tried to fight the arousal, tried to keep control of her body.

Fire burned through her, every nerve tingled with awareness of him. A gush of heat flowed from her core. Every instinct screamed to take him, take her mate, make him hers.

His hands moved to her back, pressing into the muscles as they slid through the oil smoothly to the nape of her neck. His fingers danced over her skin like warm raindrops kissing her flesh.

"Turn over," he growled.

If his gravelly voice was any indication, this turned him on as much as it did her. Glad she was not the only one affected by the massage, she smiled and rolled onto her back wondering if he would strip her of her sports bra and shorts.

His fingers dove into her hair in a soothing rhythm. To her surprise, he continued the massage. She admired the control he must be exerting to keep from giving them both a "happy ending."

His fingers danced over her scalp, their movements choreographed in a sensual waltz. Her lips parted in a contented sigh which brought an answering smile to grace Demetri's face.

"Like that?" he purred beside her ear, his dark voice sliding like velvet down her spine.

God, YES!! her brain screamed as more heat curled through her, sending an answering rush of moisture.

She lay boneless on the table. Her muscles wept in relief as Demetri stretched her head first to one side then the other. She'd not experienced a massage before, had always thought them wussy, but now she understood why everyone raved about them. Never had she been so relaxed and yet turned on at the same time, her body a dichotomy of sensations.

****

Demetri worked his fingers through the soft black strands, reveling in the feel of the silky locks on the digits. There were but a few places on her he had not touched. As he worked, he committed the feel of her to memory. He wanted to know every inch, every spot she liked to have touched.

The only places he had yet to feel were her most private ones, the ones covered by clothes.

Her arousal perfumed the air. She enjoyed his touch. He had been so close to her most special place, he almost lost the battle not to give into the urge to explore her more sensitive parts. Only when he reminded himself this was an exercise in getting her to trust him, did he find the strength to move up to her back. He would not betray her trust, even if she were as excited as he.

Demetri stilled his fingers on her scalp. "Better?"

"Oh, much." Tatiana eyes fluttered open to look up him with total satisfaction. "I'm not sure I can move."

"So don't." Demetri smiled.

"I need to go get a shower and get dressed. Christina and Juliette are dragging me out to some dress shop to get fitted for my bridesmaid dress."

Demetri helped her sit and steadied her as she hopped down from the table. "I know. Nicholai mentioned something about that last night."

They made their way through the home in companionable conversation while Demetri escorted Tatiana to her room. She pushed open the door and turned to face him. "Thanks for the massage. It was great. You know you could make a living doing that." The toothy smile she gave him warmed his heart as she continued. "I guess you'll be going back to your townhouse now."

"Why would I do that?"

"So, you can get a shower and rinse the oil from your hands."

Demetri placed his palms out in front of him and wiggled his fingers at her. "I do need a shower, but I'll get one here."

Confusion drew her dark brows down. "Here. Why not at your place?"

"Well for starters, my clothes are here not at the townhouse."

"Why?"

A mischievous grin lifted one corner of his mouth. "Anyone ever tell you that you are curious female?"

"Uh-huh. My father used to say that all the time."

"Wise man, your father."

"Not wise enough," Tatiana murmured under her breath.

Curiosity furrowed his brows.

She quickly continued as if hoping to avoid any questions about her statement. "So why are your clothes here?"

"Because I'm staying here, in the room next to yours."

Tension bunched her shoulders.

Chapter 22

Jara slid the sketch pad across the bed toward the four demons standing on the other side. "Does this place look familiar to anyone?"

"Looks like a plantation," murmured one of the guards as his gaze raked the sketch.

The princess crossed her arms over her chest and paced the room in frustration. "No kidding. Aren't you a smart one?

"I didn't ask what it was. I asked if it was *familiar* to anyone."

She smacked the male on the head. "I know it is a plantation. I know it is in Savannah, Georgia. What I don't know is where in Savannah it is located."

Lane clasped his hands behind his back. "We could go to Savannah and show the sketch around. Maybe someone will recognize it."

Jara pinned him with a hard stare. "And how long do you think it would take asking random people throughout the city until we found someone who knows the place? By the time we discovered where it is, the bloodsucker might be gone again. We need a faster way to locate him."

"How about checking public property records?" suggested a guard with blond hair.

Jara stopped her pacing. With wide eyes, she crossed the room toward the male. When she approached, self-preservation kicked in, and he retreated until the wall hit his back. An appreciative grin drew the corners of Jara's mouth up. She always found it pleasing when a subject demonstrated an appropriate amount of respect.

"What is your name?" she asked, closing the space between them.

"Cyrus." The male's voice lowered along with his eyes.

"Well, Cy, you might just be the most intelligent demon in the room...after me of course." Jara placed a hand on his muscular chest over his beating heart. It quickened under her fingers as she expected. "Tell me, do you know how to check the property records?"

Before the blond could reply, Lane stepped forward. His eyes blazed with jealousy, and his hands fisted at his sides. "We would need to know the vampire's name to check the records."

Jara spared him a glance before dropping her hand from the guard's thick chest. "Do you know the bloodsucker's name?" The abashed look on the scientist's face answered for him so she continued after a heavy sigh. "Does anyone know the vampire's name?" she asked turning to face the remainder of the group.

The largest of the guards squared his shoulders. His commanding presence garnered her attention. "I believe I might know its name."

"Tell me," she demanded.

"The night of the escape, I was coming around the complex heading for my motorcycle. As I rounded the corner I heard an engine and two people talking. When I realized it was the vampires, I started to run for the couple. I got there in time to see the prisoner mount my bike and the female called out to him to hold on, calling him…" His voice trailed off for a moment as he struggled to recall the memory. "…Romanoff."

The princess clapped her hands in elation. "Romanoff. Is that a first or last name?"

The burly male shrugged his massive shoulders. "I would assume it is a last name, but who knows. It would be like a bloodsucker to have a strange first name."

Lane's anger pulsed in the room. His lowered eyes flitted from side to side. "There must be a way to locate the vampire." His eyes rose from the floor to look hopefully at Jara. "Why not get a map of Savannah and try using the scrying stone to find the street where the home is located?"

Jara tsked. "That would be a great idea, except for the fact I have already expended too much energy by scrying twice in the past twelve hours. Do you wish me harm, Lane?"

Lane shook his head. Repulsion shown on his face. "Of course not. I-I wasn't thinking."

The blond guard pushed away from the wall. "Most public records can be found online. How about we do an internet search for property records in Savannah belonging to the name Romanoff?"

Her eyes lit with excitement, and another smile came to her lips. "Now there is a male who is thinking. Finally, something helpful. Who has a computer?"

She watched the males shake their heads in unison. Jara couldn't believe the ineptitude she was forced to suffer by her subjects.

"I think the lobby has a computer for guests to

use," Mr. Big and Burly suggested, earning an approving nod from the princess.

"Great. Cyrus, you seem to be the smartest one in the group. Be a dear and go to the lobby to research the records."

The guard left the room to do her bidding.

Satisfied for the moment, she sat down on the bed. Clicking on the television, she lay against the headboard to wait while the males settled on the remaining bed and one of the chairs.

She didn't have to wait long. Before the second commercial break Cyrus returned, a smug look on his face.

"Well?" she inquired expectantly as he closed the door to the room.

He held out a hand containing a few pieces of paper. "There are only three properties located in the Savannah register to someone with the name Romanoff."

Jara leapt from the bed and snatched the papers from his hand to peruse them. After reading them, her eyes linked with his as he spoke. "None of those properties appear to be the one in your drawing. One is a townhouse and the other two are modest homes located in the heart of the city."

"Hmmm." Jara tapped her chin with a thoughtful finger, the tip of her red nail hitting against her lower lip.

"I had a thought, if you'd care to hear it," offered the blond guard. A nod of her head gave permission for him to continue. "We could put the three addresses under surveillance, each guard could take one of the homes. Maybe we'll get lucky, and the vampire will show."

"That might work. Perhaps the bloodsucker was visiting the plantation at the moment I did the scrying. He might know the owner or have been there for some other reason."

"It is sensible to assume he knows people in the town where he owns a home," Cyrus offered then sat in the nearest chair.

"Good work, Cy. You did well."

His chest filled with pride at the compliment. "Thank you, Princess."

Looking down from where she stood, she rested a hand on the guard's arm appreciating the feel of his thick bicep beneath her fingers. "No need to be so formal. Call me Jara."

She graced the blond with a genuine smile. Lane stiffened.

"I think I would like to be alone now," she announced, returning to lie on the bed. "We'll leave for Savannah in the morning, that way we can set you three up at the possible houses before nightfall."

The guards rose in unison, then marched toward the door.

"Cyrus," Jara called out sweetly.

The guard stopped then faced her. "Yes?"

"I'd like you to stay. I want to…talk about the boon you have earned this evening." She glanced over at the scientist still sitting on the opposite bed. "You can go, Lane."

His body went rigid with anger as he thrust his arms into his sports coat with more force than necessary and stalked to the door, slamming it when he left. Jara giggled playfully at Cyrus, knowing the sound of her laughter would carry through the thin door. She did so enjoy playing games.

****

Tatiana ran her lathered hands over her body, the sensual feeling enhanced by the oil still on her skin. Her thoughts returned to Demetri for the hundredth time since beginning her shower. Each caress of fingers brought a longing for the touch to be his.

She wanted his hands teasing her body, cupping her breasts. Breasts that despite their size seemed heavy and full tonight.

She breathed deeply and blew it out while she stepped under the stream of water to cool her heated skin. She admired Demetri's restraint. She had been so aroused during the massage, she almost rolled over and demanded he take her on the padded table. Tatiana scented Demetri's arousal, sure in the knowledge he too wanted to mate. However, he had somehow restrained himself, seeking only to pleasure her, keeping his talented fingers on the exposed parts of her skin, never dipping under her clothes.

This male continued to surprise her. She found him honorable.

Not only had he not taken advantage of her earlier this evening, but there was the incident after his rescue when he had refused to feed from the pregnant woman. He had been in great need both times, and yet he found the fortitude to deny himself.

Damned impressive.

Tatiana dumped a glob of shampoo onto her head and began massaging it into her scalp. Her mind instantly returned to the massage session. With a moan, she closed her eyes and indulged in reliving the sensation of Demetri's fingers on her scalp. The memory sent a flood of heated moisture between the juncture of her thighs.

"Snap out of it," she murmured, letting the cool water wash the suds down her body.

Stepping out of the shower, she toweled herself dry then gave her strands a brisk towel dry. After running a brush through her hair, she trekked to the closet in her bedroom to choose some clothes.

What did one wear to go to a bridal shop? She had no clue. Since whatever she wore would no doubt need to be removed so she could try on the bridesmaid dress, she decided leathers were not the way to go.

Picking a dark blue tee shirt and jeans, she hurried to dress then stopped by the kitchen to down a pint of blood. She stood in the kitchen, enjoying the taste of the AB negative goodness while dreading the coming activity.

The image of a possible bridesmaid's dress came to mind, and she groaned. Weren't bridesmaid dresses always ugly and frilly? Hideous creations meant to make the bridesmaids look bad, so the bride would look better.

In her imagination, the dress was neon green, with a ruffled skirt and a big material rose on one shoulder. She cringed at the image and took another sip from her glass.

At least there is one saving grace to this evening. Demetri will not be coming with us.

A little time and separation from the potent male was exactly what she needed, even if it meant trying on a fugly dress.

As if on cue, Demetri sauntered into the kitchen,

looking freshly showered with his hair slicked back from his face. Her gaze scanned his body starting with the black boots, up his matching jeans, over the white tee shirt that stretched over a defined chest to finish their trail on his handsome face.

Their eyes met, his nostrils flared. "AB negative?" he asked, eyeing the glass.

She smiled around the rim of her glass. His eyes moved to her neck to watch her swallow the liquid.

"Yes, want some?"

His heated gaze flew to her lips. "You know I do."

He prowled toward her. Her heart raced in her chest. Its wild rhythm drove a rush of blood to flush her face.

He closed in quickly, only a handbreadth of space between their bodies when he stopped. Cupping her face between his hands, he leaned forward closing the distance between them. His tongue flicked across her lips.

"Ummm, that's good," he purred against her mouth before his tongue darted back out once more to blaze a path over her lips.

Desire coursed through her veins, heating her blood until her body flamed. Her lips parted in invitation.

Finding herself leaning into him, she allowed him to indulge in a long, slow exploration of her mouth. His body against hers drove her mad. She struggled for control when blood rushed to her ears, dulling the sound of a low moan. Hers? His? She didn't care, lost in the passion of his kiss.

Her arms wrapped around his narrow waist, pulling him forward to pin her back to the counter. His hands encircled her back. He pushed his hips into hers, allowing her to feel the hard evidence of his arousal.

While her mind protested quietly in the background, her body had plans of its own. It knew what it wanted, what it needed. It recognized its mate and wanted him with fierce desperation.

Demetri broke the kiss. His lips blazed a trail down her jaw to her neck. Laying tiny kisses on the delicate flesh, his lips stroked the fire within her, sending sparks of pleasure through her body.

"I thought you wanted some AB negative," Tatiana panted as one hand weaved in his hair to hold him to her.

His tongue flicked across the vein in her neck. "I do," he growled, his breath ghosting over her skin. A shiver wiggled down her spine. "Do you think I don't remember the type of your blood? You are AB negative. My favorite. I've never had any sweeter than you."

The tips of his fangs trailed over her flesh. Her head lolled on her shoulder, exposing the side of her neck to him fully. Inviting him to feast.

His soft lips pulled back. Her heart raced faster at the anticipation of the thrust through her skin.

"Hey guys. Ready to g…" the sound of Christina's southern drawl trailed off as she emerged from the stairs leading from her suite.

Demetri withdrew from her neck and glanced at the indentations in her flesh she knew were there before turning his eyes to the red head standing across the kitchen.

"I'm sorry," Christina sincerely apologized. "When I heard two sets of footsteps traipsing around up here, I thought it was Tatiana and Julie. I'll just go downstairs. You guys go back to what you were doing." She winked at them before a mischievous grin played across her lips.

Tatiana released her grip on Demetri. Her mind finally took control over her body, and she pulled his hands from her to scoot out around him. Putting some much-needed space between them, her mind began to clear from its erotic haze.

The taking and giving of blood was intricately entwined with sex for most vampires, and she was no exception. If Demetri had sunk his fangs into her, she probably would have allowed him to sink other hard parts of himself into her as well.

"We were just—" Tatiana's sentence was interrupted by Marcus' mate.

"Oh, you don't have to tell me. I know what you two were just." Smiling, Christina purposely let the sentence hover unfinished.

Tatiana fought her body for control, slowed her breathing and the rhythm of her heart until she felt almost normal. Demetri's close proximity made controlling her body difficult. Wanting more space, she crossed the kitchen to join Christina. "Let's go. The sooner we get to the shop the sooner we can get the fitting over with."

"I'll just run upstairs and get Julie, then we will get under way."

The female warrior nodded in acknowledgement and watched the red head dematerialize.

"She does like to show off." Demetri's tone noted his amusement. He meandered to the refrigerator, withdrew a pint of blood, and downed it in one long swallow before throwing the empty bag in the trash.

"Yeah, she does," Tatiana agreed. "Of course, I know another vampire who likes to show off as well."

"Why, *kotik kisa*, whoever do you mean?" A teasing grin spread across his handsome face.

"Gee, I wonder," she replied, the sarcasm dripping from her voice. "Did you just call me what I think you called me?"

"Yes." He chuckled, the sound resonating from deep within his chest to wash over her. "I called you *kotik kisa*. I used it as a term of endearment."

"I'm not sure I like being called a kitty cat."

"Your eyes remind me of a cat. They are wild and fierce like a tiger."

Tatiana decided she could live with the analogy and graced the male with a genuine smile. This man had potential.

Best not to dwell too much on that.

Demetri glided across the kitchen. Taking her upper arm in his strong hand, he led her down the hall to the foyer to where Julie and Christina waited for them.

Tatiana remained silent as the group made its way through the heavy oak door and down the wraparound porch to the car waiting in the drive.

After sending her senses flowing out over the land in search of threats, she took a deep breath, savoring the feel of the humidity on her face. Not as thick as home, but much better than the lack there of in Wyoming.

She allowed Demetri to open the passenger door for her and hand her into the car before closing her in. Tatiana took in the leather seats and wood grain interior. The car bespoke of wealth, and a new car smell surrounded her

Christina slid behind the steering wheel, then Julie hopped in the back seat behind Christina. Surprise turned Tatiana in the seat when she heard the back-passenger door open. Demetri sank down into the leather seat behind her.

"I thought you would be staying here."

"You aren't the only one who needs to be fitted for wedding attire. Nicholai requested I stand up for him at the wedding. I need to be measured for a tux. Of course, I would have preferred to remain in the kitchen with you, but duty calls."

Tatiana's cheeks flushed as she silently gazed out the window, watching the Spanish moss sway from the oak trees that lined the gravel drive. By the time, they reached the wrought iron gate at the end of the drive, she decided the Fates must be working against her, probably enjoying her misery. Not only was she on her way to try on a bridesmaid dress, but she had not escaped being near Demetri. Quite the opposite, in fact, since his presence wrapped around her as they drove.

A string of curses flowed through her thoughts.

Damn him! Well, if you can't beat 'em, torture 'em. A naughty smile pulled at the corners of Tatiana's mouth.

Chapter 23

Demetri observed Tatiana from his seat. She appeared pensive. Hopefully, she contemplated what occurred in the kitchen. Their time together certainly was on his mind. She responded readily to his kiss, no doubt in large part to the natural chemistry between heartmates, but he didn't mind using that to his advantage.

Tatiana turned to Christina. "Didn't you tell me the tuxes would be bright pink to match my dress?"

"Huh?" Marcus' heartmate shot her a confused look.

"You know." The female warrior's eyes widened slightly. "You told me last night that my dress is hot pink, and the tux for the groomsman would match. I think Demetri will look wonderful in hot pink. Don't you think so, Julie?"

The curvy brunette smiled, her eyes sparkled with mischief. "Oh yes. I agree. Demetri will look wonderful in pink. It will complement the color of his skin nicely."

"You are joking." Demetri's voice filled the passenger compartment. "You can't seriously expect me to wear pink."

"You're a groomsman in a wedding. You're going to have to wear whatever they want you to," Tatiana informed him.

"But PINK! There must be another color suitable

for the occasion. How about black? I think a black tux would look fine with a pink dress." Demetri's suggestion hung in the air a moment, giving him hope the women were considering the recommendation.

When Christina spoke, the hope was dashed. "I'm afraid the pink tux has already been ordered. You'll just have to live with it. It is only for one day."

"The bridesmaid and the groomsman have to match," chimed in Julie. "It's southern tradition."

Demetri stared out the tinted window of the car. He'd agreed to stand up for his cousin. He would not back out of the agreement. His honor would not allow it. However, he couldn't wear a pink tux to fulfill his duty. Some men wore pink and that may be fine for them, but he didn't wear the color. He preferred black combat gear to a tux any day, especially a *pink* tux.

Holy hell what have I gotten myself into?

His mind raced, seeking a solution. Surely, he possessed enough intelligence to figure a way out of this predicament.

While they drove, Demetri continued to ponder the options, occasionally drawn from his pensiveness by a question from one of the women to which he absently grunted an agreement. His thoughts never returned fully to the car but stayed ahead of them in the shop.

With luck, I'll come up with a solution by the time we pull into the parking lot.

He did not.

Inside the dress shop, Tatiana's sexy lips gaped open at the opulence. Grand chandeliers hung from the ceiling with crystal teardrops dripping from them that sent prisms of light to dance off the marble floors. A well-dressed woman greeted them then ushered them down the hall into a large room.

Effeminate furniture sat in front of a large full-length mirror. The brocade upholstered couch with spindly legs beckoned witnesses to observe the brides scrutinize their reflections in the capacious mirror. The three arched openings in the room, each flanked by round decretive columns, drew the eye to the clothing hung on long racks. Through the first archway were the bridal gowns, the next housed the bridesmaid dresses, and the third opening contained the tuxedos.

The saleswoman led Tatiana into a dressing room. When she disappeared from his sight, his chest tightened.

Demetri propelled his senses out to scan the store and the surrounding area, looking for anything unusual. Assured everything was fine, the Alpha relaxed.

A young lady approached with a tape measure draped around her neck.

"Good evening, sir. I'm Dora. Might we get you measured for your tux?" She ogled him, her gaze roaming his body before she pulled the tape measure from her neck. "Let's start with the chest. Hold out your arms please."

Demetri stretched his arms out in a "T" formation to allow the woman to measure around his chest. Dora wasn't hard to look at, and if he wasn't mated he'd have been tempted to see where the evening might lead, but he only had eyes for Tatiana.

Tatiana emerged from the dressing room in a strapless chiffon gown. The black shade of the gown perfectly complimented her dark hair. The material flowed around her long legs when she walked, dusting the floor. A jeweled detail gathered the black material under her bosom to create an empire waist which emphasized her breasts in the most delectable way. She'd never looked more beautiful.

Yearning drew him. A physical sensation pulled his chest. When the attendant released her arms to measure a new part of his body, Demetri stalked toward his mate. His purpose for being in the store forgotten the minute he had seen Tatiana, he moved behind her to gaze at her reflection.

Their eyes caught in the mirror. He knew she would see the desire in his eyes. Everyone probably did, but he did not care. She looked beautiful in the gown. Arousal hardened his body.

He ran his finger along her bare shoulder, memorizing the sight of the creamy flesh that pebbled with gooseflesh under his touch.

"You are stunning," he growled next to her ear.

A hand lowered to trace the jeweled design under her breasts. His thumb brushed across one nipple, causing it to strain against the material of the dress. Enjoying the obvious effect, he was having on his mate, his hand traveled across the design until his thumb found her other nipple. A light touch and it matched its twin, sending burning desire throughout his body.

Tatiana trembled under his touch. Her arousal tickled his nose. Her eyes closed as if pleasure rushed through her body like a mighty flood.

"Open your eyes," his gravelly voice commanded. "Look at yourself in the mirror."

She obeyed, as his hand splayed then moved down the dress to cover her stomach.

"Do you know what you do to me?" he asked, his hot breath flowing across her ear. "Your eyes draw me." His eyes captured hers in the mirror, demanding her attention. "Your scent calls to me." He moved his head, nuzzling her neck, inhaling deeply to take her delicate aroma into his lungs.

"I want you," he murmured against her neck. "I *need* you."

In the mirror, he noticed movement behind them. Focusing on the reflection, he witnessed Juliette leaving the dressing room.

Tatiana tried to clear her throat. The second try worked. "We have company," she whispered.

Juliette wore a floor length gown of light pink chiffon with a delicate lace overlay. Its empire waist was adorned with fresh water pearls lined in three rows. She strolled across the room, the gown swaying gently.

Reluctantly, Demetri allowed Tatiana to pull from his embrace. Taking his hand, she led him off the raised platform on which they stood so Nicholai's heartmate could take their place.

"You look beautiful, Julie," Tatiana complimented the woman. "The lace bolero puts the dress over the top. Very pretty."

"You should see Christina." Julie twirled in front of the mirror. "Her dress is more traditional than mine. Since this is my second marriage, I thought pink would be more appropriate than a white gown."

"It is a good choice," Demetri offered. "Nicholai will love it."

Julie's smile reached her eyes. "Thanks."

Her eyes flicked from her image to stare behind her.

The couple turned to watch Christina float toward them, her ivory colored gown flowing behind her. With the full skirt and cathedral length train, she looked like a princess. Swarovski crystal beading that matched the designer heels on her feet adorned the strapless gown.

"Wow," Demetri murmured on a soft breath.

Tatiana released his hand, but his grip tightened, refusing to relinquish her fingers. He pulled her close to whisper in her ear. "She cannot hold a candle to you. You are far more beautiful to me."

The female warrior blushed under the proclamation. She tried once more to pull her hand from his. This time he reluctantly allowed the freedom, and she took full advantage moving away from him to sit on the delicate observation couch. Demetri wondered why she retreated.

"Sorry we are late for the party," a male voice called from the back of the room. Marcus and Nicholai entered from the hall. Two squeals and a blur of movement had the men laughing.

Christina grabbed Juliette and ran back into a dressing room as fast as her preternatural speed could take them, trying to keep their future husbands from seeing them in their gowns. She peeked her head out of the door to the dressing room to properly chastise Marcus as Julie changed out of her gown. Julie then left the room to dress down Nicholai while Christina changed.

The whole thing entertained Demetri. He chuckled.

"You really shouldn't laugh." A small burst of air escaped Tatiana's smiling lips.

One brow rose on Demetri's forehead. "You should take your own advice."

The pair laughed. The young vampires completely deserved what they got from their mates. Demetri understood very little about human wedding traditions, but even he knew the groom wasn't supposed to see a bride in her gown before the wedding.

Wondering why the heartmates had not used their mindlinks to lash out at their mates in private, Demetri glanced around to see who might be listening and found the two employees of the shop standing with their mouths gaping wide in disbelief. He pushed into their minds to discover they had both witnessed Christina's flight from the room.

When Tatiana went to change out of her dress, he quickly rearranged their memories, wiping the event from their minds. Next, he distracted them by suggesting they were both needed to finish his measurements.

Following them into the tuxedo room, he stood stoically while the two women knelt before him and ran their measuring tapes along the inseam of his jeans.

"Nice." Marcus entered, nodding down at the woman. "I wouldn't let Tatiana see them doing that." The smirk on his face raised one corner of his lips.

He walked around the older vampire. Demetri heard him pushing hangers over the metal clothing bar. "So, how's the fitting going? Did the attendants have you try on a tux yet?"

"No," Demetri ground out between clenched teeth as one of the women bumped her hand against his groin.

"Oops, sorry." She batted her eyes up at him, earning her a raised eyebrow from the warrior.

The women stood in unison, one wrapping the tape around his waist, as Marcus returned to slip a jacket onto Demetri's shoulders. After shrugging into the confining coat, Demetri looked down.

"I think not!" A sea of pink flowed down his arms.

Nicholai walked into the room. "But you are supposed to match the bridesmaid."

"The bridesmaid is wearing black. I would be happy to match her." Demetri allowed the jacket to fall from his shoulders, catching it in his hand before it hit the floor.

Marcus returned it to the rack. "You'll be matching Julie's gown instead of Tatiana's dress."

"I most certainly will *not*."

"But you promised to stand up for me." Nicholai pulled a pink shirt from a rack and held it up in front of Demetri. "Besides pink complements the color of your skin. You must match. It is a southern tradition."

Demetri's eyes narrowed. His cousin's words were an exact copy of what Nicholai's heartmate said during their car ride to the shop. He suspected foul play.

"I know you are jesting, cousin. Even your taste is not so bad as to pick a pink tux. Though Marcus' tastes are rather questionable." He crossed his arms over his chest, daring Marcus to deny his quip before continuing. "You and the women had me going for a while."

Nicholai's young face lit with a wide smile that reached his amber eyes. "Sorry cousin, I am afraid we could not help making you the ass of the joke."

"You mean butt of the joke," Marcus corrected the Russian's English before he slapped Nicholai's shoulder in camaraderie.

Unable to contain their laughter, the joyous sound burst from both Marcus and Nicholai. Deep chuckles filled the room along with a distinctly feminine one.

The warrior glanced in the direction of the high-pitched laugh.

Her arms crossed over her tee shirt, Tatiana leaned against the decorative column watching the entire discussion. Laughter shook her body, jiggling her breast in a way that brought a smile to his face. Demetri joined their laughter.

"I must say, Romanoff, I expected you to react badly about the tux. But you took it in stride. I'm impressed. You keep surprising me."

In a good way, he hoped.

Christina and Juliette joined the group followed by the shop attendants, one of whom toted a tray with fluted glasses, while the other held a bottle of champagne.

"Would anyone like a glass of champagne?" offered the woman who had bumped Demetri's jewels.

"None for me thanks." Christina waved off the offer. "I'm driving."

Julie glanced down at her watch. "None for me either, thanks anyway. It's getting late."

Christina noted the time. "Oh shoot! We were having so much fun, I lost track of time. We have to get you over to the counseling center, Demetri."

Puzzlement furrowed the ancient vampire's brows. The jovial smile faded from his face. "Why?"

"Don't you remember what you agreed to do in the car? We need to get over there, so you can try on the costume and make sure it fits."

"What costume? I don't remember agreeing to anything about a costume." Demetri's mind raced back to the car ride. He remembered everything with perfect clarity until he had been told he would have to wear a pink tux, after that he vaguely remembered something about the counseling center and him agreeing to something, but the details eluded him.

"You agreed," Tatiana assured him. "We all heard it. Christina asked you if you'd be willing to wear the costume for the kids' Easter party and you agreed."

Dread crept up his spine. "Exactly *what* did I agree to, Tatiana?"

Pinned under his steel gaze, Tatiana squirmed. "I hope after the tux joke that this isn't his breaking point," she murmured under her breath, just loud enough for Demetri's preternatural hearing to pick up.

She swallowed, like she tried to gather her courage.

"Well. Umm." She shifted her stance.

Anticipation got the better of him. "Spit it out, woman."

Her eyes narrowed ever so slightly. "You agreed to be the Easter Bunny."

Chapter 24

Demetri trailed behind the women, ruminating about his predicament as they ambled down the hall of the counseling center to Christina's office. He could not believe he had agreed to portray an Easter Bunny, not even when he had been so distracted in the car. It was simply not something he could do.

He wouldn't be caught dead dressing up in pink ears and bunny tail. Those were great for Playboy Bunnies, not him. No way would he be playing Peter Cottontail. Not. Gonna. Happen.

He slowed his pace when the sound of a soft voice reached his ears. The Alpha peeked into the room to his left. Inside, a woman with short hair and a soothing tone invited the listener to relax. She had a way of calming the soul, and Demetri stilled in the doorway to listen to her speak.

"Abuse is never acceptable, regardless of the circumstances," she said to the circle of women sitting around her. "When a person has been abused, they may come to believe they have no control in their life and no ability to make decisions. The first step in healing is to recognize you can regain control. Control can look very different for each person, and that is okay."

A petite blonde sat wringing her hands in her lap. Her eyes remained cast down to the floor when she spoke. "It is hard to take control when the one abusing you has all the power, Catherine."

Catherine nodded in acknowledgment. The ends of her brown hair danced over her shoulders. "You can take back the control, Lilly. It may be that you take control by allowing yourself to surrender, but as I said control can look different for each person."

"That doesn't make sense," another woman said.

The leader of the group glanced in her direction. "Sometimes the route to taking back control of your life is in surrendering to what you cannot change. Accepting you were abused, surrendering to the emotions that come with the acceptance. Surrendering to the rage, the pain, the sorrow can be freeing because it is through acceptance that often people find a will to change their lives. Find the courage to stop being a victim and become a survivor.

"In my case, I was kidnapped and abused by the man who held me. Once rescued…"

Demetri didn't need to hear the rest of her story, for he knew it well because he'd been there when she was rescued.

Catherine had been kidnapped and tortured by a former Alpha who had turned rogue named Michael. After Michael had been killed, Demetri and Tatiana took Catherine and several other women to the hospital for treatment. Of course, he eased her memories of the event, specifically wiping anything pertaining to vampires, and rearranging the memories so she believed a human had been her captor.

During the battle with Michael, he'd accidentally wounded Tatiana, and she had taken some of his blood to help heal. The memories twisted his gut. She kept herself from him, knowing they were mates. Had he really been so awful to her that she didn't want him for a mate?

Sure, he might be a bit old-fashioned, if memory served she'd referred to him as chauvinistic. He had to concede, he had some strong beliefs in the differences between men and women.

He had always believed that since males were naturally stronger, faster than females they should stand up and be the protectors. His strong sense of honor demanded he protect those weaker than himself.

But Tatiana didn't want his protection. She believed herself to be the strong one. The woman could fight and handle a weapon. She certainly had no problem with self-confidence.

Perhaps he'd underestimated her abilities. He had to admit, right now between the two of them, she was the one in better shape physically, thanks to those damned demons. She had more stamina, stronger muscles, and probably could kick his butt in a fighting ring.

But his strength had improved and would continue to do so until it returned to its peak condition. It would take time to get there which was okay because anything worth having was worth working for.

And he wasn't afraid to work for something he wanted.

The sound of Catherine's voice pulled him from his reverie. "So, by accepting what had happened was not my fault, I could move forward, embrace the future and open myself up to the possibilities. I could take what the future had to offer and make my life what I wanted it to be." She made eye contact with each person in the room before continuing. Her eyes locked with Demetri's when she spoke. "I surrendered to gain control."

His mind absorbed the words. A calm settled over him. Catherine was right. To gain control he needed to surrender.

If he allowed Tatiana to take the lead, he could win her. She was used to being in control of every situation just like him. He recognized that part of himself in her. He could use the knowledge. Allow her strength to forge their bond rather than forcing it on her. It was not a weakness to do so, but a way to show her he trusted her.

He pulled from the doorway and continued down the hall, intent on seeing his mate to begin this new approach, but a colorful room distracted him from the goal. He entered the room, his eyes taking in the murals containing fanciful images of unicorns and rainbows. Clouds drifted along the ceiling. He swore, if he stared long enough, the fluffy white puffs actually moved. The artist had done an amazing job of creating a dream world in the room.

Shelves lined the space, holding multicolored bins of toys. Rectangles of red, green, blue, and yellow repeated their patterns inviting little hands to take the treasures held within. Dolls folded from one of the bins, draped over as if trying to escape.

"Excuse me."

Demetri felt a tug on his jeans and looked down onto the most precious face he had ever seen. A little girl with long black hair and chubby cheeks gazed at him expectantly. He sensed she was a vampire instantly. "Yes?"

"What is your name?" she asked.

"Demetri."

"Hi, Mr. Demetwi," the child greeted, the smile on her face producing an answering grin on his.

"What is your name, little one?"

She fisted her hands on her hips, reminding him very much of a miniature Tatiana with her black hair and the temper flashing in her light eyes. "I'm not wittle. I'm twee."

She held up three fingers.

Demetri knelt. "Wow, three years old. You *are* a big girl. What is your name? No let me guess." He rubbed a thoughtful hand over his chin before continuing. "Is it Sassafras?"

A childish giggle rewarded the silly guess. "No."

Demetri chuckled. "Is it Rasputin?"

"No, my name isn't Wasputin." The little girl shook her head with such vigor her dark strands covered her face, causing her to wipe them away with a tiny hand.

"I give up then. What is your name?"

"My name is Webecca," she answered, grabbing his hand. "You want to play dolls with me?"

The warrior rose and allowed her to lead him over to the bin holding the dolls. She pull two from the container.

"Rebecca," he repeated. "That is a pretty name."

"I know. Mommy used to say it was a pwetty name for a pwetty girl."

Noticing they were alone, Demetri asked, "Where is your mommy?"

The little girl's eyes clouded with unshed tears. "She's gone."

"Gone where?" Demetri's heart clenched at the

sight of a lone tear sliding down her chubby cheek.

"Daddy says she's in the Gweat Beyond." Rebecca handed him one of the dolls to wipe the tear away with the back of her freed hand.

"I'm sorry," Demetri mumbled, following her to the middle of the room. They sat on a colorful carpet.

"It's all wight. Daddy says he loves me enough for both him and Mommy."

Demetri mirrored her cross-legged position, making the doll dance along the floor. "What happened?" He instantly regretted the question, especially if it brought the child any more pain.

Rebecca made her own doll dance in time to Demetri's. "She was taken by bad people."

Demetri studied the child. She stated her mother's fate so succinctly, as if she had recited the abduction numerous times before. A throat cleared from across the room.

Tatiana leaned one shoulder against the door jamb, her arms crossed over her ribs.

Demetri couldn't help but notice the similarities between the two of them. Their hair was the same shade, blue-black like a raven's wing. Their eyes evidenced fiery personalities. He gazed back at the child instantly feeling like he looked at their future.

He wanted a little girl with Tatiana's beautiful features, just with a little less stubbornness. Demetri rolled his eyes. Yes, definitely less stubbornness than her mother. He wasn't sure he could handle two Tatianas.

A male approached and turned sideways to squeeze between Tatiana and the doorframe.

"Excuse me," he said to her before turning his

attention to the child. "There you are, Rebecca. I told you to wait for me in the lobby while I signed in. You shouldn't be wondering around by yourself, little princess."

"I'm not wittle!" she protested as her father picked her up.

Turning to Demetri, the male gave him an assessing stare. "I hope she was no trouble."

"None at all. We were just talking about her mother."

A clouded expression took the male's face. "We lost her last year. We were on vacation, visiting her sister in Wyoming when she went missing."

"I'm sorry."

"The thing was she was pregnant. We were going to have a little boy. So close to having Rebecca. We couldn't believe how blessed we were." The father's words stopped in his throat at the memory.

Rebecca reached her tiny hand up to run it along her father's jaw. "It's otay, Daddy. You still have me."

He hugged his daughter to his chest. "I certainly do, baby," he whispered.

"Let's play," Rebecca offered in the innocent way children do, as if everything was better if you just played. "Mr. Demetwi has the boy doll." She wiggled in her father's arms. "But there are more girl dolls. I go get one for you."

"Here, your father can have my doll," offered the Alpha. "I have to go talk to Miss Tatiana, anyway. I can't play anymore."

Rebecca's lower lip popped out in a pout that would make any man cave. "But *we* were playing."

Demetri rubbed a hand in her hair, messing the

tresses. "And now I need to go. But you can stay and play with your father."

Demetri handed the man the doll.

"Come on, dear. You have bothered the man enough for one day."

"It was no bother," Demetri assured the father, the sincerity in his voice left no doubt as to the truth of the statement. "Rebecca is a sweet child."

A smile graced the father's face for the first time that evening, bringing with it a glimpse of the pride he felt for his daughter. "She is that. Just like her mother."

Demetri crossed the room and took Tatiana's hand. He led her down the hall and into Christina's office.

Closing the door softly behind them, he turned to face Marcus' mate. "What's the story with the little girl?"

"He means Rebecca," Tatiana supplied, keeping her fingers locked with his.

Christina sighed. "It's confidential. I can't say."

The Alpha's eyes narrowed. "Her father told us her mother disappeared in Wyoming, and she was pregnant. Stephan and I were searching for a female vampire who had been taken in Mason's Bluff. We never found her. Is that her daughter?"

Christina nodded. "Poor little thing has had such a hard time coping with her mother's loss. It took her six months of therapy to finally start speaking again. When she first started coming here, she had selective mutism."

"What's that?" asked Demetri.

"It's someone who speaks only in certain situations or to certain people," explained Juliette. "I had a student one year who was a selective mute. She sang beautifully in my chorus class but wouldn't talk in any of her other classes."

Christina opened a door and disappeared inside. "I really appreciate you agreeing to be the Easter Bunny, Demetri. The costume won't fit Marcus, or I'd make him do it."

She emerged with a carcass of white fur draped over one arm.

Taking the faux fur from her outstretched arm, Demetri held the outfit in front of his lean body. He instantly realized why he was the best choice for the costume. It was long, well over six and a half feet, but not wide, requiring a thin male to play the part.

Christina tucked her hair behind her ear. "I have someone to play the bunny in the morning for the party we are having for the human children, but he could not make it later in the evening for the party for the vampires. I just couldn't break the children's heart by not having the Easter Bunny arrive with goodies for them, and it's not like they could come to the morning party." Noting the disdain on Demetri's face she added, "Rebecca is signed up to be there, and she is so excited about seeing the Easter Bunny. It's all she's been able to talk about during our last few sessions."

His gray eyes flicked to her face, his brows narrowing. "Low blow, Christina. You do not play fair."

How could he disappoint that sweet, cherub-faced child? She'd suffered much loss in her young life. He couldn't possibly add to it by denying her the Easter Bunny. And she wouldn't be the only one looking forward to seeing it. Other children would be expecting to see the bunny too, other young ones needing a little happiness in their sad lives.

Just like that he knew he would do it.

Christina gave an insouciant shrug of her shoulders. "As I said the other night. All's fair in love and racing...and getting someone to wear a bunny costume."

"Well, come on, try it on," Julie prompted. "We're dying to see if it fits."

With a disgruntled noise forced from the back of his throat, Demetri reluctantly put each leg in the costume.

He'd wear the damned thing, but he didn't have to act like he liked it.

After tugging it on his arms, Christina moved behind him to zip it up. The costume fit a little snug, but the zipper closed much to his chagrin. "How do I look?"

"Unfinished." Christina handed him the head.

Demetri took the oversized noggin between his hands and stared into the face. A big pink nose with protruding whiskers drew his attention first. His gaze traveled upward to a set of googly eyes that shook from side to side. His eyes next landed on a set of two-foot pink ears at the top of the cranium.

"You have got to be kidding." He donned the huge head and found himself staring out the rabbit's mouth, two oversized buck teeth partially obscuring his view.

Julie appeared in front of him, holding out a sizable Easter basket. "Here, don't forget this."

Taking the basket from her, he crossed the room. The oversized feet were cumbersome especially when the toothy head obstructed his vision. "I need to see myself. Where is the bathroom?"

"I can do better than that. Here." Christina pulled a full-length mirror from behind her desk. "I've been so busy with the opening of the second center, I sometimes have to change here before going out to meet with someone about the wedding, so I keep this mirror here." Her eyes darted to Tatiana's face before she pushed on. "Marcus has been trying to get me to back off and take it easy. He says I'm working too hard with all I have to do for the wedding, but I can't delegate these things, so I just ignore him and keep on going."

****

As Christina placed the mirror before Demetri, Tatiana tensed. *This is it.*

Demetri would take one look at himself in that ridiculous costume and refuse to honor his commitment. Not that Tatiana would blame him.

He hardly looked like a fierce male warrior in the get up. A deep chuckle emanated from the male, shaking the googly eyes. She did not keep the surprise from her face and joined in the laughter along with the other females in the room.

"What ya think?" Christina asked, still holding the mirror.

"I think I look ridiculous, but I'll do it for the children."

"Nicholai said you would keep your word." Julie glanced down at her watch. "We need to be getting back to the house. The boys will wonder what happened to us."

Christina put the mirror back behind the desk then grabbed her keys and purse. "Here let me help you out of the costume so we can go."

"That's okay," Tatiana said. "You take Julie back

to the plantation. I'll help Demetri out of the costume then we'll dematerialize there."

"We don't mind waiting," offered Julie.

Tatiana shooed off the offer with a wave of her hand. "No. You guys go on. We'll probably get there before you do."

"All right then." Christina started toward the door.

"Bye," the women called in unison as they left.

Tatiana moved behind Demetri and closed the door to the office with a thought, locking them in as she slid the zipper down. Placing her hands on his shoulders, she took the heavy material from him. Her hands moved down his arms as she did so. She knelt behind him to pull the material from his legs.

Demetri stepped from the costume and removed the enormous head. Placing the cranium on Christina's desk, he turned and looked down at Tatiana on her knees before him. He swallowed hard at the sight.

He wrapped his fingers around her arms to lift her to her feet. Surprise made her brows rise. Instinct told her to escape the hold. Before she acted, he kissed her. The feelings from earlier came rushing back with a heat that consumed her body. In the kitchen and in the dress shop, she'd wanted him so badly. Now they were alone and thanks to the fact of the locked door they weren't likely to be disturbed anytime soon.

He took her breath away with a kiss that was both gentle and passionate at the same time. She relaxed into him, allowing the sensuous feel of his body to wash over her.

His tongue did not dart between her lips when they opened. Instead it hovered just out of reach as if he waited for her to make the first move. Overcome with lust, she gladly responded to the invitation, running her tongue sensuously over his, tasting him thoroughly.

He allowed the exploration, allowed her to lead the dance of their tongues. The control was very sexy.

His grip on her arms tightened slightly as if he struggled to keep his restraint. Admirably, he remained still to allow her kiss.

She pulled back, breaking the kiss, and put her fingers over her tingling lips. His kiss was as magical as his massaging fingers. Her body felt heavy, achy. This male wore down her resistance with his potent sexuality and surprising attitude. She found herself drawn to him more as the day progressed.

Each time he showed his sense of humor or took something in stride, he ingratiated himself to her a little more. The tipping point had been the little girl.

The Demetri she knew would never have sat on the floor playing dolls. He never would have dressed up in a ridiculous looking costume just to bring smiles to children's faces.

Maybe Demetri was a new man, changed by the torture he suffered. She knew better than most how a traumatic event could change a person. The torment she had suffered in her youth had forever changed her. Perhaps Demetri was no longer the overbearing male she remembered.

"What happened to you, Demetri?"

His eyes bored into hers; his jaw ticced. "You know what happened. You saw me on that table."

"No, I don't mean physically. You've changed. It's like you are a different person. How are you handling this so well?"

He paced away from her, the topic clearly making

him uncomfortable. "If it seems like I'm handling this well, it is because I learned long ago life goes on, no matter what terrible things happen. It may horrify you, but then you realized you can step back onto the train and let it take you down the tracks to your destination. Let something else take control and just cruise for a while."

"Like pretending everything is all right, until one day it actually is."

He paced back to her and cupped her face in his hand. "You are too insightful about this, Tatiana. I know you have suffered some abuse. Tell me about it."

"I don't want to discuss it." Tatiana's tone allowed no negotiation as she fisted her hands on her lean hips.

His eyes searched hers. A flutter danced in her mind, a light touch searching her memories. Recognizing Demetri's mental touch, she slammed a barrier down into place, blocking him from her mind.

"Stay out of my mind, Romanoff!"

Demetri struggled to still the grin that threatened to take his face. "But it is such a beautiful mind. I cannot help but want to be in there."

He pushed once more against the barrier in her mind. Her anger amplified at the intrusion. They had been having such a nice evening and now he was being pushy, not taking no for an answer.

Since he had fed several times, he was strong, much stronger mentally than she. It wouldn't take long for him to break through her barrier and take the information he sought. She simply wasn't ready to share that yet, not with him. She needed to get away from him before he forced it from her.

And so, the old Demetri has returned, she thought,

dematerializing before his eyes, leaving only a wisp of black smoke to waft through the fingers of his hand.

Chapter 25

Cyrus sat in the rental car crouched down in the driver's seat, ruminating about his predicament. It had been two days since they had left Mason's Bluff. Two days of doing surveillance on each of the properties. Unfortunately for him, they had yet to spot the vampire, and that had Jara in a rather foul mood, which did not bode well for him since his idea brought them here.

Jara clearly held him responsible for them being in Savannah. It wasn't fair. She'd located the vampire here. In fact, she'd tried scrying for him since they arrived, and the stone indicated he remained somewhere in Savannah. Since they had been unable to locate his exact whereabouts, Jara's temper and frustration rose with each passing minute.

Gone was the lover who had taken him to amazing heights with her skills, replaced by a fiery tempered bitch that enjoyed taking out her anger on others. She banished him from her presence, telling him once he had found the bloodsucker she would allow him to be with her again, as if she were the only woman who would have him.

His eyes darted to the townhouse across the street. For days, he had been watching the place for any signs of life. Still during the day and dark as pitch at night, no one had come or gone from the premises as far as he could tell.

He had snooped around of course, materializing into the home during the day when he was sure the vampire would be asleep. Going through the home, he found the kitchen's pantry stocked with canned goods, but nothing in the refrigerator. Upstairs, clothes hung in the closet and some lay folded neatly in the dressers but sheets which should have been on the bed were instead tucked into a linen closet in the hall.

The house appeared dust free as if someone had been cleaning the place, everything in its rightful spot, but everything seemed too perfect. No magazines strewn about or bills left out to be paid. It was as if the house awaited the owner's arrival, but the owner was nowhere in sight.

The sound of his stomach growling its hunger brought his eyes front and center. His hand patted the beast. "I hear you. I know just the place."

Luckily, he'd put in the contacts which changed his red eyes to blue. He licked his lips in anticipation when he brought the engine to life and pulled from the curb.

After a couple of turns, he slid into the parking lot beside the three-story brick building in Savannah's historic district. The front of the building had matching bay windows stacked on top of each other, one on each floor. The porch boasted carved columns which supported its roof and wooden rocking chairs that beckoned patrons to sit and talk a spell.

Cyrus strolled through the front door. A mixture of breads, meats, and veggies permeated his senses. His mouth watered. Normally his kind avoided human contact whenever possible, but sometimes the risk was worth the reward. And this little place was definitely worth it.

The meals here tasted unbelievable. They served good old-fashioned food. The collard greens, biscuits with gravy, and country fried steaks all pleased his pallet, and the cornbread was worth dying for. Literally.

A hostess led him to one of the round tables near the back, past a staircase cordoned off by a velvet rope.

"What's up there?" He pointed to the stairwell as he slid into a chair.

"That's a VIP section," the hostess answered. "It doesn't open until dark."

Cyrus glanced out the window behind him. "So, if I wait a few more minutes, can I be seated up there?"

The hostess graced him with a pleasant, but somewhat condescending smile. "I'm afraid there is a process to getting up there. Everyone needs to apply for admittance. The owners do a screening. It takes a while to get approval."

Now that piqued his interest. "Sounds exclusive. Do many people get approved?"

"I couldn't begin to know. They keep the list very private."

Cyrus was intrigued. If the owners were exclusive, it meant the list of approved patrons would be small. The fewer people allowed in a place, meant fewer germs.

"Can you give me an application, please?"

"Sorry only the owners give those out."

"Then may I speak to the owners?"

"They aren't in."

Cyrus blew an exasperated breath. "When do you expect them?"

"They usually roll in about the time the VIP section opens. I guess they like to keep the same hours as their…" Rolling her eyes skyward, she put her fingers in the air making quotation marks to emphasize her next words. "…exclusive clientele."

The hostess glanced back over her shoulder at a couple who had entered the restaurant. "I need to go. Your waitress should be here shortly."

While she scampered off to fetch the couple, Cyrus slid his chair closer to the table and tucked his legs under the floor length tablecloth. He ran a hand over the white material, noting the softness. The demon moved the china plate slightly, so it sat squarely before him and lifted one of the silver forks to inspect it. The place setting and stemware bespoke of wealth as did the richness of the tablecloth. They may serve a home cooked meal, but they did it with class. He couldn't help but wonder just how much finer the dining upstairs might be.

After ordering a meal, he took his time to peruse the dining room. The Victorian period wallpaper depicted a flower design that appealed to him. Electric sconces made of iron filled the room with soft ambient light to complement the lit candles centered on the tables, each of which sat in a bulbous glass dome surrounded by sprigs of fresh greenery and Baby's Breath. Completing the ambiance, soft orchestral music played in the background.

Yep, this place is definitely worth the risk, Cyrus decided when his waitress brought him a basket of bread and placed it on his table along with his drink. He ripped the bread with his fingers, buttered it lightly, then popped it into his mouth savoring the buttery goodness.

The rest of his meal tasted just as decadent. The pot

roast was so tender he ate it with a spoon because when he tried to stab it with his fork the tines had pulled right through the meat. The dessert was a chocolate soufflé with white chocolate mousse, done to perfection.

He could not help but wonder if the food was the same upstairs. He had difficulty imagining anything better being served, but he wanted to know.

After glancing out the window, he beckoned the waitress over to his table. "Are the owners here yet?"

"I don't know. Why? Was there something wrong with your meal?"

Cyrus shook his head. "No. The meal tasted great. I just hoped I might speak to the owners about applying for the VIP section."

"Oooh," sighed the server, clearly relieved. "I'll check."

Cyrus stretched his legs under the table, crossing them at the ankles, and settled back in the chair to wait. Hands laced across his full belly, he indulged in one of his favorite pastimes, people watching.

His skills of observation had been honed over the years. It was one of the things that made him such a good guard. He paid attention to the details, watched people's body language. More than once his eyes had gained him valuable information. Tonight was no exception.

He forced himself to remain still, appearing relaxed, as he watched three men walk through the door. The first two in the door were of little consequence to him though he noted the predatory way they moved. The last one, however, set him on edge.

His face seemed familiar, but a little fuller than before. His hair had been duller, dirty and matted not shiny and healthy, but it was definitely the same man. Not a man, he reminded himself.

A vampire!

His eyes tracked the trio. They moved in unison across the room to the stairs. A burly man now stood next to the velvet rope. The shortest of the males approached the bouncer who nodded once in acknowledgement and unchained the rope allowing the trio to pass.

At the top of the stairs the former prisoner opened a mirrored glass door to a foyer area, encouraging his companions to enter before him. A beautiful blonde hostess greeted them from behind a podium with a smile.

The jovial group left his sight when the door closed behind them.

His mind replayed the scene adding the conversation he had had earlier with his hostess as the background music. *They usually roll in about the time the VIP section opens. Doesn't open until dark. Screening process done by the owners. Very private. I guess they like to keep the same hours as their exclusive clientele.*

His mind came to the only conclusion possible. The V in VIP stood for vampires.

He pulled the cell from his pants. This would make Jara's day. He just hoped the others could get there in time since they were spread out all over the city.

****

Demetri sent his awareness out through the building, the act as automatic as breathing. Among the human and vampiric energies, he detected several blank spots. "Do you feel that?" he asked the fellow Alphas sitting across from him.

Marcus' brows furrowed over his brown eyes. "Feel what?"

"Exactly."

"Cousin, you are not making sense. Are you sure your head is drilled on straight?"

Marcus chuckled. "You mean is he sure his head is *screwed* on straight."

"Forget about my head," Demetri growled. "Do you feel that?"

"Are you referring to the dead spots?" Nicholai ran a hand through his shaggy, black hair.

Demetri nodded his head succinctly. "Exactly."

"Do you think there are demons here?" A fierce look marred Nicholai's face. "I would like nothing better than to find some demons on which to take my revenge, not only for the one who attacked Juliette, but for your treatment as well, cousin."

Marcus faced Nicholai who sat next to him in their booth. "Whoa. Before you too get carried away, you should know the building has titanium. Big sheets of it line the rooms upstairs. That's probably what is blocking your senses." He turned his gaze to Demetri who sat across from him in the booth.

Nicholai cleared his throat. "Titanium could explain the blank spots since our senses can't penetrate it."

A pretty vampire approached the table. She squatted beside the table, giving the males a nice view of the bosom peeking out of her low-cut shirt.

"How may I help you this evening? Would you like to start with drinks?" She flashed a demure smile which showed the tips of her fangs.

Marcus spoke first. "Bring me three fingers of Lag."

"I'll take a vodka mixed with some AB negative." Demetri's deep voice drew the woman's attention. "Make sure the vodka is cold."

"Is there any other way to serve it?" She gave a wink.

Demetri's answering grin reached the slight lines by his eyes. "No, there's not, but most Americans don't seem to realize that."

"I'll have the same, except make the blood O positive," ordered Nicholai.

"Right." The waitress tapped her pencil on her pad and stood. "Okay, so that was a Lagavulin and two truly Bloody Marys, one with O pos and the other with AB neg. Got it. I'll be right back."

Nicholai turned his attention to the male sitting across from him. "So, Demetri, Juliette said I needed to talk to you."

That cannot be good. A groan escaped the warrior's lips. "Are you sure now is the best time, cousin?"

"No, but there is no time like the present."

Marcus slapped a friendly hand down on Nicholai's shoulder. "Hey, congrats. You didn't mess that saying up!"

Nicholai gave an inelegant scoff. "I do know some of the English vernaculars."

"Yeah, but hearing you mess them up is way more fun," Marcus teased as the waitress arrived with a tray of glasses in record time thanks to preternatural speed.

"Thanks, Hun." Marcus took a glass from her hand and dropped a bill on the tray.

She winked at him. "You're welcome, sexy." She took the remaining glasses from the tray one by one, handing them to the two Russians. "Anything else you boys need? I'm a full-service kind of gal."

The innuendo hung in the air for a few seconds before Nicholai spoke. "We are all mated, so we'll only be needing drinks tonight."

Looking a bit forlorn, the server tossed her hair with her hand. "Your loss. Let me know when you are ready for more drinks."

She turned to walk back to the bar, swaying her hips suggestively as she went.

Nicholai downed his drink in one swallow. Putting the emptied glass down on the table, he fingered the rim as he spoke, keeping his eyes downcast. "Speaking of heartmates…as I was saying before we were interrupted, Juliette wanted me to talk to you."

The alcohol burned Demetri's nose when he lifted his glass to his lips. Knowing he would need a fortifying sip, he took a drink and waited for Nicholai to continue. Anticipation twisted his gut.

"You know the women have been spending a lot of time together the past couple of days getting all the stuff done for the wedding." Nicholai cradled his empty glass in his hands, waiting until Demetri nodded his head before he continued. "So, Juliette has gotten to know Tatiana, and she thinks you are going about wooing her all wrong."

Disbelief widened Demetri's eyes. "I have followed your advice. I have backed down, given her the control. I have been taking things slow. I even agreed to be the fucking Easter Bunny to show her I am a man of my word. What more can I do?"

Marcus raised his glass in salute. "I can't thank you enough for that by the way. Saved my ass from having to do it."

"You wouldn't have fit in the damned costume," Demetri growled.

"Christina still would have made me do it." Marcus chuckled. "Probably would have altered it herself to make sure someone played the part. I have no idea why, but she feels it is imperative the children see Mr. Bunny during the party."

Nicholai lifted his empty glass, shaking in the direction of their waitress. When she looked his way, he held up one finger indicating he would like another before placing the glass back on the table. "Juliette said Tatiana was shocked you agreed to do it."

"Tatiana wasn't the only one shocked," Demetri muttered around the lip of his glass, then took a sip.

"She noticed you and Tatiana haven't seen much of each other these past two days. Apparently, Tatiana mentioned you tried to force some information from her mind."

Demetri's eyes widened slightly in surprise, his brows pulled down so hard they nearly touched.

What was his cousin talking about? When had he tried to take information from his heartmate's mind? They had barely spoken to each other the past two days. In fact, Tatiana seemed to be avoiding him ever since they had been at the counseling center talking about how much he had changed since the kidnapping...*Ohhhhh yeah.*

Now he remembered.

So that explained why she'd been avoiding him. She was upset about him trying to find the memory of her traumatic event.

"I was trying to find out what she had been through," Demetri confessed. "She won't tell me what happened."

Their waitress appeared and gave Nicholai his drink which he took with a thank you before handing her money. Waiting until she had left, he turned his attention back to the single male at their table. "Perhaps she is not ready to confide in you just yet."

"She is my mate. I want to know everything about her, especially if someone has hurt her. I must know what happened, so I can avenge her."

Marcus finished his scotch, setting the glass loudly on the table, and waved a finger at the waitress when she turned at the sound. "Maybe Tatiana has already dealt that revenge. She seems like the kind of gal who is used to taking care of her own problems."

"But as her mate, I have to know. I have to help her through it."

"And who is helping you through it?" Nicholai asked with a raised brow. "Have you discussed your time with the demons with her?"

"Of course not. She doesn't need to hear all the graphic details."

"Why?" asked Marcus after taking his refill from the server and handing her another folded bill.

"Because the details would be disturbing."

"No. I meant why are you not letting someone help you through it?"

"Because I'm fine."

Marcus leaned his forearms on the table. "Christina says it always helps to talk through a traumatic event. It is why she opened the counseling center, to help her and the other women who had been taken by Michael to recover. She says therapy is a crucial part of the healing process."

"Perhaps for a woman. I do not need therapy."

Nicholai took a sip of his Bloody Mary. "Do you think Tatiana went to therapy?"

Demetri pondered the question. "Probably not. But then I don't know because she won't share anything about that time. That was why I was trying to get the information from her memories." He finished the remainder of his drink in one thick swallow and motioned for their waitress to join them. Once she arrived he said. "I need another and no blood this time, just straight vodka. Hell, bring me the whole bottle."

"Right away." Her form blurred as she crossed the room, grabbed a bottle from the freezer behind the bar and returned, handing it to the surly male. "Here you go. Straight from the freezer."

"Thanks," he murmured then handed her a couple folded bills. "Keep the change."

She unfolded the bills. Her eyes widened at the amount. A genuine smile lit her face, reaching the corners of her eyes. "Thanks! Let me know what else you boys need. Anything. Anything at all. I mean it."

"We're set for now. Thank you," Marcus said, shooing her away.

He silently waited as Demetri twisted off the bottle cap with a snap of its metal seals. The vodka poured from the frosted bottle like syrup.

"Maybe you should talk Tatiana into trying one of the support groups at Christina's center," Marcus suggested.

"And how would I do that?"

"Offer to go with her." Nicholai finished his drink, allowing Demetri to fill his glass from the bottle.

The older Alpha eyed his cousin wearily from across the table. "Un-huh. And you think she would go for that, do you?"

"I think she would find it…" Nicholai paused, searching for just the right word. "…an honorable suggestion."

"I think she would find it a suspicious suggestion just as I do." He leaned forward, resting his forearms on the table. "I think you are trying to get me to go to therapy, and you are using my mate as bait."

"Sheesh, paranoid much?" Marcus tapped his empty glass. "Fill me up, Romanoff?"

Demetri sat silent as he filled Marcus' glass then his own. The alcohol had its desired effect. His mind was getting muddy.

Maybe this therapy idea wasn't such a terrible thing. If he could get Tatiana to go with him, she might open up about what had happened to her.

Demetri knew his friends meant well. If they had not been mated, he probably would have dismissed the advice. But perhaps they offered sage counsel.

"I will consider your therapy idea," he capitulated. Noticing his cousin's glass, he filled it before continuing. "But enough talk about my love life, comrades. It is unmanly."

"I'll tell you what's unmanly, using a word like love life," Marcus quipped.

Nicholai raised his glass. "To our love lives…may they be hot and sexy."

"Here, here," his fellow Alphas said in unison, raising their glasses with smiles on their faces. "To our love lives!"

They shared a chuckle while finishing the bottle then added three more to their table before their night was through.

"I'm afraid we are too drunk to drive home." Marcus leaned back against the booth.

Demetri rested his forearms on the table, hoping to steady his swaying head. "One of the benefits to being in a vampire bar is a vamp can dematerialize out of the place and no one will care."

"Payton can come in the morning to pick up the car," Marcus offered.

"Good, then it sounds like we can get out of here." Nicholai scooted to the edge of his seat.

As they stood to leave, they heard a commotion downstairs. After being assured their assistance was not needed by the waitress, they left, leaving three wisps of smoke and the bottles on the table.

****

Cyrus cringed as Jara shrieked, "Let me pass!"

The burly bouncer had obviously had enough. He grabbed her around the middle in a fierce bearhug that forced the air from Jara's lungs.

They'd been so close. Up those stairs sat the object of her obsession. All she had to do was get the guards up there to capture the creature. Instead of talking her way up into the room, she managed to talk her way into being thrown out of the restaurant.

The large man carrying her crossed the room quickly while her feet and arms flailed against him. He tossed her out the front door. Jara landed on her bottom, and Cyrus skirted the man to rush to her side, the other guards hot on his trail.

"I do not care what country you are princess of, you are not welcome here. Take your friends and go," the bouncer barked at her.

Jara appeared thoroughly insulted. "Imagine, being thrown out of a vampire bar. Why I never!"

Cyrus helped her stand and escorted her down the stairs. The other guards flanked the couple as they marched to the cars.

"I told you to let me do the talking," Cyrus admonished her.

She pulled her arm from his hand. "Cyrus, if you say one more word to me right now, I will rip you apart." Jara ground out between clenched teeth. "I can't believe the vampire was so close. 'Just upstairs' you said. 'Sure, it was him,' you said. 'Let me get us in,' you said."

Her hands fisted on her hips in ire. Anger hovered her hair away from her skull. Her eyes flashed deep red, the color of blood. "It is your fault, Cyrus, that I got upset and couldn't talk our way upstairs. Imagine you telling me you'll get us in, like I couldn't do it. You'll stay here all night and wait for the bloodsucker. Follow him to his lair. When you know where he sleeps, report in."

Fear snaked down his spine. The princess was known for her temper. It wasn't his fault she'd gotten thrown out of the place, but there was no way he'd tell her that.

He watched a guard hand her into the car, grateful she'd chosen to leave. After the others joined her inside the car, her window rolled down. The demon princess stuck her head out, pinning him with her eyes. "Oh, and Cy," her voice sounded sickeningly sweet. "Don't come to our hotel until you can tell me where the vampire is. It would be very bad for your health."

Her head disappeared into the car. The vehicle backed from the parking space with a screech and left. After it was out of sight, Cyrus climbed into his rental car, positioning himself so he had a good view of the front door to the restaurant. He turned on the radio and lowered the volume, then settled back against the seat to wait for the vampire to emerge.

"It's going to be a long night," he sighed.

Chapter 26

Tatiana's gaze traveled the room. The split-level library extended up through two stories of the home. Three of the walls had floor to ceiling bookcases with a mahogany ladder on rails that slid between the cases. The bookcases were filled to capacity with leather bound editions.

No doubt, these original editions are probably worth a fortune, she thought.

She sat in the middle of the room on a settee covered in a thin striped material. Julie perched in a matching wingback chair beside her. A round, marble-topped table with a Tiffany-style lamp separated the two women. The sound of a hitch in Juliette's voice drew Tatiana's attention from the perusal.

"I am just so grateful I found Nicholai." The brunette shifted in the chair then crossed her legs. "After my husband and girls were killed, I concentrated on getting through the days and nights. The grief was crippling. I thought I could escape it by running to England, but it didn't work."

Noticing the lift in Tatiana's brows, she clarified. "Don't get me wrong. The move gave me something to think about. I had new friends to make, new places to find. I no longer had to drive along the roads I had traveled with my family. So, in that respect, it helped a little, but they were still always on my mind.

"Instead of being in a park thinking 'this is where he kissed me for the first time,' I was in new parks thinking 'Steve would really like it here.'"

"I can understand that."

Tatiana sympathized. She'd thought of Demetri often during the year they were separated. Even though she'd been miles away trying to go on with her life, thoughts of him would creep into her mind. Much like a winding vine, her heartmate would wrap around her brain, sprouting up in the most unexpected places.

Juliette's eyes stared sightlessly out the window. "It was a living hell. One I couldn't escape. My life was one wistful moment after another. The grief overpowered me at times. Until I found Nicholai.

"He showed me it was okay to love again. At first, I felt awkward and very guilty, like I was cheating on Steve. But, little by little, I allowed my heart to open to the possibility of Nicholai." Julie's eyes glistened as she continued. "I was lucky. Nicholai understood that I had thought I'd lost the capacity for love. He helped me realize Steve would have wanted me to be happy, even if it meant I found love with someone else."

A large smile spread over Julie's face.

"Nicholai seems like a good guy."

Julie's eyes darted to Tatiana. "So is Demetri, Tatiana."

Tatiana lowered her gaze to the floor in capitulation. "I know. He is an honorable male." Her eyes rose to meet Julie's. Her face became unapologetic. "But he is also domineering and wants things his way."

Julie giggled. "Yeah, so I've heard, but it seems to me that if anyone would understand that behavior it would be you."

Tatiana's eyes widened at the remark. "What's that supposed to mean?"

"It means you and Demetri are two peas in a pod. If anyone can understand where all that controlling behavior comes from, it would be someone who is the same way."

Nicholai's mate smiled disarmingly, the only thing that kept Tatiana from leaving.

"Don't get me wrong, two control freaks together would be explosive from time to time, but sometimes amazing things happen after an explosion." A wistful look crossed Juliette's face briefly before she continued. "Look, all I know is finding my heartmate is the most amazing experience of my life. Once I allowed myself to be open to the adventure, it's been an unbelievable trip. You don't strike me as the kind of person to shy away from adventure...or difficulty."

The knowing expression on Julie's face gave Tatiana pause. Maybe Julie had a point. She'd been running from the situation with Demetri like a coward. And she never ran from a fight, it just wasn't her nature. Her fight-or-flight response was to fight.

Always.

Why was it so different with Demetri? Was it because he was a strong male? Did he scare her?

She mentally shook the questions from her mind, unwilling to examine them too closely for fear of the answers.

Fear.

It was seeping into her life, like a virus, attacking her strength and confidence.

She was a powerful woman. So what if Demetri

came on strong, she could be strong too. She could hold her own against any male, even Demetri Romanoff. Ugh! It was utterly maddening. Back and forth she'd wobbled for days on her opinion about the male.

I don't want to think anymore.

She had been doing too much of that over the past two days. Her body needed action. Training always provided a welcome outlet for her, a way to push away the world for a few hours and concentrate only on the feel of her body. She relished the physical punishment she slavishly inflicted for hours.

Since the terrible night she escaped from her captor, she had put herself through grueling workouts, honing every muscle in her body to its peak condition to make sure she was as powerful on the outside as she was in. She needed to feel that power, needed to be consumed by it. A basic workout in the gym wouldn't cut it. She needed something more intense, like combat, and knew exactly where to find it.

"I'm going to go workout," Tatiana announced, pushing off the settee.

"Didn't you work out earlier? Did I say something wrong?" The genuine concern on Julie's face was touching. The woman barely knew her, and yet she seemed to legitimately care. They were becoming friends.

"No. You gave me a lot to think about, and I think better when I'm moving."

Having changed into her leathers and made the trek across the vast estate, Tatiana opened the heavy door to the metal building and stepped inside. The room lit immediately from the bare bulbs overhead. They poured a wash of harsh light into the space, illuminating a bank of computers. Since Marcus had given her a brief rundown of the place the day before, she knew exactly which button to hit to bring the station to life.

A greenish glow cast over her when the monitors came online. The center screen flashed angrily, waiting for her command.

"Do I want to run a simulation program?" she read aloud.

"Yes." Tatiana's finger punched the Y key on the keyboard.

"Length?"

She paused a moment to consider the prompt. Tatiana wanted a thorough workout, needed to be left breathless and tired at the end, but she was also new to this so better to be safe than sorry. She typed fifty minutes onto the screen using the number keys.

"Pick a level."

She hit a number key, but the computer only beeped at her. She tried another number and got the same result. Her eyes roamed the console, landing on a dial encircled with the numbers one through ten. She turned the dial slowly clicking through each number until the arrow reached nine. That seemed to make the computer happy because it flashed a message up on the screen.

"For this series, you will need a sai and a gun," Tatiana read the screen. She smiled, looking behind her at the cache of weapons on the wall. "I can work with that."

She selected a nine-millimeter and strapped it to her leg in a leather holster before moving down the wall to retrieve the sai. She ran one finger lovingly over the traditional Okinawan martial arts weapon, following the basic form of the weapon. Her finger started at the point of the dagger-shaped metal truncheon. Next, the digit slid down the long blade to the two curved prongs called yoku that projected from the wrapped handle. Knowing they were generally used in pairs, she grabbed the twin.

She twirled them in each hand, testing their weight and balance. They felt good, like a familiar friend. A wide smile lit her face as her heart sped up in anticipation of combat. She felt alive, looked forward to seeing what the simulation room would bring.

Tatiana opened the door to the large room and winced when the harsh light from overhead assaulted her eyes. She heard the swish of the door whisper shut behind her, followed by the sound of a bolt sliding into place.

"There's no escape now, mwaahahahahaha," she joked, doing her best impression of an evil laugh. "Well, do your worst."

Her taunt echoed in the vast room. She stepped forward and felt the tile beneath her foot lower. A fissure opened quickly. The floor disappeared before her eyes. She pushed off from her small foothold, flung the sai out before her to free her hands and jumped to the other side of the gap. The sai skittered across the floor on the other side of the hole.

She landed against the side of the hole, her arms stretched across the floor while her body hung suspended into the opening. She clawed at the ground, her fingers seeking purchase. The toe of one boot found a slight crevasse in the concrete, giving her the boost she needed. Tatiana pushed off; the muscles of her leg straining under the leather, giving her just enough leverage. She shifted her leg up onto the ledge. As it crested over the opening, she spun her body out of the hole and rolled into a crouched position.

Her senses pushed out into the room, searching for the slightest movement. Tatiana listened for the tiniest sound that would indicate from where the next attack would come. Her blood rushed through her veins as much from the adrenaline as from the physical exhaustion. The world narrowed around her, her eyes and ears sharpened. The thrill of the fight surrounded her, and she welcomed it with open arms.

She stood slowly and retrieved the sai from the floor, taking one in each hand. Holding her arms out from her body, she turned in a slow circle waiting for the next attack.

She did not have to wait long.

A noise from above drew her attention. Looking up, she had but seconds to register the sandbag dropping from above. She slashed the bag in half, so it swung past her on each side of her body. Two more bags swung down on each side of where she stood. Tatiana stepped back, allowing them to hit together. A whoosh of air brushed her face from the near miss. As the bags ricocheted off one another and momentum took them in opposite directions, Tatiana did a round off between them.

Her hands shot out, using the truncheon to stab the bags. She let the bags take her weight. The female warrior kicked her legs over her head, one foot contacting with a third sandbag that had dropped behind her. The force of her kick split the bag, sending sand raining onto the ground below.

Tatiana pulled the sai from the bags and dropped to

the floor. A roundhouse kick, followed by a slash of a sai deflated one of the bags. She cartwheeled twice and landed a powerful kick into the other. As the sandbag swung from the momentum of her kick, Tatiana twirled the weapon in her hand, its blade reflecting the harsh lights from above. She brought both blades across the bag in an X pattern. More sand fell to the floor.

A large bag with a bull's-eye painted on it dropped several feet to her left, bouncing when the length of rope hit its apex. She faced the bag. Her eyes tracked the bouncing movement. Tatiana's muscular thighs pushed off the floor, but they had no momentum. Her boots slipped in the sand. Knowing she wouldn't reach the bag, she spun the blades in her hands and hurled them across the room. They hit the mark on the bag.

Tatiana twisted her body and shuffled her feet like a young ice-skater to keep her feet under her in the slippery sand. Finding her balance, she moved deeper into the chamber. The only noises in the building were the sound of her own breath and the soft sound of rushing sand.

She moved forward on silent feet, her eyes darting from side to side, hand hovering over the grip of the nine-millimeter. She flicked open the hood of the thigh holster with her thumb, ready to draw the weapon when needed.

Columns pushed up through the floor, spaced several feet apart. She advanced between them, turning as she went to make sure nothing popped up behind her. The sound of metal froze her in her tracks. She turned. A large metal square painted with a silhouette of a man hurtled toward her at preternatural speed. The weapon was in her hand before her mind thought to put it there.

Backing away, she emptied the magazine into the target.

Noticing the slide of her gun had locked back, she did a series of back flips to get away from the pursuing silhouette. The gymnastic move gave her enough space that she had time to eject the magazine and reload.

Cocking the gun, she fired, her aim true. The blasts from the gun competed with the sharp noise of the bullets hitting the target. Gunpowder tickled her nose. A second target swung down from the tall ceiling. Tatiana leapt onto one of the columns and took aim as it descended. She peppered the second silhouette with holes until it came to a stop. She spun the gun in her hand, a smirk lifting the corner of her mouth.

"Damn, this is fun."

Tatiana jumped to the floor. She held the gun in front of her with a straight arm, her legs crossing in front of each other as she stalked over the ground. Her eyes scanned the room, looking eagerly for the next target.

With a loud click, the lights in the room went off. Darkness enveloped the space. A digital voice broke the silence. "You will need no weapons for the remainder of the simulation."

A spot light clicked on, its light showing on a far wall. Above her, something moved along a metal track. It slid to a jerky stop, and two ropes dropped from the ceiling, suspended from the track.

She prided herself on trying a large variety of training techniques. These included various martial arts, fighting styles, and strength training. Tatiana not only used weights to increase her strength, but also aerial silks and ropes from time to time. She found they not only improved her strength but also increased her agility, both of which came in handy during combat.

Tatiana unstrapped her holster then laid both it and the gun on the ground. Next, she removed her boots and padded barefoot to the ropes. She climbed a rope halfway and looped it around her foot, creating a hold. Taking the second rope in her other hand, she wrapped a rope around each wrist a couple of times. She flexed her arms as she kicked loose the foothold and dangled in midair.

Suspended, like a bird in flight, Tatiana began a routine on the ropes.

Chapter 27

Demetri materialized in his room at Marcus' plantation, immediately crossing to the suite bath. He splashed some cold water on his face, hoping it would sober him up. Vodka made his brain a bit hazy. His mind replayed the time at the bar. He had needed to get a little perspective where Tatiana was concerned, and now he had it.

He'd been rather brutish with her. If he was to be honest, he had to admit even the first time they met he'd acted like a bully, forcing her to spar with him just to prove he was bigger, stronger. Of course, the behavior had earned him a kiss, albeit a dangerous one.

A smile graced the thin face reflected in the mirror as he remembered the first time they sparred. Her athletic body pressed against his. The sensation of her soft lips had been heaven until he had felt the tip of her blade press into his neck. Her catlike eyes had flashed angrily at him when he pulled away.

He chuckled.

His tigress warrior deserved respect. What she did *not* deserve was his high-handed treatment.

His gut twisted. He'd taken her for granted, assumed she would desire to be his heartmate and understand their mating was inevitable. He should have known his tigress would fight the pairing. She fought everything with a fiery passion that got his blood boiling.

He had been going about this all wrong. Tatiana was the kind of woman who met aggression with aggression. He needed to back down, let her come to him as if she were a wild animal he needed to tame. He smoothed his hair back in a leather tie and went in search of his heartmate.

Finding Julie in the library, he slipped into the room. "Hello, Juliette."

She looked up from her book. "Please call me Julie or Jules. Juliette sounds so formal."

Demetri nodded. "As you wish. Have you seen Tatiana this evening?"

Julie smiled and closed the book around a finger to save the page. "I have. She and I had a long conversation…about you mostly."

Demetri flinched. He could only imagine what Tatiana might have said about him.

"Do I want to know what she said?"

"I'd never break a confidence. Sorry. But I can tell you she left here with a very pensive look on her face saying she was going to work out."

"Pensive look?" the Alpha repeated. "Pensive good or pensive bad?"

Jules laughed, the sweet sound brought her heartmate to the room.

"And what is so funny?" Nicholai placed a charming kiss on her forehead.

"Demetri would like to know if Tatiana had good things to say about him."

"If you want to know, cousin, why don't you go find her, and ask the woman yourself?"

A genuine smile lifted the corners of Demetri's

mouth. "I think I'll do that. Julie said she was going to work out."

Confusion drew Nicholai's dark brows down. "I just came from the gym. I had to go down to get this." He shook a bottle of the massage oil and gave his mate a pointed look. "She wasn't in the gym."

Demetri sent his awareness flowing through the house. Feeling the energy of everyone except Tatiana, he pushed farther out onto the property, over the fields to encompass the newest addition. It was there he sensed her. A shiver of dread raced down his spine.

Find her? Nicholai asked.

Yes, she is out in the combat simulation building.

By herself?

Yes.

You must go to her. She should not be there alone. There is no one to spot her if she is training.

Demetri dematerialized from the room immediately.

His form coalesced in front of the computer station. When the Alpha read the message flashing on the monitor, his heart seemed to drop to his toes.

'Warning; level nine confirmed, safeguards off.'

His heart beat a furious rhythm. Tatiana was in danger.

Demetri dashed to the door and pulled. It moaned under the pressure of the pull but did not open. He gave the door another hard tug. Still the damned thing did not budge.

He crossed back to the computers and peered out the one-way glass that separated the computer station from the simulation room. His racing heart skipped a beat when he noticed the gaping hole in the floor. His eyes tracked up the length of the room to several shredded bags hanging limply from ropes. He didn't miss the skid line in the sand below.

Questions flooded his brain. Had she fallen in the slippery sand? Was she lying in there hurt? And just what the hell did the computer mean by the safeguards being off?

The dark room forced him to strain his eyes to see a series of targets with bullet holes. He allowed himself hope that Tatiana was the one to put the holes there and not some automated gun. Next, he imagined a semi-auto shooting through his heartmate to pepper the target behind. The hope crashed to the ground.

He clenched his eyes shut against the mental image, horrified. Panic gripped him in its suffocating hold, making it difficult to draw air into his lungs. He forced his eyes open, desperately searching the room for some sign of Tatiana.

A spot light hit the far wall. He saw the outline of his mate. She stood. That had to be a good sign.

Relief flooded his body, bringing with it an adrenaline dump that made his hands shake. Under his watchful gaze, she unstrapped something from her thigh and laid it on the ground before taking off her boots.

His relief was short-lived when he saw her pull herself up the ropes and hang suspended between them. She would break her neck. With no safety net below her, a fall wouldn't kill her, but it would certainly do damage.

She began a warm-up on the ropes. Tatiana moved with an effortless grace, twisting her body to wind the ropes around her. Catching one behind a knee, she held the other with both hands stretching her body out between them. She turned in on herself and thrust back out, spinning like a coin on its side.

The ropes slowed, and Tatiana moved again, her body a flowing concert of muscles as she stretched from one hold to the next. Awe softened the tension in his shoulders. Never had he seen such a beautiful sight. Her movements were controlled, precise, their fluidity painting a picture of perfection.

With each shift of her supple body, his apprehension gave way to amazement. She was alluring. The sight of her body moving in sensual ways enticed him. The speed of the movements would have been barely perceivable to the human eyes, but his eyes tracked every one. The vision she created mixed with the roller coaster ride of emotions to create a heady combination that hardened his body.

****

Like a cirque artist, Tatiana worked the aerial ropes, coming to a rest suspended between the ropes in a full split, a foot purposely tangled in each rope. After bringing her hands to the ground for support she raised her legs into a handstand and untangled her feet. Not ready to stop just yet, she climbed the rope again.

Twisting one of the ropes around her leg, she pinned it in place with her other thigh and let go. She dangled upside down, only the strength of her legs keeping her there. Carefully she released the pressure between her thighs, circling the rope as she descended slowly toward the floor while still inverted.

Movement along the wall garnered her attention. Her eyes tracked as small square cavities slid open in a line up the wall. Anticipating what may come, she quickly changed positions. Tatiana wrapped the rope around her waist, then twisted her body rolling up the rope, so she ascended the line just in time to avoid the series of arrows that shot from the wall. They chased her up the rope, the final one nicking her leg.

She allowed the line to hold her weight at the roof. Hard puffs of air pushed from her lungs from the effort while she blocked the painful nick from her mind. The sound of movement along the opposite wall drew her gaze. Her yellow eyes widened when she noticed identical squares sliding open on the wall. Beginning at the ceiling, another series of arrows flew in her direction. Releasing her hold on the rope she rotated down the material. With her legs held straight from her body like a ballerina spinning on a jewelry box, she tumbled toward the floor as fast as the line would allow.

Her hands gripped the rope, one above her body the other below, to stop the descent just before she reached the floor. She hung suspended only a few feet off the ground. More air rushed from her lungs.

"Session terminated," the disembodied electronic voice said as the lights came on in the room to replace the spot light.

Tatiana closed her eyes in relief. Her muscles burned from the abuse, but the awareness of the limbs growing stronger and more agile felt good. She concentrated on her body, the sensation of the rope in her hands, the way it constricted around her waist. Her awareness heightened when the air stirred around her like a gentle summer breeze. Warmth surrounded her, cocooned her in its softness. *Softness* and *strength*, she amended sensing a subtle, coiled strength just beneath the surface.

Her eyes snapped open. Struggling to focus in the harsh light, Tatiana blinked several times before realizing a pair of blue jeans with a very manly bulge right at eye level stood before her.

"Demetri," she said on a breathy sigh, her eyes rising to meet his.

The intense look on his face, something between anger, fear, and hunger, made her swallow. She couldn't tell which emotion ruled, wasn't sure she wanted to know. He looked like he could take her head from her shoulders or maybe devour her body with his mouth, either way he hovered over her like a predator wanting its prey.

She twisted vertical and released the grip on the ropes when her feet touched the ground. She intended to be on level ground to deal with this male.

"Do you have any idea how stupid it was to run a simulation with no one to spot you? You could have been injured." Demetri's voice was harsh, heavy with a mixture of passion and anger. "When I saw those arrows shooting from the walls to chase you up and down the rope, when I noticed one had nicked your incredible thighs, everything but your safety was forgotten. I had to get to you. Now seeing you safe, knowing the simulation is over and you are out of danger, I don't know whether to throttle you or kiss you."

The passion in his steel eyes betrayed him. He cared for her. It was plain to see in the depths of his stormy eyes. Her heart softened toward the warrior. She cupped his chin with her hand.

"I'm fine. See." She turned in a circle holding her arms away from her body. "No harm done."

Demetri knelt before her, his large hand circling her thigh. "What I see, is that you were scratched."

Using the tear made by the arrow, he ran a finger inside the leather pants and traced the light pink line.

Tatiana's body trembled, whether from the ropes or from the male kneeling before her she was not sure. The light touch from her mate sent a river of desire coursing through her blood, the sound of her heart pounded in her ears.

"See it's fine. I've almost completely healed." His hands ran up her thighs. "What do you think you are doing?"

Demetri looked up from his task. "I think I am making sure my heartmate is uninjured." His hands traveled around her hips to the zipper on the back of the pants. He lowered it, the sound of the slide sinful. Demetri began to peel the leathers from her hips, but her hands grabbed his.

"Hey," she protested, but the sound of his voice stilled the rest of her challenge.

"I need to see you, Tatiana. See with my eyes you are truly all right. See that my mate is not harmed."

His need pulsed from him like a beacon, surrounding her in its intense light. Growing up, she'd heard stories about heartmates possessing an unnatural need to know the other was safe. Perhaps it was self-preservation because when one heartmate died the one left behind often chose to follow his mate into the afterlife.

If he needed to see for himself, she would allow it. Modesty didn't concern her. Not when Demetri's presence overwhelmed her. His touch, his scent, his voice—all called to her.

Her hands peeled from his. The action giving him permission, Demetri continued his course without saying a word. He pulled the pants to her ankles, lovingly caressing each as she stepped from them, leaving only her black panties and leather top. His hand traveled up the calf of the uninjured leg. His fingers brushed over her skin in a gentle caress. Higher it traveled, searching for any sign of injury. He touched the inside of her thigh; the muscle twitched slightly beneath the pads of his fingers. His hand left her flesh for the briefest of moments then it encircled the other calf and worked its way up the injured leg.

"When I saw the arrow slice your leg, I realized you have become the most important thing in my life. The thought of you injured tore my heart from my chest. Don't ever do that to me again, woman. My heart could not take it."

He leaned forward and ran his tongue down the fading line on her leg. Tatiana did not need the healing properties of his saliva to aid in the regeneration, but she didn't protest the gesture. She couldn't. The moment his warm tongue began laving moist kisses along her leg she'd been lost to the sinuous sensation. Her voice failed her when she tried to speak. Instead, a low moan passed through her lips.

"I want you, Tatiana." His breath ghosted hot against her thigh when he spoke. "I want to lay you down right here and make you scream my name."

She closed her eyes at the sound of his raspy voice. By the heavens, she wanted that too. She'd never wanted anything more in her life. Did she dare? Was Julie right that the bond between heartmates was so special it could overcome all obstacles?

If she allowed herself permission to explore this relationship with Demetri, might she find a love like Julie and Nicholai's? She had never had much use for the emotion.

In her experience, love was obsessive and destructive. But maybe it could be precious and giving. Christina and Julie certainly made finding your heartmate seem like the best thing in the world. They had made her reconsider her stance on the concept. Having a heartmate had some redeeming qualities. One of which was the amazing way he could make your body feel.

She jumped when the backs of his fingers brushed against her core. A sensation akin to electric shock coursed through her body. Tatiana reached down, grabbed him by the shoulders and pulled him to his feet.

"Okay."

He waited, possibly expecting to hear more, but she offered no other words.

"Okay, what?" he asked as confusion furrowed his dark brows.

"Lay me down and make me scream your name."

Chapter 28

Demetri closed his eyes and sent a silent prayer of thanks up to the heavens. He'd expected his invitation to be turned down. Braced for the rejection which did not come, Demetri had reminded his inner beast to let her be the one in control. When they made love for the first time it would be her decision. Oh, he might stroke the fires a little, but she would be the one to pour gasoline on it.

Demetri slid a hand around her waist and pulled her body against his. He leaned down to feather soft kisses along her jaw. By the time he had reached her lips, his mouth met hers in fiery passion.

His emotions lay raw and spent from the roller coaster ride they took while watching Tatiana. One minute lust coursed through his veins when she moved sensually on the ropes. The next his heart was in this throat as he watched the shooting arrows. Lust ruled once more.

His warring emotions forbid him from being gentle. He felt tempestuous and inflamed, his body's urgent demands riding him hard. He needed to be fierce, almost punishing, and Tatiana seemed to revel in every second of the searing kiss.

A soft keening sound escaped her lips. The sound was like a sexy melody to Demetri's inner beast. He gripped her tighter against his body as he tried to rein the beast in. He wanted this woman. She was his mate, the other half to his soul. And he found her personality as intriguing as her body was sexy.

He broke the kiss. His gaze raked her body. Her long, lean legs, chorded muscles, and thin waist all drove him mad with passion. The way her hips swayed when she walked, the slight bounce of her small breasts. She was walking sex. It made his mouth water.

Sheer perfection, he thought.

His hands slid up her back, making their way around her body to cup each breast. They were barely a handful, but they made his shaft jump in response. Perfectly round, they rested lightly in his palms, like delicate china—beautiful and stunning. His thumbs brushed across her nipples. They pebbled under the thick leather.

"So responsive," he mumbled, backing her body until she hit the wall.

His hands left the globes long enough to open the bustier and peel it away, then they were back touching the creamy globes that beckoned him so. His mouth replaced one of his hands. He nipped at the breast before taking it between his lips to suckle.

Tatiana pulled the chord from his hair, freeing the strands. She ran her fingers through it and pulled back in surprise.

"You got a haircut."

"Um-hmm," he murmured around her soft skin. "It was too long."

He pulled away from his ministrations when a thought struck him. "Did you prefer it long?"

She ran her hands through the strands and made it frame his face. It fell just to his shoulders. "It's perfect," she breathed.

Cupping his face with her hands, she drew him in for a kiss. An emotion he could not name took him, working him into a frenzy as his mate kissed him. She deepened the kiss, inviting him into her mouth to explore and taste. His tongue ravished her, driving her need higher.

Tatiana's hand left his face. She pushed away from the wall, used the momentum to turn their bodies and pinned Demetri. She pushed into the kiss, changing it from a gentle loving gesture into something carnal and demanding. Her tongue traveled into his mouth to taste her lover. She pulled back and clasped his face between her hands. She licked her lips.

"Fates above, you taste of spice and maleness…with just a hint of vodka."

"Is that bad?"

"Exactly what I would expect from my Russian. Delicious. Addictive."

Her mouth descended on his as her hands worked blindly at his clothing. In a rush, together they unbuttoned his shirt, so she could slide it off his shoulders before she helped him out of his pants.

Thank the Fates, I went commando, he thought as she lowered to her knees and removed his jeans.

She threw the offending cloth on the growing pile. Her eyes roamed his body.

"You are healed," Tatiana announced, noting how there were no more visible marks from his torture.

Demetri gazed down at her with a hunger in his eyes that spoke of his need. He had to be inside her, feel her heat wrap around him. She looked so sexy, kneeling before him like she awaited a command. Waited for him to take control.

He gritted his teeth, fighting the instinct.

She is the one in control, he reminded himself. *Let her take control.*

His shaft jumped when she took it in her hand and leaned forward. She licked the length of him, swirling her tongue around the sensitive tip while her hand worked up and down in a tantalizing rhythm. Up and down, in and out. The combination nearly drove him to his knees.

He fought his beast for control. It wanted to grab her by the hair, thrust his hips at her, taking her mouth like he would take her inner core. Sweat broke out on his forehead from the effort to remain still. He clenched his hands at his sides to keep from thrusting them into her hair.

The effort was rewarded as she worked him masterfully, sending a wave of desire coursing through his body. She built speed. The combination of sucking and rubbing caused him to throw his head back and growl with need.

Who had said something about letting her have control? Was it Marcus or Nicholai? It didn't matter who had said it but whoever it was had been right. Giving control in the bedroom could be amazing. The sight of her working his length pushed all thoughts of others from his mind. He was close, so close to spilling his seed.

"Tatiana," he warned, his accent pronounced. "You are about to push me over the edge, woman."

His patience spent, he lost the inner struggle. Demetri grabbed her under the arms and stood her before him. Taking control, he pushed a punishing kiss against her mouth. His tongue thrust between her lips, demanding entrance. Their tongues battled, pushing back and forth between their mouths, each struggling for dominance.

His mind hardly registered her moving against him. Her skin was there, then not. Her hand brushed his arm then was gone. Something touched his other arm. He didn't care. The kiss garnered his full attention until she pulled away. The smile on her face touched the fire in her eyes.

"I wasn't done." Tatiana placed her arms by her sides.

Demetri's eyes narrowed. She held the ropes in her hands. His arms pulled behind him. Realizing he'd been restrained, he knew a moment of panic until she dropped to her knees.

"Be still." She wrapped the ropes around each of his thighs, pulling them tight as she went. They forced the blood to his upper extremities making his erection thicken before their eyes. To his surprise, it pulsed in time to his heartbeat.

She tucked the ends of the ropes under her knees and went back to work. Tatiana locked her hand around the base of his thick shaft, then leaned forward to taste him once more. His mate groaned. The vibration moved up his shaft. Demetri arched, his head thrown back on his shoulders in complete ecstasy.

She had complete power over him and seemed to delight in the heady knowledge. Oh, he could break away from the ropes, if he wanted, but he didn't. Allowing someone else to be in control stimulated him. Surrendering to her freed him. He didn't have to think, only feel. The silkiness of her mouth drove him higher.

Not knowing when she would decide to stop, exhilarated him.

When he struggled against the ropes, she glanced up at him. Tatiana drew him into a long, slow glide of her mouth. She rolled her tongue around his velvet steel, circling the tip before letting it free of her hot mouth. She continued to stroke a hand along his most manly part as she fit her other hand to the shape of his hip. Long fingers traced the lines of his muscles, caressing and massaging him until he whimpered with need.

"Tatiana, please!"

Fates above, she was going to kill him. He couldn't take anymore. Nothing had prepared him for this. He accepted her caresses with carnal pleasure, his lips parted as he watched her ministrations.

She released him from the bonds and ran her hands over his muscular thighs to aid the circulation. A low growl garnered her attention from the task.

Demetri's fingers went for her panties. With a quick tug, the material gave under the pressure and tumbled to the floor.

His fingers slid into her core, testing her readiness. She moaned at the invasion. It was all the encouragement he needed. He lifted her from her feet, spun them and pinned her back against the wall. Her soft creamy skin pressed against his chest. Tatiana wrapped her legs around his waist, positioning her core above his erection. She took the hard power of his need in her palm.

His hips thrust upward, impaling himself inside her moist core to the hilt in one hard push. And just like that their power reversed. He now held the control. A delicious moan escaped her kissed swollen lips as he drove into her. Their flesh pounded, the sound muted only by the rush of blood in his ears. She met him thrust for thrust, their intensity increasing as did the pressure in him.

He inserted a hand between their bodies and rubbed tiny circles on the sensitive spot between her folds. She straightened, leaning back against the wall. When the orgasm took her, she cried out his name.

Soft gasps of need pushed between her lips as Demetri continued his attack. His body invaded hers, a thick, hard fullness that brought waves of pleasure so intense he struggled to stay in the moment. As he moved, he became lost to everything but the passion building between them. Tatiana clenched around him while she rode another crest of ecstasy to reach another climax.

Her arms wrapped about his neck, crushing her against his chest. As he continued his aggressive thrusts, she breathed hard for several minutes.

Catching her breath, she said, "I need to feel you flowing within, take all of you into me."

Her fangs lengthened from her gums and poked into her bottom lip. Her eyes tracked the muscles in his neck as they strained from his effort. The vein hiding just beneath the surface pulsed in time with his heart, in time to the rhythm he set for their bodies.

Along his neck, her lips slid. The scrape of tiny fangs against his skin drove him mad. He thrust harder, loving the way her body trembled with pleasure. Her teeth breached the flesh. The slight pain added to the ecstasy.

Her suckling drove him wild. The feel of her

wrapped around him while taking his blood was his undoing. Her blood called to him, and he refused to deny himself its pleasure.

His fangs slid from his gums demanding satisfaction. They found their mark at the base of her neck. He barely registered the sinful moan that vibrated against his lips as her sweet nectar flowed down his throat. He drew at her neck, taking her essence into him.

His hips thrust ferociously, almost brutally, their bodies crushed against one another. He sensed her in his mind, experienced the sinuous sensation he caused in her body. Her next orgasm crescendoed. It built until she pulled from his neck and threw her head back to scream his name once more.

He wanted it to last forever, but the feel of her inner muscles gripping him pushed him over the edge. His body rode the crest of the wave and had no choice but to fall over the precipice. His release boiled up through his balls and pulsed through filling her, branding her in a way far more primitive than his mark on her neck.

He stood holding his mate, his forehead resting against hers, their hard breaths mixing. Reluctantly, he lifted her and separated her from his body, instantly bereft at the loss. "We better get back to the house."

"Yeah, wouldn't want someone to come down here and see us like this."

Demetri noticed the flash of emotion that crossed her face, unable to name it. What was she thinking? What was she feeling? Was she regretting what they had done? The questions pinged around his brain while he dressed. Suddenly, he realized what their exchange meant.

They exchanged enough to create a mindlink. He felt it. Her emotions and thoughts were there in the back of his mind.

She watched him from the corner of her eye as she donned her shirt, saddened by the fact they had to get dressed. She would have been quite content to remain naked in his arms all night, but they really did need to get back to the house before the sun rose.

Tatiana tugged her leather pants up her beautiful legs. Why were those damned things so much easier to remove then put on? Of course, the lack of underwear didn't exactly help or the fact her muscles now screamed in agony from the abuse they had suffered at her hand this evening.

I could give you another massage, Demetri offered, zipping the fly of his jeans. *The last one seemed to help.*

Tatiana smiled at the memory. "Yeah, it helped all right." To herself she thought, *it about drove me out of my mind with lust.*

Never a bad thing between heartmates, Tatiana. I hope my touch will always be able to drive you out of your mind with lust.

The shock on Tatiana's face would have been comical if he had not experienced the mixture of emotions that accompanied it when she realized they had been communicating through a mindlink. He remained a quiet shadow in her mind, watching it process how the connection had happened. As it dawned on her they had exchanged enough blood during intercourse to establish the link, her hand raised to her mouth with a gasp.

It's all right, kotik kisa. *We are heartmates it was*

inevitable that we would create the mindlink.

Panic quickened the pace of her heart. She had just decided to give Demetri a chance to be her mate. She wasn't ready to know everything about him yet, and she definitely wasn't ready for him to know everything about her. Her panic turned to anger.

"Don't call me a kitty cat. And stay out of my mind."

"I can't stay from there anymore than I could stop breathing. I am sorry but being a part of each other's thoughts is natural for heartmates. You know that. You now have access to my thoughts as I have to yours. Nothing can be done to change that, and I wouldn't change it if we could. I love being in your mind."

He sent a comforting warmth over the link to sooth her mind and monitored her reaction.

She found the sensation nice, like being held in her mother's arms as a child. It gave her a sense of peace and tranquility. Due to the mindlink, she realized the feelings were meant to provide a sense of comfort not to be intrusive or highhanded. Even though she read Demetri's intent, she still found having someone in her mind too similar to the time she had been controlled.

She couldn't help the way the intrusion made her feel, like the room was closing in. Another male now had the ability to control her. The thought made her stomach roll.

Shhh. You do not need to worry, Tatiana. I would never try to use our link to control you. It is inconceivable to think any heartmate would do such a thing! To know someone once did such a terrible thing to you infuriates me.

Someone abused her! He tramped down the

growing anger. "Please tell me about what happened," he requested purposely speaking aloud to demonstrate he would wait for her to tell him rather than pull the information from her mind.

"I can tell you are not searching my mind. I appreciate the gesture, Demetri." She crossed her arms around her waist in a bracing hug. "I know you could easily take the information if you were so inclined."

"I would not do that, *kotik kisa*. You will tell me when you are ready."

She sighed. "Let's go back to the house first, then I will tell you what happened."

He reached for her hand, grateful when she allowed their fingers to interlace. Demetri escorted her back to Marcus' home, careful to stay out of her mind while they walked. He wanted to give her privacy. Let her be the one to decide when and how he learned about what had happened to her. It was a struggle. Demetri's instinct screamed at him to take the information that was his right to know as her mate, but honor won, and he restrained himself. He just hoped she would not change her mind, for he wasn't entirely sure what he would do if she did.

Chapter 29

Tatiana allowed Demetri to lead up the stairs, her feet sluggishly taking one step at a time. They were headed to her room to discuss the ordeal she'd been through in her youth. She didn't want to relive the awful memories. Dreaded it really, but she knew it was important for her heartmate to know the terrible truth. Having put the trauma behind her centuries ago, the thought of dredging the memories up like a decomposed body from a swamp made her stomach turn. But she owed it to her heartmate to share the story with him.

Owed it to him. A smirk came to her face. *Oh, how the mighty hath fallen.*

She shook her head; grateful Demetri did not see the action. It had only been a few days since she'd found him in the warehouse, but it seemed like a lifetime. She had always been drawn to him, at least physically, even before she discovered their destiny. Every minute in his presence strengthened the bond between them. At first, she believed the bond was simply chemistry in action, but now she knew better.

The past few days she had gotten to know him through actions and deeds. Demetri was an honorable male, willing to put personal pride aside to keep a promise. He had been so tender with the little girl at the counseling center, feeling genuinely guilty for not being able to find her mother. He took on the troubles of the world and blamed himself when he could not solve them.

As much as she hated to admit it, she could not blame the feelings for him on chemistry. And now that they had established a mindlink, it would be even harder for her to remain neutral about the man. His feelings for her poured over the link.

Demetri cared deeply for her, wanted to protect and care for her. Tatiana realized those were his motives behind the chauvinistic behavior. The knowledge made it easier to forgive his tyrannical behavior—not condone it but forgive it.

And the sex had been amazing. Mind-blowing. So hot, the passion still burned in her body.

Demetri glanced over his shoulder, one brow raised. Tatiana met his eyes, defying him to disagree.

I do not disagree that we were amazing and mind-blowing, but I must disagree on one thing. I did not have sex with you. We made love, he corrected through their link. He continued trying to quell the anger building in her mind. *Forgive my intrusion on your thoughts, but I cannot bear you thinking what we shared in the simulation room was anything other than me loving you.*

Reaching the door to her room, Demetri opened it, and indicated she should precede him. As she passed through, surprise made Tatiana misstep. She wasn't as upset as she thought she should be to discover Demetri had been monitoring her thoughts. In fact, it felt natural to have him there, like a familiar friend holding your hand during a time of hardship who sat quietly letting you go on and on about your life. No judgments, just quiet acceptance.

Maybe this is the connection my mother talked so much of in my childhood. Her mother had described the relationship between heartmates as a connection so deep you could wrap it around you, let it keep you safe in its love. But she and Demetri barely knew each other.

You can't love me, Romanoff. You hardly know me.

Search my mind, kotik kisa, *if you do not believe me.*

Demetri's long strides took him across her room to the bed. He sank onto the mattress then leaned against the decorative pillows resting against the headboard. Demetri stretched his legs out, crossing them at the ankles.

In stark contrast, Tatiana prowled the room like a caged tigress, her movements agitated, sharp. She accepted his offer, diving into his mind to find it open to her, all information there for the taking. The honesty of his love increased the speed of her pace. He cared deeply for her, wanted to protect her, see to her every need.

The emotions made her feel desired, cherished. It had been a long time since she had felt special to someone. An unsettling feeling twisted her stomach.

Wringing her hands, she pulled from his mind. The female warrior was unaccustomed to the emotions she sensed from him. They made her uncomfortable, added to her agitation. Her pace quickened again, her steps eating up the floor as she walked from one side to the other, every bit as fluid as a lion. And just as caged there in the room with him.

Demetri laced his fingers over his chest and settled deeper into the pillows. "Tatiana." The quiet timbre of his voice drew her from her thoughts. "Come sit beside me."

"No thanks. I'm good over here." She continued the pacing as she spoke. "I'm not sure where to begin."

Demetri lay stone still. *I know you are struggling to share your tale.*

Yeah, that was the understatement of the century. She had no idea how to start. *Give me a minute, Romanoff.*

I can do no other than give you what you need, Tatiana. You are prowling. You need to ease yourself. Listen to the sound of my breath.

Her mate took deep, even breaths as he sent a tranquil reassurance to her mind, encouraging her to follow his lead. He sat patiently, waiting for her to calm.

Tatiana stilled and locked eyes with Demetri from across the room. She matched her breathing to his, slow and steady. Demetri's calming presence in her mind gave her the peace she needed to begin the story.

"I had just come of age. My parents had taken me to our local fête. It was the usual event. All the eligible females donated blood to the eligible males at the party to see if any of them were a heartmate.

"We lived in a small town in Russia at the time, so the event was rather tiny. Only local vampires attended."

Demetri nodded his encouragement, remaining silent as she continued.

"There was a male there, named Sammael, who was several centuries old. He tried to woo me. We danced and chatted for a while. He mentioned he had watched me grow up. He owned a home near our property and would often cut across our land when going into town.

"Sammael seemed harmless enough, chatting with my father, dancing with my mother. He appeared to be a perfectly respectable gentleman. Everyone liked him."

Tatiana shook her head at the memory. How naive they had all been.

"When it was time for the males to taste our blood, he drank all the other female samples first, leaving mine for last. After tasting mine, he announced I was his. We were heartmates. Everyone congratulated us. My parents were ecstatic, so happy for me. 'Imagine getting lucky enough to find your mate during your first fête', my mother said while she hugged me to her."

A dark chuckle that held no humor burst through her lips. "Lucky. Ha. Luck had nothing to do with it."

Demetri's eyebrows furrowed over his steel-gray eyes. He cocked his head. "What do you mean?"

Tatiana's face clouded, and she cast her gaze to the floor. "The bastard lied. Sammael knew we were not heartmates. I found out many years later that he had once had a heartmate. She had been put to death when the local villagers discovered she was a vampire, making him turn rogue from her loss. So, he knew exactly what to say to my parents to make them believe I was his mate. He knew the right way to express the supposed feelings he had for me as a result of our,"—She put both hands in the air making finger quotes around the last word in her sentence—"bond. He whisked me away to his home that night, claiming his emotions for me were so strong he could not bear to be without me one more night. My parents did not resist. I can't blame them, he did seem completely sincere."

"Did you not protest?"

Tatiana moved to the bed. When she sat, the mattress sunk under her weight. Her eyes captured Demetri's, willing him to understand. "I was young, Demetri, and he seemed so sure. I didn't know what it was to have a heartmate. He was good looking and charismatic. I didn't realize what I felt for him was simple attraction and not the pull between heartmates."

A low growl emanated from the Alpha's throat. "He took advantage of your innocence. Tricking you into believing you cared for him more than you did."

"Yes. Once he got me to his home, all was lost. As I said, he was centuries old, much more powerful than I was both mentally and physically. As soon as we arrived at his home, he tried to…" She looked away, unable to meet her mate's gaze. She took several deep, steadying breaths before continuing the tale.

"He tried to take me to bed. When I protested, saying I wanted to get to know him better before we were together, he pushed into my mind and took control of my body. He marched me down the stairs of his home to his bedroom and forced me to—"

Demetri took her hand in his, squeezing it when she struggled to continue. His eyes were like Florida storm clouds, swirling with shades of gray that matched his turbulent emotions. "I don't need the details, Tatiana. I get the idea."

She stretched out beside him, keeping her hand in his. "I tried to run away. He caught me before I even got off the grounds. After that he either kept me chained to a bed or under his mind control at all times."

"Did no one ever come to see you? Try to help you?"

Tatiana sighed heavily, unshed tears burned her eyes as the memories pushed in. "My parents came of course. But Sammael would refuse them entry unless they dispatched notice ahead they were coming." She put a staying hand on his chest when Demetri started to protest. "It was a common courtesy at that time, so my parents thought nothing about the request, especially when every time they saw me I was under his control telling them how wonderful our life together was. He would force me to tell them I loved him with all my heart, that I was happy there with him. That the servants treated me well."

Demetri's body tightened as his anger rose. He struggled to keep his voice even. "There were servants in the home? Why did they not help you?"

Tatiana shrugged before settling on her back. She stared at the blue canopy over the bed.

"I was never really sure. Maybe he had them under his control. Maybe he threatened them. Or maybe he just paid them well enough it earned him loyalty. I never found out why they wouldn't help me, but they never did. Every time he left the house, I tried to escape. I asked them so many times to help me, but they never spoke to me, let alone helped me. After a few decades, I stopped asking them to help."

"Decades!" Demetri did not keep the anger from his voice. He pushed up onto one elbow, staring down at her with fiery eyes. "How long did you suffer at his hands?"

"I lost track of the exact amount of time. The nights began to mesh into one endless night. Every night the same routine occurred. He would wake, force me to perform in his bed, telling me he loved me as he was forcing me to comply with his wishes." She turned on her side and faced Demetri. Her eyes looked into his beseechingly. "You have to believe me, I never stopped fighting him. I never gave him what he wanted willingly."

Demetri pulled her into his arms and rested his chin on the top of her head. Emotions poured from him. He felt nauseated. Her story ripped his heart from his chest.

Fear wound its way into her brain. Would he think her somehow less worthy? Too weak to be his mate?

"Tatiana, I know you would have fought him with everything in your power. You are a fighter, like me. You would never have given him what he wanted no matter how much easier it would have made your life. I know better than most what that is like. No matter what the demons did to me, I never cooperated."

He believed her. Somehow, he did not see her at fault for what happened. She pulled it easily from his mind.

Tatiana relaxed into his hold and sighed contentedly. She'd never told anyone the details of her captivity before. Sure, her therapist had heard the gist of the story, but she had never before allowed herself to speak of the details of the mistreatment.

A weight lifted from her shoulders. She had confessed her most shameful secret, and her heartmate understood. He did not judge her. In fact, just the opposite, he commiserated with her. The knowledge gave her the courage to continue.

She snuggled into the warmth of his body, allowing his arms to give her the strength. "Eventually, one of the servants died in a stable fire so Sammael needed to find someone to replace him. He found someone on one of his trips to the coast. She came from China, sold to Sammael by a slave trader. Her name was Ming, but only I knew that because no one in the house ever cared enough to find out her name. To Sammael and the other servants she was simply Girl."

I know it is difficult for you to share your story.

His admiration flowed over their link. Tatiana blinked her tears away when his hand stroked her back in silent support. He remained silent, allowing her to continue unabated.

"Ming and I developed a trust over the years as only two people in a dire situation can. Eventually, she trusted me enough to teach me Kung Fu."

Tatiana pulled back from Demetri's chest and stared up at him with a sad smile. "I remember the first time she taught me a kata. I felt so powerful as my arms and legs moved through the series of punches and kicks. We worked for long hours when Sammael was not home. I practiced every movement over and over.

"I kept it a secret. Luckily, Sammael found me so inferior he never searched my memories. He believed in his ability to control me, to the extent he didn't care what I might be doing when he wasn't there."

A sharp pain lanced over Demetri. She entered his mind to find out why. He was thinking that she had been betrayed by those who should have protected and loved her. First her parents, then her supposed heartmate. He would devote his life, or even his death if necessary, to making sure she never hurt again. To avenge her for the wrongs done to her.

"I will kill the bastard for what he did to you!" Demetri growled. The sonorous sound came from deep within his chest cavity. "I will garrote him with his own viscera."

"What does that mean?"

"I will gut him with a dull knife and strangle him with his own intestines."

"You are about a century and a half late. I have already disposed of the male."

His chest expanded with pride. "I should have known you would find a way to best a vampire who possessed superior abilities. You are truly amazing, strong and capable. How did you kill him?"

Tatiana gave him a sanguine smile, the sharp ends of her fangs indenting her bottom lip. "As I mentioned, he was much older than I. He stayed awake long after the pull of the dawn forced me to sleep. As I aged, I became more powerful and began to force myself to stay awake.

"Often, he would be out at the whore house until after dawn, choosing to dematerialize into his bedroom after the household staff and I would be asleep. He thought to keep his indiscretions from the staff that way."

Tatiana wrapped an arm around Demetri's waist. "I continued my training with Ming. She helped me develop my mind as well as my body. Eventually, I became strong enough to stay awake after the dawn."

Darkness sealed the room with a soft whisper of metal sliding into place as the shutters covered the window and balcony doors. They would be safe from the sun's rays while the dawn painted its pink light across the sky.

"Please continue," Demetri prompted before pulling her close.

"One night I broke a leg off the chair in our room. I

got lucky, and it fractured with a point on one end. After cramming several books under the chair to hold it upright so Sammael wouldn't be suspicious, I tucked the stake under my pillow. I thought I was dead when Sammael got home and sat in the chair to take off his shoes, but the books held, and he never realized what I had done.

"I stilled my mind, using all of the skills I learned from Ming to make it appear like I was asleep in case Sammael tried to control me. Luckily, he was more interested in sleeping than me, so he crawled into bed and fell asleep quickly. Once I heard his breath even out, I took the stake and pushed it through his heart."

Tatiana hid a yawn behind her hand. Her body needed to rest after what she had put it through earlier in the simulation room. Between the workout and Demetri, she'd be plenty sore in the evening.

"I can tell you are fighting to stay awake to finish your story, but even a tigress warrior needs to rest."

Tigress warrior. I like the sound of that.

She easily read Demetri's own lethargy. A yawn threatened to take him as he burrowed his face onto the top of her blue-black hair.

"You are the most amazing woman I know, Tatiana." Demetri released her just long enough to pull the blanket from the bottom of the bed to cover them. "You battled a monster in your own home, then went into the world with no one to stand up for you, to watch your back. I hope you believe it when I tell you that you will never have to battle alone again. I will always have your back."

Tatiana realized they remained fully clothed, but quickly decided she was too weary to get out of bed to change. Her muscles ached, her brain ached, even her heart ached. Dredging up the long-buried memories made her emotional. There was a reason Tatiana never brought the memories out to examine. Her anger had fizzled as she spoke, replaced by exhaustion. She felt utterly drained.

Too tired to talk, she used the mindlink to communicate. *Thank you, Demetri. I know you will have my back. You'll probably never let my back out of your sight.* His chuckled told her she was right. *Now if you don't mind, I think this amazing woman is done talking. I'd like to get some sleep.*

For the first time since she had begun her tale, Demetri smiled wide enough to show his white fangs. *I would like to stay here with you if it's okay.*

She stretched languidly, curling against the warmth of his body. *I wouldn't want you sleeping anywhere else.*

****

Ringing rousted Jara from her beauty sleep. She stretched drowsily then rolled away from the warm body lying beside her in the bed. In the darkened room, her hand flopped about on the nightstand, searching blindly for the phone. Finding the offensive thing on the third smack, she picked up the receiver and silenced the screaming apparatus. Bringing it to her ear, she bit out between clenched teeth, "This had better be good."

Silence met her demand.

"Hello?" she said loudly enough to make the male next to her stir.

"This is Cyrus. I have news."

Excitement made her push up into a seated position with her free hand. "Tell me you found the vampire."

More silence from the demon on the other end of the line. "Cyrus, you did follow the vampire to his lair, didn't you?" Her anger stirred, turning her eyes red.

"I'm following someone now."

"The vampire?"

"Not exactly."

She blew out an exasperated breath. "It is too early in the morning to play these games. Are you following the bloodsucker or not?"

Jara's hand clenched down hard on the phone.

"I'm following a guy who looks a whole lot like Michael Gouch."

"Who?"

"You know, the actor who played Batman's butler on the sixties TV show."

"I never watch TV."

"You're kidding!"

The burly guard rolled her way, wrapping a beefy arm about her waist.

"I most certainly am not. I have no time to waste on something as asinine as TV. It irradiates your brain you know."

"Actually, it doesn't."

Jara gritted her teeth. "Did you call to discuss television or to share some important news? It had better be the latter."

"I called to let you know I waited all night for the vamps to leave, but they never did. This morning I noticed a lone SUV in the parking lot of the restaurant. The old man just came to get it. I believe he works for the bloodsuckers. He certainly looks like he might be a butler."

"When you know more, let me know."

"Are you planning on staying at the hotel today?"

"Yes, we will be meeting later to devise a plan of attack so once you tell us where the vampire is we will be ready."

Brakes screeched over the line. Cyrus let a series of vile curses flow.

"What is it?" Jara swatted the male hand making its way up her body, heading for her breasts.

"I caught a red light."

"You better not lose him." Jara stood.

She paced beside the bed. Her latest lover rolled onto his back with a moan. Were those Cyrus' fingers tapping on the steering wheel in irritation she heard in the background?

"Don't worry. I'm sure I can find him again. I know the direction he was heading."

Jara heard the sound of the rental car's engine when Cyrus left the light. "You see him?"

"Hold on…let me get around this guy…Yeah, yeah there he is. I found him. He is heading out of downtown."

"Don't lose him again, Cyrus. We are counting on you to bring us the location of the bloodsucker. I don't have to tell you what will happen if you don't."

Cyrus' silence told her he was processing the implied threat. "I know you do not tolerate failure. Hopefully, this guy will lead me to the vampire."

"You better hope so."

Chapter 30

The water sliding over her body felt delicious. Tatiana braced her hands on the wall of the shower, standing under the stream. She luxuriated in the way it washed over her, taking the slippery shampoo suds down the drain. She'd been so exhausted the prior evening she went to sleep without showering, but today was a new day, and she felt wonderful. Only her thoughts marred the otherwise perfect experience.

Since she awoke her mind had been racing, replaying the previous night like a record skipping on a turntable. Over and over the scene between her and Demetri ran through her brain. It was supposed to be just sex.

But it wasn't *just* sex. It had been glorious, hot, sensual sex. A beautiful expression of heartmates coming together as one. An amazing experience that still had her body humming, wanting more. She would have thought she'd be drained from the night before, but her body felt energized. Maybe it was taking his blood. Maybe it was him. She had expected it to be just a physical act, an urge that needed to be sated.

But she found her need had not been sated at all. In fact, just the opposite.

Being with Demetri was addictive, and she wanted more. Much more. Her well-intentioned plan shot to hell by the male lying in her bed. The act had been much more than physical. It had been intimate, pulling them into each other's lives. Tying them to one another.

A smile graced her face. She could no longer deny her feelings. They refused to allow her to confine them. They poured from her heart to engulf her, bringing with them a sense of tranquility and peace she'd never experienced.

She spent decades living alone, isolating herself from others so she would not be hurt again. Sex was supposed to be impersonal, but who was she kidding? One night with her mate had taken down the barrier to her heart.

Damn that male!

He had swept into her life, and in just a few days, he'd broken through her defenses. Completely overwhelmed her. Made her desire him. Crave him.

His scent remained on her skin. Fainter now, but still there. She inhaled the husky musk into her lungs. Her sexuality had lain dormant for decades, now it demanded satisfaction. It demanded her heartmate. She pressed her thighs together, relishing the pressure on her sensitive core.

She pushed away from the shower wall, turned off the water with a twist of her wrist, and toweled off. Opening the door to the bath, she padded over to the bed and looked down at her mate who remained clothed from falling asleep while cradling her the night before. Her heart swelled with emotion, betraying her true feelings for the male.

She was his as he was hers. Their bond could no longer be denied. They were heartmates in every sense of the word. He was the other half of her soul, he completed her. She had never expected to find love.

Never wanted it—until now.

Her mate loved her; she had felt it in his mind. His love, his motivations were all there for the taking. It was a heady sensation, knowing someone would give their life for you. Always see to your protection and care. She understood.

She would die for that male. Being in his mind allowed her to see the real Demetri. She now understood him fully. What she perceived as chauvinistic had been coming from a place of caring. He didn't want women to risk their lives because he saw them as precious, not inferior.

Demetri stirred under her watchful gaze. His eyes darted behind their lids, and his dark brows furrowed. The lines on his face deepened. His mouth drew into a tight line. His head thrashed from side to side.

Sweat dotted his skin. His hands bunched in the sheets.

Demetri's head turned to her side of the bed as his eyes flew open. He looked at the empty pillow beside him.

"Tatiana," Demetri called out and reached across the bed to touch the vacated spot.

She quickly put a reassuring hand on his shoulder. "I'm here."

The relief on his face touched her heart.

He pushed into a seated position, dangling his feet off the side of the bed. The warrior rested his elbows on his knees and buried his face in his hands. Breaths left his body in hard exhales as he fought to calm his racing heart. He pushed the palms of his hands into his eyes with great pressure as if he tried to force disgusting images from them.

Tatiana gently cradled Demetri's face between her hands then lifted his head to force him to look at her. She didn't need to ask him what he had been dreaming about. The images played in his mind.

She fought to keep her emotions in check. She saw what had been done to him, experienced the torture. Anger boiled in her veins. Outraged by what he had been forced to endure at the hands of his captors, she tasted revenge. But he didn't need the anger. He needed her to comfort him, someone to be his solace in the world.

Let me take your demons away, she offered, running her fingers through his silky hair before brushing it back from his face.

Fates how I want that! I want to get lost in you. Shut the world out if only for a short time.

His arms wrapped around her waist and hugged her nude body to him. He buried his face in her bosom. It cradled his cheek as her hands moved behind his back.

She felt his world narrow until only they remained.

You have become my everything, Tatiana. My reason for living. I found my life in your arms.

His thoughts melted her heart. The sincerity of his words traveled through the link.

His shirt already unbuttoned, Tatiana slid the material off his back. The pads of her fingers played deliciously over his skin as she did so. Her nimble fingers made quick work of the fasteners on his pants. He lifted his hips, helping her to disrobe him. Tatiana made a show of it, going excessively slow as she pushed the material down his thighs to help him out of the jeans. She ran her fingernails back up his thighs when she stood.

She stilled, taking in his body with her sensual gaze. His shoulders seemed a little broader. His flesh now stretched taunt over new muscles and sinew. The whip-lean body was giving way to the familiar burly build. His thighs were slightly thicker, muscles more chorded. Though he was still lean, he was muscular, like an actor playing a superhero in an action movie. His muscles rippled as he took her in his arms.

Demetri lay back on the bed, taking his mate with him. His flesh on her bare body sent a wave of pure ecstasy through her. Her legs straddled his hips, placing her hot entrance on his long shaft, bathing him in her moist cream. She'd never tire of how he felt against her, the feel of him under her was heaven.

Tatiana eased her hips up to slide a hand between their bodies. She took him in her hand, stroking from the base to the tip. Urgency spurred her on, her grip tightening—the expression on his face her reward.

She was achy, needy and there was only one thing that would satisfy her. Him. She slid his shaft inside, seating herself fully on its thickness.

Need drove them hard and fast. The sound of skin slapping together filled the room, music to their ears. The steady rhythm increasing tempo as they came to the crescendo together. Time blurred until finally they tumbled over the precipice, his roar of ecstasy rivaling her own.

"You're beautiful," he breathed then lowered his lips to take her mouth with a gentle, loving kiss.

Demetri looked at her with awe in his eyes. Tatiana glowed with vitality and health from everything he gave her. She collapsed on top of him and exhaled in a shudder.

Too soon she shifted off, separating his still-impressive shaft from her sex.

Demetri rose from the bed in a fluid, graceful movement.

"Where are you going?"

"I need to shower and feed. Company will be arriving soon."

"Oh yeah, I forgot about that."

Demetri looked at his mate over his shoulder, a boyish grin on his lips. "Was I so good that I drove all other thoughts from your mind?"

She chuckled. "Don't let it go to your head, Romanoff." Tatiana crossed her arms over her stomach.

Noting she did not deny his prowess, his chest expanded with male satisfaction. Demetri leaned down and placed a light kiss on her forehead. "I wouldn't dream of it, my tigress warrior. Besides, if I ever did, you'd be right there to put me in my place."

She smiled warmly at him. "You better believe it."

Chapter 31

Heaven. He found Heaven in the arms of his heartmate when they make love. And Heaven smelled like the ocean. Her scent had surrounded him, taking his troubles and vanquishing his nightmare.

Now Demetri followed Tatiana, watching the sway of her hips as they meandered down the grand staircase in Marcus' home. He reluctantly tore his eyes from the sinuous movement to note the people walking through the front doors.

"Stephan," the warrior called out to his longtime friend.

The Alpha leader's sapphire eyes flew to him. "Demetri," he greeted stepping around his heartmate, Katrina, when she stopped to give Marcus' valet a kiss on his cheek. "You are a sight for sore eyes, old friend."

The two Alphas clasped forearms in greeting. "Damn, it is good to see you. You had us worried for a while."

Demetri nodded. "Thanks to my mate and Alexander, I am back safe and sound."

Stephan turned his attention on Tatiana. "Thank you, Tatiana. Alex told me you were invaluable in finding Demetri. He also happened to mention all your fighting escapades. If I remember correctly, I believe he said you fought like the third tiger on Noah's ark.

"We are going to need more warriors on the

Council. Would you consider leaving VES to join our ranks?"

A strangled sound came from Demetri's throat, a mix of a bark and a growl. "You can't be serious." Much as he tried since he knew it would anger Tatiana, he did not quite keep the disbelief from his tone.

Tatiana shot him a warning glance, her yellow eyes blazing with fire. "I appreciate the offer."

But you won't be accepting it, Demetri sent over their mindlink.

Tatiana crossed her arms over her chest. *Annnnnnd the old Demetri has returned. Just when I thought we were making progress.*

Demetri swallowed hard. They had made progress in their relationship. But even he realized their mating might still be a bit tenuous.

Tonight was supposed to be fun. The Alphas and their mates had come into town and were planning to go out for the evening to celebrate the impending weddings. *We can speak of this later. Now is not the time to get into it.*

Fine, later then. But I warn you, I will not be dictated to.

Stephan scrutinized the silent play between the couple. As if wanting to ease the building tension, he said, "Listen, take a few days to think about it. I know you probably don't want to quit VES. I don't need an answer tonight. Tonight is for fun. I understand you ladies are going to go to a spa."

Stephan laughed when a disgruntled expression took Tatiana's face.

"By the Fates, I don't know why Christina and Juliette wish to go there," she complained. "They said something about getting a mani pedi, whatever the hell that is."

Katrina sauntered up to the trio with graceful strides. She pulled her fingers through her long blonde hair. "A mani pedi is a manicure and pedicure. You know, getting your fingernails and toenails polished." Tatiana visibly shuddered while Kat continued. "We're also getting massages and facials. It should be fun."

Tatiana pursed her lips. "I guess a massage would be nice." Memories of the massage Demetri had given her poured into her mind.

Make sure it is a female masseuse. I do not want another male touching you.

She smiled demurely. One shoulder lifted in a shrug. *We'll see.*

You'll do more than see, unless you wish some poor man to lose his life this evening.

Relax, tiger. I don't want anyone to die just so I can have a massage. I'll make sure the masseuse is a woman.

Payton approached the group. "If you all would be so kind as to follow me. I believe everyone else is waiting for you on the back porch. Miss Christina requested refreshments be served there this evening."

The older gentleman led them down the hall and pushed through the kitchen door. Grabbing a tray of hors d'œuvres on the way past the granite island, he opened the back door to the home, the tray balanced on one hand. He beckoned the couples through.

The porch boasted a cozy feel. Painted white to match the siding on the house, it looked like summer— warm and bright. Wicker furniture dotted the scene, some of which sported cushions with a floral pattern.

Soft light from candles cast a chipper glow.

The space was abuzz with activity. Marcus stood next to Christina who sat in a wicker rocking chair. His hand rested on the nape of her neck while they spoke with Alex. In a corner of the porch, Vladimir stood quietly observing the group, his hand absently scratching Connor's large, furry head as Nicholai spoke to him.

A little farther down, Julie handed a drink to a man Demetri did not recognize. The Alpha was surprised his cousin wasn't near his mate with another man talking to her. He noted the way they exchanged easy smiles.

The man possessed the build of a warrior. He stood feet apart, legs braced like he was ready to bound into action at the slightest provocation.

Noticing on whom Demetri's eyes had fallen, Stephan said, "You haven't met the newest addition to our team. Let me introduce you."

Demetri followed behind their leader. His eyes sizing up the male while they walked. Stephan had added a new member, probably to replace Michael he reasoned. Their leader also invited Tatiana to join the team. Was Stephan adding to their team for a reason? Was there a threat he had not yet been told of?

They stopped in front of Julie and her friend. "I'd like you to meet Desmond Wright. Desmond this is Demetri Romanoff," Stephan introduced them.

The male shook Demetri's hand in a firm grip. "DW to my friends." he said, his British accent sounding like he had just stepped out of Buckingham Palace. "Nice to meet you, old boy."

"You look familiar."

Stephan put a hand on Desmond's broad shoulder.

"He should. Desmond is a big movie star."

The newest Alpha chuckled. "Hardly. Now, I mostly just produce. My production company keeps me plenty busy."

"I've always wondered what a producer does," Tatiana commented, coming to stand beside Demetri. She slipped her hand into the back pocket of his pants.

"I basically shepherd the production from start to finish. I do it all; from securing the rights to coordinating the post production. I even get my hands dirty now and then. Just this past week I worked with my pyrotechnic crew, helping to rig some explosives on the set."

Julie gasped. "I had no idea you did that. Isn't it dangerous?"

"I guess." Desmond's shoulders lifted in an insouciant shrug. "But I hired the best, and they taught me well."

Vlad passed behind the group murmuring for them to excuse him as he moved to the table containing the tray of hors d'œuvres. He popped one of the tasty treats in his mouth then leaned back on the balustrade, bracing one foot against the decorative gingerbread carved in it. Connor sat at his side, his tail wagging.

"May I get you a drink, sir?" Payton asked with a smile, always happy to serve.

"Nyet." The gruff timbre of his voice matched the expression on his face. His sturdy face sported the usual dark goatee around a mouth set in a taut line. His black eyes held an intensity that made most men cringe. "I mean, no," he muttered in English, his thick Siberian accent pronounced.

Marcus smiled. "Payton, my man, you have done a

lot today. You picked up the SUV from First Bite, then stopped by all the vendors to pay them for the wedding. You even stopped by the counseling center to pick up the loan papers for Christina's new center. You've done more than your fair share. Please take the rest of the night off."

"I am fine, sir. I don't mind staying to help with your party."

"Nonsense. We will be leaving in a few minutes anyway. The girls are going to the spa and us guys are heading to First Bite. There is really nothing more for you to do."

Payton bowed in acquiescence. "As you wish. I will just clean up the kitchen before I retire."

Christina shook her head, sending her auburn locks flowing around her shoulders. "I swear the man has more energy than I do. We can't get him to take a break. He is forever doing stuff for the wedding. I don't know what I would have done without him."

Marcus rubbed his fingers along the nape of her neck, the gesture possessive, yet loving. "Sweetheart, you know he is happiest when he is being helpful. He is loving the fact we decided to have the wedding so quickly. It has given him a lot to do."

"Oh, Jules," Christina called out to her friend as she went to walk by. "Hold up, sweetie. Where's Samantha? I expected her to come into town tonight."

Julie rolled her eyes.

What's the eye roll about, Demetri sent to his cousin, knowing Nicholai had caught it as well.

Most people in the world know her sister, Samantha, as a super model who lives in New York. To Juliette she has always been her overbearing sister from Virginia.

"She is running on Samantha time as usual," explained Julie. "She called saying she'll be late and would meet us at the spa."

"I was afraid she wasn't going to be able to come on such short notice," Christina said. "You're lucky she didn't have a modeling gig lined up."

"Mmm-hmm, real lucky." Nicholai's mate did not keep the sarcasm from her voice. "I have to admit, I'm a little worried my sister will find a way to upstage Christina and I on the big day. Samantha always has to be the center of attention, unlike my friend Penny who would have loved to be at the wedding. I wish Penny could have come."

"Why couldn't she?" asked Alex.

"She's too far along in her pregnancy. The doctors wouldn't let her fly all the way from England."

Alexander swirled the whiskey in his glass in silent contemplation. "Why don't we broadcast the wedding over the internet? I could work with the videographer to rig something up. Penny could watch via a secure site."

"You could do that?"

"Sure, piece o' cake. Weddin' cake that is," he quipped in his southern drawl.

"I hate to break up the party, but it is about that time," Nicholai observed as Desmond, Tatiana, Katrina, and Stephan joined their group.

"Let the good times roll." Alex lifted his glass in salute then downed the rest of his whiskey in one long swallow. "Smmmooooth," he commented. His rough voice earned him a chuckle from the group as his eyes watered from the burn of the alcohol.

The Alphas saw the ladies into their SUV. Marcus

handed Christina behind the wheel of the girl's ride as Stephan and Demetri made their way down the gravel drive. Stephan turned to him throwing a companionable arm around his shoulder. "So, I hear you were the next of us to fall. Congratulations. I have to admit, my old friend, I have a hard time seeing you and Tatiana together."

"It is proving to be a challenge. One you did not help by offering to let Tatiana to join the Council."

"I think she should consider the offer. Tatiana is one helluva fighter. She could be a huge asset to our team. With a pretty face like hers, she can gain access to all kinds of places we can't with our ugly mugs."

Marcus shook the keys to the SUV, a mischievous grin reaching his eyes. "Speaking of ugly mugs and pretty faces, we best get going before they give our reservation away to someone else."

Chapter 32

Alex strolled behind the petite hostess, watching the sway of her hips appreciatively, as she led the Alphas down the hallway of the third floor. "You reserved a room, Marcus? I figured you reserved a booth down on the second floor. I bet we're in for a treat!"

Stephan cleared his throat, a disapproving look on his stern face. "I thought we agreed to keep this classy. Drink one hundred-year-old scotch, smoke some Cuban cigars, maybe play some poker. Please tell me you did not arrange for a stripper or worse."

"I don't think our heartmates would approve," Demetri championed the sentiment.

Alex grinned. "You know what they say, Demetri, when the cat's away—" He chuckled.

"Yeah, but my cat is a saber-toothed tiger." The banter earned Demetri a laugh from the group.

"Here you go, boys." The hostess opened one of the doors wide with a smile playing across her full lips then stepped back, allowing them to enter. "Enjoy."

"My God, Marcus, what have you done?" Stephan took in the room with a scathing glare.

A neon purple glow bathed the room. The ceiling, painted a light purple, was adorned with dark purple markings best described as similar to the lines of tribal tattoos. A faux leather couch, the gaudy upholstery in shades of light and dark purple, circled a silver pole. The walls of the room matched the shade of purple on the couch, making the room look like the inside of a Vegas party bus.

Marcus raised his hands in supplication and shook his head. "I swear, I didn't request this. When I called to reserve the room, the person on the phone asked if there was a special occasion. I told her it was a bachelor party. She must have assumed this is what we would want."

"Well, I, for one, think this is a great room. Hell, it even has its own workout station." Alex grabbed the stripper pole and swung his muscular body around it to demonstrate.

Stephan turned to the hostess. "Do you have another room available, perhaps?"

"Sorry, but they are all booked this evening. I could put you downstairs if you like."

"The Bachelor Brotherhood can make this room work," announced Alex, surveying the room.

"Bachelor Brotherhood?" asked Vlad.

"Yeah, we're the Bachelor Brotherhood," the blond Alpha informed him. "You know, a group of guys who are all bachelors. At least for tonight. What happens in the Brotherhood stays with the Brotherhood."

Desmond stepped forward. "I agree. We can make this room work. We are, after all, the Bachelor Brotherhood. Look, there is space for a table in the middle of that U-shaped couch." He turned to the hostess. "Could you arrange to have a poker table brought in?"

"Of course, sir. I'll see to it right away." The female vampire left, closing the door behind her.

Demetri instinctually launched his awareness out from his body. Sensing only the energies in the room and nothing else thanks to the sheets of metal lining the space, he muttered, "Damned titanium."

The men settled on the purple couch to wait and thankfully they did not have to wait long. Within minutes, a beefy security guard came into the room carrying a hexagonal table. Two waitresses followed close behind. The blonde server placed a silver aluminum case in the middle of the table. She opened the case for their inspection. Doing her best game show model impression, she ran her hand over the two decks of playing cards, five dice, and the numerous chips within. Next, the brunette server entered with an amber bottle and a box of cigars. After she placed them on the table, a series of people streamed into the room each placing a chair around the table then leaving.

"The night is looking up." Nicholai crossed the floor and removed a cigar from the box. He smelled the barrel, running it under his nose as he inhaled deeply. "Mmmm. That's what I call a good cigar."

The men took their cue from Nicholai, each joining him at the table.

In record time, with drinks before them and a lit cigar between their fingers, they began the game.

Nicholai opened the bidding with three chips. "Now *this* is more like it. Good friends, a friendly game. I think our heartmates would approve."

Stephan threw some chips in the middle of the table. "I call…Speaking of heartmates, I still can't believe you and Tatiana, Demetri. I thought you would be the last of us to succumb to amore."

Nicholai smiled, smoke wafting between his lips.

"You should have expected such. Our family is renowned for being lovers. Is that not correct, cousin?"

"Maybe your side," Demetri taunted. "My side was better known for fighting than loving."

"Are you trying to say I cannot fight?" Before Demetri could respond, Nicholai continued. "For if you are, I will gladly take you out back to the love shack."

A boisterous laugh left Marcus' mouth. "I think you mean woodshed. You'll take him out back to the woodshed."

Alex leaned on the table. "A love shack is entirely different from a woodshed, Nikko. Best not be mixing those two up."

The grouped laughed.

Vladimir ran his hand over his dark goatee. "I call." He tossed in his chips. "And my glass needs a refill."

Desmond poured the remainder of the bottle in the Alpha's glass. "So, Stephan, I hate to bring up business, but you mentioned earlier you wanted a report on what we found."

Demetri gave the team leader a questioning look. "Report on what?"

"I asked Vladimir, Alexander, and Desmond to go back to the warehouse where you were held to see if they could find anything about the demons."

"And," Demetri prompted, throwing his chips on the pile.

Desmond spoke up. "We didn't find anything of use. The place appears to be abandoned."

"You didn't look hard enough," accused Demetri, his tone as sharp as a two-edged sword. "They *must* have left something behind that would give us some idea of where to find them."

Vlad leaned forward, his hands cradled his glass in a well-practiced maneuver. "I swear to you, Demetri, we turned the place upside down."

Alex nodded, took a draw from his cigar, and blew a cloud of smoke over the table. "We got lucky. They hadn't changed the keypad code, so we got right into the place. Everything was pretty much like we left it, but the office was cleaned out. There wasn't even a partial phone number to be found. Believe me, we looked."

Demetri's fist pounded down on the table, sending the chips jumping. "There must be *something* there to tell us where to find those creatures! I'll go. I'm sure I can find something. I will have retribution."

Stephan met his angry stare, the warriors locking eyes. "We all want retribution for what was done to you, Demetri. And we will have it. I vow before you and our brethren we will avenge your torture. But tonight is a night to have fun, not plot revenge." He tapped a finger on the lip of his glass. "Tonight is for celebrating. Two of us are getting married day after tomorrow. Now I say we order three bottles of their best vodka, and let the good times roll."

Demetri tapped the ashes from his cigar. Stephan was correct. This night was for fun, not his ire. He took a deep breath and pushed his anger down, burying it until he needed it again. He met each of their eyes in turn while he spoke. "I'm sorry, comrades. I did not mean to ruin the party."

"I think it is still salvageable." Alex rose. "Deal me out of this hand. I'll be right back."

"Where are you—" The sound of the door closing

behind Alexander cut Marcus' question short.

Stephan shuffled the cards with the expertise of a blackjack dealer. "I hope he isn't going where I think he's going."

"Think he is arranging a surprise?" Desmond cut the deck then handed it back to their leader.

"Yeah, of the long, curvy variety." Stephan dealt the cards with a flick of his wrist.

Vladimir whistled low. "We can only hope." He pushed his chips into the middle of the table. "All in."

"Too rich for me. I'm out." DW threw in his cards.

"Me too," Nicholai chimed in before laying his cards face down on the velvet table.

Music started playing, a loud rap. Its deep bass reverberated off the purple walls. The chips danced on the table. Over the speakers, the rapper chanted, "back that booty up now, and let me see your hips shake." The lights pulsed in time to the music as a disco ball dropped from the ceiling. Its spinning mirrors sent prismatic rainbows dancing around the room.

The door opened. A hand slipped inside waving a tulle veil attached to a plastic headband. "I heard someone is getting married," a husky, effeminate voice called out from behind the door.

"Ah-oooooooooooo." The wolfly call came from Vlad's throat as he threw back his head to howl his approval.

"Let's see you, love," DW encouraged. "Come on in. The stags are waiting."

The blond came through the door, dressed in only a plastic firefighter hat, red boa, and...

red boxer shorts?

The white veil twirled in his hand as Alex made his

way over to Vladimir, thrusting his hips in time to the music. Catcalls and laughter erupted in the room. The blond Alpha leaned over, doing his best impression of an exotic dancer, and stretched the headband over Vlad's head. The Alpha's goatee contrasted nicely against the white veil.

Vlad clenched his teeth. His fists tightened on the table as if he had the impulse to punch the young Alpha. "If you wish to leave here tonight on two working legs, do not put that thing on my head."

The scowl on the Alpha's face made Alex pull the bridal veil back. He gyrated his hips from side to side, his arms in the air, dancing his way to Marcus. After snapping the headband on his friend's head, he hooked his fingers around the red boa, twirling the ends out from his body as he wiggled his derrière in Marcus' face.

Marcus laughed, the sound honest and loud. He smacked the blond on his butt with the hand holding his smoldering cigar, sending ashes raining down. "You go girl, shake that thing."

Alex looked down at his friend over his muscular shoulder and wagged his light brows. Grabbing the brim of his plastic hat, he gave a nod of his head then jumped across the room in one bound. He landed on the silver pole and swung his muscular body around it. Alex falling to the floor with a crash garnered another laugh from the group. With the next beat of the music he was on his feet, jumping into his vacant chair at the poker table. He shook his bum, thrusting in time to the music. Turning around, he hooked his fingers in his boxers and pulled them down, mooning the group.

"Did not need to see that," Desmond joked,

looking away, his hand in front of his eyes.

"Nor I," Demetri agreed, a pseudo smile on his face. "I'm going to go order us some more drinks. Although no more for him. Alex has obviously had enough." He pushed away from the table. "I'll be right back."

"You cannot leave now, cousin. You will miss Alexander's grand finale." Nicholai took a bill from his wallet and stuffed it in the waistband of the dancing Alpha's boxers.

"Somehow I'll manage."

Demetri slipped out into the hall, breathing a deep sigh of relief. The guys were having a good time, but he didn't feel very jovial. His anger lay just beneath the surface, making him edgy. He had not expected Stephan to send other members of the team to do recon in Canada. The thought of other people in the place, witnessing the evidence of the horrors that occurred there, set his teeth on edge. He reached out to Tatiana automatically for comfort, surprised by how natural it felt to do so.

What are you doing, kotik kisa*?*

I'm getting a massage. The sound of her voice in his head softened his stormy gray eyes.

It better be a female masseuse. He received an impression of a smile from his mate.

It is, and you'll be happy to know she is nowhere near as good as you are. You really could make a living by giving massages, you know.

His chest swelled with pride. His mate loved his touch. It was there in her mind. She loved the way he held her, loved the way he gave himself to her when they were in bed. Loved the way he thought about her.

She loved *him*.

She didn't yet realize it, but he had found it in the deep recesses of her subconscious. He had discovered it as he lay holding her when she had shared her darkest secret with him. Her feelings for him were kept deep, like she was afraid to admit they existed, but they were there, and he was determined to connect her with her feelings for him. And he wasn't above using anything at his disposal to achieve his goal.

Her voice purred into his mind. *Demetri, I have just spent an hour having a woman rub oil all over my body. Does that give you any ideas?*

Oh, I have plenty of ideas where you are concerned. He allowed the images of a few such ideas to flow through their link.

Not nice. Now I'm all hot and bothered with no male to take care of me.

He got the impression she was stifling a giggle. *Just wait until you get back to the plantation. I'll be there to take care of you.*

Promises, promises. We'll see if you can deliver, big boy.

Oh, my big boy will deliver, woman. Don't you worry about that.

Her laughter curled around his mind in velvety softness. The tension melted from his shoulders. His breath came easier to his lungs as he allowed the sound of her giggle to take the last of the anger. Fates, how he loved that woman!

I'd better go. The masseuse just told me I'm late for the pedicure, not that I'm anxious to get it done, but I guess the girls are waiting on me.

Then I will let you go have your girl time. Demetri

got the distinct impression of a smug look from his mate. *Have fun, my tigress warrior. I will see you later.*

Safe travels to you, my Alpha warrior. I'll see you in a few hours.

****

Sensing Demetri was now at ease, Tatiana cut the mental connection to her heartmate. His edginess had flowed through their mindlink. She contemplated asking him what was wrong, then realizing what it might be, she decided it was better not to open that can of worms since they had agreed to speak of it later.

No doubt he was still upset Stephan had offered her a position with the Alphas. If Demetri didn't want her working for the Vampire Enforcement Squad, he surely wouldn't want her on the Alpha Council. The memory of Stephan's invitation warmed her. No female had been a member of the Alphas. Ever. It was an honor to be chosen. Once she proved herself, she could pave the way for other strong females to join.

Of course, leaving VES would be hard. She'd miss her coworkers. She had developed some friendships in her years there, especially her partner, Ty. It was not an easy decision, and she needed to think it over. Luckily, Stephan had been considerate enough to give her some time. She just hoped Demetri would be reasonable if she decided to take the position. For it was *her* decision to make. It was her life, and if he wanted to be a part of it, then he had better accept she was her own woman.

Tatiana drew the robe tightly around her body and knotted the tie at her waist. She padded down the hall from the massage room to the beauty parlor. The smell of acrylic nail polish and acetone burned her nose. Through watery eyes, she spied the women sitting beside one another, their feet soaking in bubbling mini tubs.

"Tatiana, you made it." Christina's drawl sounded as smooth as hand churned ice cream on a summer's day. "Come, we saved you a seat."

She sat in an empty chair sandwiched between Juliette and Katrina. A quick sweep of her eyes informed her they were one person short. "Where is Samantha? I thought she was supposed to join us."

"Pbbbbbbbbtttt!" Julie blew a juicy raspberry. "She left a message on my cell while I was getting my massage. Sami isn't coming. She said something about having a headache."

"You sound like you don't believe that."

"I love my sister, but I don't much like her. She is a brat, always has been. If I had to guess, I'd guess she is tired from the flight and simply decided to stay in and watch TV rather than make the effort to get all done up to come here."

"But she wouldn't have to do much to come here," Katrina observed. "We were getting massages and facials. It's not like she would have worn makeup or anything."

"Ha! You don't know my sister. She never walks outside without an hour-long makeup job. She won't even go out to get the mail without makeup on. And it's not as if she needs it. She's beautiful. Her skin is flawless like yours."

"That's only because of what we are," Katrina whispered in the brunette's ear. "If Christina and I hadn't converted we would need make up too. Why haven't you converted yet? You're planning on it, right?"

Julie kept her voice low. "I'll convert after the wedding. I've been too scared to do it. For a while, I was afraid Nicholai might change his mind about marrying me, and then I would have to live an eternity without him, but now I'm just plain scared. Nicholai said it hurts a lot."

"I can understand that." Christina leaned toward Julie. "It is not exactly fun to go through. But it's kind of like childbirth because the reward is worth the pain."

"Stephan can help you through it." The Alpha leader's mate offered. "He did me. It's kind of like morphine. He can't make the pain go away, but he dulls it enough that you can deal with it."

Relief took Julie's round face. "That's sweet of you to offer, Kat. Are you sure he won't mind?"

"Not at all. Stephan will be happy to help you through. He thinks the world of Nicholai and is glad he found you. He'd do anything to help you two have your happily ever after."

Julie turned her thoughtful gaze on Tatiana. "Speaking of happily ever afters, how are things going with you and Demetri?"

"Things were getting better until Stephan asked me to join the Alphas tonight."

"Stephan told me he was going to ask you." Katrina shifted in her chair, turning in Tatiana's direction. "I bet Demetri didn't take that very well. I know he doesn't want you fighting."

Christina leaned toward Tatiana, letting the arm of the padded chair take her weight. "Poor thing. It must be hard having Demetri for a mate."

"He's an honorable and good man. I could not ask for a better mate." The shocked look on Christina's face mirrored her own thoughts.

Who is Christina to judge Demetri? She belonged with him. Demetri was her mate, the male she wanted to spend the rest of her years with. She had no idea when or how it had happened, but she wanted to be with him. She'd be willing to live with his sometimes abrasive ways because she realized they came from a place of love and concern.

Tatiana's outrage built. She struggled to voice her thoughts without having a bite in her tone. "He is a brave male, a fierce fighter. To protect me, he would put his life before mine. It is not hard having him for a mate, it is a blessing."

"I'm sorry." The red head appeared properly contrite. "I didn't mean any insult. I just meant Demetri is a scary man. I mean...I'm sure he is a good man, but he looks like he could eat a rattle snake and spit out the venom."

Tatiana opened her mouth to defend him again, but closed it without a word when four human women in lab coats came over and sat on a little stool in front of each one of the heartmates. As her attendant pulled her right foot from the mini tub and went to work, Tatiana closed her eyes, longing for this torture to be over so she could be in her lover's arms.

****

Cyrus fought the urge to cringe while Jara paced the room. Her long blonde hair crackled with magical sparks of ire. He had informed her that he had been unable to locate the vampire.

He had followed the black SUV all day. Damned thing went all over town. He had to run three red lights to keep it in sight. In fact, another car almost hit him during the effort, but he never stopped following it. Unfortunately, he looked away for only a moment, but it was a moment too long, for when his eyes returned to the road the SUV had vanished.

Jara did not take the news well.

"You mean to tell me you lost the car!" she screamed.

"But there is some good news too." Cyrus gave a weak smile and hoped it appeared encouraging. "I followed it to a bunch of places. It stopped at a bakery, a flower shop, a caterer."

Jara placed her hands on her hips. "And what is so good about knowing that?"

Lane cleared his throat. "It sounds like the bloodsuckers are planning a party."

Cyrus nodded approvingly at the male demon standing behind him. "Exactly. I bet we could find out where the party is by going to the vendors. The vehicle also stopped by a counseling center on Bull Street. Maybe the party is going to be there."

Jara's fingers twitched by her sides. Little blue arcs danced along the tips. "And that gets me my vampire how exactly?"

"If we discover where and when the party is, then we will know where the vampire will be and when. We could spring a trap."

"So, are you going to be the one to get me the information from the venders?"

Cyrus didn't like the way her sarcasm dripped from her voice. "I could," he replied cautiously.

A malevolent cackle burst violently from between Jara's lips. Her face contorted with rage. "You, Cy, couldn't even follow an SUV. Thanks to you, we still don't know where the vampire is staying. We still don't know how we will catch him. We don't know much except how inept you are! You are useless to me. An inept, useless demon, who is not worthy of his demonic life!"

Jara's eyes glowed blood red. Her hair stood out from her head as power swirled around her, fueled by her outrage. She looked terrifying, standing in front of him bathed in blue light. Her lissome form heaved with each breath. Crackling hair stood away from her head like she touched an electromagnet. But her eyes frightened him the most. He had never seen anything look so wild and untamed.

Her stare burned, held him still. Her fingers flexed. Blue sparks of electricity arced wildly from the tips. She raised her arms, pointing those deadly fingers at him.

When the current flowed from the tips of her digits, Cyrus' self-preservation kicked in. Heat pulsed white-hot over his skin as he dodged the near miss and dropped to the floor with a bone-jarring thud. The hit knocked the air hard from his lungs, causing them to burn as he struggled for oxygen. The sound of a blood-curdling scream turned Cyrus' head. Time slowed as it does in a moment of great terror.

When Jara's power reached Lane, a blue light bathed the scientist. His eyes widened. Fire engulfed his legs and traveled north until it silenced Lane's horrified scream. A blackened charred corpse stood in the scientist's place for a second before it turned to ash and collapsed to the ground. A heap of piled ash and a bit of gray dust in the air were all that remained of the man.

Gathering his wits about him, Cyrus drew in a

gasping breath of air. His eyes met Jara's—hers blazing with anger, his wide in disbelief.

He needed to escape before she succeeded in killing him. He dematerialized, the sound of Jara's incensed scream in his ears.

Chapter 33

Jara glanced up from where she sat at the elegant desk in her hotel room.

"Oh, it's you," she commented to the guard entering the room. "I was hoping Cyrus had come crawling back. We never got to finish our conversation last night. Has anyone heard from him?"

She glanced around at the two guards in the room expectantly, a wicked glint in her eyes. With Lane dead and Cyrus missing, she was down to only two guards. Her brother, Varrick, could not be told of their situation because as far as he was concerned, she was still in the Canadian compound with Lane experimenting on the male vampire, so she had no choice but to revise their plan.

The bigger of the two guards answered. "I haven't heard from him, have you?" he asked, looking at his cohort.

"I haven't either. Sorry, princess."

Jara huffed her displeasure at the news.

"The two of you aren't enough to capture the vampire alone."

"What about asking King Varrick for more men?"

Jara shook her head. "Not possible."

Jara did not want to face Varrick's wrath should he discover not only had the vampire escaped, but she had been going behind his back for days trying to find the bloodsucker. Having the vampire on the loose was a liability. He might lead more of his kind to their complex in Canada or worse find a way to trace them to the mountain compound in Mason's Bluff.

"My brother will be most displeased. He will probably find a way to blame me for this mess."

But it wasn't her fault. She hadn't been the one to lead the vampires to the warehouse. She hadn't been the one to lose track of the vampire's SUV. It certainly wasn't fair to blame her for Cyrus getting her so angry that she fried Lane by mistake, taking away their best hope for finding a cure for their immune systems deficiencies.

"He might even banish me from the demon community. I can't let that happen. I'd miss our underground compound in the mountain at Mason's Bluff. My spacious room, with its obscenely expensive furniture, is fit for a queen, which I was until my brother found his mate.

"Now his mate keeps him distracted, and he neglects his duties. I've mentioned as much to him on a few occasions. He probably would love the opportunity to throw it back at me, claiming I did not pay attention to my duties with the vampire experiments."

She could not—would not—give him the opportunity.

"I must find a way to make this right."

Find a way to keep her brother from ever discovering the escape. She needed to come up a way to clean up this mess, leaving no one to tell the tale.

A devious plan formed in her mind.

They could kill the vampire instead of retrieving him. Even if the two guards left could capture him, he would be of no use to them. Lane was dead. With no scientist to conduct the experiments, she no longer needed the subject. She would claim a catastrophe took out the warehouse and all within. Maybe an explosion.

"Leo, where were you just now?"

"I just returned from the counseling center on Bull Street."

With a tap of her hand, she motioned for the large guard to sit across the desk from her. "And did you find anything interesting? Cyrus seemed to think that the vampires were having some sort of party."

Leo nodded. "They were having an Easter party. There were children everywhere."

Jara's brows furrowed. "During the daytime?"

"Yes, but I did notice a sign on the wall saying that there would be a second party scheduled for this evening at ten o'clock."

Jara's eyes narrowed, her lips pursed. "A second party. Ten o'clock seems awfully late for a child's party. Why would they do that?"

She impatiently tapped a finger against her chin. Her mind raced through the possibilities until her eyes widened in realization. "Unless they were having a second party for the vampires. They wouldn't want the baby vamps with the human kiddies now would they."

She clapped her hands together, rubbing them in earnest.

"That would make sense." The expression on the guard's face did not support his statement.

"But?" Jara prompted when he hesitated to say more.

"But it doesn't gel with what I found out at the caterer."

317

"And what was that?"

"When the caterer closed the shop to make a delivery, I materialized inside. I found three events listed in his books, a kid's birthday party next week, a corporate event at a local company in two weeks, and a party tomorrow night. A wedding at a home address. So, I ran by the home addresses." Leo smiled wide, showing his white teeth. "And you'll never guess what *kind* of home the wedding is taking place in."

A wide grin spread across Jara's face. "A plantation," she guessed.

"Um-hm. And I just happen to know exactly where and when the wedding will be."

Unable to contain her joy, Jara jumped up, rounded the desk, and sat in Leo's lap. She gave him a tight hug around the neck. "Do you know what this means? We have two opportunities to take the vampire out. If he shows at the counseling center tonight, we'll kill him there. If not, we'll get him at the wedding tomorrow. We can't fail."

The largest guard cleared his throat. "I thought we were trying to capture the vamp."

"I've changed my mind. With Lane gone, he is of no use to us now."

Leo shifted Jara on his lap, clearly uncomfortable with the princess being so intimate. "Lane is gone? Where did he go?"

"You don't want to know," muttered the guard sitting on the bed. His eyes briefly darted to the gray smudge on the carpet.

Jara pushed out of Leo's lap to pace the room. "We need a way to kill him. Something he can't heal from."

For several minutes, the fall of the female demon's

footsteps were the only sound in the room. Leo's voice brought her to a stop.

"How about a bomb? Surely a vamp can't regenerate after getting blown up."

"That's not a bad idea. Do you know anything about making a bomb?" Jara asked.

Leo shrugged his muscular shoulders. "How hard can it be? A fuse, some wire, a clock, a little C4, and we're good to go."

The other guard scoffed. "Good luck finding C4. It's not like you can go into the local grocery store and pick some up."

Leo thoughtfully stroked his chin. "How about dynamite then? There are enough farms around here. Surely some local place will sell dynamite. Don't farmers use it for blowing up beaver dams and stuff?"

Jara's eyes brightened. "Leo, you just became my favorite guard. We don't need anything pretty, just effective." Jara returned to her chair at the desk. "I wish one of you knew how to make the device."

"You'd be surprised what you can find on the internet," Leo replied. "I'm not as good as Cyrus, but I doubt I'll have any trouble finding directions on how to make the thing."

****

Tatiana observed Demetri zip up the leather jacket he borrowed from Marcus. It was a little large, but definitely a better fit than it would have been when he first arrived at the plantation. He'd amassed muscle at a good clip, finding several times a day to work hard in the gym. Taking Tatiana's blood helped as well. At over four hundred years old, her blood was powerful, giving his muscles the energy to grow, strengthen.

The Alpha swung a leg over the motorcycle and tugged on his helmet. "You coming anytime this century, woman?"

Tatiana pulled her helmet down over her dark hair, the blunt ends sticking out from under it like twigs in a nest.

"Hold your horses, Romanoff." She straddled her bike.

Demetri shifted the bike from its stand and rousted the thing with a kick of his booted heel. He gunned the throttle. "My horses want to go," he called over the roar of the sports bike.

Tatiana started the motorcycle she borrowed from Marcus with a push of a button. The black beast growled to life. "Well, what are we waiting for then? I bet I can get to the counseling center before you."

The howl of her engine made further conversation impossible when she revved the machine.

They tore off down the gravel drive, the bikes fishtailing. Bits of gravel spit out behind them. Demetri gunned his engine and took the lead. He flashed her a brilliant smile when he passed, making it almost worth being second place. But not quite.

As they rounded out of the gated fence onto the road, Tatiana cut under him to regain the lead.

He shook his head. *Life will never be dull with you, tigress warrior. You are a fierce competitor, but then so am I.*

The Alpha took his motorcycle off-road and up the grassy hill that hovered next to the asphalt. With a boyish grin of delight, he twisted hard on the throttle. Tatiana looked up just as he jumped the bike over her head and landed with a bounce in front of her on the road.

She revved her engine. Popping a wheelie, she brought the front tire of her bike within a foot of Demetri's back.

He glanced over his shoulder to see the spinning wheel looming at his face. Demetri gunned the engine, lying low over the tank. Tatiana followed, curling her body onto the bike. They raced down the roads, the lead changing back and forth between them several times before they reached Bull Street.

Coming to a stop beside her mate at the counseling center, Tatiana removed her helmet. She shook out her hair as she brought all hundred and ninety-eight horses to rest by turning off the bike. She kicked down the stand before leaning the bike to one side. Watching Demetri dismount, she appreciated the way his roped muscles played under the fabric of his pants.

He unzipped his jacket and approached her with sure strides, his hand held out to assist her in dismounting the bike. When she took the proffered hand, his fingers wrapped around hers, strong and warm. She hooked her helmet on the handle bars, loving how the night air flowed over her, bringing with it the smells of the city. There was a real sense of freedom in riding, a call of the wild that made her body tingle.

"Nothing like a ride, huh?" Tatiana smiled and wagged her dark brows.

"A ride to my doom," he joked dramatically, laying his free hand over his heart. "I think you should give this man a dying wish."

"But you aren't dying."

"I might just end up dying from embarrassment.

And you don't know what my wish would be. You might like it, you know." The wicked gleam in his eye sent a shiver down her spine to her belly, making it do a little turn.

"Mr. Demetwi!" A tiny form ran to him with welcoming arms wide and black curls bouncing. Rebecca wrapped her tiny arms around both his legs in a fierce hug. He laid one hand in the middle of her back and patted it in greeting.

"Hello, Rebecca." He looked down into those sparkling eyes. She lifted her arms. Her fingers wiggled with excitement. Demetri scooped her up, resting her on his waist. Her little arms circled his neck as his eyes met with her father's across the lawn. The two nodded to each other in acknowledgment.

"Miss Chwistina said you would come. Daddy said you won't, but I said yes 'cause Miss Chwistina said so."

Tatiana smiled at the picture her mate and the young girl made. He was being very amiable, looking like a practiced father, completely at ease with a child in his arms.

"Well Miss Christina was right. He's here."

Rebecca glanced her way briefly, but quickly turned her attention back to the male holding her. Tatiana could understand why. He had a way of drawing a female's attention. She too found it hard to notice others in the room when near him.

"Mr. Demetwi, did you know the Easter Bunny is coming?" she squeaked with anticipation. "Want to play dolls until he comes?"

"I'm afraid I can't play today, little one. I have to go…get the Easter Bunny. He's a friend of mine you know."

Her eyes widened in awe. "You know the Easter Bunny!"

Tatiana did not keep the smile from her lips at the wonder on the child's face.

"I've heard he is a very sweet bunny." She winked at Demetri behind Rebecca's back.

Demetri narrowed his brows and pursing his lips in a faux scowl. "I'm not sure sweet is the best way to describe him. I prefer to think of him as loyal and trustworthy."

Rebecca wiggled against him, her youthful energy coursing around her body. The Alpha put her down.

"What do you tink of my dwess?" She turned in a small circle with her arms out to her side.

"It's very pretty," Tatiana replied.

"I think you are too young to be worried about how you look in your dress," Demetri chastised softly, a grin threatening to take his face. The comment earned him a smack on his shoulder from his mate.

Rebecca gasped and covered her mouth with her hand. "Ohhhhh. Daddy says you shouldn't hit people."

"Yeah, Tatiana. Don't you know you shouldn't hit people," the Alpha quipped.

I'll show you a hit, heartmate. Tatiana fisted her hands on her hips.

But I'm more of a lover than a fighter. Nicholai was just saying so last night. A low chuckle slid through her mind like silk.

The female warrior turned toward the child. "Your father is correct. It is usually not okay for children to hit each other."

Usually? Demetri sent over their mindlink.

I don't believe in always or nevers.

I hope that doesn't apply in thinking about us because we will always *be mates and I'll* always *put your needs before my own. I'll* never *cheat on you. And most of all, I'll* always *love you.*

Love crossed their link, flooding her mind with the sincerity of his declarations. Tatiana's heart did a little flip in her chest. He had a way of surprising her. She never would have expected Demetri to profess such romantic feelings. She certainly wouldn't expect him to tell her he loved her today.

Today she expected him to be irritable, unhappy because he was about to be completely humiliated by putting on a bunny suit. Instead, her mate appeared completely at ease.

Rebecca kneeled in the grass. "Look, Mr. Demetwi, a nightcwawler."

Demetri grinned. "I see. He's a fat worm isn't he."

Rebecca nodded vigorously. Her curls bounced around her round race while she played with the curly worm.

Tatiana gazed at Demetri while he bent at the knees to observe the interplay.

In the past few days, their mindlink had given her extraordinary access to the information in his mind. He had been so open with her, allowed her complete access to his mind, even though he could have easily put a mental barrier to stop her from exploring. She'd seen images from his childhood, watched the way his parents had been rather cold in their aristocratic ways. She witnessed the night he converted Nicholai and his sister Natasha. Experienced his grief when he had not been able to save their mother.

He'd even allowed her to take information about his time with the Alphas. They were his family, his brothers. Only his loyalty to her matched his loyalty to the Council.

We are a tight team and would give our lives for one another, Demetri sent, then placed the worm in his hand so Rebecca could get a closer look.

The Alphas loved one another in their warrior way. They would give their lives for each other if need be but fought hard to keep it from becoming necessary. They had been through horrific battles, but the grotesque memories in his mind did not scare her. Instead they inspired her.

She wanted that kind of comradery. She wanted to be part of their exclusive group.

The sound of Christina's voice broke her reverie. "It's time for the Bunny Hop Race. Come line up over here."

Rebecca and Demetri stood.

"Bye." Rebecca waved, then skipped off to join the other children.

"Bye," Tatiana and Demetri called out in unison after her.

Demetri laced their fingers then headed for the counseling center. Lost in thought about joining the Alphas, Tatiana allowed him to lead down the hall.

Demetri closed the door to Christina's office. "What are you thinking about?"

"Nothing much."

He brought her hand to his chest, resting it over his heart. "Please tell me."

"Why don't you just take the information from my mind? I know you are in there."

A sad smile drew his lips tight. "I'd prefer you chose to share the information with me."

Emotion played over his face. She'd hurt him. "I didn't mean to imply—"

He drew her into his arms. The warmth of his body surrounded her, taking the words from her throat. "I'm sorry, Tatiana. Sorry I was such a bastard toward you in the past. Forcing you to sleep, taking things from your mind without your permission. I do not wish to cause you any pain, and I certainly do not wish to remind you in any way of Sammael."

She wrapped her arms around his waist, enjoying the feel of his roped muscles beneath his tee shirt. "You are nothing like Sammael, and if I ever hear you compare yourself to that monster again I will kick your ass."

He chuckled, the sound sonorous. "Duly noted, my tigress warrior. Now I think it is about time the Easter Bunny makes his appearance. If I'm late Marcus' mate will probably kick my butt."

"She'd have to get through me first."

The Alpha leaned down to plant a tender kiss on the top of her head before releasing her. "I have no doubt you'll always have my back."

She removed his costume from the closet, then turned with the white fluffy suit in hand. Her eyes locked with her mate's. Her mind automatically flowed into his to glean the thoughts behind the expression on his face.

He believed she would watch his back. He found her to be a fighter, a fierce one. Her passion unmatched. He felt what she lacked in physical strength, she easily made up for in cunning. He found her to be thoughtful, strategic in battle. Like his fellow Alphas.

She *was* similar to the warriors he fought with, he thought. Smart, brave. She could push down her pain to continue the fight no matter the odds. He had to admit Alex's assessment of her skills were spot on. She fought like the third tiger on Noah's ark.

Tatiana smiled. *So maybe there is room on the Council for me?*

Demetri straightened his shoulders. "I couldn't allow you to be in any extraordinary danger. You could help us with research and recon, you've done enough of that for VES. You're quite good at it, actually."

Tatiana grimaced. He was considering her bid to join the Alphas, but only if she stayed out of the more dangerous situation. He had no intention of allowing her to be a real member of the team. There wasn't another Alpha that stayed behind during a battle because the danger was too great.

"Look, Romanoff. I know what you are thinking. And you can stop right now. If I join, it will be as a full member of the team. I'll be on every mission. You can't think to leave me behind. I want to be there, to watch your sorry back, if for no other reason."

She threw the suit at him. He caught it easily with one hand. As he put his legs into the costume he whispered, "I'd rather have you watching my front."

He mentally transmitted the sensation of him caressing her breast, his tongue licking across her nipple. Her right nipple pebbled before his eyes. Tatiana damned her body for being so responsive to its mate. Even when she was angry with him, she wanted him.

"Stop that," she snapped, then brushed a hand over

the breast to wipe the imaginary mouth away. "Don't distract me with sex, that's how you got out of having this conversation last night."

A wicked grin spread across his handsome face as he lifted the costume up and shoved his arms through. "You can't tell me you didn't like my little distraction. You orgasmed so many times you passed out."

A flush crept up her neck, and he flashed her an endearing look. "I didn't pass out, you bored me until I fell asleep."

Demetri leaped across the room before she blinked, coming to rest directly in front of her. He took a lock of Tatiana's hair between his fingers and thumb, bringing the silky strands to his nose. He inhaled its ocean scent deeply into his lungs. His hand crept around to the back of her head.

Demetri's fingers fisted tightly in her hair and jerked her head to the side, holding her exactly where he wanted her. His lips descended onto hers in a surprisingly gentle kiss. His mouth brushing hers, his tongue not demanding entry.

A small moan escaped her lips, the erotic contrast between his hard hand and soft lips dissolved her anger. Her warrior, hard but soft. Fierce, but gentle. She melted into his body, wanting more, needing more. More of him. More of his love.

She wrapped a leg around his thighs and pushed her core against his arousal. Tatiana rubbed against him like a cat.

He pulled back from her slightly, so close his lips brushed hers as he spoke. "You did not fall asleep. Woman, you should not lie to me. It makes me want to prove you wrong. Throw you onto Christina's desk and pound into you until you scream my name to the heavens. Fuck you until you pass out just to prove you did not fall asleep."

Her womb clenched at his crude description. Ragged breath sawed heavily from her lungs. Only the feel of the soft faux fur under her fingers allowed her brain to function. "I'd love for us to learn which of us is correct, but you have a job to do, bunny boy."

A deep sigh pushed from his full lips. "A rain check, then. We'll settle this later tonight, when we are back at the plantation."

Tatiana knelt before him. His shaft jumped in response to the sight.

"Put these on," she instructed, before pulling two ginormous shoes closer. Her fingers daftly undid the laces on his boots, pulled them from his feet, and replaced the manly boots with the effeminate, oversized pink shoes.

"Fates above, what did you talk me into?" He wiggled one of the large shoes at her.

She chuckled. "You know what they say about men with big feet."

Tatiana straightened and made her way around to his back. She zipped up the costume, noting how a recent increase in bulk made the suit extremely snug. Another day or two and it would not have fit. "They have big—"

Rather than finish the sentence, she reached around cupping the length of him in her hand, giving the steely appendage a squeeze.

"Have mercy, Tatiana. You just said I have a job to do."

She rubbed down the length of his shaft before her

hand dropped from his body. "You're right. Sorry." The sarcasm oozed from her voice. "I'd hate to get you all hot and bothered."

"I'm always hot and bothered around you. You don't need to touch me."

I'll remember that tonight when you try to prove which one of us was correct, she teased, lifting the giant head from the floor of the closet. *My job will be much easier if I don't have to touch you.*

His fingers brushed hers when he took the rabbit head. Something akin to electric current passed between them, pulsating, firing all their nerves at once. Desire danced between their bodies. She shuddered from the erotic sensation.

"You'll be touching me, Tatiana. You can't keep your hands off me." The devilish grin on his face produced an answering smile of her own.

She casually shrugged her shoulders. "What can I say? When you are right, you are right. Now put this thing on so you can get this over with. The sooner you do this the sooner we can get back to the plantation to see which of us is correct."

Demetri donned the head, sending the googly eyes circling wildly.

Honoring his word, Demetri played the Easter Bunny with all the grace and ease of the breed. The children took turns sitting on his lap, so he could give them a colored egg. He didn't flinch when one of the children brought a chocolate covered hand down across his arm turning his white fur brown. Nor did he protest when a baby was thrust into his arms, screaming at the giant bunny while her mother took a picture. Demetri even remained calm when one little boy wet himself and the urine flowed down the leg of the costume to puddle around the overly large plastic shoe.

Tatiana stood off to the side, watching in amazement as her mate took it all in stride. Admiration softened her expression from the way he remained calm and composed.

After allowing Tatiana to help him out of the costume, they made their way outside to join the festivities. Rebecca came running as soon as she saw them. "Mr. Demetwi, the Easter Bunny was here. You missed him." Her lower lip stuck out in a small pout.

"That's okay, little one. Remember, he is my friend. I have seen him plenty of times."

"Here." She lifted a colored egg up in her hand. "You have my egg."

Demetri shook off the offer with a wave of a large hand. "That's okay, you keep it. He would want you to have it." He tumbled her soft, black locks with a twist of his hand on her head.

"Look." Tatiana pointed across the lawn. "Miss Christina is calling everyone over to have a duck race."

"What's that?" asked Rebecca.

"I'm not sure. Why don't you go check it out? I bet it will be fun." She smiled down at the girl, watching after her as she crossed the lawn.

Rebecca tripped, falling face first toward the grass. In a blur of movement, Demetri caught the child before her knees or hands hit the ground. Her mate held the child away from him, inspecting her for any signs of injury. Satisfied she was fine, he put her down, and sent her on her way with a gentle pat on the head.

"You keep surprising me," Tatiana commented when Demetri came to her side. He brought his arm around her waist, tucking her against his side.

"In good ways, I hope."

"Mostly." The comment earned her a questioning lift of his brow. Not wanting to elaborate she daftly changed the subject. "Look at them. Christina has them doing the funniest things."

The children were currently racing across the lawn toward a finish line, bent over at their waists, their hands wrapped around their ankles, and their little butts in the air as they waddled toward the line. When two of them let go of their ankles, Christina made them go back to the starting line to begin the journey again. The sound of adult laughter mixed with childish giggles until most everyone laughed so hard tears rolled down their faces.

Demetri bent his head and planted a kiss on his mate's temple. "One day, Tatiana."

"What do you mean?"

He captured her with his gray eyes, letting her see the sincerity there. "One day, I want a little Demetri and a little Tatiana to be giggling like these children."

She couldn't have been more surprised. Having children never occurred to her. The world seemed like too cruel a place to bring an innocent into it. She assumed Demetri would feel the same. "You want children?"

"Only with you. What do you say we go back to the plantation and start working on them?" His lips slid to her ear to nibble there.

She pulled the lobe from his lips to look at him. "I'd say we have a lifetime to worry about having children."

"You might be carrying my child even now." His

hand splayed over her stomach protectively.

Emotions ran through her like a herd of turtles. She couldn't be pregnant!

Could she?

It's not like they'd used protection. Because it was difficult for most female vampires to conceive, she had never even considered the need for protection. She had been with Sammael for years and thankfully never conceived. It had not occurred to her it could be different with Demetri.

She would make an awful mother. A child wouldn't fit in her life. She was always off on assignments, risking her life. And she liked it that way. She didn't want to be a mother. Not yet and maybe not ever.

An uneasy fear turned her stomach. Her muscles tightened beneath her skin. Demetri's hand dropped from her stomach, but he retained his hold around her waist, needing to keep her close. He flowed into her mind, finding her concerns.

Don't worry, Tatiana. If it is to be, it will be. Whatever the future holds for you, for us, we'll get through it. I'll support you in all things. His hand drifted down to pinch her bottom. He nuzzled her neck, his lips passing softly over the pulse in her vein. A tremor coursed through her body.

The outskirt of her mind registered he'd distracted her again, but in that moment her body didn't care. Passion zinged through her veins, building a conflagration of fiery lust and desire. Her body ached with need. He had a way of making her like that. Making her forget everything but him. Being with him. Having him inside her.

His teeth nibbled at her ear. Hot breath blew across the lobe in a heated rush, sending an answering rush of moisture below.

His words whispered in her ear. "Come back to the plantation with me. I want to be alone with you. I will worship your body, make it writhe beneath me until your screams fill the room."

She found herself nodding, even though a part of her wanted to examine the issue he was trying hard to distract her from. She tucked the thoughts about having a baby away, vowing to pull them back out to examine later, preferably at a time when Demetri was distracted and not in her mind.

Tatiana needed to be sure her feelings were her own, and she was beginning to merge so completely with Demetri at times it could be hard to determine where she ended, and he began. And right now, a lot of lust and longing flowed between them. Their desire built until she led them to their bikes. The female warrior wanted to have him all to herself, knowing his sensual promise would be fulfilled.

Chapter 34

Demetri stood in front of the mirror in their room, automatically sliding the black silk tie beneath the stiff collar of his shirt while Tatiana move absently around the room. His heartmate met his eyes in the mirror and smiled as she came up behind him.

"I'll do that," she offered, sliding around his body to take the tie from his hands. He surrendered it willingly, glad to have help. It was a small task, nothing really, but to him it was something special.

Tatiana wasn't the type of woman to do what in his day had been considered wifely duties. She would fight to the death for him, but she wasn't inclined to cater to her man. He fought the grin which threatened to take his face while her elegant fingers worked the dark silk into a knot at his neck.

"What?" she asked.

"Nothing, I am just thinking about how beautiful you look."

And she did. He loved the way the black strapless evening gown clung lusciously to her slight curves. The empire waist pushed her breasts up to tempt him, made his body stir. It ached with need, even though they had just finished making love an hour ago.

"Well, don't get used to seeing me in this. I don't do dresses."

"Hmm, that's a shame, because they definitely do

you." He wrapped his arms about her waist and drew her into the heat of his body. Lowering his lips to hers, he took her mouth in a passionate kiss. Using his tie to pull him closer, she melted into him and deepened the kiss.

Their tongues indulged in a long, slow exploration. Their tastes mingled until they became one. The delicious scent of her arousal stirred his passion. Her legs trembled when his hands slid down to cup the firm curve of her bottom and pulled her closer to feel his excitement.

He was the one to break the kiss, leaning back to gaze down on her beautiful face. Tatiana was a vision. Her lashes lay against pale cheeks. The dark crescents fluttered open. Her yellow eyes, clouded in a sensual haze of desire. She hungered for him, wanting what only he could give her. It nearly did him in to push away from her tempting body.

"You need to finish dressing, *kotik kisa.* It is almost time."

Her hands dropped from his body in a slow sinuous slid down his chest. She glanced with disdain over at the panty hose lying on the bed.

"Florida girls don't wear hose. I hate those things. It isn't right. They're like wearing plastic wrap around my legs."

The Alpha straightened the tie, then smoothed it flat against his white shirt. Next, he buttoned his black tuxedo jacket over the shirt. "I'm sorry, for your discomfort, but you know what they say about when in Rome."

"But we aren't in Rome, we're in Savannah." She picked up the nylons by one leg and walked the fabric between the fingers of her hands to bunch the material. "Actually, Savannah's way worse. Did you know you aren't supposed to wear white here after Labor Day? I mean, come on, that's stupid. Down in Florida, people wear white all the time."

Demetri moved behind her and placed his hands on her, catching the dress around her hips. He steadied her while she grudgingly pushed one leg and then the other into the hose.

"Sounds like there is a lot of freedom in Florida."

Tatiana jumped up and down, pulling the hose over her hips then shimmied the skirt of her chiffon gown down over her legs. "There is. It is such a diverse group of people there that everyone is free to be who they are. No etiquette or values are imposed on everyone like there is here."

Demetri went to one knee and slipped a black, high heel shoe onto her foot. He wound the long laces around her calf. After anchoring them into place, he could not help but notice the way the shoes made her legs look long, sexy. Tramping down on the iniquitous thoughts the shoes elicited, he tugged her dress down to cover the sight. "I think I'm glad your bridesmaid dress is long."

"Why?"

"Because, if those beautiful legs were on display all night, I'd have to fight every male at the wedding for staring at them. Those shoes are sexy as hell."

Tatiana's laugh slid over him in a silky glide.

"I think Julie called them fuck-me-shoes."

One dark brow rose. "Sounds like a plan to me."

He picked her up by the waist and threw her onto the bed, his body following to blanket hers. He braced his weight with his arms on either side of her head as her hands came up to lie against his chest. "Demetri, we don't have time for this. Remember?"

He forced a heavy breath between his lips. "Fine," he capitulated. "But I want you to wear those to bed tonight."

His arousal jerked against her stomach at the command. A sinfully wicked smile stretched her painted lips. "They'll go well with the bunny costume. Don't you think?"

A vision of her from the previous night flew into his mind. She had surprised him after they had arrived at the plantation from the counseling center by having a bunny costume of her own. She emerged from the en suite bath wearing a ruffled black and white tuxedo bodysuit. The corseted outfit came complete with black elbow-length gloves, a fluffy tail, and black bunny ears headband. Where his bunny costume had been cumbersome and funny, hers was sleek and sexy. The thought of adding the black stiletto heels to the outfit had his most manly part jumping for joy.

He pushed from the comfort of her body, smoothing down his tux with a tug of the lapels. You realize every time I look at you tonight, I will be thinking about you in the costume wearing those heels."

His eyes devoured her hungrily, drinking in the sight of her.

"Good, then I will not be the only one feeling excited."

"Why? Do you think I look good?" He swept a graceful arm down the length of his body.

"You look—"

When she hesitated, he pushed into her mind to

338

glean her thoughts.

Tatiana found handsome not nearly an adequate description of how he looked to her. His face no longer appeared pale or deathly gaunt, his body no longer spectrally thin. The gleam in his eyes was wicked, but not feral. She no longer saw signs of the pain or weakness he endured; just the opposite, in fact. Now he exuded a commanding strength and confidence, an allure that made her heart speed up and her legs go weak. He projected a raw sexual appeal that made desire career through her body, stirring her inner passion until she ached with need only he could satisfy.

"Tatiana." The sultry tone of his voice as he said her name sent a rush of answering heat to her core. "You must not look at me like that, thinking those thoughts. We need to go downstairs now, or we might not make it down at all."

She didn't try to argue for her mind realized he was right. She hungered for him with an unquenchable appetite. Her mouth salivated for the taste of him, his kiss, his body. His blood.

Demetri moaned. She was killing him. If they didn't get out of the bedroom soon, his self-control would falter, and they might not make the wedding.

Tatiana put her hand in his and allowed him to lead her down the stairs. The house buzzed with activity. People scurried about like ants in a mound.

Workers carried flowers through the home, taking them to their destination with haste. The video crew prepped their cameras to make sure not a single shot was missed. People from the catering company in white shirts and pink bow ties moved about, gathering food onto the trays and pouring drinks into glasses.

Payton brushed by them with a murmured excuse me, obviously on his way to oversee the activity in his kitchen. Only Alexander seemed to be taking the preparations in stride. He meandered through the foyer, laptop in hand.

"Hey guys," he greeted, typing on the keyboard.

Tatiana pulled her fingers from Demetri's hand to point at the computer. "Why the laptop, Alex?"

"Just making sure the secure live feed is working." He turned his attention from the pair to the computer screen. "You seeing everything okay, Penny."

"Yes, it's spot on, Alex. Can't thank you enough. It's brilliant," a disembodied voice with a British accent said.

The blond Alpha's smile reached his eyes. "Glad to do it. The feed will be on a slight delay, but you won't miss a thing." Alex nodded in dismissal to the couple as he strolled away talking to the laptop.

Christina passed him when she came down the hall in a strapless ivory gown, the crystal beading sparkling.

"There you are!" Marcus' heartmate greeted. "I was afraid you had backed out after what I had said at the spa."

Demetri shot a questioning look to his mate. *What did she say?*

Nothing, don't worry about it. We worked it out. All's good.

"I know you didn't mean it like it sounded, Christina."

"You seemed pretty mad."

"I was upset," Tatiana admitted. She laced fingers with her mate. "But I'm over it. Since you've gotten to know Demetri and even asked him to walk you down the aisle, everything's good."

"So, you're okay with Demetri escorting me?"

"I think he is a perfect choice."

What am I missing here, Tatiana?

Nothing. I'll tell you later. She sent to appease him.

I'll hold you to that.

I wouldn't expect anything else. Tatiana's exasperation flowed over their mindlink.

Christina took Demetri's hand in hers. A small growl emanated from Tatiana's throat. Demetri sensed jealousy and shock at the emotion from his mate.

There is no need for your jealousy, kotik kisa.

Tatiana beat it down hard. *I know Christina is no threat, especially since she and Marcus are mated. I don't know what came over me.*

I am flattered you are protective of me, Demetri sent.

Don't get cocky, Romanoff. Tatiana coughed into her hand to cover a smile.

"Come on you two." Christina pulled Demetri's arm. "It's almost time. We have to get out back."

With the exceptionally long train of Christina's wedding gown draped over her arm, the trio hustled through the large home to one of the two tents set up on the property.

Demetri gently led Tatiana to the white tent where Juliette stood waiting for them in her light-pink, chiffon gown. The tiny white pearls around the empire waist were complemented by the bouquet of flowers she held which boasted matching pearl accents.

"Hey guys." Juliette gave them a wide smile. "I'd like you to meet my father, Bob Saint-John. Daddy these are my new friends, Tatiana and Demetri, and of course you already know Christina."

"Pleased to meet ya both." The farmer shook each one's hand in turn. "Julie Bug's told me a whole lot about ya."

"It's a pleasure, sir," Demetri said. "Any relation to Juliette is a relation of mine."

"Julie mentioned Nick's cousin would be attending. Guess you're him."

Demetri smiled, hoping it came off friendly and respectful. Juliette's father seemed quick minded, figuring out he and Nicholai were related with only the one comment from him. "Yes, I am Nicholai's cousin."

"If you and your cousin are any indication, guess size runs in your family." Bob turned to his daughter. "Sorry honey, looks like you'll be birthing some big babies."

"Daddy!" A blush crept up Julie's neck.

The sound of music cut off their chuckles, ending any further banter. The wedding planner shoved a small bouquet into Tatiana's hand and ushered her inside the tent to stand between two tall pedestals each of which supported a large flower arrangement. The planner closed the curtained opening behind her, cutting Demetri off from his mate.

****

Tatiana started down the aisle. Rows of white chairs filled with guests all staring at her lined both sides. Delicate pink rose petals dusted the white runner beneath her feet. It led to the dais waiting at the front of the tent where Marcus and Nicholai stood, looking dapper in their similar tuxedoes.

Marcus wore a three-button notch jacket. Its silk lapels matched the stripe down the legs of his pleated pants. A white silk vest coordinated with his white bow tie. Nicholai's tux was similar to Marcus', with the exception of the accessories. He wore a more traditional design with black silk cummerbund and matching tie.

Making her way down the aisle, she counted the candelabras that flanked her, shocked to discover there were twenty of the things casting a delicate light over the guests. Pink roses and white hydrangeas draped from the arms. The couples had spared no expense. The flowers alone cost a fortune. They must have bought out every flower shop in Savannah to cover both tents.

When she reached the front, Tatiana took her place across from the grooms. Nicholai gave her a wink, clearly noting how uncomfortable she felt having had all the attention on her during the trip down the aisle. She blew out a steady breath of relief. The hard part was over. She just had to stand here and hold the brides' bouquets for the remainder of the ceremony. Piece of cake. She graced Nicholai with a tight smile.

When the music changed, his gaze flew to the back of the tent. His bride entered on the arm of her father. Nicholai's intense eyes tracked every step. His anticipation built as she approached. His love showed on his face. The corners of his mouth turned up in a broad smile that reached the sparkle in his eyes. His gaze took in the delicate blush gown, and the coordinating lace bolero that almost hid the spaghetti straps on Juliette's shoulders. He seemed to be memorizing everything down to the slightest detail as if he wanted to remember this moment for the rest of his long life.

Julie handed her bouquet to Tatiana then turned her attention to her heartmate. When their eyes locked, the world seemed to fall away, leaving only the two of them. As Julie's father handed her off to Nicholai, the music changed once more.

Marcus stepped around the couple to watch his bride be escorted down the aisle. Christina flowed over the scattered petals. Her strapless gown, with its hand-embroidered, fitted bodice, shimmered from the reflection of the candles on the crystal beading. Her full skirt and cathedral-length train, glided around her.

Marcus' dark eyes locked with her emerald ones. She moved like a dancer, fluid and light. Graceful in her sultry strides. Tiny wisps of her auburn hair fell from her chignon around her delicate neck and face. The smile she wore for Marcus widened as they approached.

Tatiana's eyes locked with Demetri, and her heart skipped a beat. He looked handsome, dashing really. The cut of his jacket emphasized his broad shoulders and narrow waist to perfection.

Do you see my cousin, Natasha?

Tatiana glanced around noting the guests. Of course, Vlad and Alex had chosen to sit near one another. Close to them was Desmond, his arm around a woman who was crying, presumably Juliette's mother since her father had just sat down next to her. A pretty woman sat to the left of Julie's father. In all probability, she must be Juliette's sister, the super model Tatiana had heard so much about. There were also several people there she recognized from the counseling center.

Nicholai's sister, Natasha, sat near the front looking saucy as usual with her wildly colored hair. Tatiana never knew what color her hair would be when she saw her. She changed the color as often as most people changed their clothes. For this occasion, she opted to wear her long hair down, dyed black with only a strip of dark purple near her face.

She was a free spirit, the type who would go skinny dipping in a frozen lake. She often wore fire engine red lipstick that stood out in stark contrast to the black dog collar choker with skulls and crossbones she usually wore around her neck.

I'm relieved to see she has replaced her choker with a strand of large gray pearls and decided to wear a simple black dress instead of the tee shirt and jeans she typically opts for.

An improvement in my opinion, Demetri sent.

Obviously, Vlad agrees, given the way he is watching Natasha discretely from the corner of his eyes.

What! Demetri's outrage poured over their link.

Concentrate on your duties, Romanoff. You have a job to do. There will be time later to deal with Vlad.

Arriving at the dais, Demetri waited for Christina to give Tatiana her flowers then handed his charge to Marcus, placing her hand in his before taking his position next to Tatiana.

Juliette and Christina look beautiful in their gowns, but they do not compare to you, Tatiana. You are absolute perfection. I'd love to run my fingers along the jewels under your bosom. He clasped his hands behind his back as if to keep himself in check.

Holy hell, her heartmate was walking sex. Her core clenched. His naughty thought planted a sensual picture in her mind. Just as she contemplated doing something about the need he created, the sound of Nicholai's voice drew her from the thought.

Nicholai's large hands wrapped around his mate's delicate fingers. He gazed into her honey brown eyes when he spoke, the conviction in his sturdy voice evident as he professed his vows. "I pledge to you my faithfulness, never to forsake you. I pledge to share a lifetime of eternal, boundless love with you; to care for you, take into my protection all that is yours. I pledge to love you until the end of days, with an unselfish devotion. On this night, my heartmate, I pledge my life to you, to be your partner in all things, for all of time."

He had chosen the traditional vows of the breed, and Juliette repeated the pledge to him, promising to give her life to his as her eyes glistened with unshed tears of happiness. At the minister's prompting, Juliette took her mate's hand in hers and slid a platinum band around his ring finger saying, "I, Juliette, give you this ring as a symbol of our never-ending love and pledge to each other this day."

Nicholai reached up, wiping a lone tear from her cheek with the pad of his thumb before taking her hand to slip a diamond-encrusted band around her finger. He captured her with his amber eyes, and the rest of the world seemed to dissolve from around them as he spoke. "My dear Juliette, I give you this ring as a symbol of our *never-ending* love and of my pledge to you this day."

A tear slipped down her cheek. He caught it with his lips in a gentle caress.

"I love you, *lastochka,*" he whispered against her cheek.

"Now, now. It isn't time for the kissing just yet," the minister admonished him with a friendly grin. "Marcus and Christina still have to say their vows."

The guests chuckled, Nicholai tucked Juliette to his side and patiently waited for the other couple to have their turn.

After Marcus and Christina exchanged similar vows, the couple each took a turn to slide a ring onto the hand of their mate as the minister prompted them to proclaim their rings to be a symbol of their never-ending love and pledge.

The two couples turned to face their guests. The minister's loud voice rang out behind them. "Today these two couples have joined their lives to one another before this company. May their days be long, and may they be seasoned with love, understanding, and respect.

"Their miracle lies in the path they have chosen together. May they enter this marriage with the knowledge that…"

The smell of smoke wafted on the breeze, drawing Tatiana's attention. The odor light but noticeable to the vampires in the tent. Noses scented the air. Eyes darted around the room. Heads turned left and right looking for the source. It was not a woodsy smell, more man-made, like plastic or wiring burning.

A scream came from the back of the tent, silencing the minister and earning a collective gasp from the guests.

Tatiana's eyes raked the back of the dwelling until she saw smoke rolling in wispy waves like ghostly fingers from the laptop Alexander had been fiddling with earlier. Desmond jumped into action, his long strides taking him to the computer.

"Penny, did you scream?"

The woman on the screen screamed her answer, obviously seeing the smoke and thinking the tent was on fire. Flames began licking the screen, consuming Penny's image as the laptop ceased to function.

Desmond snatched the flowers from the pedestal standing next to the opening of the tent. Ripping them from their vase, he threw the blooms to the ground. As flower petals scattered, Desmond dumped the water from the vase over the computer, dowsing the flames. When the steam and smoked cleared, Alex stood next to him.

"Quick thinking," the blond Alpha muttered, pulling the plug from the extension cord. "Must have been the battery. I've heard of them catching fire, but I've never seen it happen before."

Desmond placed the vase back on the pedestal before turning to face the guests. "Problem solved. Just a little issue with a laptop. You know how it is with technology; it never works when you bloody well want it to."

A nervous giggle spread through the crowd.

Marcus cleared his throat to garner the attention of the group. "If I might have your attention please. I would like to recommend Nikko and I get on with the kissing, so we can get out of here and start the party."

Without waiting for approval, he bent his heartmate over his arm, giving her a long, passionate kiss that left her breathless. Over her groom's shoulder, Christina watched Nicholai cup Juliette's face between his hands before he gave her a gentle loving kiss that caused a blush to creep up her neck to rosy her cheeks. The guests clapped and cheered when the two Alphas picked their brides up in their arms and carried them out of the tent. Demetri and Tatiana walked behind the couples, their arms linked, followed closely by

Juliette's mother and father who led the guests from the tent across the lawn to the reception.

Only Alex stayed behind.

"I'll be right back," Tatiana told Demetri.

"Where are you headed?"

"Back in to see what happened."

"I'll go with you."

They tucked under the flap of the tent.

"I can't believe the stupid thing caught on fire." Alex scratched his head. "I've never had that happen before."

Demetri shrugged, his tux stretching tight across his broad shoulders. "These sorts of things happen."

"I guess." Apprehension played over Alex's face.

Tatiana's eyes met Alex's over the smoldering computer. "Let's just hope this doesn't start a trend for the rest of the evening."

Chapter 35

The burning laptop left the sharp taste of stale smoke in her mouth. Tatiana stepped from the tent and took in a long breath of fresh air. Slow steps allowed the cool evening air to surround her. The aroma of freshly cut grass and the sweet smell of flowers swirled about her. Flower petals carpeted the manicured lawn. They released a heady perfume of roses that tickled her nose. Water flowed, the sound soft as it cascaded down from a manmade waterfall into a crystal blue pond. She closed her eyes, drawing in another deep breath. The slight humidity felt good on her heated skin, like a misty rain that fell to warm her flesh.

Demetri's fingers laced with hers, anchoring her to the earth when her thoughts threatened to transport her away. She looked down at their hands, his long fingers entwined with hers, wrapped around to hold her tightly to him. He brought their hands over his heart. "Tatiana, you are far away. What are you thinking about?"

That was her mate, always aware of her, a constant shadow in her mind. She smiled up at him. "Aren't you reading my thoughts?" she whispered as they continued toward the reception tent.

I try not to intrude. I'd hate to make you upset with me.

She got the distinct impression over their mindlink he was teasing. *Teasing* her. She never would have thought him a jokester.

Why stop tonight? Her quip earned a legitimate smile on his handsome face.

Spending time with him was always full of discovery. She had been so wrong about him. She hadn't believed he could be charming or warm. Maybe it was because they always fought, struggled against each other for dominance.

I didn't exactly give him a fair chance of showing his true colors when we first met. I just assumed the worst.

She did that—assumed the worst of everyone and moved on. It was easier that way. It meant she never had to care. No one ever disappointed her or hurt her.

I'll never hurt you, Tatiana. Not intentionally.

I know. She gave his hand a reassuring squeeze. *I know you now, Demetri. You may be a badass, but you have a good heart.*

He brought her hand to his lips and nipped her fingers with his fangs. *Don't spread that nasty rumor around. I have a reputation to protect.*

Your secret is safe with me.

Their eyes locked over their hands. Her breath hitched in her lungs at the love on his face.

And you are safe with me. I pledge to you my faithfulness, never to forsake you. I pledge to share a lifetime of eternal, boundless love with you; to care for you, take into my protection all that is yours. I pledge to love you until the end of days with an unselfish devotion. On this night, my heartmate, I pledge my life to you, to be your partner in all things for all of time.

Her heart did a flip in her chest as her breath left her lungs in a rush. He had just pledged himself to her with the words of their breed. Those words were sacred, honored, a promise that would never be broken once uttered. He was hers. Forever. She knew he meant the oath. The wealth of his sincerity flowed into her mind mixed with his love for her.

His head lowered slowly, eyes locked on her full lips. Their breath mingled, becoming one when his lips brushed hers.

"Hey guys. There you are." Marcus' booming voice shattered the moment into a thousand pieces. "We were wondering what happened to you."

"We just wanted a little air," Demetri informed him, watching as Marcus' long strides quickly brought him to the couple.

Marcus gave his fellow Alpha a conspiratorial wink. "More like a little time alone."

"That, too."

"Well, you'll have to get some alone time later. Everyone is asking about you guys. The wedding planner is having some sort of fit. I don't know, it's time for a toast or something. Anyway, Demetri's services are being requested."

"What if I happen to need his services?" Tatiana asked, trying to sound playful, but the husky timbre of her voice fooled no one.

A boyish grin lifted the corners of Marcus' mouth. "I'd say he's a lucky man."

Demetri growled, it was low, a playful warning, but a warning none the less. "Let's go. Lead the way, Marcus."

The trip to the reception tent was a quick one. The doors to the tent stood open wide. Classical music from the ten-piece orchestra poured from the opening as they approached. A long Lucite table met them just inside the tent. It looked gorgeous, filled with floating white, cream, and pink roses as well as votive candles. Suspended over the table, hanging from crystal beading, were the place cards, most of which had been picked off by the guests who were already seated at their tables. Tatiana noticed the names left hanging. Alexander Hall and Samantha de Clare hung on the sparkling strand next to their cards.

"I thought Juliette's last name was Saint-John. Who is Samantha de Clare?"

Marcus rolled his eyes. "That is her sister's professional name. She insisted we use it. Made Christina change it at the last minute. I thought Payton would pop a gasket when he found out. Poor man, I think he has finally been worn out. I'm going to give him a long vacation after this."

"Who's getting a long vacation?" Christina asked, coming up to join them. Marcus put an arm around her back and rested a hand on the nape of her neck, massaging the tension there in a slightly possessive gesture.

"Payton. I'm going to give him a month off once everyone leaves the plantation."

"That's perfect. He can be on vacation while we're on our honeymoon."

Tatiana plucked Demetri's card from the beads and handed it to him. "Where are you guys going?"

"To Europe. I've never been."

"I want to show Christina my home in Italy, then we'll tour some of the other countries. We'll stop by Germany, of course, maybe see Stephan and Kat while we're there. Then on to France, Spain, England."

Tatiana pulled her card from the crystal strand, sending it swaying to create beautiful prisms along the wall. "Sounds lovely. Are Nicholai and Juliette going with you?"

Both Marcus and Christina laughed. Christina spoke first. "No. I don't think either Marcus or Nicholai wanted to share a honeymoon."

"He would be put to shame by my sexual prowess. I wouldn't want to embarrass him on his honeymoon," Marcus teased, glancing down at his watch. "You better find your way to the table you two. The wedding planner is looking for you to make a toast, and she is a real stickler about timelines."

Demetri raised his hands in surrender. "Wouldn't want to piss off the planner."

Marcus leaned forward and muttered conspiratorially, "You have no idea." The younger Alpha straightened and offered his arm to his mate. "Ready to go back to our table, *cara*?"

Christina linked her arm in his, allowing him to escort her to their table at the head of the tent. Tatiana and Demetri followed behind the newlyweds, giving her time to take in the opulent setting.

From the ceiling, crystals swayed gently casting a soft reflective light that danced around the space. They complemented the smaller crystals which hung from the flower center pieces on each table.

The tables, set with beautiful gold silk tablecloth underlays, were covered with champagne colored silk fantasia linen that boasted hand-beaded pearls and crystals. Three-foot high crystal vases dripped flowers in shades of pink, white, and ivory over the tables.

Did you prepare a toast?

Demetri nodded his head. *I thought of a few things to say. Nothing is written down. I figured I would wing it. I must admit, now that the moment has arrived, I'm a little nervous.*

You can handle it.

Demetri handed Tatiana into a chair tied with a big champagne bow.

Thanks for the vote of confidence. His chest swelled a little as he sat.

The statement was sincere. Tatiana believed he could handle not only the toast, but anything life threw at them. She had the utmost conviction in him and his abilities.

The DJ handed Demetri a mic and he cleared his throat. "When Marcus and Nicholai approached me and announced I needed to come up with a speech for tonight, I didn't know what to say. Luckily, our stag party provided lots of fodder."

Demetri paused and looked around the room. "Ummm. It would seem that last statement has made some squirm in their seats. As well it should."

A picture of Alex on a stripper pole flashed onto the screen located behind the dance floor. The audience roared.

Tatiana burst out laughing at the ridiculous image of Alex dressed in short shorts wearing a veil on his head and swinging a boa around the silver pole.

However did you get that picture and arrange to have it displayed? She sent Demetri over their mindlink.

I got the owners of First Bite to send me a screen shot from their surveillance cameras.

Tatiana shook her head. *Alex isn't the only one*

with tech skills, I see.

Demetri smiled before he continued. "Given Alexander's penchant for cross dressing at the bachelor party, I was a little worried he might upstage the brides today. Luckily, for the grooms, he did not."

He waited for the laughter to die down before going on. "It is my understanding that traditionally I should *sing* the praises of the grooms and mention their *numerous* good points. Alas, I'm terribly sorry, but I can't sing, and I won't lie." More giggles sounded from the crowd. "However, what I can say is this."

"I would like the brides to each place one hand on the table." Demetri waited for Christina and Juliette to comply then glanced from Nicholai to Marcus. "Now grooms, if you would be so kind as to place your hand on top of your brides' for the remainder of this speech."

Once the males did as he asked, Demetri proceeded, "In all seriousness, it has been an honor to be your best man today and watch two men I care about marry their heartmates. Nicholai, you are a very lucky man. Your Juliette is beautiful and intelligent. The love you two share is beyond measure. I can tell the two of you will be immensely happy together."

He turned toward Marcus. "You, comrade, should be thanking your lucky stars. Christine has a heart of gold and beauty that outshines her heart. She deserves a good man. So, count yourself lucky that you got to her first."

Tatiana joined the crowd in a chuckle.

Demetri glanced over the audience. "It makes me happy to see so many people here from around the world. Nicholai, Juliette, Marcus and Christine, seeing so many people to go all this effort to celebrate this day with you is a credit to you. I'm sure everyone sitting here agrees with me when I say your love for one another fills the room and makes our hearts sing with joy. I'm sure we all can agree that these four individuals make two perfect couples."

Several people used their silverware to clink their glasses and the couples kissed.

"Now in case you are wondering why I asked the boys to place their hands on top of the brides', I will tell you. As my final duty as best man, I have given the grooms the last five minutes in which they will ever have the upper hand over their heartmates."

Very cute, Tatiana sent over their link while the audience laughed. *I certainly hope you intend to give me the upper hand in our union.*

We shall see, kotik kisa. A corner of Demetri's mouth lifted in a sly smile while he picked up a glass of champagne from the table beside him.

"And so, it gives me immense pleasure and much relief to invite everyone to stand, raise a glass and join me in a toast to the happy couples."

Once everyone complied, Demetri lifted his glass and turned back toward the head table where the newlyweds sat with big smiles. "May you have long and happy lives together. May you forever hold one another in your safe keeping. May you be blessed with children and may your love outshine the brightest star. Salute!"

Demetri tipped his glass toward the couples then took a sip.

After taking a sip of her wine, Tatiana smiled, and a warmth blossomed in her chest that had more to do with Demetri than the wine. Her confidence had been well-placed. Pride for her mate and the amazing way he'd come up with an entertaining and funny speech off the cuff made her smile.

After the toast, Demetri was asked to DJ for the special dance of the evening. The first couple he introduced on the white dance floor was Christina and Marcus. After their dance, they exited, and Demetri ushered his cousin and his wife onto the floor. Julie looked especially beautiful in Nicholai's capable arms. They swirled around the shiny floor under a spotlight from above that cast their initials onto the floor.

"Let's take this up a notch," Demetri's suggested as the song ended, cutting off the orchestra with a wave of his hand. "Everybody dance now."

Music boomed from the DJ's speakers, the deep bass line pounding its rhythm.

Happy to be people watching rather than dancing, Tatiana glanced over to her left. Samantha and Alex joined the fun on the dance floor.

"Hey Sami," Julie greeted.

"Hi Jules. Great wedding."

"Thanks."

"Yeah, looks like you spared no expense. Nicholai must be loaded."

The expression on Julie's face made Alex spin her sister away to avoid any potentially ugly conflicts. They twirled in front of Tatiana and she couldn't help but overhear their conversation.

"So, you are enjoying the wedding?" Alex placed his hands upon Samantha's thin hips.

"I suppose it's nice enough. Juliette seems happy."

Her partner nodded. "Yeah, Nicholai too. So, do Christina and Marcus as far as that goes."

"Did you see Christina's dress? But, of course, you did. How could you miss it? The train was huge. Too big really for the venue."

"It's not so big now," Alex nodded toward Christina who was dancing with her husband.

"No, it was bustled up after the wedding. I bet that took a long time. But the designer is good, you can't even tell there was a train. She just looks like a big puff ball."

Tatiana cringed inwardly at the comment. If she didn't need to hide her preternatural hearing, she'd be tempted to give Sami a piece of my mind.

Luckily, Alex pulled her close and whispered. "That's not nice."

Samantha leaned back, surprise on her face, as if no one chastised her like that. "I didn't mean—"

"I know what you meant. And as long as Christina likes the dress, what does it matter? You aren't the one getting married, she is."

Looking sufficiently rebuked, Samantha let the hurt show. Tatiana blinked, and it was gone.

The music changed, the new song pounded a fast beat. Demetri danced his way across the white floor toward his cousin. Tatiana smiled. Her mate looked like a natural. His moves were current, modern.

I'll be damned. Demetri is an excellent fast dancer.

Katrina sat down into the empty seat beside her. "Your man can move."

Tatiana pushed some uneaten food around on her plate with a golden fork. "Yeah, he can. I had no idea."

"I did," Katrina informed her, watching a server remove all but the gold charger from the table.

Tatiana raised a questioning brow. "You did?"

"Yeah. He and I danced together." When jealousy flashed across Tatiana's face, she quickly amended the statement. "It was a long time ago. Before he met you."

"Excuse me ladies." Payton squeezed between their chairs and the next table.

"Payton." Kat reached out her arm, stopping his movement. "You did a great job. The wedding is awesome."

He looked down on her with genuine warmth. "Thank you, Miss Katrina. I'm glad you are enjoying yourself."

"I've asked you for over eight years to call me Kat."

A knowing smile acknowledged the request before he scurried off in Demetri's direction murmuring something along the lines of "couldn't do that, miss."

****

As he boogied over to his cousin, gyrating his hips to the music, Demetri's eyes tracked Payton. That man never stopped moving, which was especially impressive for someone his age. He turned on the floor, stopping to face Juliette and Nicolai who were dancing so close they were practically in the same space.

"Hey now, break it up you two. This isn't the prom you know."

"Then why are you acting like a chaperon, cousin?" Nicholai spun Julie and pressed her bottom against his groin. His hand held her to him, fingers splayed wide over her stomach. He moved with her in a sensual flow of their bodies.

Julie batted at his hand. "Stop that," she hissed. "Mama and Daddy are right over there."

Nicholai bent his head; his lips brushed her ear.

She melted against him, laying her head on his shoulder.

"Cousin, I don't think—" The loud sound of an explosion stopped the Alpha's admonishment.

The concussion from the blast rocked the ground. The tent glowed red around them.

Dammit!

Demetri thought a vile string of curses, chastising himself. He had been so consumed with Tatiana and his duties at the wedding, he forgot to be vigilant about his surroundings. Not once this evening had he sent his senses out looking for threats.

A few of the guests screamed. He immediately located Tatiana. Her eyes snapped to his. They moved as one, making their way through the crowd until they were side by side at the opening to the tent.

Another explosion erupted, and the tent glowed orange. Guests hurried outside, eyes gazing upward as a third explosion burst into the night, sending sparkling embers of yellow and blue to light up the night's sky. A series of thumps launched another round of mortars into the air, each exploding with a different burst of color.

"Isn't it beautiful," Christina exclaimed, drawing her husband's arms around her. "The fireworks were Marcus' idea. Desmond helped to rig them up when we decided to do them at the last minute. He's a pyro genius."

Demetri watched as color bathed the spectators. Shades of purple, red, orange, and blue danced over their faces like lights in a disco.

"Ohhhhh, look at that one," Marcus' heartmate exclaimed.

With a series of crackles, light exploded all around

them, turning night into day. The colors so vivid many had to avert their eyes.

Connor barked beside them, clearly agitated by the display. His ridge stood along his back, and his ears lay flat against his head while he paced. Vlad appeared from the shadows to rest his hand on the dog's head. Their eyes met. The dog settled, lowering his hind legs to sit on his haunches, clearly soothed.

Seeing the transformation in the canine, Natasha approached. "That was amazing. You have a way with animals."

Vladimir kept his attention on the Irish Wolf Hound. He shrugged his shoulders, but his hand never left the animal's head. "I didn't realize anyone was watching."

"I was," Natasha admitted. "That was really impressive. He calmed right down under your touch."

Vladimir's eyes lifted to her, pinning her with his intimidating stare. "My touch can do much."

Natasha shivered.

What the hell? thought Demetri. *She better be shivering from the cool air.*

Vlad stared at her like she was his prey, like he wanted to devour her. Why didn't she put some distance between her and the warrior? It was as if his gaze held her fast. She moved a step forward instead of back, closing the slight distance between them with a ridiculous look on her face. Demetri pushed into her mind to discover the cause.

Fates above! Demetri grimaced at what he learned.

What is it? Tatiana sent, sensing his discomfort.

It's Natasha. She thinks Vlad is handsome. She actually believes his secretive aloofness is, and this is her word not mine, intriguing.

Tatiana laughed.

You'll not think it's so funny when I pound him into the ground.

Oh, stop the big brother act. It's her life. She should be able to live it.

She can live it, just not with Vlad. He's not right for her.

Tatiana laid a hand on his forearm. *I believe the same could've been said about us.*

That's ridiculous.

Her laughter slid through his mind like a silk scarf. *Why not talk to her before you jump to conclusions that would result in beating Vlad's ass during what should be a happy event? I'm sure Nicholai would appreciate not having to separate you and Vlad at his wedding.*

Demetri pulled his eyes from the pair and gazed into his mate's yellow eyes. *Thank you, heartmate. I think I'll take your advice.*

That would be a first. Tatiana winked then looked up in time for the next mortar to explode.

Demetri shut down their mindlink and opened the link he shared with Natasha.

Natasha, are you enjoying the fireworks?

Her attention snapped to Demetri. *Yes, they are breathtaking. I'm having trouble breathing.*

His gaze narrowed, his brows pulling down over his gray eyes as he watched his cousin carefully. *Why do I get the impression it is something besides the fireworks that is causing you distress?*

Demetri, get out of my mind. It's nothing. Just the fireworks. They scared me a little when they went off.

You are sure that is all it is. Perhaps there is

someone here I need to have a talking to.

Stop with the father routine! I'm fine. I'm a big girl and can take care of myself.

I will always look out for you, Natasha. You are my blood, and I love you.

I love you too. Now get out of my head and start paying attention to your mate.

A sense of caring for him and appreciation for his concern came over the mindlink, then she snapped a mental barrier down to keep him out, but not before she also sent the impression of her love. Though he could have broken through, he allowed it to remain in place.

They smiled at one another around the throng of guest separating them on the lawn. Natasha turned back toward Vladimir to discover he'd left. Both he and Connor had vanished into thin air.

Demetri let out a sign of relief.

Payton pushed through the crowd, a silver tray clutched against his chest. Natasha reached out a delicate hand to capture his arm as he tried to pass. Demetri focused his preternatural hearing on the pair.

"Have you seen Vladimir?" she asked the older gentleman.

"Yes, miss. Mr. Starikovich headed toward the house, taking Miss Juliette's hound inside."

A wide smile spread across her pretty face. She leaned over and gave the valet a peck on his cheek. "Thanks, Payton. You're the best."

Yeah, thanks, Payton. Leave it to the butler to know where everyone was.

As Natasha hurried off toward the house, Marcus announced the time to cut the cake had arrived. Before Demetri could protest, Tatiana dragged him by the arm into the tent saying, "I must have cake."

After the cake was cut and the champagne drunk, the guests escorted the two couples around to the front of Marcus' home. Amid a barrage of well wishes, the newly married couples paired off, each tucking into the backseat of an awaiting limousine. The guests cheered and waved behind them as they took off down the long gravel drive at a snail's pace, allowing the couples within to wave back at the crowd. Under the veils of Spanish moss swaying from the oak trees lining the drive, Marcus and Christina, stood up through the open sunroof of their ride and waved, while behind them Nicholai and Juliette leaned out an open window from their limousine.

Demetri removed his jacket and wrapped it around his heartmate before tucking Tatiana under his arm. "This wedding giving you any ideas?" he whispered against her temple.

"It was a perfect night, almost makes a girl want a wedding of her own."

"Say the word and I will marry you tomorrow."

Tatiana opened her mouth to most likely make a sarcastic reply. A blast halted her voice. Color burst forth into the sky, raining debris over the limos. Demetri expected to see them jerk from the force of the explosion, but they continued their slow procession down the drive. Confetti drifted lazily down to blanket the vehicles and the occupants within with slips of brightly colored paper.

"Confetti cannons," Desmond supplied, coming to stand beside them. "They were Christina's idea."

Tatiana slipped an arm around Demetri's waist. "They made one helluva mess. Payton will have a coronary."

"That he will," Desmond agreed. "You two staying here tonight?"

Demetri nodded his head. "I thought we'd stay here one more night, then switch to my place tomorrow. It's near First Bite. I figured we could go there for our first meal when we rise tomorrow. Maybe celebrate the fact the wedding is finally over, then move our things into my townhouse after we eat."

"Why don't you join us, Desmond?" Tatiana offered.

"I wouldn't want to intrude."

"Nonsense, I'd like you to join us," Demetri assured him. "It will give us a chance to get to know each other a little since we will be working together."

Desmond's mouth twitched. "Ah, you mean it will give you a chance to feel me out. See if I'm worthy to be an Alpha?"

Demetri smiled, a genuine smile that reached the faint lines by his gray eyes. "Something like that."

"Very well, then. Tomorrow evening. First Bite. At say, eight o'clock?" The newest Alpha stuck out his hand and smiled.

Demetri grasped his forearm in the way of the warrior. "See you then."

Tatiana rolled her eyes at the display. *You don't have to be so macho, you know. A handshake would have sufficed.*

You love it when I'm macho. You think it is manly. Demetri sent to her, watching Desmond weave his way through the departing crowd into the house.

Come. Tatiana tugged on his tie, leading him like a dog on a leash. *I'm taking you upstairs, so you can show me just manly you are.*

Her arousal, flowed over him, mixing with the delicious smell of the ocean he adored. The scent of her desire lured him closer. He went with her gladly. Hell, he almost howled his approval, watching her swaying rump as they made their way to their room where he spent the rest of the night showing her just how manly he was.

Chapter 36

"...brocade, silver fish, willow, and chrysanthemum, but my personal favorite is the crosette because that one is a series of smaller explosions within a larger one. You get a lot of colors, more bang for your buck."

Tatiana sat across from Desmond listening to him discuss the fireworks show from the previous night. Demetri's large hand rested on her thigh, discretely concealed by the long white tablecloth covering their table. His fingers traced small circles along her inner thigh as if to declare his possession, branding her as his. And Fates help her, she liked it. She felt loved, cherished. She was his just as he was hers.

Tatiana leaned forward, taking her glass from the table. The act brought his hand a little farther up her thigh, sending a sizzling shot of heat up her leg straight to her inner core. Her stomach tumbled. This male turned her liquid, made her body melt with merely his touch. She couldn't get enough of him, no matter how often they made love.

It had only been a little over a week since she had found him in that awful warehouse, but it had been more than a year ago she discovered they were mates. And now she realized their bond had begun as soon as they met. She began loving him that first day. When his large body had pinned hers against the wall, something stirred. A tiny spark ignited within her and had grown into a raging conflagration of feelings.

What she had with Demetri went beyond love. It was a tangible force, a connection so deep it could never be severed, a meeting of two halves becoming one. One love. One soul.

Her life would be unbearably empty without Demetri to complete her—to love her. A tremor snaked down her spine at the thought.

I'll always be with you, kotik kisa. His hand squeezed her leg, sending a fresh wave of heated desire into her belly.

I might just hold you to that, Romanoff.

I'd hope you would.

She gave him a sly, sexy glance, her eyes full of mischief while she drank a sip from her glass. Demetri watched her throat work, the way her lips closed around the cool water, the ice bumping against her mouth until she took it between her teeth and sucked it in with a sensual slide between her full lips.

His hand slid a little higher on her thigh, and Tatiana gave him a knowing smile having gleaned his thoughts. He wanted her. Wanted to lay her over the table and sink into her warm heat until he became lost in her.

Desmond cleared his throat. "I think it is time for me to take my leave."

"But we just finished our meal," Tatiana said. "Are you sure you have to rush off?"

The newest Alpha glanced at Demetri, noting the intensity on his face. Her male looked almost as if he was in pain. Tatiana realized Desmond must sense the sexual energy pulsing between Demetri and her. It had been growing as they dined, and DW had appeared more and more uncomfortable as their meal progressed.

"I'm sure." Desmond motioned for their server. "I'm paying."

"No. I've got this," Demetri assured him.

"I don't think so," Desmond challenged with a smile, meeting the Alpha's eyes.

Demetri's eyes narrowed. "I think—"

A scream stopped Demetri's retort. Somewhere a tray dropped, sending china to the floor to break into a thousand pieces. From the third floor, a vampiric couple ran down the stairs in a blur, followed by two employees.

Demetri rose, put on a burst of speed, and intersected one of the workers. His hands wrapped around her arms like steel bands, preventing her from moving even as she struggled hard against his grip. The woman's fear perfumed the space. Her eyes were wild, her body tense.

"What's wrong?"

"I…there…"

Demetri shook her slightly, then pinned her with his stare. "Slow down. Take a breath."

The commanding timbre of his voice brooked no argument. The female vampire forced a deep inhalation.

"Let it out." Demetri waited for her to comply before continuing. "Now tell me what is wrong."

The server trembled, her legs going weak beneath her. If Demetri had not been holding onto her, she would have collapsed. "Up there…on the third floor…a…"

"A what?" Demetri demanded, his tone as sharp as the dagger he had hidden beneath his jacket.

"A bomb!"

Tatiana and Desmond stood, sending their chairs flying to the floor. Tatiana arrived beside the girl first. "What do you mean a bomb?"

"A bomb. You know as in *boom*. We've got to get out of here."

Tatiana nodded. "You dematerialize. We'll get the customers out."

"Wait," Desmond commanded. He laid a hand on the server's shoulder. "Where is the bomb exactly?"

"Third room on the right."

"Right. Got it." Desmond sprinted up the stairs.

As the waitress dematerialized from his steely grip, Demetri let a series of Russian curses flow from his lips. "Tatiana, you get the customers and employees to safety. I'll go help Desmond."

Her eyes locked with Demetri's. "You're not going to try to dismantle the bomb, are you?"

"Actually, I have some munitions training. With what Desmond seems to know about pyrotechnics, we might just be able to save this place. Now move."

Demetri disappeared in a blur of vampiric speed up the stairs, forestalling the argument on her lips. Knowing the civilian lives were a priority, she set to work running from table to table on the second floor encouraging those stupefied into befuddlement to materialize to a safe place. The few she encountered who could not yet dematerialize she sent downstairs, telling them to get as far away from the building as possible.

With the floor cleared, the female warrior ran down the stairs to the ground floor of the restaurant. She pushed her senses out, searching all signs of life.

Everyone was human except for a few of the serving staff. She held her speed in check, forcing herself to go at a human pace, going from table to table asking the patrons to leave. Most refused to take her seriously.

Anger boiled in her veins. This wasted precious time.

She captured the gaze of one stubborn man. "You will leave. Go home. Now!"

He grabbed his wife round the arm and drug her from the premises despite her protests.

Tatiana pulled a similar routine with the others. Slowly, one table at a time, the patrons left. Each with the same blank look on their face.

Demetri, what's going on? She pushed into his mind to garner the information. She saw a crude device. Some dynamite, wire, a travel alarm clock. *Looks like something out of a movie.*

She grabbed a remaining human and captured him with her stare.

Precisely what the rookie thought. Desmond thinks he knows how to disarm it.

Tatiana sighed. *But you aren't going to let him do it are you.* It was a statement not a question.

Fear for his safety slid up her spine. Its icy tentacles wrapped around her brain until only room for thoughts of him remained.

Tatiana lost the grip she had on the human's mind. The man stared at her, his eyes wide with wonder and outrage.

"Excuse me, miss." The man looked at her expectantly. "Can I help you?"

The VES agent blinked, coming back to her full awareness. She captured him with her eyes. *You have paid your bill and want to go home. Leave quickly. Now!*

Immediately, her thoughts returned to Demetri.

Demetri, I'm coming up once the last of the humans are out of here.

No! I want you to dematerialize back to our townhouse where it is safe.

No way, Romanoff! I'm not leaving you.

He poured his concern for her safety into her mind. The power of his fear coursed through the link. It was all-consuming, just as her concern for him was.

Tatiana, I need to know you will be safe. My worry for you is distracting me from this task. The device is a little more complicated than we first thought. I need to be able to concentrate.

You need to get out of there.

I'm going to have to block you.

Don't you dare! I have to know you are all right. At least let me stay in your mind so I can see what is happening. I'll keep my thoughts to myself.

No, it is too dangerous. I'll send you my impressions, let you feel my emotions so you'll know I am fine. It is the best I can do.

Fine. She'd take anything she could get. At least if she could feel his emotions she would know he was alive. *But I'll tell you this, Alpha, you better be safe. If you think the thing is going to explode get out of there. If you blow yourself up, I'll kill you.*

I love you too, my tigress warrior.

****

A deep chuckle was the last sound Demetri sent across their mindlink. He turned to Desmond who knelt beside him.

"Looks like it's pretty standard. What do you think, rookie?"

The English Alpha nodded. "I think if you cut the blue wire the timer will stop."

Demetri slid the dagger from its sheath. Sweat dotted his brow as his anxiety rose. With a steady hand, he sliced through the wire. The two males watched the timer expectantly, surprised when it continued its count down.

"What the hell?" Demetri wiped his brow with the back of his hand.

"There must be a duplicate. The pyro guys on the set would sometimes do that, build a duplicate into the explosive device to make sure we got the shot."

His fingers traced the wires on the device. They led between the sticks of dynamite and under the bomb.

Desmond bent down to take a closer look. "I think I see it. Cut the red one."

"You sure? Because a minute ago, you said it was the blue."

Their eyes met over the device. Time was ticking away. They had less than five minutes to either deactivate the damned thing or dematerialize from the room. They needed to act fast, a decision must be made.

Desmond nodded with absolute certainty on his face. "The red."

Demetri sliced through the red wire, the sharp blade going through like water through fingers, smooth and easy. The timer stopped its count down.

Relief poured through them. Demetri sat back on his heels and breathed heavy sighs of relief while Desmond began to take the bomb apart piece by explosive piece.

Demetri's thoughts turned toward his mate. Tatiana was a brave woman. If he'd allowed it, she would have been right here with him. And if he was honest with himself, he would admit a part of him had wanted her there. Her presence steadied him. He didn't like denying her, making her feel unvalued by refusing to allow her to help.

She wanted to be in the action, and he could certainly understand that. It was wrong of him to keep her from the council. Tatiana was smart, capable. And he could be there to ensure her safety.

Desmond's sharp gasp pulled him from his reverie.

"Shite!" the Brit exclaimed, finding a clear cylindrical container with two black lines on it. The bubble inside moved when he lifted a stick of dynamite. "It has a bloody failsafe!"

Chapter 37

Tatiana ushered the last of the humans from the building. They scampered across the freshly cut lawn like insects toward the parking lot. Tires screeched and the smell of burning rubber wafted in the air as people hastily made their retreats. To her left a vampire couple dematerialized before her eyes. She glanced around impatiently to see if any of the humans had noticed. Seeing no one who needed their memory wiped, her thoughts returned to her mate.

She focused on their mindlink, remained a quiet shadow on the fringes of his mind, careful not to distract him from his task. Thank the Fates he allowed his emotions to flow over their link! Reading them let her surmise what was happening. He was concentrating hard, determined to save lives. Save her. He's placed concern for her safety above his own.

His relief flowed over the link like a cool breeze to take the heavy feelings of concern and pressure away. Things were going well. Demetri no longer worried.

Tension eased, lifting the weight of her fear for Demetri from her body. Tatiana took a deep breath.

A second breath. A third.

Suddenly, Demetri's anxiety increased. Her muscles bunched, halting a leg mid stride. A moment of unmitigated fear crossed their private channel then the world exploded around her. The blast threw Tatiana to the ground with such force, her face dug into the earth. The smell of burning flesh stung her nostrils. Pain radiated in her limbs, her back.

Her next thought was of him.

Demetri!

No answer came through the mindlink.

Tatiana pushed up on unstable arms, her muscles protesting the movement. She took a breath to steady her shaking limbs then turned to face the carnage. The explosion deafened her ears, except for a high-pitched ringing. Heat singed her lashes and hair. The assault of the caustic fumes twisted her stomach.

My heartmate!

The desire to find him took her body, demanding action. Her eyes scanned the burning inferno. The brightness of the orangish-red color hurt her eyes, making it difficult to see. She squinted to make out an image of the building through the hazy smoke. The third and second floors were completely gone, vaporized into the ashes that floated in the air. Luckily, the first floor remained relatively intact. The front doors were blown from their hinges, allowing her to see inside.

The sight of fallen beams within spurred Tatiana into action. She pushed to her feet and headed toward the building. Her mate might be trapped under the debris, burning alive.

She quickened her steps and shoved down the pain that burned throughout her body

Her sensitive nose registered the smell of gas in the air a split second before another explosion rocked the ground. Flames licked at the dark sky. She should have guessed the restaurant would have a gas line. It was not safe to go in there, not that it would have done any good. The second explosion destroyed the first floor.

Despair dropped Tatiana to her knees. A single tear escaped her eye as regret, anger, and overwhelming sadness mixed. The septic whirlpool threatened to pull her under. The world went quiet. A deafening silence screamed through her mind.

Tatiana reached out to her mate once more over their link, desperate to find something, anything. She opened her mind completely, searching for the smallest sensation, even pain from Demetri would be welcomed. She would take anything as long as it meant he survived.

Dark, black, nothingness.

Nothing!

She had never thought such a mundane word could rip her soul apart. Grief crushed in. Tears rained down her cheeks like the ashes from the air, forming soot-blackened streaks which dropped heavily down to the charred grass on which she knelt.

"NOOOOOOOOO!" She threw her head back, the scream clawing from her throat.

****

Jara jumped up and down for joy. "I told you we would get him."

Leo closed the door to the hotel room and smiled. "We certainly did."

"I can't believe we happened to see him going into that restaurant."

The other guard nodded. "Thank goodness we decided to go back there to eat after we didn't get to the plantation in time."

"I know," said Jara. "When we had trouble

assembling the bomb and didn't get it done before the wedding, I didn't think we'd get another opportunity to kill the bloodsucker."

Leo sat by the desk. "But the Goddess blessed us. I'm just glad we had the bomb assembled and ready to go."

Jara clapped her hands. "Oh, me too. The explosion was—"

"Glorious," supplied Leo with a gleam in his eye.

****

She had wasted so much time. For over a year Tatiana had known he was her heartmate. For more than a year she refused to allow herself to love him. That amazing male, so honorable, a tenacious fighter and gentle lover. And what was she in return? A coward. Afraid to take a chance, afraid to give up her life for him.

That was no longer the case. She would trade her life for his if the bargain could be made with the Fates.

But she could not trade places with her mate. Instead, she'd have to live with her decision to waste what little precious time they would have had. She wanted to rip her heart from her chest, join him in the afterlife.

She buried her face in her hands. Sobs racked her body. Despair pushed in on her, robbing her lungs of air. She took long gulping breaths. Her body tried to live even as she wanted to die—traitor.

Soon, she vowed, she would join her mate. She would search the afterlife until she found him. They would have their time together if not in this life, then the next. She would make sure of it. She silently cursed the Fates for their cruelty. Were they trying to teach her a lesson? Were they punishing her for keeping herself from him?

Why? Why did I let my fear keep us apart? I knew my heartmate was out there. I knew the other half of my soul was mine to seize, to grab hold of and yet I didn't because of Sammael. I allowed that bastard to continue to keep me prisoner even from the grave!

She hated herself in that moment, all the rage from her captivity mixed with the feelings of losing Demetri. She turned the toxic emotions inward, sending another wave of grief and self-loathing through her body.

Tatiana lifted her face from her hands to stare at the burning remnants of the building. The inferno delivered sickening miasma into the air. She breathed it in deeply, searing her lungs. Finally, physical pain that matched the pain inside her.

Physical pain she could do. It was like a familiar friend coming to comfort her and take away the emotional torment. She concentrated on the pain, reaching for it. Needing more, she held her eyes open against the onslaught of heat. Her vision blurred. She didn't move, instead stared straight ahead, absorbing all the pain her body offered.

The inferno licked at the charred remains of the building, its hungry mouth eating away at the bits of wood. Like her life with Demetri, the restaurant went down in flames. She observed the scene through a haze of pain that clouded her vision, the sight too difficult to look at through clear eyes. Her mind blessedly blurred her view, or perhaps in her need to hurt she had allowed the heat to damage her eyes. She didn't know, didn't care.

Time stopped. Images of Demetri played through

her mind. The first time they sparred. The way he looked at her as he had come down the aisle. His tender interaction with the children at the counseling center. The feel of his flesh pressed against hers as he held her after they made love. The taste of his kiss.

When the last of the images played, Tatiana bent her head. Had she knelt there for minutes? Hours? She didn't know. Time had lost all meaning. If her time could not be spent with Demetri, she wanted no more of it.

She slowly pushed to her feet and willed her legs to support her weight. Her hands fisted at her sides as she squared her shoulders. Finding herself swaying slightly, she locked her knees to hold herself upright. She took one more look at the blaze. There was nothing more to hold her here, to hold her at the site of her lover's death. Nothing to hold her to this plane.

Determination turned her. She was alone now. One foot pushed forward followed by the other. Step by step, she put distance between her and the building. At least physically. Nothing would put distance between her and the mental image of the building shattering. She knew that with certainty. As long as she walked this earth, she would forever remember the feelings associated with watching the structure burn down in front of her. Watching as the metal and wood collapsed down to bury Demetri's body—if there was a body to bury.

She could only hope his death had been quick. The thought of him suffering turned her stomach. She wrapped an arm around her waist and bent over to heave the contents of her meal. She straightened before wiping her mouth with the back of her hand. Tatiana forced her body to take her from this place, refusing to allow herself even the slightest weakness. She knew what she needed to do.

End it.

End the pain. End the sorrow. End the torment of losing him.

She found herself picturing Demetri once more as she gradually made her way across the blackened lawn. The handsome features of his face, his chorded muscles. The way he swaggered when he stalked toward her with hunger in his eyes. How his presence wrapped around her every time he came near, bringing with it a visceral awareness she belonged to him.

She could almost feel Demetri, as if he was coming back for her, like his spirit was surrounding her to comfort her as best it could. She wrapped her arms about her waist and turned to take one last look at the all-consuming fire.

A shadow emerged from the blaze, gliding in her direction. The form, veiled by the smoke, continued toward her. She blinked, trying to clear the ethereal image in her vision.

She watched the dark form continue on its path closer. It widened fazing into two distinct shapes. It couldn't be!

Did she dare to hope?

She sent her mind racing along their mindlink again.

Demetri?

Pain flowed across the link, followed by a deep voice. *My tigress warrior, are you all right?*

Relief flooded her. New tears poured down her cheeks. Elation made her streak across the lawn and jumped into Demetri's arms, wrapping her arms about his neck. The movement brought a flinch to his body.

She pulled back as far as his strong arms would allow and looked into his face. It was bright red in the few places where the skin shown from under the black soot. She reached a hand to gingerly wipe away a stripe of black from his cheek, noting the way his mouth drew into a tight line as he winced in pain.

"You're hurt. Let me go so I can help you." Concern furrowed her dark brows.

"I will be fine. I am more concerned about you. Are you okay?" Demetri's assessing gaze raked over her body when he released her from his hold.

"I'm fine." Tatiana slipped her arm around his waist, then pulled his arm over her shoulders. She glanced over at Desmond who walked beside them in silent contemplation.

"You need any help, DW?"

"No, Tatiana." His voice sounded raspy from the smoke just as Demetri's had been. "I can manage. Take care of your mate, he took the brunt of the explosion."

Her eyes darted to Demetri. His clothes matched Desmond's, torn and charred with some of the material still smoldering. Wisps of smoke rose from his skin while they made their way to their vehicle.

Desmond crawled into the passenger seat then Tatiana helped Demetri lie down in the back. After getting them under way, Tatiana looked back in the rearview mirror at her mate, catching the reflection of his steel-gray eyes.

It will be okay, kotik kisa, Demetri sent to her along with soothing comfort. *I will live to fight another day.*

The female warrior now understood why he didn't want her to work with VES for she wished he would never go out in the field again. She wanted him home with her, safe—never again putting his life at risk. She knew what it was to think she had lost him, and she couldn't go through that again! The thought of possibly losing him brought bile to her throat. She swallowed hard, willing herself not to vomit a second time.

Shhh, quiet your mind. Demetri reached forward and touched her shoulder in reassurance. *I will not be going back out tonight.*

I'd like it if you never went back out again.

A smile graced his lips, cracking the charred skin. *I'm glad you are concerned for my safety, but you know better than most, that not fighting is simply not something I can do. We are warriors, Tatiana. Fighters. It is who we are; what we do. To deny ourselves the fight would be like trying to stop breathing. We were born to battle.*

Coming to a stop at a light, she glanced back over the seat at her mate. "We? So, you are saying that you are okay with me going back to VES?"

"I'm not sure VES is the best place for you. I'd rather have you by my side where I can watch your back."

"You mean keep an eye on me."

"That too." Demetri's chuckle became a cough, producing a black mucus he spit into his hand.

"Here." Tatiana grabbed a towel from under her seat and handed it to her lover.

"Light's green," Desmond observed wearily, pointing at the traffic light as a horn honked behind them.

Tatiana hit the gas. "You heard that right, Desmond? Demetri agreed to let me be in the Alpha Council. You'll be my witness."

"He won't have to witness. I will not stop you if you wish to accept Stephan's offer to become an Alpha."

"Not that I'm complaining about the new and improved you, but you must have hit your head pretty hard in that explosion." Tatiana quipped, turning right.

"Actually, he did more than hit his head." Desmond turned to look at the female warrior. "When we realized the bomb was going to explode, he tackled me, sending us both toward the window. The blast turned us around in midair, and Demetri was slammed into the thing, taking the brunt of the impact. It rendered him unconscious."

Tatiana wasn't sure she wanted to hear all the gory details, but DW continued anyway.

"I spun our tangled bodies, shielding Demetri as best I could from the debris as we plummeted to the ground. We hit hard, the landing knocking the breath from my lungs. I rolled over and covered Demetri's limp form as the fiery fragments rained down over us. Luckily, a large piece of titanium, probably from one of the rooms upstairs, fell on us. It shielded us from the brunt of the heat and fire."

Demetri moaned, shifting back to lie on his side. "He makes it sound worse than it was."

"How would you know? You were unconscious most of the time?" Desmond bantered.

Tatiana laughed.

A blithe smile raised the corners of her mouth. Everything would be all right. Demetri and Desmond would recover, they just needed to feed and rest. Both were already starting to heal in just the short time they had been on the road. Her mate had said she could join the Alpha Council. She felt lucky to have such an incredible mate. And as soon as he had recovered, she would show him just how grateful she was.

Chapter 38

Leo rolled over and draped an arm across Jara's naked chest as he had most every evening since they killed the damned bloodsucker. "So, princess, have you given any thought to what I asked you earlier?"

Jara smiled. "Actually, I have. You want to know what's next. What we are going to do now that the vampire is dead, and Lane is gone."

Leo pushed up onto an elbow and ran a finger down her cheek. "As much as I have enjoyed the past few days, we must consider what our next option will be."

"I can't go back to my brother's compound."

Leo nodded. "I know."

Jara worried her bottom lip between her teeth. "I want to kill more vampires."

"Me too. But how? It will take us forever to find them all."

Jara's gaze drifted across the room as she silently contemplated his statement.

"We may not have to find them." A gleam twinkled in Jara's red eyes when they locked with his. "There was a tome I read as a child, long ago. If my memory is correct, there may be a way to kill them all at once."

Jara pushed from the bed, pulled a gown over her thin frame, and turned on Leo. Her hand fisted on her hips. "Well, don't just lie there. Get up. We have work to do."

Leo rose from the bed. "Right now?"

"Right now. I need you to get me the scrying crystal. I have someone I need to find." An impish grin took Jara's face.

****

A week had passed since the explosion at First Bite. Desmond had recovered enough to return to England while Demetri and Tatiana had remained at Demetri's townhouse in Savannah. They had been taking their time, getting to know each other in all the little ways. Demetri now knew the toothpaste she preferred, of course it was a brand he couldn't stand, so they each had their own tube by the bathroom sink. He supposed that was a good metaphor for what their lives together would be like. There were bound to be a lot of times they would have to agree to disagree, and that was okay. As long as they ended their day together he could live with the compromises. Tatiana was worth it, and she felt the same way about him.

Demetri lay in their bed looking down at Tatiana who still slumbered peacefully beside him. Her black hair made for a stark contrast to the white pillow. He drank in the sight of her like a man dying of thirst, savoring every ounce. Her tapered hair fell over her brow, shadowing her eyes. His finger trailed down the pert little nose which sat above her lips, lips that were full, held slightly apart in sleep. She had a delicate, rounded chin. But the most striking feature on her face hid beneath her lids—those amazing cat-like eyes, with the greenish-yellow tint in the irises. They could hypnotize a man, draw him in, make him lose himself in her gaze.

The soft sheets of their bed covered her body like a glove, outlining her supple form. She possessed a lithe muscular frame which gave her a graceful feline gait. Her small round breasts pushed at the fabric. His libido automatically registered the curves beneath the silk, following them down to the tiny waist. He trailed his finger up the length of her strong legs, hugged lovingly by the sheet.

His hand snaked out, reaching for the sheet down low. His fingers walked the fabric down her body, exposing a little of her flesh at a time to his view. A tantalizing striptease of sorts, which hardened his body. Demetri's mouth watered for a taste of her. His heated gaze roamed every exposed inch, memorizing each nuance.

His hunger rose, his inner beast needing its mate. She was so smooth, deceptively soft. Her strength flexed close beneath the surface of her creamy skin. It shot him into a spiral of need for her. Need for everything about her.

Need for everything she was.

He ran the pads of his fingers lightly over her flesh, blazing a trail from her belly button to the underside of one breast. His hand cupped the creamy mound, kneaded it with loving fingers. Tatiana stirred beneath the palm of his hand.

"Feeling better I see," she teased, pushing against the palm. When she scissored her legs, he slipped into her mind, seeking their connection. Pressure built between her thighs. Her body burned with need, need he created by his touch. She burned, and desire poured through her veins like hot lava.

"Much," he murmured against the breast not cupped in his hand. He sucked her nipple into the warmth of his mouth, swirling his tongue over the pebbling bud. It puckered, seeking the sensuous sensation of the moist cavern.

Her fingers fisted in his dark hair and laced in the silky strands to hold him to her in desperation. He drove her body higher, sending her reaching for the precipice with his ministrations.

Demetri leaned back to gaze down her body as his hands kneaded then caught her nipples between the pads of his fingers and thumbs to pinch them lightly. Tatiana arched her back hard, the pleasurable pain pushing her over the edge, wringing the climax from her as she covered his hands with her own.

His shaft, hard as steel, pulsed and throbbed against her thigh, looking for an opportunity. He ruthlessly denied it, choosing instead to shimmy down the side of her body. The sensation of his flesh against hers nearly pushed him over the edge of restraint. He refused to give into the demands of his body, instead seeking to draw her pleasure out and make certain she believed no other male could love her like him.

His fingers slipped out from under hers. She moaned her displeasure. But a startled gasp quieted the protest when his hand dropped down over her stomach to slip between her legs. She pushed her mound against his hand, shamelessly seeking his touch.

Her legs spread wide as he settled between them. Demetri draped her legs over his shoulders. He lowered his lips to her core then gave it a long sensual lick. His mouth closed over her sensitive nub, sucking it into the warmth of his hot mouth. Tatiana covered her breasts with her hands, squeezing them in time with his licks.

Demetri feasted on his mate. Took her delicious taste into his mouth, feeding from her as she thrust her hips against him in wanton abandonment. She breathed his name, the sound a pleading need as her hand found his head. She held her to him, encouraging him to increase the pace. He could do no other than oblige the invitation. Demetri set a furious pace, the action drawing a long moan from Tatiana. Her head twisted on the pillow from side to side.

He pushed a finger into her feminine core, twisting it while his tongue went back to kiss her nub. She groaned. Her body clamped around his finger. He withdrew, inserting two instead and pushed her over the cliff of ecstasy. He pumped his fingers into her as he drew another orgasm from her with his talented mouth. A rush of her sweet cream rewarded the effort.

She lay panting. Her hard breaths thrusted her breasts in delicious invitation. Holding her legs to his shoulders, he edged up her body to take one of the fleshy globes between his lips. His tongue swirled around the peak, drawling tiny circles around her nipple.

"Demetri!" Tatiana fisted both hands in his hair, desperate with need to feel him inside her.

Instead of giving his mate what she wanted, his lips blazed a fiery trail of kisses upward to close on the delicate skin of her throat. Demetri crawled over her body, the feel of her flesh against his chest an added pleasure.

Her pulse called to him. It beat hard just under her skin. His fangs ached with need as he adjusted her legs on his shoulders.

The slide of his fangs into her delicate flesh sent her careening toward another climax. He took long drawls, taking her deep into his mouth. The supple pull propelled her over the edge of the precipice. Her orgasm flew up her spine, sending fire to singe every nerve which then passed over their mindlink

Demetri pushed deeper into her mind until he found her love for him. She realized he deliberately took this slow, loving her with his body in a way that would prove she belonged with him. And she wanted this, wanted him to take the lead, wanted to give him the control.

His shaft jumped against her core in response. He grasped the thickness in one hand and pushed the tip inside her slick opening. His breath caught in his throat as he slid his steel through the velvety folds. Throttling the need to simply impale her in one hard thrust, he amassed all his hard-earned self-control and pushed slowly inside, savoring the way her body wrapped around his tip to fist him in a wet, tight grip. She convulsed around the mushroomed head. It drove him higher. Needing more, he slid home. Inch by luscious inch he filled her, stretching her, until she milked his length.

Tatiana arched, and he gradually withdrew. Her core clenched around him, the contact adding another sinuous pleasure to her orgasm, drawing it out. She moaned at the contrast. Innnnn. Ouuuuut. Each plunge and withdrawal tantalizingly slow.

Demetri braced his weight on his hands. His hips pistoned gently as she floated back to earth. His only thought to bring her over the edge once more. Her calves squeezed his ears. He lowered himself until her supple, naked body crushed beneath his. Her legs still over his shoulders allowed him to be seated fully within her. Looking into her eyes, he watched her pleasure build with each long thrust.

This is going to be a long, slow ride. kotik kisa.

A soft keening cry escaped the back of her throat, as his thick shaft slid inside in a long silken glide, only to inch out again. She threaded her arms around him, holding him to her, riding his powerful thrusts. Trapped beneath him, Tatiana's claustrophobia should have been screaming, but he drove all thoughts from her mind besides the feel of his body.

She inhaled, breathing his exotic scent deep into her lungs. It drove her hunger. Half crazed by desire, she lifted her head to find his lips.

Their lips locked in a passionate kiss. She poured all her love for him into the kiss. Their tongues dueled with a ravenous intensity that had them thrusting deeply between their mouths. The pressure built inside her, deep and full, increasing with every lunging thrust. Her legs dropped from his shoulders to circle his waist, changing the internal pressure.

She came again, screaming into his mouth. Maddened, she released his lips and buried her face in the curve of his jaw. His pulse pounded against her lips. Incited, her fangs pushed from her gums. She sank deep, letting the richness of his blood spill into her mouth. Demetri moaned, the low sound rumbling against her lips. But she scarcely noticed as his blood flowed into her mouth with the hot blaze she had come to associate with him, like a shot of straight vodka sliding over her tongue.

Still feeding, he rolled her over until she was

spread over his body, impaled on his shaft. His hold tightened as she continued to feed from him. One strong arm wrapped around her back. His other hand held her hips still as he took her.

She couldn't move, constricted by the bands of steel wrapped around her. Her breath quickened, anxiety pushed in. Tatiana licked the wounds on his neck closed and struggled against the oppressive hold. Sensing her discomfort, he allowed her to push away and brace her palms on his chest. She looked down at him, pleading silently with her eyes for him to understand.

It's all right, my tigress warrior. I've got you. Trust me. His arms wrapped around her and gently brought her back down to his chest. His thrusts slowed a little, allowing her time to accept him, decide to trust him.

And she did. He sensed it in her mind. Everything receded until only he consumed her. In that moment, she turned herself over to his keeping, trusting him with her body. Her love.

The knowledge drove Demetri's body harder, ratcheting his need to sate his hunger for her. He turned them once more, so she again lay under his body. He unleashed a sensual storm inside her. She felt truly free for the first time in her life. Free to love another. Free to trust another.

Her hips slapped against his as she pulled his head down for a ravenous kiss. She thrust her tongue into his mouth, demanding he match her intensity. Tatiana writhed beneath him, her hand fisted in his hair, her mouth eating hungrily at his. One hand clawed at his back as her body rushed for the rapture.

One of Demetri's hands wrapped around her back,

the other fisted in her hair. He pulled her head to the side, his hold keeping her exactly where he wanted, anchoring her in place, while his gaze burned a brand over her. His fangs lengthened, and he lowered his lips to the delicate neck. His teeth scraped back and forth. Demetri's tongue darted out to taste. One lick. Two.

The anticipation drove Tatiana higher. Her hands slid down his back, leaving scratches that trailed to his buttocks. Grabbing his lower cheeks, she held on for dear life. She thrust her hips to meet his, needing more. More feeling. More contact.

More pleasure, the thought crossed their link

Demetri was more than happy to oblige. His hands tightened, drawing her head further to the side. The muscles of her neck chorded tight. Her blood was his to take, a willing offering. His fangs pierced the tender flesh.

"Demetri!" Tatiana screamed the climax.

She bucked wildly against him. The sensuous sensation of his sucking against her neck added to her pleasure, took her higher still. The orgasm rolled through her body in endless waves of ecstasy. She rode each wave to their crest as her inner core pulsed.

Demetri's tongue lapped at the small wounds to close them before he pulled away, gazing onto the face of his mate. Her eyes were closed, her lips parted. The soft mewing sound coming from the back of her throat spoke to his inner beast, calling to it, begging it to join her on her plain of ecstasy.

He could do no other than answer the call. His hips rutted wildly against her. Pushing deep, seating himself to the hilt with each thrust. He allowed the muscles of her core to milk his climax from him. It built into a powerful surge. Pressure pushed it through his shaft until he emptied into her, pumping his seed as he threw back his head and let out a mighty roar.

His hips slowed, eventually coming to a stop while the couple struggled to breathe. This had been an amazing demonstration of their love and trust in one another, something he intended to repeat often. Their bodies pulsed with the after effects of their love.

Still seated within the warmth of her body, Demetri braced his weight on his forearms and looked down into Tatiana's eyes, noting the wide grin on her face. "Why are you smiling?"

"What's not to smile about?" She wrapped her arms around his back.

A smug grin graced his handsome face. Without separating from her body, he turned them so she once more draped over his body.

Her hand cupped his face. "I love you, Demetri."

He'd waited centuries to hear his heartmate say that. His chest expanded with love for her. He knew she loved him, but to hear the words from her lips made his heart sing.

"For over six hundred years I have existed on this earth. Not until I met you, have I truly lived. I love you with all my being. My very soul." A thought occurred to him. "Do you want to get married?"

"This again?" Tatiana did not keep the incredulity from her voice.

"Christina, Juliette, and Katrina all wanted their heartmates to marry them in a formal ceremony. Do you not wish to do the same?"

A playful smile lifted the corners of her mouth. "I think you just want to get me back into a dress again,

Romanoff."

He leered suggestively at her. "I do like the way you look in a dress." He gave her bottom a gentle squeeze. "And out of one."

She laughed and swatted his chest with her hand. "You know we don't need a wedding. The bond between heartmates is greater than any ceremony."

"I know, but I thought I'd offer. I want you to be happy."

She snuggled against his chest, resting her cheek on his shoulder. "I am."

She sent her love pouring into his mind as she spoke, *I pledge to you my faithfulness, never to forsake you. I pledge to share a lifetime of eternal, boundless love with you; to care for you, take into my protection all that is yours. I pledge to love you until the end of days with an unselfish devotion. On this night, my heartmate, I pledge my life to you, to be your partner in all things for all of time.*

His arms tightened around her, needing her skin on his skin—her soul on his soul. He felt the bond form around their hearts, forever connecting them in a way far greater than any marriage license could. She pledged her love to him in the most sacred way possible.

The harsh sound of Demetri's cell broke the tender moment. Recognizing the ring tone, he separated their bodies and rolled out from under her to pad over and retrieve the pesky thing from its place on the top of the TV.

"Hello," he barked.

"Who is it?" Tatiana whispered, stretching languidly out on the bed.

He covered the receiver with one hand. "Stephan."

She lay quietly observing. The conversation was quick, efficient, very Alpha-like with few words being exchanged.

Demetri turned, punching off the phone, the expression on his face a mixture of excitement and resignation. "Get dressed."

Tatiana rose from the bed. "Why?"

"Stephan believes he knows who blew up First Bite," Demetri informed her, making his way over to the dresser to pull out some clothes. "We have an assignment."

"We? As in you and me?"

"You don't have to sound so excited about it." Demetri gave her a quelling glance. "I'm still not sure I like the idea of you on the Council."

She ambled up behind him and wrapped her arms around his waist in a hug. "I know, but you are a good mate, and you would rather have me where you can keep an eye on me."

He snorted then turned in her arms and wrapped his around her in turn. "Just promise me you'll be safe."

She grinned up at him. "I will."

"Yeah, right." He gave her a rather hard smack on the bottom. "Get dressed, woman."

A few minutes later, dressed in her usual leather bodysuit and shit-kicker boots Tatiana looked every bit the *femme fatale* he knew her to be. She shrugged into a leather duster with her usual grace.

"Ready to go?" Demetri sent love and caring over their link like a velvet caress.

"Of course."

"Me too." Demetri let out a wistful sigh. What he

really wanted was to crawl back into bed with his hot, sexy vampire, but that could wait.

After all, they had plenty of time for that.

Forever, in fact.

Tatiana holstered her weapon then thread her fingers through his. "Let's go get 'em."

She flashed her pearly fangs, sending a jolt of heat coursing through his blood as he thought of where those teeth would be by morning.

But for now, they had an assignment to complete.

Together.

Tatiana indulged a wide grin that brought a sparkle to her eyes. They were partners. He'd fight to the death for her. Be there to protect her, care for her. And she wouldn't want it any other way. He would have her back and she would always cover his.

A perfect team.

A perfect duo.

The perfect Alpha pair.

A word about the author…

Born in Virginia, Brenda Sparks now resides in the Sunshine State with her incredibly supportive husband, and beloved son. Balancing her professional commitment to the local school district with her writing is challenging at times, but writing suspenseful paranormal romances is a passion that won't be denied. Her idea of a perfect day is one spent in front of a computer with a hot cup of coffee, her fingers flying over the keys to send her characters off on their latest adventure. Brenda loves to connect with readers. Please visit her at www.brenda-sparks.com.